Wild About My Scotsman

The Butlers' Romance Series
Book 4

Amber Cooper

Kilted Hero Press

To Jess
Because you saw him first

Contents

Introduction and
a note on content.

Welcome to Butler world, part four. All the books can be read as standalone or in order. Before you do read, a word about the content and steamy bits.

This book deals with or touches on the topics of grief, terminal illness (Motor Neurone Disease) and historical miscarriage. There are several open door sex scenes in this book as well as profanity within and outside of these scenes. If you think you may be offended or affected by any of this, then please do consider whether this is the book for you. It should also be said that this is balanced out with plenty of fun and laughter. It's definitely not all doom and gloom.

I truly hope you enjoy Sean and Cherry's story.

Amber xx

Glossary

Here are a few words, phrases or other detail that appear in the book that are used in Scotland, Ireland or the UK in general.

Aff yer chops: Drunk

Belter: Exceptional or amazing (person or thing)

Bunnet: A cap

Calm doon: Calm down

Cowp: A dump

Gallus: Cheeky, mischievous, bold

Get tae: Go away. Short for get tae fuck/get to fuck

Gobshite: Someone who talks nonsense

Hee haw: Nothing

Mibbes aye, mibbes naw: Maybe yes, maybe no

Scooby: Clue

Stookie: Plaster cast

Thae: Those

Chapter 1

Sean

Sean Butler had never met a wedding crasher or a woman who made him want to commit to anything, but right now he got the distinct feeling he was staring at a two-in-one package.

Surely, though, women you could spend forever with didn't flirt combatively with security before strolling into the glittering New York City ballroom where your eldest brother was getting married, throwing your concentration off course with their sparkling sequinned dress, high-tops and dark-golden mermaid waves, then make a beeline for the vol-au-vents.

Surely forever started differently to this.

There was one way to find out.

Sean excused himself from chatting to the bride's uncle and strode across the room, the kilt swishing at his knees providing a welcome breeze. Whose idea was it to have a Scottish wedding in New York in July? Even the air con wasn't providing relief.

And this woman's presence notched up the mercury one thousand percent. As he approached, their eyes locked, hers flashing with surprise yet holding a playful readiness. Adrenaline he'd never felt before coursed through his veins. Was he ready for this? Whatever 'this' was?

'Evening.' He met her dead-on. She could be a friend of the bride, Bea, but why not head to your friend rather than the French pastries?

'Good evening.' The woman fanned her mouth, now full of food, and he noticed the lack of wedding ring. 'Catering have done themselves proud here.'

'Aye, they have.' *Nice attempt at deflection, you wee chancer.* 'Bea's over there, if you want to chat to her.' Sean motioned indiscriminately over his shoulder. It didn't matter because this woman didn't know Bea.

'Ah, great.' She nodded as if grateful of the direction. 'I'll pop over and see her shortly.'

'I'll tell her you're here. Your name is?'

'Sorry, I'm so rude.' The interloper held out a perfectly manicured hand. Sean detected a hint of a Scottish accent underneath lacings of American. 'Cherry. Cherry Paradise.'

He laughed. 'Aye, right.' That was the name of a shampoo scent or a tray bake, not a human being. At least not where he came from. In Sean's part of the world, women were called Elspeth McKay or Fiona Gilmour, not Cherry Paradise.

'Aye,' she said. 'That is right. And yours is?'

'Johnny. Johnny Castle.' Watching *Dirty Dancing* on a loop with his sisters had finally borne fruit.

She cocked a brow and almost certainly stifled a smile. 'I see.'

'Good. And like my namesake, I like to dance. You coming?' Sean should have been asking her to leave, but here he was holding out his hand. There were two ways to deal with this situation, and the dancing version was less disruptive than eviction. The Butler family had dealt with a lot of pain, since the recent death of Sean's father after a long-fought battle with Motor Neurone Disease. Cal and Bea's big day would not be marred by the dramatic ousting of a wedding crasher.

Even one who was hotter than an NYC summer.

Sean hadn't expected her to agree to dance. The visions he had were of a sparkling figure dashing into the night, handbag full of vol-au-vents, his question still hot in her ears. But after grabbing a glass of champagne from a passing server, she downed it in one and followed Sean onto the dance floor.

The music was an eighties' power ballad, *Take it on the Run* by REO Speedwagon, made for bouncing off the walls in high-ceilinged spaces like this.

'May I?' Sean motioned to Cherry's hand. She nodded, and he took it in his own, surprised at how small and soft it was – a contrast to her bold presence. The heady scent of honeysuckle drifted into his senses. Heady suited her. She seemed like the kind of woman who took life by the reins, including crashing other people's weddings.

'So, Cherry Paradise, I'm pretty sure you don't know my brother, so how do you know the bride?' Sean asked as they melded into one another and the music.

'Oh, I don't.' Cherry quirked her head sideways and smiled like she'd won a game Sean didn't even know they were playing. Did she know that now they were dancing, now that he could smell and feel her up close, kicking her out had become an impossibility because there was something more powerful than a summer cyclone in this tiny space between them?

Some sort of intoxicating chemistry swirling around that made you adjust the way you breathed.

She knew this. It was there in the cobalt sparkle of her eyes, in the soft bounce of her high-tops as she moved her feet in time with his. Cherry Paradise knew that Sean would vouch for her as his plus-one in a second rather than risk her leaving. Because letting her go meant never finding out what the hell this feeling was. Where it could go.

'As I thought. Do you know anyone here?'

'I know you. Kinda.'

'And I'm the person you know the best?'

'Yes.'

'You make a habit of crashing weddings?'

'Nope. But I'm staying in the hotel, and I heard on the grapevine that this one was Scottish, so I thought I'd take a peek. And then honestly—'

'You do honesty?' The urge to laugh was palpable.

'Honestly...I saw something I liked the look of.'

'The buffet?'

'Nope. It was...' Cherry threw her glittering gaze up and down Sean's form, from the tip of his heat-mussed hair to the toe of his Ghillie brogues. 'This gorgeous man in a kilt. What can I say? I'm a sucker for one. And this particular one – I couldn't look away. Can't.' Her glossed lips parted, and she searched his face, making a laboured point of enjoying the view by biting on her bottom lip.

'I saw you looking at the food.'

'That is true, and I tell you what, I'm still hungry.'

'Oh, aye?'

'Very much so. You have the most beautiful green eyes, Johnny Castle. Women must tell you that all the time.'

'On occasion,' he admitted. 'And you can call me Sean. Seeing as that's my name.'

'Okay, Sean. You can call me Cherry. Seeing as that's mine.'

He roamed over her face as if searching for signs she was lying.

'Oh, don't dull those gorgeous greens with such cynicism. Cherry is my name.'

Sean nodded and watched her steadily, as if waiting for the rest.

'And Paradise is also my name. Look...' She retrieved her driver's licence from a small crossbody bag, holding it up for Sean to inspect. And sure enough, unless she was an elaborate counterfeiter, then he was facing Cherry Paradise.

'Okay, Ms Paradise.' Were you after some kicks and decided to crash a Scottish wedding? Are you homesick? I detect a half-Scottish accent, although that name doesn't sound very Scottish.'

'To answer your questions... Firstly, I was curious. I am also homesick for Scotland.' Cherry curled her fingers partway around Sean's bicep. 'There's a lot to love about it. And the name is of Greek origin, from Paradisopolous, since you asked.'

Sean darted his brows upward. He was on a fast-track tour of this woman – five-star so far. The reflection of the sparkling chandelier in her cobalt eyes surrounded with sweepings of blue glitter eyeshadow seemed to sum up her whole character. His attention dropped to her lips. Luscious cherry-coloured gloss was begging for a tongue to swipe over it.

If she wanted a man for the job...

He bet she tasted as a sweet as cherries, too. Her gold dress dazzled the corners of his vision, and something near her cleavage caught his eye.

'What's that?' Sean motioned downwards.

'Those are boobs.'

He laughed hard. 'I meant the little bit of paper stuck inside your dress. Is that your shopping list?'

'Kind of. That's my bucket list.'

'People still write bucket lists?'

'I can't speak for people, but I have one. Don't you?'

'Not officially, no. There are things I want to do, but I haven't written them down and stuck the list inside my underwear.'

'Are you wearing underwear?'

Was she for real? This conversation might be the best one Sean ever had. 'Not tonight, no. Kilt equals no underwear. It's the rules. You should know that, being Scottish.'

'Just checking for my records. You should put a bucket list in your underwear – when you're wearing some. It will remind you never to let go of your dreams.'

'Hmm, okay. Thanks for the advice.'

'You're welcome.'

For a moment, they danced without talking. Sean loved the way this rocket of a woman felt in his arms. The way her smaller frame fit into his, her head flush with his upper chest.

He would admit, at least to himself, that he needed something like this. A woman to dance with. To hold. Over the past few years, he'd watched three of his brothers find the love of their life: Cal with Bea, Jamie with his fiancée, Alicia, and Niall reunited with his childhood sweetheart, Carli. Sean believed it would happen for him, although living and working in the small Scottish village of Kinshore, he had to wonder how. There was nobody there he could see being 'the one'. He'd considered and re-considered them all. The love of his life was not in Kinshore.

But could it be that she was right here, on this dance floor in New York City?

Had he met his match?

Steady on there, Seany. You might be getting ahead of yourself.

But that was what Sean did. That was his MO. He got ahead of himself, always had done. He was not a man for measure. Sure, he was good at providing it for other people's problems. Giving a good listening ear to serious issues and offering subjectivity. But with his own decisions, Sean went ahead and made them. And something told him this woman did the same.

'You're thinking about my bucket list, aren't you?' Her voice drifted up to him like syrup spun round a spoon, the soft contours of her face glowing.

'It's one of the things I'm thinking about,' he admitted.

'I can tell you about it, if you like.'

Ordinarily, if someone offered to share the contents of their bucket list with Sean, he'd suddenly realise he'd left the oven on, or the surf was too good to miss, but this was different. Hell yeah, he wanted to see what was on her list.

'Is swimming with dolphins on it? Visiting the Taj Mahal?'

She laughed. 'Nope. But sleeping with a man in a kilt is. All my non-Scottish friends think it's outrageous that I've never done that.'

This got Sean's attention. 'Right.' He lowered her arm but not her hand. 'Let's get a drink and sit down.'

It was strange to think that, less than two hours ago, he was innocently sitting at this table listening to his brother Jamie give a best man speech. It was brilliant, full of laughs – wry observations and funny anecdotes about family life. When there were seven siblings, there would always be stories, and the Butler family had plenty of those.

And now here was a new chapter. Was it daft to think

like that? He'd known this woman less than ten minutes, but in that time, he'd been more stimulated – physically and mentally – than in any previous relationship. The plates of the planet were shifting.

Sean's planet at least.

'Drink?' He grabbed a champagne flute from a server and placed it in front of Cherry.

'Thank you. So this is your family?' She surveyed the large ballroom, apparently awestruck.

'Aye, not all of them.' There were at least one hundred people in the room. 'Bea is American, so most of these folk are her friends and family. And there's a fair few oldies back in Kinshore who couldn't make the journey. We'll have a wee Scottish shindig for them.'

'Kinshore? Where's that?'

'Kintyre. Wee village, about 2000 folk. Near Camp-beltown.'

'Ah, the home of Butler's Whisky.'

'Aye, that's us. My dad ran the company until he passed away recently.'

'Oh, wow. I'm sorry to hear about his passing. Butler's is great stuff, and I'd have loved to tell him.'

'Thank you. He'd have loved to hear that. Now, tell me about your hopes and dreams.' Sean nodded to the piece of paper still wedged between Cherry's cleavage and her dress.

'Ah yes, those.' She retrieved and unfolded it. 'Here we go. Oh, and if you can help me achieve any of these, let me know.'

'Will do.' Sean winked, and the temperature of the smile returned his way nearly knocked him off his chair. He took the list and flattened the paper onto the table with his palm.

'You could use your notes app on your phone for this,' he said.

'Ah, where's the fun in that? Plus, you'd never have asked me about it if it was there.'

'Very true. Okay, what have we got? Let me check for dolphins and the Taj Mahal.' Performatively, he ran his thumb down the page.

Cherry giggled, a cute contrast to the bold-as-brass exterior she'd exuded so far.

'I see you've got "crash a wedding" on here,' he noted. 'Guess you can cross that one off. Okay, wait... Is there anything on here that isn't about sex?'

'Crashing a wedding isn't about sex. At least not yet.'

Sean whipped his head up. *Bloody hell!*

'You've got having sex with a man in a kilt, an NYPD officer, an FDNY officer, a Canadian Mountie, a cowboy, a younger man, under a waterfall and in an elevator. Am I missing anything else?'

'Not on the sex front, I don't think.' Cherry sipped her champagne. 'Do you like the list?'

'It's entertaining. What else have we got? "Get married in Vegas", "marry the love of my life". And what does the wee star next to that mean – hung like a blue whale?'

'Exactly that.'

This got another powerful laugh. 'I presume all the cowboys, NYPD, kilted men, etcetera, have to meet the same criteria?'

She shrugged. 'Preferably.'

Sean shook his head, but the grin on his face betrayed how amusing he found this. 'Okay, to the less X-rated section of the list: learn to surf, adopt a cat/kitten, learn to cook, write a book, sex in a vineyard... I must have missed that one. "Win the World Series"... Are you a baseball player?'

'No, poker.'

'You're a professional poker player?'

'Yes.'

'Well, that makes sense.'

'Does it? How so?'

'You don't strike me as the type to have hot chocolate and Hobnobs in the office at eleven every day. I mean, you could be blowing off steam from all that, I suppose.'

'No, poker's been my full-time job since I was twenty-five. Twelve years. That's what I want to write a book about.'

Sean did the calculations in his head. She was thirty-seven. She didn't look thirty-seven. Five years older than him. It was nothing. Before now, he might have considered it something, because the last older woman he'd dated hadn't exactly worked out, but things had changed. In the last twenty minutes.

'Is poker what brought you out here?' he asked.

'Kind of, yeah. I mean, you can't stay in the States because you like to play poker, but I've had enough money to support myself and got visas that way. And I was in a relationship with an American guy.'

'I'm guessing not a cowboy or NYPD officer?'

'No, another poker player. So I stayed. When I'm not travelling around the world playing, this is where I spend most of my time. I've come close, but the World Series has eluded me. Any woman, actually.'

'Sorry to hear that. But there's still time.'

'There is, although I'm not sure it matters all that much to me now. I might scrub it off the list. Replace it with some-thing more important.'

'Like what?'

'I don't know. What can you offer me?'

Sean angled his chair facing Cherry's, his feet planted apart, the heavy weight of his kilt preventing things getting explicit, although he already knew he wanted explicit with this woman. He wanted everything with her. The sex, the dances where he held her, watching her win poker games, taking her home to meet his family. Hell, he was ready to take her around this room and meet them right now.

'I'll tell you what I can offer you, Cherry. Instead of kicking you out for crashing my brother's wedding, I'm going to ask you to stay as my plus-one. We can talk and dance some more. Maybe we'll find a quiet elevator. Tomorrow, I'll take you for breakfast. Then, if you're lucky and I'm lucky, you can marry the love of your life, who will also be wearing a kilt. Not in Vegas but at City Hall, which is like Vegas but with more class and fewer Elvises.' Sean worked hard not to mirror Cherry's smile. Did that mean she was keen? Who knew he did such a fine line in romantic hyperbole? He continued, 'Then you can move back to Scotland with me, where I'll teach you to surf, take you to a secluded waterfall that I know and get you a kitten.' Possibly he was going over the top, but she was enjoying it. 'That'll cover about five points on your list. Oh, and you can put a wee star next to all of them, in case you were wondering.'

She burst out laughing. 'If you do say so yourself.'

'I'm only going on what I've been told.' Did that sound big-headed? Hopefully, she would know he was playing it for laughs.

Cherry shuffled her seat close to Sean's, so her knees were hitting the front of his chair. She leaned her hands on his knees, her own apparent delight mirroring the amazement Sean was experiencing.

'I have a hunch it's the truth,' she said. 'Guess I'll find out in the elevator or on our wedding night – whichever comes first.'

Holy smokes. She wasn't exactly batting back his idea.

'If we get married, I'll keep my surname,' she added, jumping way ahead of any considerations Sean had.

'Of course. Why leave paradise behind?'

'I should have put "sex with a whisky heir" on my list.'

'Ach, I'm not a whisky heir. I just make the barrels they put the stuff in. My brother Jamie runs the show now.'

'Ah, a cooper. That would explain the biceps.' Cherry leaned forward and squeezed Sean's arm again, the heat from her small hand shooting to behind the scenes of his sporran. He would need to be careful, although something told him Cherry wouldn't mind if it became obvious what she did to him.

'I could marry a man with arms like these,' she said.

'If you're lucky, I might let you,' Sean joked, knowing that he'd be the lucky one if anything as outrageous as marrying this woman came to be.

Chapter 2

Cherry

Cherry might just have met the man of her dreams. Including dreams she'd forgotten she ever had. Wangling her way into a random Scottish wedding this evening, because of the promise of men in kilts and the long-forgotten feeling of home, was only meant to be a ten-minute thing. Cross another item off the bucket list by standing metaphorically on the solid Scottish land her bones understood. Give them a small break from the restlessness of the road.

But now she was thinking about forever with this guy. This kilted man who felt like sex and the safety of home at once. The kind who had her reaching for something to steady herself the second she saw him, so rattled she nearly toppled into the buffet table and pretended it was intentional by grabbing the first thing she saw – vol-au-vents.

And the way he talked, he made it sound like all the fantasies on her list could become a reality of his making. He said yes to so many things. Didn't hold back. Cherry needed that in her life.

Surely all this was insane. You didn't think about

forever with someone you'd met an hour ago. Her mum had with her dad, but Cherry wasn't like her mother. She dealt in practicalities – decisions made by consulting probability and consequences – while her mother operated on whispers from the universe. Cherry played poker. Her mum read tarot cards. One was real, and you won from skill and odds calculation; the other was mystical waffle. For years, she had used her maths degree and psychology to make poker her full-time job. Yet so many people saw it as less than tarot.

But the universe was whispering something to her about Sean Butler. What would her mother's tarot cards say about this? Would she see forever in them? Would they bring up an indication of marriage – such as the Lovers or the Empress – or something more ominous, like the Scythe, pointing to caution over making rash decisions?

For goodness' sake, Cherry. Examine the evidence and make a rational decision, like you do at the poker table.

But Cherry's emotional compass was spinning like a roulette wheel. North could be anywhere. Although, something about Sean Butler felt like a giant magnetic pull towards a place her needle could rest awhile.

Maybe forever.

They danced some more, stopped and refreshed themselves with champagne. Laughed a lot – about what she wasn't exactly sure, but Sean made her abs ache in a very good way.

The one thing she hadn't done much of was eat. The room was spinning, and Cherry knew as she excused herself to go to the bathroom that, even in trainers, she was teetering. But no way was she going to bed. The frustration of the tournament she'd crashed out of was mellowing into the background, helped by champagne and Sean Butler. The words of her ex as she lost her final stack – 'You're a busted flush, Cherry' – weren't ringing so hard in her ears.

After reapplying her lipstick, Cherry spritzed perfume onto her hair and on the pulse points on her neck.

For a moment, she stood outside the ballroom, concealed from its occupants. What if she didn't go back in? Ignored the starlight in her brain and went to bed? She'd wake up in the morning, drink some orange juice and go for a walk in Central Park. Maybe go to the gym. Get refreshed and screw her head back on for tomorrow's tournament.

Follow the rational route.

But there was a man inside that ballroom whose sweet skin smelled like oaked whisky barrels and whose laughter rumbled right into her heart, making her feel like she was the centre of his universe.

Poker hadn't given her anything resembling that in a long time.

There was no competition.

As Cherry stepped back into the ballroom, she stared at Sean unfiltered. He was gesticulating expressively whilst chatting to someone. But, as if he sensed she were there, he turned. His smile lit the way back to him. Cherry tried to keep her cool, but it was impossible. She gave a little wave and strode over.

To her future husband.

Don't be daft.

But he'd said it. *'You can marry the love of your life.'*

Something in her gut wanted to marry him. Maybe it was the champagne. Or the promise of happiness after so long without it. To have this feeling for the rest of her life.

'Hey, would you like a whisky?' Sean held up a tumbler of amber liquid, the ballroom lights dancing over the surface like the sparkle in his eyes.

Cherry took the glass and sipped. 'Mmm, Butler's.'

'Okay, my family name coming out of your mouth like that might be a little arousing.'

She laughed. 'I know quality when I taste it.'

'I'm impressed.' Sean stepped closer, his sensual, woody scent clouding her mind. 'Tell me, are you an instinctive poker player or one who does all the maths in your head?'

Cherry swilled the whisky. 'Oh, I never decide in poker on instinct. I consider all the evidence, all the possibilities, read the other players. There's too much at stake to wing it.'

'And does that carry into the rest of your life?'

'Hmm, mostly. Although, tonight, I kind of sailed in here on a vibe. Something was calling me. Someone maybe.'

Sean nodded an understanding, took the whisky from her hand, placed it on the table and led her onto the dance floor again. She wouldn't fight being close to him. She might be addicted already.

'You smell delicious,' he burred in his rich Scottish accent. 'Like honeysuckle.'

'How does an adult man who isn't a gardener know what honeysuckle smells like?'

'We used to have it in the garden growing up. I'll never forget that smell, and now I certainly won't. You, Cherry Paradise, smell as good as you look, and you look incredible.'

'The feeling is mutual, Sean Butler.' She was transfixed. 'I don't know whether to look at your legs or your kilt or your face.'

'Why not all three? You've got all night.'

As they danced to another slow song, Sean's gaze dipped to the oval-shaped golden pendant around Cherry's neck. 'What's in there?'

Unclasping the vintage locket she always wore, Cherry lifted it for him to see. 'It's a tiny photo, but that's me and my dad at my third birthday party. My mum's the blur with the cake in the background.'

Sean rested the locket on two of his fingers and examined the picture, the warmth from his hands radiating to her heart.

'Your dad... He looks like an American soap star; that's some 'tache. Was he an actor?'

Cherry laughed. 'No, he was a police officer, but he retired early after being injured in the line of duty. And he'd have loved the actor comparison.'

'He's not around anymore?

'No. He died when I was thirteen. Massive heart attack.'

'Fuck, I'm sorry.' Softly closing the locket, Sean placed it back against her collarbone. He pressed his hands a little firmer into her back. A protective hold that softened the edges of that need in her. 'I know what it's like to lose your dad, although I did have mine for thirty-two years.'

While it was sad that he'd lost his father, it was a comfort that he understood her pain. 'I don't think it's easy whenever you lose them, especially if you were close...' she said. 'Were you?'

'Mmm, aye.' Sean's focus drifted to something across the ballroom. 'Losing him was like losing a limb. He taught me to surf, kind of a metaphor for everything else in life – the best stuff is hard won and all that.' He dipped his chin and brought his focus to her again. 'He was a good man; watching him go was horrendous.'

'I'm so sorry.'

'Thanks. Were you and your dad close?'

'We were. Because he retired early, he always had time for me. I was his shadow. We grew veggies and plants on his allotment, fed the ducks, learned about birds and butterflies.

He taught me to play poker. I was like *Cherry the Champion of the World*.' She laughed at the comparison to one of her favourite books, for the way it idyllically captured her memories.

'He sounds like a good guy... What about your mum? You have a similar relationship?'

Cherry brushed some invisible lint from the white cotton shirt covering Sean's remarkably muscular shoulder – an action she realised was something her mum had done to her dad. '"Get on" might be a bit strong. As long as we don't spend too much time together, it's civil. I love her but, my God, we're different.'

'She's not a poker player then?'

Cherry would need to be careful not to rant about her mum. *Keep it brief, keep it upbeat.* 'No. She's Pamela Paradise, Mystic and Colour Consultant – and that's for your wardrobe *or* your aura. When my dad died, she absorbed herself in reading people's futures with tarot cards, telling them not to wear pumpkin because they're "a winter" and stuff like that. Just as well she lives in Scotland and I travel around the States. We're better thousands of miles apart.'

'You're actually selling her to me; she sounds fun. And I detect a fair bit of love for her in your voice.'

Slowly, Cherry blinked, not giving too much away. Who was this guy with his astute observations, seeing into her very soul?

'Are you on the road a lot?' he asked.

'A bit too much.' She tried to maintain a reasonable distance from Sean, not to press too close, stay cool and detached, but the heat of him drew her in. 'Poker is losing its edge. Or I'm losing mine. I have these dreams about going back to Scotland...pinning my kids' macaroni art to the fridge…cooking hearty casseroles, even though I can't cook for shit, or meet a decent man to have said kids with.'

Sean's mouth curved upwards – she could tell at her honesty rather than her circumstance. 'Do you need a man for that stuff?' he asked.

The volume of Cherry's laughter turned the heads of several people dancing nearby. 'Okay, where is your mother? I need to thank her for raising you and ask her permission to marry you.'

'It's true though, right?' His expression was so sinfully earnest that she could have kissed him there and then.

'It is mainly true. But it's not all about biology. I'd like someone to be part of the journey.'

'And your ex. He's…?'

'An alcoholic. Still plays poker, badly. Drinks too much and sways around tables, putting people off their game. There are reasons he's like that, but it's hard to sympathise when he's such an arse to people, me included.'

Sean sighed, pulling her a little closer, the rough wool of his kilt brushing her leg. 'Alcohol is a fucker. My uncle Archie was an alcoholic. Drinking killed him, lost him his wife to his brother and left a permanent mark on our family. His sons – my brothers – are lucky to have grown up with our dad. We were all lucky…'

Cherry caught the tendon in his jaw flexing as he trailed off. 'You okay?' She was glad for the focus to be drawn away from her.

'Aye… Aye. Cal is the first of my siblings to get married, and we're doing it without my dad. All a bit weird, but it's not meant to be a time of me sobbing into my whisky or, even worse, your whisky.'

'Sob into my whisky all you like.' She imagined drawing her glass under his chin, like with buttercups in the school playground. If it weren't for the neat brush of stubble, the golden glow of the drink would surely reflect off his skin.

Sean smiled. 'I'd rather focus on moving forward and making things better for other people. My siblings and I are cycling a hundred miles down the Kintyre Way in September for an MND charity.'

'That's incredible.' A philanthropist too. This man kept on giving. 'I can't wait to meet them.'

And she'd said the right thing because Sean's face illuminated. 'No time like now,' he declared. 'Come on...' He tugged her away from the dance floor into a whirlwind of Butler siblings.

Cherry tried her best to remember the names. There was Cal, a bar owner, and his new wife – a stunning redhead – Bea. Jamie, the second eldest and CEO of Butler's whisky. Niall was a keen surfer, like Sean, and his partner in crime as teenagers. And then came the triplets: chilled vet Nate, exuberant actress Cara and Eilidh, a teacher, who seemed possessed of an untamed energy. Clearly a lot of alcohol had been consumed, but handshakes and hugs were offered. The only person Sean didn't introduce was his mother. But that was fine because meeting the mother was the big gun.

'Did you know,' Cherry said as they danced again, 'that there was this psychological study in the nineties where the participants asked one another a list of questions, stared into each other's eyes for three minutes and some of them fell in love?'

Sean leaned in, everything else fading out again as his voice vibrated in her ear. 'I didn't, but go on...ask away.'

'I can't remember all the questions, but one is: Tell your partner something you like about them already.'

'Hmm, okay...' Sean wasted no time. 'I like your hair, I

like your sex-crazed bucket list and I like that you're not afraid to go after vol-au-vents when you see them.' He winked at her. 'Your turn.'

A smile lifted Cherry's mouth before she spoke. 'I like that you've not entirely dismissed me for ram raiding your life tonight. That you're a "yes, let's" type of guy. And as previously discussed, I like your gorgeous, swimmable green eyes that I'd go skinny dipping in if they were lakes.'

Sean lifted his brows as if to give her a better view. 'I've never heard that before. Come skinny dip anytime.' He glanced at the table then back to her. 'Want to do it now for three minutes? See if you fall in love with me?'

'You bet I do.' Cherry let him lead her back to their seats, where she placed her tumbler down, looked at him and was slammed with a realisation.

Staring into this man's eyes for three minutes was an entirely superfluous part of the process of falling in love with him.

It was like wondering what cards your opponents held when you were already staring down at a Royal Flush.

The second the elevator doors closed, their lips collided, tongues entangled, hands everywhere – Sean's hands sliding over her backside, hers buried in his hair.

'Fuck, Cherry.' He pushed her up against the gunmetal wall, the heavy fabric of his kilt hot and scratchy against her knees, the furnace of his skin burning through the white cotton of his shirt. Everything in this tin box was rising – the temperature, the glowing numbers ticking upwards as they rose through the floors of the hotel and the heat between them.

Clutching at the shirt, Cherry tugged Sean towards her,

needing to feel him – badly. And feel him she could. There was enough there for its magnificence not to be tempered by the barrier of his kilt. How far they could go was out of their hands, but who cared? The only thing that mattered was this moment with this incredible Scotsman, whose evening she had serendipitously ambushed. Everything else was background noise.

'You sure you want to do this?' Sean spoke hoarsely into her ear as he ran his touch inside her dress. Damn, no man's hand had ever felt as good as this. One of Sean's placed on her thigh was doing more for her than the whole body of anyone she'd been with in the past.

'Yes...' Cherry grasped at his kilt. 'I want this. I want to fuck in an elevator with you, Sean Butler.'

'Let's get those items checked off your list then.' He hoisted her dress up, and she lifted her leg and hitched it over his hip. He'd be able to see now how wet she was through her white underwear.

And to see his face as a low 'fuuck' emerged, it soaked her even more.

'Jesus, Cherry, you're this wet for me already. Say you'll marry me.' He did at least meet her eye as he spoke.

'Yes, I'll marry you.' Cherry lifted the edge of Sean's kilt. Absolutely she would marry him because look at what she'd get for the rest of her life. The Butler genes played a strong game, it would seem.

But something changed in Sean's expression. Seriousness took over. What had she said? She dropped the kilt.

'I'm not doing this here,' he said.

'What? Why?' Cherry lowered her leg, suddenly feeling exposed.

'Because it should be better than this. The first time. It won't be a quick fuck in a lift with someone else walking in and seeing you with your leg round my waist. I know that sounds daft and possessive, because I've known you a few hours, but... Well, I dunno what's going on, to be honest. I just know I'm not doing this with you here.'

He must have clocked her confusion.

'I'm serious, Cherry. I know we've joked about getting married, but it doesn't feel like a joke. It should, but it doesn't.'

'Are you religious?' What guy who was ready to have sex in an elevator stopped as the ride was beginning?

Sean stroked her dress down over her hips. 'I think I might be about to get pretty fucking religious about you. You deserve better, Cherry.'

On a curious head tilt, she asked, 'How do you know what I deserve?'

'Okay, I phrased that wrong. I want to give you something better. How does that sound?'

She couldn't deny that it made sense, but it didn't make it any less surprising. 'I don't know what to say. No man has ever said those words to me before.'

'Well, that's a fucking disgrace.' Sean traced the line of her jaw with his fingers. 'But here we are, and here I am with my words. You can decide whether to find out if they have substance or not.'

The sincerity in his eyes blew Cherry away. Men could lie. Men did lie. And she had fielded a thousand lies from less than a handful of men. But most of the time, she'd known they were lying – poker had given her the skill to discern a thousand tells. Sean Butler was either entirely sincere or the best liar of the male species she'd ever met.

'Okay, so what are we doing then?' She adjusted her breasts inside her bra cups. 'Going to bed in separate rooms with a cup of hot cocoa?'

At that moment, the elevator doors pinged and slid open. Level twenty-five. Where Cherry's room was located.

'Let's get off.' Sean reached for her hand.

'Or not.'

Ignoring her dig, he moved out of the lift and into the corridor. 'Come on. I'll walk you to your room.'

Outside Cherry's room, her hand still in Sean's, she sensed him watching her as she unlocked the door with her keycard. She swung round and leaned against it, pushing it open with her back, gaze fixed on him, lips parted, lids laden, anticipating his response. This seductiveness had worked in the past.

But Sean examined her with a pained expression that suggested he was fighting against every atom of desire in his body. He wanted her, but he wasn't going to take her. The man had principles. She should admire him for that.

But, hell, she wanted him. Like, achingly wanted.

'Are you coming in?' she asked. *Goddammit, say yes.*

'No. Do you have a pen in your bag?'

Cherry sighed, fished into her bag and handed Sean a ballpoint pen.

He lifted her hand to his. 'Here's my room number.' Sean wrote the number 3707 on her skin, and next to it his name. If you wake up and still feel the same as tonight, come get me. I'll take you to breakfast.'

Cherry considered the rather surprising number. 'It almost looks like love,' she said.

'Pardon?'

'The numbers: three, seven, zero, seven. They almost look like L, O, V and E, when you're reading upside down.'

Sean looked down at her hand still resting in the confident hold of his own, considering her observation. He ran the wide pad of his thumb under the numbers. Low-level electricity zinged through her.

'Aye,' he murmured deeply. 'It's all a bit backwards and upside down, but it does kind of look like "love" alright.' The dismissal or humouring that Cherry had expected wasn't there. Only a man on exactly the same page.

Only a concurrence that this could indeed be love, delivered in an encrypted way but there to see if you knew how to decode it.

Chapter 3

Cherry

The following morning, Cherry woke up with Sean's room number still on her hand and an aching desire to find him. Not to mention an aching between her legs that had to be sated in the shower before she pulled on a sky-blue summer dress, flip-flops, whipped her hair into a messy bun and made her way to room 3707.

As soon as Sean opened his door, the aching returned. Here he was – fresh-out-of-the-shower hair, cargo shorts and a white shirt. So tall – at least six four – with solid legs, muscular arms, and innumerable tattoos. Cherry was a goner for a man with tattoos, and Sean had them by the armload.

'Morning, Paradise.' From the energy in his voice, you wouldn't suspect he'd sunk as much alcohol as he had the night before. Maybe it had all been smoke and mirrors. Or he was one of those people who easily bounced back.

'You don't seem hungover,' she said.

Sean grinned. 'Hangovers are a state of mind. Also, I only drink quality whisky, and a lot of water when no one's about. The sight of you might just cure any hangover, though.' He glanced down the corridor towards the lift. 'I was googling ways to make elevators stall. I think I can get us a good three minutes before the alarm goes off.'

Cherry lifted a questioning brow. Was he serious?

'I'm joking. You want to hang out, though? You were the first thing I thought about when I woke up, and I think we should do New York today. You up for it?'

She said yes. Of course, she said yes.

First was brunch at Bubby's – a New York institution. Facing each other with two giant stacks of pancakes, hers laden with blueberries and his caramelised banana and walnuts, Cherry realised not only how hungry she was, but how curious she was about Sean.

'Who would be your ideal dinner guest?' she asked amid the lively hubbub of the sun-drenched diner. 'That's one of the questions to make you fall in love, by the way. Just for full disclosure.'

'Ah, thanks for letting me know I'm part of your experiment.' Sean stabbed his pancake stack with his fork. 'You have a willing participant. And to answer, I know I'm meant to say my dad or Jesus or something, but my honest answer is Hercules the Bear.'

Cherry snorted with laughter, grateful she hadn't yet taken a bite of food.

'You know who I mean?'

'I've a vague idea. He was a celebrity bear or something?'

'Aye. Bought as a cub from the Highland wildlife park and raised by a wrestler and his wife. Disappeared while filming a Kleenex ad in the Hebrides but was found fifteen stone underweight because he was too tame to eat any wildlife he could have preyed on. And they re-nourished him with shrimp and Advocaat. That's what I'd serve at the dinner party, with a wee dram for after... What about you?'

Cherry lowered her fork, which she realised had been poised mid-air while Sean talked. 'I'd love to meet Poker Alice,' she said. 'She was a legendary Old West poker player who outplayed the men, smoked cigars and carried a 38 revolver, which she used to reinforce her rule about never playing on Sundays.'

'Jeezo! She sounds more terrifying than a grizzly.'

'She wouldn't scare me.' At last, Cherry managed to take a bite of pancake. 'She might scare Hercules, though.'

'Aye. He was a big softy.' Sean smiled. 'How's the pancake?'

'So, sooo good. You like?' She nodded to his stack, caramel drizzling down the remaining side.

'I love.' Sean's eyes sparkled as he stared right at her while stabbing another piece of pancake off his plate.

Cherry almost forgot to keep chewing. Without ungluing her gaze from his, she asked another question. 'Would you like to be famous?'

The answer came fast. 'Nope. My family is well known enough in Scotland, and in Kinshore, sometimes it feels we're like the Kintyre royal family or something.'

'Ooh!' Cherry loved the concept of somewhere so small and Scottish having its own royal family. And of Sean being part of it. She bet he was one of the eligible princes on the peninsula.

'I'm not bragging,' Sean said, 'but folk know us. My mum gets invited to open garden centres and stuff. One of the reasons Cal had his wedding in New York was so folk wouldn't be offended if they weren't invited. God knows how Jamie will cope when it's his turn. He's the CEO, so that makes him the king. I'm one of the spares.' Peering down at his food, Sean seemed to realise how little he'd eaten. 'God, I don't half talk a lot, sorry.'

Cherry tucked her fork into a wedge of his pancake and cheekily scooped it up. 'I like listening.' She slid the fork into her mouth. 'I want to know all about you. And these questions are fun. Not that we need a conversational crutch.'

'Aye, we don't, but it is fun. So, would *you* like to be famous?'

The answer to this was definitive. 'No. I'm well known in the poker world, but besides a decent bank balance, I'm not sure what it's given me. It's bad enough on the circuit for a woman, without the wider media latching on with their "poker wild woman" garbage. Also, I dated a minor celeb back in the day, and getting papped sucks.'

'Ah, right.' Sean didn't ask who the minor celeb was, for which Cherry was grateful, seeing as he was more of a major celeb nowadays. She was also touched that where most people would fish for a name, Sean did not.

As they emerged, pancake-happy, into the Tribeca sunshine, Sean interlocked his fingers with hers, pressing their hands together. It was hard to concentrate when he asked, 'Where to now?' All she could think about was how protective this simple gesture felt. But as they walked through Lower Manhattan, chatting away, she relaxed into the feeling. He was such easy company.

'Seany,' she said as they were cruising out to the Statue of Liberty, 'would you really marry me today, if you could?'

Sean glanced up from the river he'd been staring into, eyes bright but serious. 'Aye, I would. Not to sound like a nutter, but I found out from Google that to marry at City Hall, you have to wait twenty-four hours after getting a licence. I'd do it, though.'

The other passengers were occupied by the Statue of Liberty, but Cherry was fixated on Sean. 'Me too.' He made the outlandish seem normal by committing to his chosen direction. But did he regret his choices? She wouldn't marry him if he might change his mind next week.

'What would your family say?' she asked. Their reactions could hold the key to whether this was a sustainable approach.

'That's easy. "Calm doon, Sean, take your time, don't rush into things, why don't you think about this for a bit, consider your options, be more Jamie, be more Cal, blah, blah, blah."'

'Ooft! Have I hit a sore point?' Cherry had no siblings, but she could understand that in a family of Sean's size there might be unfair comparisons.

'Ha, no. Well, maybe, aye. I might be a little bit jaded by being underestimated all my life. I have this thing where I do things fast – whether it's buying a new washing machine or a house or moving to London at the last minute – and people don't get it because that's not how they operate. So they think I'm headed for calamity. Add things like dyslexia and poor focus and, well, I suppose I've spent a lot of my life being underestimated for what I understand. There's an accepted idea of intelligence, and it's not a lad who has trouble spelling and hammers bits of wood together for a living. But they don't know what goes on up here.' Sean tapped at his temple.

Cherry wondered if she'd happened upon the most reflective man who hammered bits of wood together for a living. It was admirable how honest he was about his "stuff", and how he didn't shy away from his challenges. 'Those things sound hard,' she said. 'Dyslexia is tough... And ADHD?'

'Ach, dunno. Never been tested. But listen.' He read her concern. 'If you're worried that marriage would be a hare-brained decision I'll backtrack on, the chances are slim.'

This was interesting, but how did he know? Like, really know. 'Marriage is different from a new washing machine or a move to London,' she said.

'Yeah, it is, which is why I wouldn't go into it lightly. This is a slow-paced decision for me. It's been nearly twenty-four hours since we met. Would be another two days before we could get hitched here.'

Cherry considered how many times the sun would have to set and rise before that could happen. 'Feels like ages. In the meantime, all you've done is intrigue me. I want to know more about what goes on up there.' She raised her hand to Sean's temple. 'Every neural impulse that makes you Sean Butler.'

Sean lifted his hand to meet hers. 'I'll tell you all about those impulses. And likewise, Cherry Paradise.'

After the cruise, they caught the subway north to Columbus Circle and walked into Central Park, where they meandered the numerous pathways, the rich smell of cut grass mingling with the aroma of hot dogs and honey roasted nuts, all enveloped in searing summer city heat.

'What's your mum like?' Cherry asked as they passed a mother trying to placate two squabbling children.

Sean seemed to laugh at so much in life, and this question was no exception. 'Really? Is that question on the fall in love list, too?'

'It might be, but I'm curious.' She rubbed the back of her neck, clammy in the heat, and noticed the loose strands of hair stuck there. 'People's relationships with their mothers intrigue me, possibly due to my own being a bit mercurial. Also, it can tell you a lot about a man.'

'No judgment then.' Sean walked tall with the confident air of a man who couldn't care less about being judged. 'My mum's great. She's weathered a lot. Escaped her first abusive husband, raised seven kids – three of whom were adopted at once – helped grow the distillery with my dad, dealt with the premature loss of him to a horrific disease. We're all protective of her because we know what she went through to get where she is today, but she's a trooper.'

Amanda did sound like a powerhouse of a mother. 'Seven kids is amazing,' Cherry said. 'What was it like growing up with six siblings?' She would have loved even one, had often dreamed of the hubbub of brothers and sisters barging into each other's rooms, staying up all night giggling. Home would be a place you felt crowded but never lonely.

'I think the only word is mental.' Sean chucked some loose change into a busker's guitar case. 'It's quite nice having a big family, now we're all grown up, although I'll maybe stop at two when I have my own.'

'You want kids then?' She hoped she didn't sound like a clingy female trying to pin a man down. But Sean's response suggested he heard nothing of the sort.

'Aye, definitely. You said you wanted to stick their pasta art on the fridge, didn't you? Your kids' pasta, that is? Or mine. Or ours. Who knows?' He slung his arm around her shoulder.

'I did say that.' Cherry was comforted by the closeness. 'I want a full-length portrait of me, with slender penne limbs and a mix of wholewheat and normal spaghetti hair, framed on the fridge. Or in the Met.'

'It will happen; you just have to believe.'

It was uncertain if this was a response to the Met idea or

the pasta on the fridge. Either way, Sean sounded convinced.

'Yes, well, so they say... So you're after a country wife then?'

He stopped on the path, moving out of the way to let people pass, but perhaps it was an excuse to look at her with a suggestive smile. 'What's a country wife? If she's like you, then yes.'

Cherry pretended she hadn't thought about this a million times already. 'I think she's someone with child-bearing hips who bakes scones barefoot and is sexy in wellies on the school run.'

'Hmm.' Sean feigned contemplation, but the corners of his mouth lifted again in amusement. 'I like a good scone, and...um, childbearing hips...' He brushed down the cotton of her dress at her hips with reassuring palms. 'But she doesn't have to be from the country. In fact, I might prefer something different. I just like the idea of a family. A house filled with love, you know?'

The sweet scent of roasted cashews and summer heat wrapped around them. Sean's character, and the image he conjured up, was so visceral that Cherry was almost in that home with him. She saw the two of them standing by a Scottish hearth, holding each other. Fast forward to winter, if that were the case.

'Yes, I know what you mean,' she said. What he wanted was what she wanted too. The sticking point for some time had been how to make it gel with her itinerant poker career. But Sean seemed to shift the pieces of her life puzzle so that the end picture became clearer. Achievable, even. Something that felt this right couldn't go wrong, surely.

As the afternoon drifted on, they lazed under a tree on the Great Lawn in Central Park, Cherry's head on

Sean's lap, the sense of being completely at ease and totally electric with arousal not passing her by for a moment.

'Cherry.' He stroked the hair at her temple.

'Mm-hmm.' She was too warm to do anything more than murmur.

'Would you sit up for a second?'

The seriousness of his tone brought her round. She shuffled up to face him. What was going on? There was something in those green irises that she hadn't yet experienced. A wavering. A seriousness underpinned by uncertainty. Was he about to say that he was terminally ill? Already had a girlfriend? A wife?

'Cherry, will you marry me?'

Cherry's heart ricocheted, and her breath hitched so tight she nearly choked. *Oh my God!* They'd talked about this but, somehow, Sean had managed to take her completely by surprise.

'I'd get down on one knee, but I don't have a ring and... Well, this isn't the most conventional proposal anyw—'

She grabbed his face, the words bursting out of her. 'Yes! Yes, of course I'll marry you, Sean.' There was no need for a bended knee or a ring to know the answer. Sure, they could go back to Scotland together and be boyfriend and girlfriend, but that seemed lacking somehow. Juvenile. Her feelings for Sean were not juvenile. They were whole, fully formed and very adult.

He searched her face as if to check she was serious. 'Oh, thank fuck. I was scared for a second that you'd say no—'

And true enough, she saw traces of hesitancy. So far, he'd exuded only confidence, but there was a disquiet there from putting himself on the line, mixed with relief that it had all turned out okay. He needn't have worried.

'As if I'd say no. I'm besotted with you, Sean Butler, and being your wife would be an honour and a delight.'

Sean's unerring confidence flowed back in, in the form of the most gorgeous smile Cherry had ever seen.

'Besotted is a good word,' he said. 'In case you haven't noticed, you have knocked me off my size thirteens, Cherry Paradise. And I can think of no greater honour or delight than being your husband. Let's get a licence and get ourselves married in a New York minute.'

Two days' later, under an inferno of July sunshine and a small blaze of pink confetti, Cherry and Sean tripped down the steps of City Hall and into married life together.

'Welcome to your new husband, Mrs Butler.' Sean held her waist as she tipped back, teetering on one white Manolo.

'Thank you, Mr Butler. Welcome to your wife.'

And as her husband kissed her, Cherry knew she'd married the right man. She would never tire of Sean's kiss. If she hadn't known the moment she laid eyes on him that he was her forever, then the kiss on the dance floor had well and truly communicated that. His strong hands, rough from crafting thousands of whisky barrels, were tender on the nape of her neck. The soft touch of his lips was at first gentle and slow – a contrast to the feelings ricocheting back and forth between them. It was a rare find, a man who recognised that even when fireworks were going off like a hundred Hogmanays, the kiss had to be different. The kiss had to communicate sparks but also feelings.

Sean Butler knew this.

And Cherry was melting for him.

Melting for her new husband. And just melting. New

York City summer was in full-on pizza oven mode. How was Sean coping in his kilt? She at least had on a white dress. The twenty-four-hour period from the marriage licence being granted to the wedding taking place had afforded her the chance to shop for a beautiful ankle-grazing, cap-sleeve gown. And they had bought each other rings – hers white gold with iridescent diamonds, his a yellow-gold band. Sure, she had just married a man she'd known less than a week, but the dress and the ring mattered. Although, not nearly as much as the fever for the man. That was the most important thing, and she well and truly had that.

'How many photos do you want?' Sean's older brother, Jamie, asked from the foot of the steps. Not wanting to upstage Cal and Bea or worry his mum, Sean had recruited Jamie and his fiancée, Alicia, as witnesses to the wedding and sworn them to secrecy. They could announce the marriage to everyone else back in Kinshore. 'And do you want one where you look feral for each other?' Jamie added.

Like wedding bells, Sean's laughter rang through the cut and thrust of the NYC traffic. He spoke to his older brother without taking his eyes off his wife. 'Let's try to keep them classy, shall we? One the kids won't cringe at down the line.'

Cherry almost had to bat back tears with her carefully mascaraed lashes. That he was talking about a family created a bubble around them. This was more than merely an impromptu marriage. Sean believed in her, the same way she did in him. The kids comment worried her a little but, my God, he made her feel whole, loved, vital.

As for his family, she wasn't sure they had the same faith, at least not quite yet. She'd witnessed the conversation outside the venue between Jamie and Sean. A short but serious discussion where Jamie had inquired if Sean knew what he was doing. Sean placated him by admitting it seemed insane, but he'd never felt clearer about anything in his life.

'Are you sure it's not the grief proposing?' Jamie asked. 'Why don't you guys date for a while? Have a proper wedding back home where everyone can be there.'

'Don't worry, J... We want to be married. And we can have a party in Kinshore at some stage.'

Jamie put his hand on Sean's shoulder, stood back and observed him, inspecting for signs of madness maybe. But there was an admiration there, too, from an older brother to a younger one. 'Never thought I'd see the day my wee brother beat me to the altar. By the way, you look a lot like Dad today.'

'I do?' Something shimmered in Sean's gaze, and Cherry saw how much his father had meant to him. She wished Jimmy Butler could be here to see his son marry.

'Where to now?' she asked after the photoshoot was done. 'Wedding breakfast?'

'Oh, aye, wedding breakfast. In my hotel room, where I am going to devour my wife.' Sean pulled her in tighter. 'There is no chance we aren't feral for each other in these photos.'

Cherry suspected he was right. Here she was, marrying a man she deliberately hadn't slept with. It was laughable. But the kiss and illicit moments in the elevator told her everything she needed to know. Hell, the kiss told her the past, present and future all at once. That and what she got a glimpse of under his kilt before he'd called time on things.

• • •

'Won't your family be wondering where you are?' Cherry toyed with the belt buckled around Sean's kilt as he slotted the key card into the hotel room door.

'Nah, they'll be too busy panicking about getting to the airport on time.' The door clicked open, and he spun round, simultaneously kissing and tugging her into the room. It swung closed behind them with a clunk.

'Shouldn't you be doing the same?' Cherry murmured, not especially bothered about airports or check-in times. All she cared about was getting this man's – her husband's – kilt off.

'Takes five minutes to chuck my stuff in a suitcase and five minutes to hail a cab. What I'm about to do to you, on the other hand, might take a while...'

'I can't wait. Glad you booked a late check-out.'

'Mmm, me too. We do need to get you on the same flight, though. Might involve some last-minute admin and packing.' Sean's mouth lingered at hers.

'Ah, well, I love a mad dash to the airport.' Everything Cherry needed for now was in the suitcase she was travelling with. The rest could be sorted out later.

'Fantastic. I love your attitude.' Sweeping her hair back, Sean dipped his head to plant tender kisses on her neck. 'Now, do you think we can still fit in consummating this marriage?'

'I think it should be a priority.'

'Good.' He slid down one strap of her wedding dress.

And then the shrill siren of the hotel fire alarm sliced through the air.

Chapter 4

Cherry

Squat, green static mobile homes decorated the clifftop caravan park like rows of tightly packed shoeboxes, but the expansive view across the glimmering Firth of Forth gifted the site a luxurious spaciousness.

Pamela Paradise's home was easy to distinguish from all the others because there were more plants than a garden centre on the porch and a weathered garden gnome sitting sentry at the front door.

'That's Lucky Gordon.' Cherry pointed to the gnome with her toe. 'He guards the premises, keeps away evil spirits. Forgets to take out the bins.'

'I see.' Sean tilted his chin at the gnome. 'Alright, Gordon?'

'By the way, you don't have to pretend he's real for me,' Cherry whispered. 'But my mum will love you for it.' She rapped on the frosted glass panel of the caravan door, took another glance at the view and a deep breath, before the door swung open and her mother appeared, resplendent in a tapered-leg, turquoise-green jumpsuit. It was more 'forty-year-old at a fondue party' than 'sixty-five-year-old at a caravan park', but she had been forewarned that her daughter was bringing a special guest. Although Cherry had not mentioned that Sean was her husband.

'Hey, Mum. You're looking well. That colour suits you. What is it? Aquamarine?'

'Aqua Cyan, darling. And thank you. Come on in.' Pam gave Sean a once-over, as if assessing him for sartorial suitability, before ushering them up the steps and into the lounge. 'How wonderful.'

Not much inside the caravan had changed since Cherry was last here at Christmas. The same Royal Doulton ornaments festooned the shelves, alongside gilt-framed photos from her childhood – ones of her mother and father, her grandparents. All that was missing were photos of Cherry... successfully adulting.

The sound of Sean clearing his throat interrupted her thoughts. It was time for the introductions she'd been dreading.

'Sorry. Um... Mum...this is Sean. Sean, this is my mum, Pam.'

Pam dismissed Sean's outstretched hand, opting instead to embrace him warmly. 'A solid Irish name that. Are you Irish?'

'Nope, although Ireland is just across the water from my home in Kintyre.'

'Ah, Kintyre. Tell me, do you ever see Paul McCartney coming and going?'

Sean chuckled. 'Never seen him once. He still owns his farm, but I don't think he's there much anymore.'

'Mum...' As nice as it might be to chat about trivial stuff all day, Cherry knew it was time to pull this Band-Aid off. 'Sean and I are...' She floundered and found the warm reassurance of his hand. 'We got married...in New York... We're husband and wife.'

As soon as the words were out, Cherry stood proud. For a moment, the scene dissolved into a past one where she was bouncing up the steps of their Edinburgh colonies house clutching another A-grade. But this beautiful man holding her hand was better than any Advanced Higher Maths buzz. She hoped her mum could still be pleased with her daughter's achievements.

Thankfully, instead of disapproval at the hastiness of the nuptials, Pam's overriding sentiment was pique at missing the ceremony.

'My only daughter, and I don't get to see her marry. I suppose this is the universe getting its revenge on me for my own wedding.'

'Mum was a runaway bride,' Cherry explained, relief carrying her onto this well-trodden path down memory lane. 'She and my dad eloped to Gretna Green when they were sixteen and got married in the old blacksmith's shop.'

'Best thing I ever did, following that intuition,' said Pam. 'Speaking of which, I knew there was a reason the High Priestess showed up in your reading yesterday.' She clung onto a remnant of control by convincing herself that she had known about the marriage.

'You don't have to do readings for me, Mum. I'm not here to know about them.'

'You're my daughter; I like to know how you're getting on. Anyway, I haven't even said congratulations to Mr and Mrs...?'

'Mr Butler and Ms Paradise,' said Sean, and Cherry caught her mum's expression of mild exasperation. Good women took their husband's name.

'Listen, we can't stay long; it's a long drive to Kinshore...'

Cherry ran her finger along the sideboard as if inspecting for dust, which she knew she wouldn't find.

'You could get a B&B nearby or rent a caravan from the site for the night.' Pam boiled the kettle, lined up three mugs and fussed around, pulling biscuit packets from the cupboard. 'Stay and keep your old mum company. Show me your wedding snaps.'

'Of course we'll show you the photos, but Sean and I... We kind of wanted to get back to his place and...'

'Oh, I see.' Pique pinched Pam's tone again, but she diverted attention from Cherry to someone who didn't bother her quite as much. 'Do you have many siblings, Sean?'

'Aye.' Sean glanced at Cherry, clearly aware that her mum was making a point.

Cherry smiled faintly as an indication that she was okay, letting him do the good-son-in-law thing.

'I've four brothers and two sisters.'

'Ah, well, that's lovely. Your lucky mother. I always wanted some siblings for Cherry, but it never did happen. And do you all live near to her?'

'Four of us live in Kinshore. My eldest brother and my two sisters are in Edinburgh, although one travels a lot for work.'

'That's nice. I've a daughter with a flat in Edinburgh, whom I see three days a year, if I'm lucky.'

Cherry held her nerve. 'It's more than that, Mum.' Although, maybe it wasn't much more. Perhaps they should stay, at least for tea, but they'd literally got off the flight from New York and driven here from Glasgow airport. Cherry couldn't bear another atrocious night of not consummating her marriage. She was pretty sure Sean was feeling the same, and their first time could not be in a manky old caravan or a dusty B&B.

'Why don't we stay for something to eat?' she suggested. This was a halfway house, which would hopefully appease her mum. And give less time for the conversation to turn sour. She squeezed Sean's hand, and he did the same back.

'Sounds good to me. If it's not too much trouble, Mrs Paradise.'

'Call me Pam. And it's a pleasure. As long as you're okay with quiche and Bird's Eye potato waffles.'

'I love quiche and Bird's Eye potato waffles.'

As soon as her mum left the caravan to borrow some waffles from 'Colin down the way', a giggling Cherry slid onto Sean's knee, and they began making up for lost time.

'How am I sitting in a caravan in Fife, about to eat quiche and waffles, when I should be at home doing things to my wife?' He dusted his lips over her earlobe, kissing her right in the spot under it that he'd discovered threw her completely.

'Mmm, welcome to paradise. I never said it was literal paradise.'

'I'm sure it is,' Sean murmured, hands coasting over the side of her breasts. 'God, I cannot wait for you, Cherry. Fuck, I need to stop; I can't be getting turned on at your mum's.'

'It's hard for me too, you know. Have you any idea how wet I am?'

'Have I what?' Sean splutter-laughed. 'Oh, just you wait, Paradise. You're going to get it so hard for that gigantic tease when I'm five hours from home.'

'So hard? You promise?'

'Aye. In fact, fuck it. We're getting a hotel. I'm booking the

Balmoral. We're going to consummate five-star style tonight.' Sean picked up his phone from the Formica table but laid it down as Pam reappeared up the steps with a box of waffles.

'Here we go,' she said. 'Nothing says welcome to the family like some Bird's Eye potato waffles. And after tea, I'll give you both a reading.'

Cherry stood from Sean's knee. 'Mum, you can just call them waffles. And we're good for the reading, thanks.' Sean didn't mind, but he had no idea how blunt her mum could be.

The quiche and Bird's Eye potato waffles were accompanied by tomato ketchup and a full-scale interrogation of Sean. Pam needed to build a full profile of where he was from, who his parents were and what they did for a living, as well as his siblings, their jobs and partners. Also important was Sean's star sign and date, time and place of birth, accidents or major operations, and any other miscellaneous detail he wished to declare.

Cherry was only grateful that the pressure was off her.

The plates cleared away and Pam disappeared to the bedroom, returning with a tarot deck – something that provoked a conditioned response of clammy hands in Cherry.

'Mum, seriously, can we not?'

'Such a sceptic.' Pam winked at Sean from across the table. 'Come on now, let's see what the cards are saying today.'

Cherry rose to wash the dishes – infinitely preferable to this. Protesting would only make her seem churlish and irrational. After all, if tarot cards were such pseudoscience, then why did she care either way?

Because what if they weren't pseudoscience? There had been things her mum had said in the past that were scarily on the money. Relationship endings she'd foretold on more than one occasion. Catastrophic loss Cherry had endured that her mum predicted would happen again – and it had. What if Sean's reading said that their marriage was doomed, that his perfect wife was prone to failure on a life-altering scale, and he should turn and head for the hills now?

She would have to let him. And that was the last thing she wanted. Because she was smitten with Sean. Obsessed. They should never have come here.

Pam laid the cards out in a spread and asked Sean to pick three.

'We'll only do a short reading,' she said. 'So as not to upset my cynical daughter.'

'Cherry, come...' Sean stretched out his arm and beckoned for her to sit with him. She relented and let him kiss her on the cheek.

Get a grip, Cherry. It's only bits of card with pretty pictures on them. Doesn't mean anything.

'Afterwards, we can play poker,' Sean suggested.

Cherry tried her best to laugh. 'If you're happy playing for crisps. Mum refuses to play for money. Thinks it leaches energy from the soul.'

Sean's large hand hovered over the deck. Cherry was distracted thinking of it on her body. It looked strong. Would have to be to build whisky barrels all day. But it would also need to know when to exercise finesse, to craft with attention to detail every curve and smooth edge of those barrels. She couldn't wait for him to explore every curve and smooth edge of her naked skin. The other hand – the one with the wedding ring on – linked into her own, settling her heart rate.

Pam turned over the first card Sean had chosen.

'Ah, the King of Pentacles. This represents a strong

man, someone who is a craftsman of some kind. Good with his hands. '

Sean nodded sagely.

Nicely played, Butler.

'He told you he's a cooper, Mum.'

'Quite cool of that card to pop up, though.' Sean was keeping her mum on side, and for that Cherry had to admire him. His manners were impeccable.

'Yep, guess so.' Cherry examined his profile while her mother selected the next card. He had the most striking jawline she'd ever seen. It could be described as defined and capable. One thing that she agreed with her mother on was that you could tell the mettle of a man by the strength of his jawline. And, by the looks of his, Sean had integrity to spare.

The second card was the King of Cups.

'Well, this is rare.' Pam tapped the card. 'I don't normally see this card for a man under forty. Here, we have a man who is strong on the outside yet compassionate on the inside. A real kind-hearted father figure type.'

Cherry sucked in a sharp breath through her nose.

Remember, it's all bollocks.

But she didn't want it to be bollocks. She wanted it to be true, except with that truth came heartache for her.

'He can be prone to failed relationships and divorce, though,' Pam added. 'Because he's an idealist. But, Cherry, he will accept you unconditionally. He's generous to a fault, but don't mistake that for him being a pushover.' She nodded pointedly at her daughter.

This was already too much. Sean was being painted as some kind of saviour who'd rescue and accept her, even if she didn't believe in herself, and who she needed to be warned not to take advantage of. Her mum was almost spelling out her daughter's shortcomings to him.

'Sounds a lot like my dad, actually.' Sean held the King of Pentacles card, examining it as if it were a photo of his father. 'He and my mum were married for nearly thirty-five years, and I'm sure Cherry and I will go the same distance.' He examined her adoringly. She admired his optimism.

There was so much that could be said, but Pam chose silence.

The final card that Sean had chosen was Death.

'Now, this doesn't mean anyone is going to die,' Pam reassured, touching Cherry's arm. 'It's much more about change. The death of a dream maybe. Letting go and moving onto new pastures. Every end is a new beginning.'

'Aye, so it is.' Sean nodded and sent an expression of such warmth Cherry's way that it broke her heart.

'As you two go into your marriage together, there will be things you have to leave behind. Not only lands and homes, but ideas about how the future looked before.' Pam's expression held such pity that it pierced Cherry with the pain of the past.

There she was again, curled up in the foetal position, a hollowed-out shell, drained of tears. And every time, her mum on the phone saying, 'It wasn't meant to be. Poker takes its toll. Life has other plans for you,' and Cherry biting back the saltwater until she could fall back onto the bed and sob herself into oblivion once more.

Pam was way out of line pushing this 'death of a dream' thing in front of Sean, but there was no point arguing. As she would say, it wasn't her telling the story; it was the cards.

Oh, for a game of poker with crisps.

'Okay, Mum. Thanks for the reading, but I'll finish the dishes, and then Sean and I might head off.'

'You've not even had coffee and Jaffa Cakes yet.'

'I know. Another time, eh?'

'Okay, sweetheart.' Pam seemed a little downcast, but she disappeared for a few minutes and returned with a folded piece of paper, which she passed to Cherry. 'I wrote this once but never gave it to you. Perhaps you might like it now.'

Cherry unfolded the paper and read.

A mother is not made by a footprint in the sand.

Love does not begin with a clasping of the hand.

I carried you inside me, your heart beating with mine.

And though I never held you, I'm your mummy for all time.

Oh, fuck. Oh, fuck. Oh, fuck.

Cherry' searched for something to hold onto. Anything. A piece of furniture. A cup. Her husband. In the end, she gripped the paper harder. Why the hell had her mum given her this now? Was it meant to be a comfort? Because all it did was throw her right back into the tragedy of the past. Did Pam want her to break down in front of her new husband? Was she trying to test their mettle?

'*The death of a dream. A dream so many women realise, but not you, Cherry. Not you. Still, have a poem to break your heart. I meant well.*'

All she could do was stare at the words and try to act normal. Not give anything away to Sean.

Oh, Sean. Beautiful Sean. Her husband to die for. The King of Cups. King of Hearts. She could hold the tears in right now, but beyond these walls, how could she carry on as if nothing had happened? It wasn't fair. It wasn't right.

Sean deserved better than this, and Cherry knew it. She'd seen the vulnerability behind his confidence; he was a man with a heart, with hopes, with dreams. He'd elevated her into the ranks of the most important women in his life. Told her how he saw his future. A house filled with love.

The thing she'd been reminded she might be incapable of offering. That, if he'd known two days ago, may have altered entirely whether he'd proposed or not.

Now she would need to do the closest thing to going back in time and changing the past.

She would have to talk to him and tell him that they'd made a huge mistake.

Chapter 5

Sean

The evening sunshine glared through the windscreen, blinding Sean physically, adding to the mental disorientation. Thank God they were still parked at the caravan site, or he'd be in a ditch by now.

Something had changed in Cherry since they'd walked the fifty feet from her mother's home, and he had no idea what was going on.

'Cher?' He reached his hand across the gear stick to hers. 'What's up?'

She was staring dead ahead, lost in thought, but her fingers moved gently across his knuckles. For a moment or two, she stared straight ahead, searching for something Sean knew wasn't outside the car. It was in her mind.

'Sorry about my mum,' she said at last, tugging her hand away.

'What's to be sorry about?' Sean leaned on the steering wheel and hoped Cherry would turn to him. 'I like her. Plus, she brought you into the world.' He tucked a strand of hair behind her ear. Was it okay to do that? She might find the gesture patronising. Despite her being his wife, he didn't know Cherry all that well. This was a moment when he wished they could fast forward and understand one another better.

But she grabbed his hand again before he had time to pull it away, brought it to her lips and kissed his fingers. 'Sean,' she murmured.

What was this? It was the action of someone saying goodbye. But they'd barely met, and nothing had gone wrong yet. Had it?

'Cherry, you're going to have to talk to me here; I don't have a scooby what's going on. Things were fine – they were great – but something's happened and the vibe has changed. It wasn't the waffles, so was it the cards?'

She turned to him. 'How do you know that?'

Sean shrugged. 'I'm the King of Cups. I know these things.'

Laughing and sighing at the same time, Cherry muttered, 'Fucking King of Cups. Fucking tarot.'

'It's all bollocks. We'll be fine. Who cares what the cards say?'

'It is, isn't it? Bollocks.' The darkness in her eyes said she desperately wanted to believe this.

'Of course it bloody is. I had my cards read once by some "mystic" in the local pub. She told me the love of my life had curly red hair and I'd meet her at sea. None of it came true.'

'See, that's the thing... Some of the things Mum has seen in her cards have come true.'

'Such as?'

'She told me not to get with Dale, said we had heartache ahead. I ignored her, and she was right. But when it went wrong, all I got was: "I told you he wasn't the man for you, Cherry."'

Sean sucked in a breath. 'She never said that about us, though.'

'No, no, she didn't. She likes you, and the cards like you.' Cherry softened. 'As weird as it might sound, I'm glad the cards like you.'

'Okay, so what's the problem?' He would admit to being confused. It seemed Cherry wasn't hesitant about him; it was something in the cards that had unearthed events from her past. Hopefully, she would talk. 'I know we don't know each other all that well, but...'

'I know enough to know you're incredible. But I'm scared. It's that fucking death card. Why did she have to do that reading?'

'Why does it matter? It was all general waffle... Hey, wasn't that the name of one of your mum's gnomes?'

A watery smile escaped Cherry's lips. 'It matters because... Can I hold your hand while I talk?'

'Of course you can. You're my wife. Hold my hand anytime you like. Tell me why that card bothered you so much.'

She took up his offer, and he noticed her lip quivering. 'Remember when I told you I'd like a pasta portrait of me in the Met?'

'Aye. I loved that idea.'

'Well, sometimes it feels like making that happen would be easier than the whole happy family thing.'

'Ah, okay. Is this to do with men?' Sean's family background, specifically his mother's history, made him acutely aware how hard things were for some women. Cherry had spoken of a troubled ex. There could be trauma there.

She rubbed at her mouth. 'Kind of men, but not really. When I was with my ex, I had...a few...' Each word landed like a weighted pebble dropping into a deep dark pond, the last one coming heaviest of them all. 'Miscarriages.'

Before Sean had time to think, she had tagged on an apology. 'Sorry, I know that's not what you want to hear. Believe me, it's not what I want to be telling you. I should have mentioned it in New York. I'm an idiot, and I apologise.'

But Sean was more blindsided than anything else, his head buzzing like he'd been dealt a blow to the temple. When he managed a response, it came out as sympathy. Far easier than considering if there were implications in this for him. Easier than packing all that in alongside the grief for his dad still sitting so fresh inside him, not to mention jet lag.

'Jeez, I'm sorry you went through that, Cherry. Really sorry. How do you even cope with one, never mind a few?'

With the palm of her free hand, Cherry massaged her heart. 'You cry,' she said. 'You cry so much. Search the internet for support. Play and lose a lot of poker. Slowly, the pain burns less, but you cry when you get triggered or it happens again. It stays with you, the grief, growing into your daily life. Miscarriage happens more than is ever talked about; it's just that it happened to me four times.'

'Four times?' *Bloody hell!* 'May I ask how far along you were?' Sean wanted to understand what she'd gone through. What she was dealing with.

'Two months for one and three months for the other ones.'

'Fuck, I'm so, so sorry.'

'Thank you. I don't deserve your understanding. I'm truly regretful I didn't mention it before. Everything felt so amazing in New York, like we were on a yellow brick road where everything would work out. Seeing my mum has brought me back to earth with a bump.'

'Aye, I can see that.'

'The thing you won't have noticed is that she insidiously infers it's my fault. With the reading, she was saying I should let go of that idea of my future, that I'm not meant to be a mum, despite me turning up here with you and being optimistic about the future.'

'Oh, Cherry, I'm sure she doesn't think that. And if being a mum is what you want, then of course you bloody deserve it.'

'How do you know all the right things to say?' She admired him as if he were some sort of wonder, which he felt anything but.

Right now, Sean felt like the most helpless man in the universe. What could he do to change any of this? He hadn't been there; it wasn't his body; it wasn't his kid she'd been carrying.

But he was here with her now. He was her husband, and he had to try to say something right. Cancel out the feeling of being a spare part.

'I don't,' he said. 'But I know these things are awful, and they can happen to good people through no fault of their own.'

'Yes, but four times usually means there's some reason. That's what my mum was getting at. She thinks *I'm* the problem. My lifestyle is the problem. "Touring around the world, Cherry. Sitting in darkened casinos until two in the morning, night after night, is no way to carry a baby to term." Her actual words. And I know other people have tough jobs and have babies, but when it happens four times, you start to think that every little thing you're doing might be the reason – from a rogue coffee to heating something in a microwave, to not thinking enough positive thoughts. So when my mum says I chose poker, therefore I need to let the dream of being a mother die, I am terrified she is right.'

'Fuck!' This was huge for Cherry.

It's huge for you too, Seany. You can't ignore that. Stop trying to.

'And the truth is, Sean... The truth is that part of me – this fragment I can't ignore – worries about several things. One is, you want to have a family – and so do I – but I don't even know if I can face the whole process of failing again. It hurts far too much. And two, even if I can cope with it, what if you can't? Dale slowly went into meltdown and you should see him now. I can't see that happen to you, Sean. I won't ruin someone else's life. I'm sorry. I was feeling positive about the future until now.'

Sean inhaled deeply, faced the windscreen, leaning on the steering wheel. This was heavy stuff, but it couldn't be as cut and dry as Cherry thought. At least, he didn't want it to be. Truth was he was disorientated. Cherry had been swimming at a different depth than he was used to. The closest he'd come to anything like this was when an ex's period came a week or so late and her worry that she might be pregnant became devastation that she wasn't. But still, his instinct was to deal with Cherry's pain. Put on her oxygen mask first.

That's not how the saying goes.

'First up, don't worry about me, Cher. I'm tougher than I look. Secondly, I get that you wouldn't want to go through that again. Did you get any tests or anything to see why it might have happened?'

'Yep. First time, they said to stabilise my diet and lifestyle. I cut back on late-night poker, embraced clean eating, and when I did fall pregnant, Dale worked and I tried to rest. But no go. Tests on me said I was fine. Dale refused to have any, said he'd clean up his lifestyle, but he didn't. My mum thinks I should have given up poker altogether, moved back to Scotland and let the clean air do its work, or something.'

'I see. So he refused to have tests or make any changes and let you take all the blame. Maybe it wasn't the poker so much as the stress of being in a relationship with an arsehole that had an impact. Or possibly, you and him weren't meant to have a kid together.' He wanted to believe this for his own sake as much as Cherry's.

'Sadly, I don't think "not meant to be" is a medical diagnosis.'

'Aye, right enough.' Sean was no doctor, and he was certainly no expert on reproductive issues. His mind was clouded, and he wanted to get home. But he wasn't about to drive off into the night without his wife.

'Cherry, come back to Kinshore with me. We can talk more there.'

'Oh, Sean.' She let her head loll back on the headrest. 'I have to be real. This is your life, too.'

'Aye, I know. So let me make the decisions about it.' He checked that she didn't look like she wanted out of the car. Kidnapping wasn't something he was keen to have on his resume.

But to his surprise, Cherry didn't protest. Instead, she reached into her bag and retrieved a cardigan, which she slipped on, rubbing her arms and shivering a little.

'Okay.' She stared out the passenger window and down the path towards her mum's caravan. 'I'll come. And google marriage annulment on the way. Drive before I change my mind.'

Ignoring the unnecessary annulment comment, Sean

pulled the car into first gear and away from the caravan site. For a while, they drove in silence, Cherry absorbed by her phone, until she lifted her head and broke the tension.

'From a basic search, it seems you can annul your marriage if you don't consummate it.'

'Right.' Sean tried to concentrate on this whilst merging off a slip road onto the motorway. 'That seems a bit drastic. The annulment.' *And the no consummation.* If they were going their separate ways, surely they could at least relieve the stress by enjoying one another for a while.

'Might be best for a clean break, though,' Cherry said. 'Divorce is messy.'

'Aye, look, chill for now, and we'll talk back in Kinshore. Get some rest while I drive.' Truthfully, he needed time to clear his head and focus on the quiet of the road in front of him. He would think about everything else when he got home.

Chapter 6

Cherry

Some hours later, Cherry awoke from a restless sleep with a stiff neck to find that they were parked in front of a large, white seafront cottage. The dashboard display said 00:23, which would explain that the sea she could hear crashing into shore was nothing but an inky mass.

'Welcome to Kinshore.' Sean caught her staring blankly into the darkness beyond the driveway lights. 'It'll seem better in the morning.'

'Thank you. I'm sure it's stunning.'

As he fetched their luggage from the boot of the car, Cherry stared at the solid, traditional Scottish home. For a second, she imagined standing at the window upstairs, a little baby on her hip as she gazed across the sands to beautiful lands.

'It is. Listen, Cherry, it's late, and we can talk after we've both had some sleep, but would you let me do one thing here, please?' Sean unlocked the house door, placed the luggage inside, then came back down the steps towards her.

'Um...sure.' Briefly, she wondered if he was about to seize an entirely inopportune moment to kiss her. But before she had time to think further, Sean was sweeping her into his arms, striding up the steps two at a time and carrying her over the threshold into his home.

'Whatever happens' – he lowered her to the floorboards – 'even if it's old-fashioned, I need to do the right thing by you.'

Cherry's heart nearly exploded, and she almost asked him to lift her up again and carry her straight to the bedroom. Despite all her personal misgivings, she had never felt as safe as she did in Sean's arms. This man would care for her. Couldn't she relent and let him? Have those barrel-making biceps at her disposal forever, ready to wrap around her whenever she needed them, like he'd vowed to do. *For better or for worse.*

How long would that last before the cracks appeared? She couldn't destroy him, see him fall apart like Dale. Better to be alone than responsible for that. But she had let him do the traditional thing, because – if there was a sliver of a chance for them – she, too, wanted the old-fashioned memory of her husband carrying her into his home.

Their home.

Her husband who, despite the miles they had travelled over the past twenty-four hours, didn't seem remotely tired or fazed by the journey or the distance she had created between them. He appeared as bright and energetic as the evening she'd met him.

'So this is it.' Sean switched on a lamp, illuminating the inside of the house. They were standing on the edge of a huge open-plan space with a modern cream and wood shaker-style kitchen to the right, a generous dining area with patio doors to the back of the kitchen. To the left was a spacious lounge with a huge pillowy couch you could curl up on, losing yourself staring out the huge windows to the sea. The whole place smelled of deep oak and salt air. It was homely and beachy at the same time.

'This is stunning, Sean. It's huge, but so cosy and cool.'

'Cheers. It was a wreck, but I've tried my best to shape it up. Still needs some TLC – more paintings, rugs and stuff. And the garden is a state, but we're getting there.'

'You did all the refurb yourself?'

'Aye. I like a challenge.'

'I love it so much.' Cherry moved around the room, gravitating to some photos on the mantelpiece. She picked up a framed photograph of what must be the whole Butler family, tapping with her fingernail at an older man in the middle, who a bore a strong resemblance to Sean and whom she recognised from some of the photos he'd shown her in New York. 'This is your dad, right?'

'Aye, that's him.' She saw Sean's eyes brighten before darkening, as if remembering his dad was no longer around. 'That was taken at one of the birthday parties my mum held for him every September. Won't be one of those this year.'

Cherry scanned the photo and found Sean. The resemblance to his dad was even clearer when side by side. Same strong build, same heartbreaker smile, same warmth that radiated through a camera lens.

'You all seem so happy, healthy and well-rounded.' *The perfect family.*

'Aye.' Sean's breath was a little laboured, like he was pondering his next words. 'My family's not exactly how it looks from the outside, though, Cher. My dad didn't marry my mum and seven healthy kids miraculously appeared. They went through the wringer on the way. As you know, Mum married his brother first and had three kids with him.'

'Yes. Cal, Jamie and Niall.' Cherry tapped at the faces of the three men she'd met at the wedding. 'Yes?'

Sean moved a little closer. 'Aye. Mum left Uncle Archie after all his shite, got together with Dad and they had me.'

'And then they adopted triplets,' Cherry continued from the memory of all Sean had told her. 'Nate, Cara and Eilidh?'

'Aye, so, we're a mishmash. A blended family, I believe they call it. My idea of family might not be as black and white as you think.' He barely blinked as he let her take this in. A sign he was deadly serious.

Cherry nodded. She knew what he was telling her. Things didn't have to be cookie-cutter shaped. But she wanted that for him. He deserved straightforward.

Sean took the frame from her. 'My dad had seven kids, six of whom weren't his biological kids, but he loved us all with equal ferocity. I might look most like him, but his influence will stay in all of us forever...' His voice cracked a little, and he scrubbed his jaw before putting the photo back on the mantelpiece, half grunting something indecipherable.

'You okay?' Instinctively, Cherry moved to him. 'It's still super new, Seany. You don't have to always be Captain Coping, you know.'

A lopsided expression appeared on his face as he plunged his hands into his pockets and appeared awkward for the first time since she'd met him.

'I love the way you call me Seany, like you've known me forever. As soon as we met, it was like we'd known each other all our lives.'

What else could she say to this? That was her experience, too. She simply smiled and tried to stem her tears.

'Anyway,' he said. 'All I know is Captain Coping. Breaking down isn't an option.'

'Why? Why can't you? I don't mean have a nervous breakdown, but grieve. Cry. Talk about it.'

'Because people need me. My mum needs me to be strong. The community needs that, too. My dad went through hell, and he didn't fall to pieces. Why should I get to indulge?'

Cherry could see now that Sean's coping approach was in part a tribute to the father he loved so dearly and part fulfilling expectations – letting everyone else grieve while he battled on stoically.

'Because it's healthy,' she said. 'You can be sad remembering someone you loved. Fall on the floor and sob one minute and then be happy at the good memories the next. Any emotion is acceptable. And he was *your* dad, so it's your right to grieve him.' This carry-on-all-stoical attitude reminded her of Dale after the first miscarriages – holding things in, pretending it was fine, being there for her but not himself. She should have made him go to counselling.

'Aye, okay. Thanks, Cherry,' Sean mumbled gruffly.

'No bother, Seany. What's your favourite memory of your dad?' Cherry might struggle with her own demons, but she had learned a lot about grief. And meant it when she said to enjoy the good memories.

'How do you pick one?' Sean moved to the window, staring out into the black, his reflection clear in the polished pane. 'Probably surfing together or the chats over a whisky when I was older. I loved those. I remember when I told him I wasn't going to uni like everyone else, and he poured me a dram and told me I could do an apprenticeship at the cooperage. He never pushed us to work for the business, though that was his ideal.'

'I bet he was so proud of you.'

'Aye, maybe. Maybe.' Sean shut down the conversation in those three words, his eyes glistening. 'Right, listen, Paradise, I get the feeling you might want to sleep alone tonight.' He scrutinised in an astute, perceptive way that made it very difficult to make a wise decision.

She should sleep alone. She wanted to sleep with Sean, but if she did that, it would muddy the waters entirely, mess her up emotionally, stymie the annulment and she'd never be able to walk away like she needed to for his sake. It would be a selfish, selfish choice.

'Fuck.'

'That's the question, isn't it?' Sean said.

'Did I say that out loud?'

'Aye, but I'm messing with you. The spare room is already made up. We've somehow gone this long without jumping each other's bones, so why don't you get some sleep, and I'll see you in the morning. The last thing I want is for you to regret any of this.'

'Do you regret it?' The question was out without a thought.

'Nope.' Sean hadn't missed a beat before answering. 'I mean, it was a bit mental, I guess.' His mouth lifted upwards into a tension-melting smile.

Cherry was glad he'd said it. 'Yes, I've never done anything like that before, you might be glad to know.'

'Aye, so let's take it easy on ourselves, okay? You, especially. Come on, I'll take your bags upstairs, show you to your room.'

In the spare room, standing next to Sean, Cherry had to fight the temptation to press herself to his wide chest and kiss him. This man – this gorgeous, broad-shouldered Scotsman – was, for now, her legal husband. How the hell had that happened? She could have him on tap if she wanted. They could be naked between those sheets in mere moments if she gave a sign – said 'let's fuck all night and not think about the future'. Everything she'd seen under that kilt, and more, could be hot and urgent against her own skin. Inside her.

What would the word or words be?

Strip for me!

Fuck me, Sean!

Fuck your wife, please! Now!

'You alright?'

'What? Oh, yeah, I will be once I get into bed. So tired.' Cherry exaggerated yawning and stretching, so much so that it must seem completely fake, and Sean eyed her like she was a little deranged.

'Aye, you'll be knackered.' He glanced at the bed.

Was he thinking what she was? God, they were idiots. No, she was an idiot who'd held back a life-altering truth from him. He was a level-headed, honest gentleman who didn't need any more heartache ripping his life apart. How could she watch him go through more pain than he was? As a wife, she should raise him up, make him the best version of himself. But her past was a wasteland of relationships she had ruined – some destroyed by her itinerant lifestyle, the last one by incessant grief. She was the common denomi-nator in the decimation.

'Bathroom is down the hall,' Sean added. 'It's all yours since my room has an ensuite. If you get lonely, you know where I am. Well, you don't, but I'm in the room next door.' He switched the bedside lamp on and the main light off, giving the room a softer vibe. 'Night, Cherry. Hope you sleep well.'

'Night, Sean. You, too.' Jeez, she was already lonely

without him, and he hadn't even left the room. How was that possible? Married for forty-eight hours, not slept with her husband yet, and missing him whilst standing in front of him.

What sort of fucked-up dumpster fire was Cherry Paradise's so-called life?

Chapter 7

Sean

'Morning!' At 8 a.m., Sean was in the kitchen, cooking breakfast and belting out a Dolly Parton song when he glanced up to see Cherry pad downstairs – a little sleep tempered but luminous, nonetheless, in black jogging bottoms and a well-worn Poker Winners t-shirt. Her hair was tumbled up in a messy bun, but she'd applied some light make-up. Or not removed yesterday's.

'You seem happy, Seany.' Cherry glanced into the scrambled egg pan before landing upon the spread of veggies on the kitchen island. 'This is healthy.'

'I'm always happy, Cher.' This was true. Sean was a genuinely upbeat person, grateful for his lot in life, despite recent loss. 'And I'm trying to be a better cook, despite still recovering from the disaster that was Scrambled Eggs Whisky Irn-Bru.'

She laughed. 'Sounds...um...'

'Like a shocker? Aye, nobody needs that. Nobody. Take a seat, and I'll bring you something nicer.'

Cherry tentatively seated herself at the table, and Sean

brought her a glass of orange juice and a plate near over-flowing with scrambled eggs, bacon, hash browns and spinach.

'Hope you like all that stuff. Most of it was in the freezer, but I'm a bit low on supplies.' With a plate of his own, he sat opposite her. Was she thinking about yesterday? What was she thinking? She was acting like there was nothing wrong, but it may be just that – an act. He hoped so. Because if she was fine and dandy with the annulment then that meant the end, but with hope of her pretending came a chance of saving their marriage.

'I love it all.' Cherry held her fork over the plate. 'I don't know where to start. Do you always do mornings hotel-breakfast style?'

'Nah. Except on the weekend after I've been surfing. I figured, after all the travel, you might want a decent meal. And I need to start eating healthy for the Kintyre Way.'

'Bad habits?'

'Kind of. When I'm at work, I'll grab a BLT from the shop, telling myself it's healthy 'cause it's got lettuce in it. Then add on some chocolate and Irn-Bru. And I'm surrounded by lads doing the same thing, so it's become a habit. At home, I try to cook something decent – a bit of a drag when I'm exhausted after work and surfing or training.'

'How many miles are you cycling again?'

'A hundred... You want to come?'

Cherry lifted a shoulder into half a shrug. Sean regretted suggesting she commit to something else with him when she wanted out of the first thing.

'Sorry... Listen...' He hoovered over the awkwardness. 'I'm going to lay it on the line here.'

'You are? At 8 a.m.?'

'Aye, I'm a "lay it on the line at 8 a.m." type of guy.

You'll find that out if you stay married to me for long enough, which is what I want to talk to you about.' It was stupidly early to embark on this conversation, but Sean had a fitful night's sleep and wanted the swarm of thoughts in his brain to calm down. Fuck off, preferably. However, in the swell of last night's insomnia, an idea had appeared that might buy them some time and some hope.

Cherry chewed hurriedly on a piece of hash brown. 'I can be out of here this morning if you show me where the bus stop is.'

'What? Don't be daft. You literally got here last night. Why leave today?'

'I don't know. It didn't seem right saying goodbye yesterday.'

'Or you didn't want to?'

Her wide-eyed expression suggested he'd hit the nail on the head. 'Yeah, I didn't want to, but nothing has changed overnight.'

If that meant her feelings about him then it was a good thing.

'Okay, I've been thinking, and I have a proposal for you. Only this one's a bit different.' Sean put down his cutlery, threw back some orange juice and cleared his throat like he was about to deliver the groom's speech he never got to. 'Look, for some reason, you're here. You could have stopped at your mum's, but you stayed in the car for five hours – even if you did ignore me by sleeping most of the time – and now we've spent our first night under the same roof as husband and wife. I won't pressure you to stay married, but I have a suggestion. It might be something you can work on while the annulment or whatever is coming through.'

Cherry laid her fork on her plate. 'Hit me, hubby.'

Jesus! 'That kind of talk is practically foreplay, so stop it. Wifey.'

'Sorry.' She glanced down at the remainder of her breakfast and returned to him, seemingly composed. 'Tell me your idea please. Sean.'

'That's better. Okay, here's the thing. I'd like you to stay in Kinshore and organise a celebrity-pro-am charity poker tournament to raise money for MND. I did some research, and it shouldn't take longer than a couple of months to set up, promote and host. Presuming you know the professionals, I can sort the amateurs.'

She shifted forward in her seat. 'Oh, wow! That's an awesome idea.' Then she leaned back. 'But... I dunno, Sean. Your soon-to-be-ex-wife hanging around like a bad smell organising a big gambling event? Not sure that'll go down well in a small town where you're seen as a prince.'

Sean choked on his orange juice. 'Seen as a prince! I likened the family reputation to royalty, not myself to a prince. You'll need to try better than that to get out of it.'

Silence from Cherry, which he decided was a good thing.

'Do I sense you coming round to the idea?'

'Mmm. Could be.'

'Come on, you love it. You said so yourself. It'll be like nothing you've ever done before, I can guarantee. Bring all your mates, presuming you know loads of poker players?'

'Yes, I know lots of people. Hmm...' Cherry examined all four corners of the room at least ten times. Was she imagining what it would be like to live here for two months? Finally, she settled back to him. 'Okay. Okay. I'll do it.'

Sean grinned. 'Great! This will be so good, Cherry. And when it's over, you can head off, I guess. Go back to your old life. Whatever you like. But with your connections and mine, we can raise a decent amount for a really good cause.'

She didn't say anything else. To be fair, she had committed to a lot and would need time to get her head around it.

'It could be good for you, too,' he added. 'Staying here for a bit, getting out of the poker touring circuit. You can still play online, but in between, you can go for walks on the beach, feel the Scottish wind in your face, eat well, sleep in the same bed every night – which is the one you slept in last night, by the way.'

'Really?' Cherry gaped at him.

'Really what?'

'You want me to do all this whilst living under your roof, and you don't expect me to sleep with you?'

Sean laughed, more incredulous than amused. Did she think this?

'I don't know what sort of guys you've been with in the past, but that's not my MO. I'm asking you to do something that means a lot to me. As much as I'd like to sleep with my wife, I want you to be okay with it. So there are no other expectations on top of that. What sort of guy would I be if I made that part of the deal?'

'I see. I just wanted to check.'

'Actually...' He thought for a second, fast-forwarding through the next two months and what this would be like for him in this tiny wee town where everyone had something to say about everyone else's business. He wasn't ready to admit to all the naysayers that his whirlwind marriage had been one giant mistake. Have people say, *Sean Butler's lost it since his father died and made another one of his stupid decisions.* And if he could change Cherry's mind then people never needed to know. 'I do have one request.'

'Please, go on.'

'Behind closed doors, you can be whoever you like. We sleep in separate rooms, if that's what you want. I won't ignore you, but I'm going to be busy, anyway – at work, training, surfing, doing odd jobs for folk. However, because I have some pride, in public, we are husband and wife, okay? For two months, we are madly in love and nothing can prise us apart. The marriage was not a mistake; it was the best fucking decision either of us made. Nobody knows we are breaking up. Nobody.'

Cherry examined him. Had he proposed a stupid idea? Was it unreasonable to ask her to pretend for two months whilst helping him raise money for the cause that was so dear to his heart? Faking it was part of her job, so it couldn't be that hard.

And he could pretend everything was fine. He did that any time he had a problem. The hard part would be trying not to fall for her any harder.

Surely, though, they could both employ their best self-discipline for the sake of charity. Fake it without making it. Or fucking things up.

Or fucking.

And to Sean's relief, Cherry seemed to be on the same script because, finally, she nodded and repeated his words back to him. 'Okay, the best fucking decision either of us made. Sure, hubby, I can go along with that.'

Chapter 8

Cherry

In the Scotland of Cherry's memories, warm and sunny days like today took on a starring role, the rainy ones sheltering in the wings. Why was it she could only remember pleasant weather from the past yet a mixture of good and bad memories?

Still, she was grateful for the sunshine. And the walking sunshine in six-foot-four human form had gone to work. Something about getting back into the swing and giving her some space.

'Feel free to make dinner if you like,' he'd said, unaware of the implications of that suggestion. 'There's a handy wee shop on the high street until I can get to the supermarket in Campbeltown. But don't engage the wifies working there with any chat about us, please, or it'll be over town in five seconds flat.'

Now, Cherry nursed a coffee at the window as she watched soft summer waves roll gently towards the Kinshore sands partly shielded by the mounds of grassy dunes. Sunlight danced on the expanse of stiller waters, glimmering all the way to the horizon. Her old life was out there somewhere. The shuffling of cards replaced by the rush of the ocean, the artificial casino lights swapped for Scottish sunshine, and a poker player in transit now in a very small Scottish village.

Don't get used to it. You're not staying.

Where was she going, though? The touring circuit was unappealing, but would settling in her old home of Edinburgh be any better? All her friends there were on the mummy circuit. What circuit was Cherry on?

The one for childless female poker players the wrong side of thirty-five that no one else is on. Cherry's female poker contemporaries were either disappearing to start families or young enough not to have to think about it. It was a lonely place to be. A friend to whom she could relate would be so welcome.

She emailed the CEO of a charity poker tournament company with a list of potential players for the tournament. Sean's brother, Jamie, was happy for the distillery to host the event, so that took care of a venue.

Like dust before a tornado, a name swirled in her mind, and her finger circled over his number in her phone. It was a gift having an ex-boyfriend as famous as this one, but Campbell Duff, Scot and Hollywood movie star, was not someone Cherry needed to reunite with. Then again, his attendance would be such a draw for the tournament. For charity. For Sean.

She could message and ask him right now.

But if she saw Campbell, she wouldn't be able to resist asking him questions about the past that, given her current predicament, bore too much weight. She and Campbell had only been together for eighteen months ten years ago, but they hadn't been without their ups and downs.

Maybe tomorrow.

There was one other thing Cherry didn't want to do. But she knew she had to.

Annul the marriage.

Start loading the caravans to take the Cherry circus out of town.

Turning her attention to the page she'd skimmed over the previous day, she learned that there was no such thing as a marriage annulment in Scotland, only the voiding of said union. The grounds for this were not applicable to her and Sean; they were both of legal age, both had consented to the marriage and, as far as she knew, there were no hidden diseases or gender transitions. And she definitely wasn't pregnant by someone else. There was only one criterion on which they could ask a court to declare their marriage void. That they had not yet consummated it.

Thank God they'd managed somehow not to sleep together. The struggle of restraint might have saved them a bunch of time, and the hassle and expense of divorce.

Although, how would anyone know if they'd slept together or not?

Because you stand in a room with the man and it's like the place is on fire. Any judge would see the electrical surge between you both and assume you've done the deed.

Would it be better to actually sleep together and get rid of some of that sexual tension?

Cherry laughed out loud at her own idea. The stupidest she'd ever had. Sex with Sean would not be like a coffee shop loyalty card – do it five times, get it out of your system and claim your gift of a voided marriage. Sex with Sean would lead to a serious addiction far worse than caffeine. One she would not be able to walk away from, in either the short or long term. With the chemistry between them and the goods his Butler DNA granted him, there was a fair chance she'd be unable to stand up for quite a few days afterwards, let alone walk away.

She downloaded and printed off the annulment form, dread drifting in like sea fret as she leafed through the sheets. How did people do this after ten, twenty years of marriage? She'd been married a few days, and reading these pages threw up a mess of regret, fear and sadness.

Nonetheless, she found a pen and filled in all the fields. Checked the fees. Ugh! But she could afford it. She left the forms by the printer in the far corner of the lounge for Sean to check over.

After a brisk walk along the beachfront, Cherry was warm enough to tie her cardigan around her waist. Now in skinny jeans and a low-cut vest top, accessorised with a baseball cap and sunglasses, she possibly suited the poker table more than a wee Scottish village.

Kinshore was a criss-cross of quaint thoroughfares and smaller cobbled laneways. The main street was lined with the usual Scottish village fare of grocer, baker, butcher, coffee shop, charity shops and a smattering of independents, but there was something different about this place. A tangible character. A warmth from more than the sunshine. People smiled and said hello as if they'd known her all their life.

As if she belonged here.

Imagine.

Sean had said he'd be home at five-ish – plenty time to get some groceries in and make something basic. Her cooking was nothing to write home about, but she could throw together some ingredients into the resemblance of a meal. If it was truly awful, she'd buy him a takeaway.

Cherry found the small grocery store Sean had mentioned. She would grab stuff for a simple pasta dish – within her limited cooking range.

Tinny pop music filtered through the shop's speakers. Behind the counter, two middle-aged ladies were masquerading as hard-working employees whilst swapping gossip. These must be the 'wifies' Sean had mentioned. The first win was that they appeared not to notice as Cherry strolled in.

Up the first aisle of the store she moved, stopping to examine the pasta sauce. Tomato and basil or tomato and garlic – how to choose? Maybe some olives would brighten things up.

As she was picking up a jar of sauce to see if there were any more exotic ingredients hidden within, conversation floated over the shelves, nearly causing the jar to slip from her hand.

'Aye, so I hear Sean Butler got married after five minutes, to some woman he met at Callum's wedding in New York. He's clearly taken Jimmy's death worse than any of us thought.'

All the muscles in Cherry's neck tensed. *Wow! News sure does travel on rails around here.*

'Aye, trauma does funny things to folk. Poor wee Sean. Although, he's not that wee anymore. Still, I cannae help but think of him as wee.'

Poor wee Sean? What the...?

'Aye, and poor Amanda. As if she doesn't have enough on her plate without having to worry about her son's love life.'

Why would Sean's mum need to worry about his love life? Cherry gripped the pasta sauce jar so hard that it was at risk of nearly slipping again. The sensible thing to do would be to return it to the shelf and leave before she heard something even more incendiary. But her shoes appeared to be glued to the floor.

'I'm giving it one month.'

Cherry's nostrils flared. One month. The fucking cheek of it. They had agreed to at least two. These idiots talked about Sean as if they knew his mind better than he did. It wasn't his fault that she had doubts about her own suitability as a wife.

'The thing about Sean Butler is he doesn't think things through,' the sharper-voiced of the two women said. 'He's always had a weakness for the ladies who drop at his feet. I mean, I cannae blame them, seeing as how he looks – the spit of his father when he was young – but he'd do well to recognise that he can hold out for the cream of the crop. No need to drop to his knees for the first woman outside of Kinshore to bat her eyes at him.'

Oh, right, so Sean couldn't possibly have chosen the 'cream of the crop' for himself.

'I heard she's a poker player. How's that going to work, with her away all the time in casinos?'

Had these women been talking to her mother?

'Sean needs a good village girl to keep him right.'

Oh, does he now? She'd raise their good village girl. Cherry chucked the pasta sauce into her basket, along with some spaghetti and a tub of antipasti from the chiller cabinet. As she reached the top of the aisle, the chat moved onto Sean's brothers – how none of them had chosen village girls, blah, blah.

Jesus, she didn't blame them if this was what the village women were like. Wait until she reached the checkout. Yes, Sean had said not to engage them in conversation, but this... this had to be addressed.

Then, as she was passing the second aisle, Cherry spotted something that lit her neural pathways like an airport runway at night.

Something that would do most of the talking for her.

In one stride, her basket was lined up under the shelf, and she was pulling forward what must have been around thirty packets of condoms. This silly wee shop was about to be cleared of all its regular, ribbed, extra-large and extra-durable latex contraception.

Cherry strutted to the counter, where the women were still working their jaws, now onto Lorraine Kelly's anti-ageing regime. When they saw Cherry, their focus shifted. Who was this provocatively dressed woman? What was she doing in Kinshore? And why did her basket contain the incongruous mix of pasta ingredients and an excessive supply of condoms?

'Afternoon!' Cherry dropped her basket onto the counter.

'Oh, good afternoon. Did you find everything you needed?' One of the women, whose name badge said 'Elaine', flitted her attention back and forth between Cherry and her shopping.

'Yes and no.' Cherry seized this opportunity. 'You don't have any more of these, do you?' She pointed to the contents of her basket.

'Do you mean the...?'

'The condoms, yes.'

'No, I'm afraid everything you see is out.'

'Ah, shame. You may think it's a little excessive, but it's my husband, you see.' God, she loved that word. 'He's kind of...insatiable.'

'Oh, I see.' Elaine laughed with little conviction and began scanning the items in Cherry's basket, handling the condoms as if they were used versions retrieved from the pavement.

Cherry thought it was hilarious how the women were more than happy to chat non-stop about someone else in public, but when that person's wife did the same, suddenly awkwardness took hold.

'Are you visiting Kinshore?' the other woman, Shona, asked.

'No, actually, I live here now. Just moved. Just married, in fact.' Cherry met the woman's eye and smiled with saccharine grace.

She watched the recognition hit. It was beautiful.

'And you're right,' she added. 'He's not so wee. So I probably won't need these.' One packet at a time, she lifted the regular-sized condoms out of the basket, piling them into a phallic-shaped tower on the counter.

Elaine, now utterly perplexed, scanned through every box of extra-large, large and durable condoms, and packed them into a bag. The total price was eye-watering, but it was so worth it to see their faces almost collapse in on themselves.

After swiping her Visa card, Cherry peered at the women's name badges as if she hadn't already clocked who they were. 'It was lovely to meet you...Elaine...Shona. I'll tell Sean you were talking about... I mean, asking for him.'

And before they had time to reply, Cherry had spun away and left the shop.

In the street, she stopped and realised how intensely her heart was beating. The rush of reckless energy. Fuck! Some people thought life in a small town was boring, but who needed to visit the Taj Mahal or sleep with a Canadian Mountie for kicks when you could confront the local Scottish gossips?

Of course, she had completely gone against Sean's request not to engage with them, and it was more than evident why he wanted to maintain the pretence of a flawless marriage. She could imagine the speed of the tongues and the damage to his reputation if they knew the truth. Well, she had protected him in that respect. No way was she having people talk about her marriage like that. About her husband.

Soon to be ex.

Until that annulment comes through, he's still my husband, and I will defend him as a wife should.

Whether Sean would be keen on everyone knowing that his defensive new wife had bought a truckload of condoms in a fit of pique was another issue altogether.

Chapter 9

Cherry

Cherry should have known news would travel as fast as it did. When Sean arrived home from the cooperage, he already knew about the incident in the shop.

'Evening.' He threw his bag down by the door and moved into the house. She lifted her head from her poker game and immediately registered her hand as lost.

Fuck!

This husband of hers.

He was standing there in battered work boots, dirty denim jeans, an equally ragged and filthy blue polo shirt with grime and oil stains on it, tattoos creeping out from under the sleeves onto his forearms. He filled the space between them with his energy. My God, he was absolute, edible, masculine drive incarnate. If not for the annulment, she'd be up there in an instant, tearing her hands through his mussed-up hair and kissing the face off him, sweat, grease and all.

'What's up, Paradise? I hear you've had quite the day.'

Sean's voice was rough, but there was a matching spark in his emerald eyes.

'What have you heard exactly?'

Play it innocent. You don't know what he knows.

'I thought you could tell me.' Sean toed off his boots, sights on her the whole time, before taking a step into the room. When she didn't answer, he looked over to the kitchen island, where the mountain of condoms sat next to the pasta ingredients.

For what felt like forever, he examined them as if he were counting each packet. Cherry was back at school, waiting to see what the teacher's reaction to her misbehaviour would be. Usually, a turning the other way. She'd heard the whispers. *'Such a shame her father dying like that; she'll never get those A-grades now.'* Well, she'd raised them that challenge, won, then gone and become a poker player. Her dad would be smiling.

Walking towards the island, Sean sunk his hands in his pockets, biceps pulsing, stirring something deep inside her.

'That's a lot of condoms,' he said.

'It is.'

'And I see you've got all the types. Large, ribbed, glow in the dark, fucking candy floss flavoured. All except regular size, right?' His mouth lifted ever so slightly.

He knew it all! Oh, Jesus. Was he amused? She couldn't say for certain. 'How did...? How did you know?'

'It's a small village, Cher. Very small. And if you draw attention to yourself, everyone is going to know about it by teatime – including your husband.'

Cherry glanced at her poker game. Her new hand was seven-two offsuit, the worst pairing in the deck, the flop making it even more of a goner. She cashed out and closed the laptop. This needed her full attention.

'You know,' Sean picked up a packet from the condom pile. 'Anyone would think that you were trying to send your husband a giant hint.' He flicked the packet with his finger like a nurse flicking a syringe they were about to inject you with. It was a disarmingly sexy gesture.

'I was trying to teach the women in the shop a lesson. They were talking about us – you – and...'

'Aye, as I said, they're gobshites, those two. Which is why I recommended ignoring them, but I appreciate you have your own unique approach.' Sean peeled the security seal off the packet, placing the cellophane wrapper on the counter. He ran his thumb over the opening of the small box. 'I can't help feeling there's a subliminal message here.' Drawing his eyes back up to Cherry, he waited for an answer.

'Is there?' she asked.

'I don't know.' His gaze never deviated from hers. 'Is there?'

Cherry swallowed. She hadn't considered it that way at all, but now that Sean pointed it out, it was glaringly obvious. It was possible to act as she had in the shop today for more than one reason. Sure, she'd been trying to teach those women a lesson, but there were other ways to go about it. She could have stuck it to them without buying the village's supply of sexual protection whilst implying that her husband was hung like a horse.

'I'm sorry for not ignoring them,' she said.

'Aye, ignore me instead, eh?'

'Again, sorry. I should have found a middle ground. Maybe said, "Excuse me, but I'm the new Mrs Butler, so could you stop being so nosey, and may I please have one box of extra small condoms and this pasta sauce? My husband and I are going to have a nice meal, and then he'll see to me with his teeny tiny penis."'

Sean burst out laughing. Fixed on her with electricity nearly sparking from him, like he couldn't quite believe her. He placed the condoms down on the counter and leaned against it.

'Aye. That might have worked. Although, I prefer the original version.'

'You do? Ah, I didn't think you were mad.'

'Of course I'm not mad. I'm impressed. I've no idea what we're going to do with all these fucking condoms, though. Guess you'll have to take them back to the shop tomorrow, so the village birth rate doesn't spike dramatically.'

Cherry brought her feet to the couch and crossed her legs into the lotus position, a little disappointed he wasn't suggesting they start working their way through the supply. With him looking like he did and being so chivalrous, they'd be through them in no time. 'Okay, I'll do that and tell them I'm dreadfully sorry.'

'Aye, make sure you do.'

'Seriously, though, Sean, I can understand now why you want us to pretend the marriage is fine. I get it.'

His face lit with surprise at her understanding. 'Aye, this place is no fun when you're the grain the gossip mill is grinding. But seeing as the current outcome is that I'm a sex god and my wife has my back, we're good for now.'

'I appreciate that. Listen.' Now seemed like the right time to mention the elephant in the room. 'I printed off an annulment application. It's over by the printer.'

'Righto.' Sean didn't even glance at the printer, choosing instead to keep staring at Cherry. 'I'll check later. I'm off to get changed for a ride.' He pushed off the kitchen counter.

Then, out of nowhere, he pulled off his t-shirt, revealing possibly the most beautiful body she had ever seen in her life. My God, the man was sculpted six ways to heaven. Biceps that swelled like the ocean he surfed on every day, a stunning Celtic knot tattooed around one of them, countless other tattoos and a natural firmness that was borne of solid hard work building whisky barrels, rather than hours spent in a stale, sweaty gym. He practically gleamed. And the abs. Oh, the abs. She could bury her face in them and lick them forever.

Sean Butler was pure perfection.

And she'd married him.

Cherry must have been gawping.

'Oh, sorry.' Sean noticed her expression. 'I forgot you were there. My bad.' He winked and threw the t-shirt over his shoulder. 'I'll see you for that pasta when I'm back.'

It was hard not to laugh. 'Forgot' her arse. And 'changed for a ride'. The man knew exactly what he was doing.

And boy did it ratchet her right up to boiling point.

Chapter 10

Sean

'Your sisters are worried, and I have to say, so am I.' On Sunday afternoon, Amanda Butler eyed Sean over her kitchen table with such seriousness that he was cast right back to being a teenager again.

'Worried about what exactly?' Sean sipped his scalding tea and decided to play innocent, despite having a fair idea of what she was getting at.

'Oh, just a little matter of finding out you are married.'

As suspected, this was about Cherry, or more to the point, the wedding. He kept up the bravado. His mum enjoyed being humoured from time to time; maybe today was one of those times.

'How can you be worried? You haven't even met her yet.'

Amanda didn't miss a beat; she was used to joking deflection from her son. 'I think you know that's my point. You marry two days after meeting her, one month after your dad's death. If I had to guess which of my children would do something like this, it would be you, but it doesn't mean I'm not concerned.

'Mum, please don't worry. It's fine. I'm fine. Cherry and I are good. I didn't tell you because I didn't want to over-shadow Cal and Bea or worry you. And then life got a bit busy. I'm here now, though.'

Seemingly placated, Amanda raised another salient point. 'And what is happening with the Tennessee job swap? Is that going by the wayside? You've been so keen for a change of scene, and it's a great opportunity.'

Sean didn't have an answer to this one. If his marriage had legs, it would be easier to decide whether he should take the job swap he had lined up at a cooperage in the States, visa pending. He would simply ask Cherry to go with him. But he wasn't keen to squander the opportunity if she'd be gone.

'Aye, I know,' he said. 'Cherry might come with me. It's all in hand, honestly.'

Amanda narrowed her gaze as if she knew he was sparing her the truth. But she stopped the interrogation, possibly due to not having the bandwidth amidst her own grief. For this Sean was grateful, as Cherry's business was her own, which made it difficult to share.

'How long before I get to meet Cherry then, rather than experiencing her vicariously through village gossip? I'd like to be introduced to the person who can give Elaine and Shona a run for their money. And possibly even my son.' Amanda lifted her mug of tea, but not before Sean caught the softening in her eye.

'Sorry.' He unwrapped the red and silver foil of a Tunnock's tea cake. 'I'll bring her to meet you soon.'

'Yes, you will. I want a sit-down dinner, just the three of us, since the others appear to have met my latest daughter-in-law already.'

'Ach, only Jamie and Alicia have really met her. I

needed witnesses and didn't want to bother you. Everyone else was a whirl round at the wedding. You're more important than that.' His mum's approval of his wife mattered, even if Cherry wouldn't be his wife for long.

'Good, I'm looking forward to seeing her put her mark on Kinshore.' Amanda bit into a tea cake herself. 'She's made a good start.'

'Aye, it's a strong beginning, alright. And she's helping me organise a charity poker tournament. For MND.'

'A poker tournament and the Kintyre Way? Isn't that taking on too much?'

'Och, you know I like to keep busy. Speaking of which, does anything need done around here? I can fix that broken door for you.'

'Thank you, darling. The door is fine for now.' Amanda pressed at her cuticles before raising her eyes to Sean, her expression flooding him with emotion. 'You're so like your dad – never stopping, always thinking of other people. I see him the most clearly in you, for obvious reasons. Make him proud, but please don't overdo it. You're grieving.'

Hold it together, Seany. For her sake.

'Mum, listen.' Sean reached out for her hand. Making his mum feel better and keeping the home fires burning was the thing. When Cherry was gone, there would still be family, and he would do them proud. 'Don't worry about me, please. Cherry is the one organising the poker tour. I'm just the tagalong guy who'll put the money in the bank. She's got so many contacts, and we could get Connor from our end. Dad would have approved.'

Amanda heaved in a deep breath, her eyes shining.

'The wedding kind of kept us going, eh?' Both his parents had wanted their eldest son to get married as planned, but Sean had known it would involve a comedown for all of them afterwards.

Tersely, she nodded as if more would be too much. 'It was a beautiful wedding. Bea was stunning; Cal was smiling...'

'Miracles do happen.'

She tilted her head, amusement breaking through the soft tears. 'Say that to your brother's face. Or don't. You know, I'll be glad to see that smile on your face.'

'I am smiling. Can't you see it?'

'Yes, Sean, I can, but I've seen you smile brighter.'

It was hard to tell if his mum suspected something about his marriage or if she interpreted the dimmed wattage of his expression as grief for his dad. Distracting her with a question that homed in on his dad's character would hopefully buoy her spirits.

'Do you think Dad would have disapproved of me marrying Cherry so quickly?' He tried to think of the dad in his most recent memory, unable to speak but still communicating through special software on a tablet. He would have told Sean what he thought. The dad of old, before he got sick, would have sat him down with a whisky and talked it through. His few questions would be sharp and incisive, getting to the crux of the matter. *'Do you love her? Are there any regrets? Is there enough money in the bank for all of this?'*

That last one could mean literally and metaphorically.

God, he missed those chats. Wished he'd written down the advice given to him over the years, stuck it in a notebook to hand down to his own children – if he had them. Although, they'd probably laugh at the things he'd asked his dad about girls.

'He would have come round, eventually.' Amanda

twisted her wedding ring, causing Sean to divert his mind to the door that needed fixing. He couldn't break in front of her, not when she was going through the worst time of her life, losing her beloved husband of thirty years. The husband she should have had thirty more years with, who should have been at Cal and Bea's wedding. Who should have proudly welcomed grandchildren into the world with her – Sean's own children, especially poignant since he was Jimmy's only biological child. And who should have been around to ask Sean, intimidatingly, what on earth he was doing marrying someone he'd known for two days.

Would Sean have married Cherry were his dad alive? Was it grief dragging him along? Were they grief nuptials – a symptom of losing the plot in a sneaky and subtle way since his dad had gone? Could this be how the tricky little fucker that was grief worked? Causing him to make a bad decision he was unable to admit?

No, Sean decided. He'd always been impetuous, making choices on the spur of the moment. Whether or not his dad were here to reprimand, there was a large chance he would have married Cherry quickly. It was how he lived his life. Not to mention, he'd never met any woman who made him think beyond next week, never mind the rest of his life, like Cherry had.

Still did.

And that was the thing – when he thought about his future, he thought about her. Saw the two of them happy, years down the line. He saw them with children too. What did that mean? Was it a premonition, or was it his brain in a pattern because that's how he'd always seen things? His parents had seven kids; why would he have none? Sean had never considered an alternative. How did you do that?

There sure as fuck weren't any support groups for men in his situation within a hundred-mile radius of here.

Unless Cherry's mind can be changed, it doesn't matter, anyway.

The focus now was raising as much money for charity and making his mum feel that her husband's death wasn't entirely in vain. Some things took precedence over others. Charity money trumped the frustration of living under the same roof as his untouchable fox of a wife.

Integrity alone would have to be the thing to get Sean through the next couple of months.

Chapter 11

Cherry

On Monday, Cherry showered and dressed and applied some light make-up. She was about to head downstairs to grab a coffee when she noticed Sean's bedroom door was open. Moving to the doorway, she scanned the room. This was the first time she'd seen it properly, everything else being a quick glimpse in the passing.

The room was spacious with smoky blue walls, oak floorboards, a jute rug and an expansive window framing the ocean. Scottish landscapes were represented in hanging artwork. Books, framed photos and a couple of plants filled the shelves along the back wall, and two vintage surfboards reclined in the corner. A large king-size bed commanded the centre of the space. Cherry stepped into the room, closed her eyes and inhaled the scent – clean, fresh wood, salty sea air and hints of a warm oakiness that she recognised as her husband.

The bed was made – badly, but made. She smiled. Dale had never made the bed which, for a grown man, was pathetic.

Perching on the edge of the bed, she ran her hands over the rumpled cotton of the light charcoal-coloured duvet and imagined Sean sleeping here. Did he sleep well? There was nothing to suggest that he didn't. Just a lamp by the bed, a curled set of earphones and a selection of books – commercial thrillers and some well-thumbed on Motor Neurone Disease.

The pain he must have gone through hoping to understand it, to fix it. I wish the outcome had been different.

This could have been her room, too. Their room. The place they shared as husband and wife. Heat coiled deep in Cherry's core as she imagined Sean's weight pinning her down, him moving inside her. What was that beautiful face like when he was thick and hard and chasing release? Would he growl as he rode her? Grunt with every possessive thrust? Talk filth about how much he loved fucking her? Loved her.

She bet he would. All of it.

Reaching for the pillow nearest the bedside cabinet, Cherry pulled it to her chest and sunk her face into it. Moaned at the intoxicating smell of her husband. What the hell was he doing to her? She'd never met a man who made her crazy like this, where the merest scent of the pillow he slept on sent a tsunami of hormones through her. She groaned into the cotton.

'Fuck, Seany, I want you so bad.'

You could have him. Phone him up now and ask him to come home from work.

I can't. I can't do no-strings with Sean. And strings would be a tangled mess. I need to take a cold shower and get a hold of myself.

Cherry extricated herself from the pillow and returned

it to its place on the bed. Time to get clean and to give herself the release she so badly needed.

An hour later, Cherry was rapping her fingers on the kitchen table and chewing her gum hard. 'Come on.' She took her impatience out on the computer screen. 'We don't all have all day.'

This wasn't strictly true; she had all the time in the world, but even playing four low-stakes poker games concurrently wasn't enough of a distraction.

After the games, she dealt with a few emails about the charity tournament, one of which involved flagging up Dale – a regular on the pro-am circuit but unwanted at this event. Then she printed off some home-made flyers for the village.

The clock on her laptop told that it was nearly noon. The morning had disappeared faster than the sun had burned off the coastal haar enrobing the village. She jumped up. It was a crime to sit at a computer when the Scottish sun was shining. Why not take a walk along the beach, grab a coffee and explore? Make a sandwich to eat in the park.

As she was pulling ingredients from the fridge, another idea hit Cherry. She could make Sean a sandwich and take it to him. It was time she saw the cooperage. And a 'madly in love' wife turning up with a packed lunch would be great for his pride.

While bacon sizzled furiously in the frying pan, she swiped butter across the inside of a pillowy morning roll. Slicing a generous amount of lettuce and cutting four cherry tomatoes, she layered the sandwich. It might be more lettuce and tomato with bacon giving a guest appearance, but Sean had said he was trying to eat healthily.

Sandwich wrapped in greaseproof paper and popped into a brown paper bag, alongside the tournament flyers, Cherry pulled on a baseball cap, laced up her trainers and made her way into the village to surprise her unsuspecting husband.

Along the way, she stopped in with her flyers at as many businesses as possible. Everyone – from the butcher to the florist, to the fish and chip shop – was happy to take some. Many mentioned Jimmy Butler's name when they saw funds were being raised for MND. 'Incredible man,' they said. 'Left a gaping hole in the community.'

'Which of his sons is organising this?' someone asked. When she said it was Sean and that she was his wife, the welcome was even warmer. Cherry understood now what he meant about his family being like minor Scottish royalty. And today's reception was so much friendlier than her interaction with Shona and Elaine.

In small-town Scotland, everyone might know your business, but they also know your name. On the road, from one city to the next, no one knows your business. Or your name.

Cherry knew already which would fill her heart more. But she wasn't used to being under the small-town microscope. The big-city lens was what she knew best.

A short time later, a quarter of a mile outside the village, on the other side from Sean's home, she hummed a tune as she walked to Butler's cooperage in the early afternoon sunshine, brown paper bag swinging by her side.

How strange that a few weeks ago she was sitting under the sickly lights of a casino, staring at a limp pair of cards. Now here she was on the Kintyre peninsula, excitedly approaching her husband's workplace with a sandwich.

Some might say it was lame to get such satisfaction from such a thing, but if this was being lame then it felt pretty good.

The first thing that struck Cherry about the cooperage yard was the sheer number of whisky barrels. Casks were stacked in huge pyramid formations, others scattered in various states of repair. Some appeared freshly made with their pale, clean oak; others were darker and more weathered, with dulled metal hoops.

The second thing was that it wasn't as quaint as she had imagined. Sure, there was a mid-size rectangular stone building, with a gable roof, which might have been the original cooperage. But set back from this was a larger, steel-clad structure, most likely the industrial heart of the operation.

The smell of earthy oak, charred wood and faint whisky fumes lingered in the air.

As Cherry stood in the yard, her ears became attuned to the rhythm of the work – the ringing of metal, the low thud of mallets, voices rising and falling, the soundtrack of sweat and grit and toil. Of men working.

Her husband was one of them.

Stepping further into the yard, she moved towards the hammering, banging and bursts of shouted instructions. The testosterone was already thick in the air. Then, as she crossed over the threshold of the main building, the July heat was replaced by the cool interior of the cooperage.

The space inside was large – nearly half the size a football pitch – and a strange combination of rustic and industrial. Whisky barrels were everywhere, and tools and machinery were scattered in what could be a random fashion but doubtless was not. The setup meant nothing to

Cherry, but she sensed that art of coopering was far more complex than one might initially think.

Men in worn-in jeans and grime-smeared t-shirts, some wearing Perspex safety shields, were hammering hoops into place, rolling barrels in plumes of steam, firing things in the searing orange heat of a kiln.

It was a hub of steady manual labour – a place of hot, sweaty men lifting seventy-kilo casks as if they weighed no more than an acorn.

She scanned the space for Sean. In an instant, she found him.

Cherry had no idea what exactly Sean was doing, but the concentration his expression held, the way the strong angles of his face were more defined than usual, suggested he was deeply focused on his work.

Was there anything more beautiful than a man concentrated on something he excelled in? Wearing heavy industrial gloves, Sean was wielding a hefty mallet and hammering the side of a whisky barrel, the corded muscles running down his tattooed forearms flexing with effort. Those rock-solid shoulders would be getting a hell of a workout inside his polo shirt.

She'd grab onto those during a workout with him.

Cherry was pinned to the spot. There was something about this man. She barely had the brain space to try to work out what it was. The warrior energy combined with the piercing green eyes was a lethal combination that knocked her into next week.

But without the person inside, she would have walked out of that wedding in New York alone.

Because Sean unlocked something else inside her. Unchecked a load of boxes she had checked as 'no' in her life.

Making rash decisions. Moving back to Scotland. Making herself vulnerable.

With his enthusiasm for life, his good-humoured energy and his emotional openness, he had her over on a barrel.

If only.

It was dangerous to think like this. If he was merely hot, it would be one thing. But he was so much more.

He was her match. In so many ways.

And this here. It underscored something else she suspected about him. A strength, a solidity, a stability. Something she'd sensed from that very first dance.

And he'd told her to act like she was madly in love with him. For two months. To help raise money for fighting the illness that had stolen his father.

Cherry did a lot of faking it in her line of work. Hours were spent disguising her inner feelings or thoughts so her opponents couldn't work out what cards she was holding. She was skilled at pretending, adding in fake tells to throw them off the scent. It was almost second nature now.

It won her a stack of money.

But acting like she was madly in love with Sean Butler would be the easiest faking she ever had to do.

And it was nothing to do with her years of playing poker.

Chapter 12

Sean

Everything about the day was too hot. From the morning tension in his boxers at the memory of Cherry padding around the house in her pyjama shorts last night – long, toned legs taunting him – to the unseasonably warm weather, to the hassle his workmates were still ladling on about him getting married in New York. News travelled like lightning in Kinshore, and Sean hadn't even been the one to deliver it to them. It was at the cooperage before he was.

'Two days?' Billy McDonald, a young apprentice, clarified for what seemed like the hundredth time. 'How it that even possible?'

'It is if she's a smoking fox and in New York,' Sean said.

'What, so in New York you can marry someone after two days if they're a smoking fox?' Billy wasn't the brightest tool in the box.

'No, you can get a licence to marry at short notice. You decide if your wife is a smoking fox.' Sean rolled a barrel over to the door, chuckling at Billy's misconstruction.

'If anyone was going to marry after kenning someone five minutes, I'd have put money on it being you, Butler,' Billy called after him.

'Thanks, I think,' Sean shouted back. 'What can I say? If you know, you know.'

And if you and your wife both know you're made for one another, but she thinks she's going to ruin your life, what does it turn out that you know?

Fuck all.

'Butler, there's someone here to see you.'

Sean looked up from the barrel he was working on, hoop driver and mallet still in his hand, and nearly dropped both of them.

Fucking hell!

Standing in the yard was Cherry, denim hugging her hips, a vest top so tight and low cut that her breasts were rising up like the paps of Jura, giant rose gold hoops in her ears drawing attention to that swanlike neck, a baseball cap affiliated to some poker website, and sunglasses shielding what he knew to be tantalising starlight in her eyes.

This was his wife.

She was a phenomenon.

Except she didn't want to be his wife.

She had a funny way of putting him off their marriage, turning up here all got up like a cooperage cheerleader.

'Alright.' Sean placed his tools by the door and meandered over to her, as casually as he could. 'You're a sight for sore eyes. How did you walk through the village looking this good?'

'I used my legs.'

'Seems obvious now you mention it... Anyway, what's up? Thought you'd be working today?'

She shrugged. 'On a day like this, it seemed like a waste, so I thought I'd visit my husband. See *you*, my darling.' She lifted her fingers to his face and let them trail lazily through the sweat and dirt that were layering there, as they did every day.

It was bloody hard to concentrate when she did that, and Sean just about managed to form words. 'Tease. It's nice to see you, though.'

'You, too. And since we're meant to be madly in love, I brought you a sandwich.' Cherry held out the small brown bag. 'Like a doting wife would.'

Sean reached for her offering, surprising himself at how much this gesture threw him. Had she really walked the two miles from his house to the cooperage to bring him a sandwich? 'Thanks ever so, sweetheart.' He peered inside the bag. 'Smells delicious.' It truly did.

'Hope it tastes as good as it smells. So, I suppose a real married couple would kiss now.' Cherry removed her sunglasses so Sean could see the flirtatious glint they'd been hiding. 'The husband thanking the wife and wishing her a lovely day and all that.'

'I thought you didn't want to be married to me.'

'I thought you wanted us to appear madly in love all the time.'

She had a point. It would be wrong to accuse Cherry of hypocrisy when all she was doing was keeping up her side of the bargain. The stipulation was his. He'd just expected any kisses to be incidental rather than orchestrated. Still, he could manage to kiss his wife.

Very fucking easily, in fact.

Leaning in and lifting and twisting her baseball cap backwards, Sean brought his lips to Cherry's. To that delicious full mouth that tasted like coconut nectar and sweet pineapple with an intoxicating twist. Before self-control stood a chance, their tongues were tangling hot around one another's and, in the middle of the cooperage yard, they were sliding into the fevered body of an exceptionally adult kiss. A kiss that could stop traffic on a freeway and the flight path up above.

Sean drew Cherry closer, sandwich bag dangling from his hand, unable to resist the soft swell of her breasts against his chest.

She was no less restrained, tangling her hand into his hair, fingernails making their presence very much known. Fuck, he was hardening already. This was way too erotic a kiss for daytime at work.

Thankfully, a chorus of male voices resounded through the yard, whooping and calling out 'Wahey!' and 'Get a room!'.

Sean pulled back, the sunlight dazing him as much as the kiss had. He didn't need to turn to know that his colleagues were watching. It wasn't often that women came to the cooperage, never mind ones like Cherry.

'We're taking the faking to the max, I see?' He ran his tongue over his lips and cupped his free hand on Cherry's hip. Reeled as he inhaled the honeysuckle blossom of her scent. This day just got so much hotter.

'Of course.' She squinted into the sun. 'No point doing things to the minimum, Seany. If you want the world to see that I'm madly in love with you, that is what they'll see. I've learned a few skills around the poker table.'

Sean nodded. As much as he hoped she would fake so hard she couldn't backtrack, he'd have to categorise that as fantasy. Cherry was well versed in detaching from her feelings. If he didn't do the same, he'd look like an idiot. He shook the brown paper bag.

'I appreciate your commitment. And the sandwich, of course.'

'You're welcome, baby. I'll have your favourite dinner on when you get home.' She tilted her hips far too suggestively for someone talking about dinner. 'Whatever that is.'

Sean's attention idled on the curve of her hip before rising to her face, where sunglasses were once again shielding her eyes.

'Can't wait to taste it,' he said.

'Me neither. Now get back to work. Oh, wait. I got your favourite juice.' Cherry pulled a can of Irn-Bru out of her bag, but before she passed it to him, she rolled it over her cleavage.

'Mmm, that's so nice and cool,' she drawled, a mischievous smile playing on her lips.

Sean had never wanted to be a can of Irn-Bru until now.

'You're a troublemaker, Paradise. Get out of here before I find a barrel to take you over.' He reached out for the can and grinned at her. She was a first-class tease, and he loved it, but if he didn't focus on some hoops and staves and listen to his workmates' drivel, his balls would be ready to explode.

A short time later, after splashing his face and neck with cold water, Sean sat down to eat the sandwich Cherry had brought him. *Made* for him, by the looks of the roll and abundant filling spilling out the sides. The local sandwich shop was never this generous with filling. And they didn't do a BLT like this.

BLT. His favourite sandwich.

Cherry had made him his favourite sandwich. Filled it

to the max, including a fuck-load of lettuce, no doubt because of their conversation about healthy eating. And walked into the village to bring it to him at the cooperage, accompanied by a scorching kiss.

She didn't do things by halves.

He'd married a belter alright.

Chapter 13

Sean

When Sean got home from an after-work run, the sexual tension coiled up within him was as pressured as the seams of the bruised storm clouds above. Fuck. He wanted his wife. And that was normal. What wasn't normal was to live in the same house as that wife but not be able to have her.

She had to feel the same way. There was no way that she didn't. The kiss at the cooperage had spoken loud and clear about how good the sex between them would be, if they were ever to have sex.

Which they would not be doing. Because Cherry thought she was depriving him of something. Thought she was responsible for his life. For how it turned out. It was sweet but also unnecessary. He was an adult, capable of making his own decisions about his future.

But it didn't feel like the future was in his hands. Cherry held all the cards, and Sean wasn't sure how to play the game. Where did you start with someone who'd been through that much trauma? And what would his arguments be to convince her otherwise? He'd tried presenting his own family dynamic to show he didn't have fixed ideas about family, but it hadn't hit home.

Thunder rumbled in the distance.

Cherry was sitting at the dining table, laptop open, deep in concentration, phone, sunglasses and an empty water glass by her side.

'You playing poker?' Sean laid two bags of groceries on the counter.

'Mm-hmm, won't be long.'

While she was engaged in her game, he took the chance to watch her. She was absent-mindedly eating a flaccid burger – some frozen crap she'd bought from the local shop. He went over to the table and lifted it off her plate.

'What's this? Eating before dinner?'

'It is dinner. I got a packet, so you can have some too.' Cherry spoke mindlessly, her attention on the game. It was fair enough; she was working.

But Sean took a bite of the burger. 'No, it isn't dinner.' It was just as well he'd gone to the shop after his run, if this was her offering.

'It is. That's mine, and you're eating it.' She grasped for the burger whilst looking at her computer screen.

Sean held it out of reach. 'Nope, Cherry. Your dinner is in those bags over there, and I'm cooking it, right after I've had a shower. Keep winning, and I'll bring you a drink.'

That got her attention. She glanced up at him, not fighting his decision to chuck her so-called food in the bin, but surprised. At what? That he cared enough to do this?

'What? I know we're both busy, but we don't have to avoid each other. We can have the occasional meal together, like adults. Right? Pasta together the other day was nice.'

She narrowed her gaze.

'It was.' Sean began emptying the shopping bags. 'You make a good pasta and tomato sauce.'

Cherry's expression warmed as she dropped her eyes back to the screen. 'Liar... But sure, Seany, a meal together would be nice.'

'Good.' He placed a glass of Diet Irn-Bru in front of her, bubbles fizzing at the edges of the glass. Thunder rumbled again, and he looked out the patio doors in time to see a streak of white lightning spotlight his jungle of a garden.

Upstairs, in the shower, Sean relieved himself of the sexual tension Cherry had ramped up in him. He couldn't fuck his wife, but there were no rules about taking himself into oblivion whilst thinking about her naked and wet, the sweet aroma of honeysuckle entwining around him like her legs. And in Sean's imagination, there were definitely no rules about what would happen under those circumstances. No rules about how loudly she would moan as he took her, about how many times she would come under him, on top of him, around him.

The hammering rush of the water on the shower floor drowned out his frustration, and as the rain clouds split open, he came hard and urgently over his hand, against the tiles, into the Cherry of his imagination.

The problem was that self-pleasuring in the shower was fine as a short-term measure, but it was like building a temporary fence after a storm when another was bearing down. As soon as Sean went downstairs and saw her setting the table in her skinny jeans and tight little vest, the tension coiled up again. Living with this fiercely beautiful creature was both incredible and frustrating in equal measure.

For a short while, they ate in silence, Sean stealing glances at Cherry far too frequently, only to find those swan-lashed eyes gaping right back. After around the seventh time of this happening, he chanced a wink, and her face broke into a smile – radiant, feminine warmth that rendered him near senseless.

Sort this out, Butler.

'Listen,' Sean grabbed onto his water glass like it was a life preserver. 'Thanks for the sandwich today; it was delicious. But please, don't do that again.'

'Don't do what again?' Cherry was all innocence. 'Make you a sandwich?'

'You can make me a sandwich, but don't come with that sandwich to my work, dressed like Betty Boop and then kiss me like you want to fuck me into next week. It's too much.'

'Oh, okay.' Now she dropped the naïve act. 'You were there too, Seany, kissing me back like you also wanted to fuck into next week, and possibly the one after that. It takes two...'

'Aye, I was. It does. I'm not laying down the law. I know I said we need to act like we're madly in love, but you are sex on two legs, and kisses like that make it messy. Very fucking messy. And the problem is that I want a different messy with you. I want tangled and sweaty and sticky and fucking hopelessly messy nights and days with my firecracker of a wife. So, seeing as we have an arrangement that behind closed doors this is a marriage on paper only, I think it's best if we keep things a bit more...um—'

'Boring?'

Sean sighed. This woman. 'Fuck's sake. You're the one who wanted out. Now you're saying it's boring if we don't practically fuck in public, meanwhile not fucking in private. That's – for want of a more varied vocabulary – fucked up, Cherry.'

'Sorry, but I am doing this "madly in love in public" thing to save your pride.'

'Aye, fine.' On this, she had a point. Today had perfectly presented their marriage to his workmates as happy and, quite frankly, horny. 'I was going to say, let's keep things a bit more sedate. Surely, we can look at each other...I dunno...fondly, without the over-the-top fondling, right?'

'Yes. I can do that. Sorry. I got carried away today.'

'We both did.'

'No more bringing my milkshake to the yard.'

'Cherry!'

'Sorry.'

'You have to stop.'

'Would it help if I moved out?'

'Would it...? No, it wouldn't. Because that wouldn't make sense. Stay here. We're both adults.'

'Alright, but it really does take two, so you need to keep your t-shirt on. I don't need any more x-rated stimulus material to help me act nuts about you in public. Keep that body hidden, for the love of God.'

Sean grinned. It was nice to know she also found him hard to resist and might be struggling like he was. He'd give her a chance to admit it.

'Aye, alright, that's fair enough. You know, we could give in to temptation and if you really don't want to stay married to me, we can get a divorce. You'd enjoy yourself.'

'Oh, the confidence. But I know you're right, and that's where the problems would start. I don't think I could walk away after sex with you, Sean. And you being the ride of the century isn't a good enough reason to fuck up your future.'

Ride of the century. God, she made him laugh. 'Jesus, okay.' He rapped his fingers on the table and decided to play along with her nonsense 'What if I'm not the ride of the century? What if I'm mediocre at best?'

This appeared to be no deterrent to Cherry.

'Sean, even if you had a micro penis and the style of an otter trying to escape a sack, I know I'd love being in bed with you. We'll both need to exercise restraint, for the sake of the bigger picture.'

Sean was too stunned to even laugh properly, despite a strong urge. 'Fine, you win,' he said and pincered a baby potato with his fork. 'By the way, there's a nice wee boutique on the High Street called Nan Gracie. You could think about getting yourself some below-the-knee floral dresses from there. And some comfy shoes. I'll give you an allowance to cover a new wardrobe.'

'Shut the front door, Butler!'

'Ha! Thought you'd be keen.'

'Yeah. You're funny.' But the warmth in her smile suggested she meant it.

The feeling was mutual. For all the back-and-forth with Cherry and the tension she was creating, having her around brought a dimension to Sean's life that was sorely lacking – the company of a vibrant and funny woman. His two sisters were as close as he got and a) they lived in Edinburgh, and b) they were his sisters.

'How's the planning for the charity tourney coming along?' He decided a change to a neutral subject was a good idea.

And it seemed to soften the tension in her frame. 'Really good. I've ordered a bunch of stuff to turn the distillery into a casino. Tablecloths, lamps, etcetera. And I've found some locals to be dealers.'

'That's brilliant, Cher. Thanks so much.' Sean loved how she was putting her heart into this project, like it meant as much to her as it did to him. 'If you're not working Friday, then the lads at work want to have a poker night with you as the star guest. I think they're hoping you'll coach them for the pro-am.' He wouldn't mind a little coaching himself and, he wouldn't lie, he wanted front row seats for his wife's thrashing of his gallus workmates.

'Oh, are they now?' Cherry's voice was laced with mischievous intrigue. 'I don't give away my secrets, you know. But sure, I'll play them. You're going to be there, right?'

'Aye, I'll be there.' As if they were getting anywhere near his wife in a darkened space without his being present. 'Cheers. They're living in some la-la land, thinking they'll learn from you *and* beat you.'

'You never know what will happen. But I'm not bringing down my game for your wee pals, so they'll need to up theirs.'

'I wouldn't expect you to. Can't wait to play with you.'

Her eyes rounded.

'You know what I mean, you wee minx. Behave yourself.'

'Could say the same about you.'

Jesus, were the next two months going to be like this? Neither of them seemed able to help themselves, and feeling like he might sexually combust was becoming a very frustrating part of Sean's daily existence. 'Oh, before I forget,' he said, it not being likely this would slip his mind, 'my mum wants us to come for dinner at the house. There's no getting out of it, I'm afraid.'

Cherry swallowed so hard he wondered if she'd let a baby potato go down the wrong way. But he knew how she felt. He wasn't especially excited about this dinner either.

'Don't worry. It's only the three of us, and she won't ask you any awkward questions. Remember, she's just about holding things together. It's a good distraction for her from thinking too much about Dad.'

Time dripped by. Sean swore he could hear every single raindrop that hit the patio outside. Every rumble of thunder on the peninsula. Maybe he should have told his mum the truth. Or made up a story about Cherry being too busy playing poker to come to dinner.

'I understand.' Cherry put down her cutlery. 'I'd love to meet her. I'll get something nice to take along.'

And of course, his immense relief had to manifest itself as a stupid joke. 'What, like five hundred condoms?'

'I was thinking more a bottle of wine or some flowers.'

'Definitely a better idea. Thanks, Cher.' *Thanks so much.*

Chapter 14

Cherry

Standing barefoot at the kitchen counter, Cherry muddled a large measure of Butler's whisky with freshly squeezed lemon juice and sugar syrup, poured it into a highball over crackling ice cubes and topped with a serving of soda water. Plucking a maraschino cherry from the jar in the fridge, she speared it with a cocktail stick and slipped it into the glass.

A long whisky sour: the perfect refreshment after seven hours sweating it out in an online tournament.

She padded out to the garden, unlatched the weathered wooden doors of the summerhouse and spread them wide as if airing her house for the spring. Inside was like a chaotic antiques sale, but she found two rickety wooden chairs, one to sit on and the other to rest her feet on. From under a myriad of random boxes, she located a small metal table upon which to place her drink. Who needed poolside in Vegas when you had this?

Facing the garden and the warm afternoon sun, Cherry picked up her phone and messaged her old Edinburgh schoolfriend Kirsty McGee. Over the years, their contact had dissipated. Looking at Kirsty's profile photo – a toddler in cute blonde bunches – she feared they may have grown apart. No harm in testing the waters, though.

> CHERRY: Hey, McGoo! I'm back in Scotland. Got married a couple of weeks ago. How are things? Xxx

The reply came quickly.

> KIRSTY: Paradise! Welcome home! Married?!Whaaaaaat?! Amazing! Congrats! Who is he? Tell me more! Send pics of the big day. So, so, so good to hear from you. Things are full on with a three-year-old and…wait for it…another one on the way! Due Christmas day. Soooo, besides snagging a husband, how is party poker queen life treating you? Let me live vicariously through you. Xxx

Cherry laughed but her heart caught in her throat. She knew Kirsty had one child, but it had been remiss of her not to prepare for another one. Of course, she was delighted for her friend, but baby news always required recalibration. And 'party poker queen'. Did Kirsty really envy Cherry her lifestyle? Or did she think that, at thirty-seven, she should have all that out of her system by now?

Those could be your own insecurities.

. . .

CHERRY: Congratulations! I'm so excited for you. We'll have to catch up before the little one arrives. I might be through in Edinburgh soon, working out what's next for the party poker queen. This is me and hubby. Xxx

She attached a wedding day photo to the text but didn't mention the annulment. It was too complicated for text.

KIRSTY: Wow! I can see why you might be thinking of ditching poker for married life. ;) Hope you're still honeymooning like there's no tomorrow. Would be so awesome to see you, if you're in town. K xxx

Honeymooning like there was no tomorrow. They hadn't honeymooned at all. What a waste.

Cherry turned at the clicking of the patio doors. There he was, her non-honeymooner in crime, in the sentience-addling workwear of dirty jeans, grease-stained t-shirt and what her gran would call tackety boots. The herculean pull towards him never seemed to abate.

'Alright, Paradise, you found the summer-cowp then.' Sean moved into the doorway of the summerhouse, eclipsing the sun with his broad frame. And as if that weren't enough, he stretched up and gripped onto the top of the door frame whilst surveying the inside of the summerhouse. A quick glance, and she could hardly miss his t-shirt hanging forward and showcasing those glorious abs and the tantalising strip of hair leading to the land of her fantasies.

Fuck! He was so disarmingly hot.

'I like this place.' She lifted the rim of the glass to her mouth to disguise her gawping. 'The junkyard aspect makes it all the more charming.'

'If you say so.' Thankfully, Sean released his hold on the door frame and some of her self-control. 'But I could sort it out for you, if you want to hang out here. Could even make it into a wee gaming den.' He pulled up an equally rickety chair, facing her, his back to the sun.

'You'd do that?' She put down her drink.

He laughed. 'I'm not offering to build a replica of the Taj Mahal. Just to clear some space in a place that badly needs tidying.'

'That's really kind.' Cherry glanced back into the summerhouse, trying to imagine working here. 'Casino Cherry – the world's most rural, one-woman casino.'

'Is that good?'

'It sounds good, although maybe it's a bit weird.'

'Oh, aye. How so?'

She let the verdant scent of the overgrown garden envelop her, cast back to her younger years. Gardens were her happy place.

'Well, having a casino surrounded by a forest of weeds and foxgloves is a break from the urban grind. But playing online is making me realise that live poker is sewn into my identity. I'm used to being a presence around a table: reading tells, sharing banter, listening to the sound of chips being raked. Online, I'm an avatar and the banter is crap. They are two completely different lifestyles. The online one's not me, not like the other one is.'

Sean was listening intently, a few creases around his eyes appearing from squinting in the light. 'You said you were jaded with live poker, though. Would you go back?'

'I am jaded. But what else would I do? I have my maths degree, although I spent a fair whack of time that I should have been in lectures sleeping off nights spent in the casino.'

'You could coach poker. Or even maths. I reckon you could sell beach umbrellas in December.'

Cherry tilted her head and smiled at him. 'Thanks. I have some decisions to make while I'm here. Anyway...' She stirred her drink with the cocktail stick. 'Poker tourney with the lads tomorrow night?'

'Aye.'

'Are they any good?'

Sean put his feet up on the edge of Cherry's footrest. It was intimate but not awkward. 'They're a mixed bag. We've got daft Billy, who plays every hand and bets aggressively. Tommy's kind of the same. The other three are a bit more cautious, but I wouldn't say patience is the name of anyone's game.'

Men who played amateur poker often wore it as a badge of masculinity. Cherry wondered if Sean would be the same. How would he behave in front of his workmates with her there? Would he ramp up the lads' act or tone down whatever his usual playing mode was?

'You want some tips?' A little test right now would give her a clue for tomorrow.

'You offering?'

'Yep. We could go through some starting hands. Of course, it depends what everyone else is holding and playing, but I can give you some scenarios.'

'I'm up for that. Grateful to have a professional coach right here.'

'Brilliant! One minute.' Cherry ran into the house, grabbed a pack of cards and laid them on the table between her and Sean, alongside the whisky sour.

'Most men don't listen,' she said, selecting two cards from the deck for him. 'They don't want to learn from a woman, so well done for not being one of them.' She gave the pair to Sean. 'Okay, let's say you're playing with me and tomorrow' night's crew. Billy has gone all in before the flop, possibly without even looking at his cards. Everyone else has folded. You're in the big blind. Would you play this hand?'

Sean glanced his cards for about three seconds. 'Aye, I'd play this. It's a good hand. It's a really good hand.'

Cherry nodded. 'Okay, in this case, you've made the right call. Billy is being a numptie, so I'd take a chance on King-Jack suited. But just so you know, with seven players, this hand's win rate is about twenty-four percent, so it's not the pot of gold you think it is.'

'Alright, Coach, I'm learning already.' Sean took the deck and, possibly to show off, shuffled it confidently.

Cherry was more impressed at the way he was taking the tuition – he was good-natured and willing to listen and learn.

'Let's try another one.' She selected a pair of twos from the deck. 'You're in the Big Blind. Everyone else has called a bet of fifty quid. Do you fold, call, raise or go all in?'

Sean chewed on his lip. 'Honestly?'

'Of course.'

'I'd probably call, at the least. I might even raise.'

Cherry slapped her forehead.

'What?' He laughed, nervously.

'You do not raise on this, Butler. If you stay in and another deuce comes up, then maybe a raise, but the only reason you're staying in is because you've paid the big blind. You can call it, but that is all, do you get it? In our game, this card would have a win rate of fourteen percent Don't be fooled by the pretty swans.'

Sean examined her with admiration and wonder. 'Sheesh, I get it.' He lifted her glass. 'Keep going. I'm having fun.' As he drank, he pulled a face. 'Phew...you know how to put the sour into whisky sour.'

'Sorry. Have my cherry to take the edge off.' She held out the cherry on the cocktail stick, but Sean planted his tongue into the side of his cheek and raised his eyebrows suggestively. 'You're alright, Paradise. I'll have your cherry another time.'

'Alright then.' Cherry found the King of Hearts and the Queen of Hearts and passed them to a delighted Sean.

'Do you know why I gave you those cards?' she said.

'I have a fair idea.'

'The first thing was to test your poker face, and you failed.' She playfully slapped his hand.

Sean's grin broadened, and he tried to rein it in.

'You can't let emotion guide you in this game, Seany. It's all about the odds. Don't be distracted. What is the win rate of this hand?'

He stared at the cards, like the king or queen might whisper the answer to him. 'I dunno. It seems good to me, so I'd say ninety percent.'

'Righto.' Cherry did her best not to laugh out loud. 'But wrong. King-Queen suited is about twenty-five percent in a seven player game. Not as much of a royal wedding as it might seem.'

'The King of Hearts seems like a strong card to me.'

'Yes, King is a strong card, but it's stronger with another King or an Ace.'

'Ach, it's how you play the hand you've been dealt.'

Something told Cherry Sean wasn't talking about poker anymore. 'In life, yes,' she said. 'And in poker, some of it. So what would you do with this hand? It's coming to the end of the night, you've lost a lot of chips, it's your turn to act before the flop after a raise of seventy quid and four others acting after you. You're tired and want to go to bed—'

'Am I going to bed with you?'

'Not if you interrupt me like that... So, what do you do? Do you stick everything in, hoping it will all go your way, or do you quit to avoid going on tilt if it all goes Pete Tong?'

Sean thought about this for a good thirty seconds. Cherry wasn't sure that he wouldn't go all in simply because of the King of Hearts aspect.

'I think I have a chance,' he said. 'It's a decent hand. At the least, I'd call.'

She nodded. 'Fair play. Yeah, I'd call this and hope something came up for me in the flop. But I'd also know when to quit if I didn't get what I was hoping for.' This hand was a bespoke test and Sean had passed it, although with a slight wobble, which she had expected. He was a romantic, guided by his heart. How could she fault him for that? And there were signs he would come through when the chips were down. She was looking forward to seeing more tomorrow night.

Cherry drained her drink and picked out the cocktail stick with the cherry on it. She held it out to Sean.

'You passed Level One. Have a cherry.'

And this time, he didn't refuse. He took the cocktail stick, stuck it between his teeth and slid the cherry off, keeping his gaze fixed on her the whole time.

Oh dear. Cherry Paradise, the poker queen, might be in a whole lot of trouble.

Chapter 15

Sean

'It's worse than I thought. These idiots genuinely think they're going to wipe the floor with you.'

'Ah, well, we'll see, won't we? They might win a few hands.' Cherry leaned on the cooperage door and, with barely any attempt to shield her actions, roved her gaze up and down Sean. 'I might be the one distracted.'

'*You* might be?' She had insisted that the poker game with his workmates happen at the cooperage straight after work. Something about testosterone firing up her game. But Sean wasn't half as concerned about her being fired up as he was about his colleagues. A lot of the lads were like dogs in heat, and although he knew her head wouldn't be turned by them, he didn't want Cherry feeling uncomfortable.

He didn't want anyone salivating over his wife.

Because she was still his wife.

A wife in tight-fitting Wranglers, Converse and an equally tight black t-shirt.

'Their distraction is our win,' she stated emphatically as if her win would be his too. She could be right. Sean was keen to witness his workmates "poker king" egos brought down a peg or two.

Thankfully, the cask warehouse – a lowly lit store stacked with whisky barrels and smoky corners – where they would hold their game was cool and still, which should keep the testosterone at a decent temperature.

'Mmm, I love the smell in here.' As they entered, Cherry breathed in the temperate air long and deep. It was far too arousing.

'You like the smell of manky wood and sweaty blokes.'

'I'd call it oaky and manly. Where are these "idiots" we're playing?'

'They'll be here. They went to get something to eat.'

Moments later, the deep sound of male laughter and the salty and sharp vinegary smell of chips permeated the cask warehouse, and Sean saw his colleagues through Cherry's eyes.

There was Billy MacDonald, a young apprentice with floppy black hair and a bravado that made Sean cringe, because he recognised it from his own younger years. Tommy Donaldson was of a similar age to Billy, shy but cocky in familiar company. Sean would have to watch him. Albie Donaldson was Tommy's brother and worked as a painter and decorator in the local area. And there were a couple of lads – Kyle and Rhys – around Sean's age, who hopefully knew how to behave themselves.

'Did anyone bring the cards?' Sean asked as everyone settled themselves on stools around the table.

'What? We thought you'd be bringing them.' Billy's eyes rounded.

'Why would you assume that, Bill?'

'Uh, 'cause your missus is a pro.'

'A pro.'

'Aye, like a professional, I mean. No' a prostitute.'

Sean had to fight to keep a straight face.

'Aye, alright, Billy. Thanks for clearing that up.'

Kissing. Poker. Sex. Sean knew what Cherry was like at one of those and suspected she'd be as skilled at the others. Tonight, she'd leave them all in the dust, like the day she'd walked in here with a sandwich.

And he wasn't wrong. But it happened so subtly that it was easy not to notice it happening at all. As Sean dealt the cards, Cherry disarmed them by warming into chatter about coopering, holidays, whisky. And once the hands were being played, she gave out tips, such as telling Billy to cool the hard betting on every single hand. 'It's not bingo,' she told him.

Amidst the chat and tips, she won hand after hand. At one point, she trapped Tommy by comparing his tone of voice when talking about his summer holiday to that when talking about his hand and worked out he was bluffing. It was a clever move.

Sean tried to work out her style but concluded that it was impossible to follow. She was like a cat – friendly and rubbing against you one minute, detached and staring you down the next. You thought you were her friend, then realised she was playing you.

Cherry never offered Sean any playing advice in front of the others, possibly not wanting to emasculate him. He'd take her advice anytime, anywhere. This was her domain, and her commanding the hell out of it was hot as fuck.

That didn't mean he would submit to her when he had a strong hand.

That time came when Sean faced Cherry heads up

with king-jack, suited. Twenty-four percent win rate, he remembered. And the flop came ten, nine, two, so he just needed a queen for a straight.

Cherry checked, suggesting she could have a straight as well. Or possibly something bigger.

But he decided she didn't and checked back.

The turn brought a queen and his desired straight. Sean stayed calm. Confident but not cocky. Not giving away his cards.

Cherry tested him with a small bet. It was a no-brainer to call it.

When the river brought the four of hearts, she bet even bigger. Still, he raised significantly.

In silence, Cherry studied him. Then slid all her chips in.

Sean met that raise then flipped over his king-jack. When she smiled, he thought he'd lost, but she turned over a pair of queens showing that she had three of a kind. Not enough to beat his hand. Her smile was for him – for beating her.

Calmly, Sean raked in the pot.

Cherry leaned back, admiration breaking through. 'Well played, Butler.'

'Thanks.' It was poker, not real life, but maybe she'd see that he listened, he learned and there was more to him than she originally thought.

'We could play strip poker,' Billy suggested as the night was drawing to a natural close.

Sean leaned back in his seat. 'Oh, could we now, Billy, aye?'

'Aye, how no? Cherry, you'd be up for it, right?'

'Ha!' Sean answered before Cherry had a chance to. 'Remind me how many hands you've won tonight, Billy.'

Billy shrugged. 'A few.'

'Right. Maybe sit and think about that for a minute. Instead of playing strip poker here, why don't you go home, sit in a chair in your bedroom and take all your clothes off? Because that is the same result you would get playing here with my wife. And, in case you've forgotten, Billy, Cherry is my wife. Do you understand? She's also a professional poker player, so the chances of your wee dream coming to fruition are slim to fucking none. I'd have thought you'd have realised that by now.'

'Aw, awright, I get the message.' Billy squirmed in his seat. 'Just wisnae sure if it was a real marriage or one o' thae random Vegas ones where folk are aff their chops and get married by mistake.'

Sean's jaw flexed. 'It's a real marriage, Bill.' He could say this knowing it was the absolute truth. Their marriage had never been about anything other than pure obsession with one another. 'And we got married in New York, not Vegas, stone-cold sober and very much on purpose.' Sean glanced at Cherry, who winked at him and softened him back into his usual good humour.

'Billy, let me give you some advice, man to man and all that.' Sean leaned forward in his seat. 'If you want to play strip poker with someone, my suggestion is to go to the pub and find some lassies who are single.'

'Aye, alright.'

'But make sure you've space for their guide dogs around the table.'

Everyone laughed except Billy.

'Alright, alright, keep yer wig on.' Billy put his palms up. 'It was only a suggestion.'

'The idea is very sweet, Billy,' Cherry said, drily, 'but there is only one man I will play strip poker with and he's sitting right next to me.' Then, in case there should be any confusion to whom she was referring to, Cherry scored her fingernails down the back of Sean's neck.

Fuck, that felt incredible. Was she doing it to prove a point to Billy or for him? Either way, she'd need to stop, or he'd be in trouble. He couldn't get a hard-on in front of his workmates. That would be a real comedown from the power dynamic he'd established with Billy.

'Let's play a few more hands, then call it a night,' Cherry added. 'I might even let you win, Billy.'

The hypnotised look on Billy's face mirrored how Sean felt every time he talked to his wife. She had a way of making you feel you were winning by simply noticing that you existed.

Chapter 16

Sean

'You were sensational tonight,' Sean said. The others had gone home, and it was the two of them, alone in the still of the cask warehouse.

'You weren't so bad yourself, Butler.'

'Ach, I was my usual average self. You, though. I've never been prouder to call you my wife. You were like sunshine, a hurricane and a snowstorm all in one.'

'Just doing my job. I'm proud to be your wife. Thank you for dealing with the strip poker thing so...entertainingly.'

'Thanks for your input.'

'No brainer, although they wouldn't have seen much, and I'm not especially interested in any of them with their clothes off.'

Sean chuckled lightly. 'Me neither.'

'You, on the other hand.' Cherry hoisted herself up onto a whisky barrel, the muscles in her biceps rippling as she did so. 'I could be persuaded.'

'To play strip poker with me?' He stepped towards the

barrel. She widened the gap between her knees, and he positioned himself between them. 'Here?'

Cherry recced the warehouse. 'As long as we have the place to ourselves, then yeah. Here seems like a good place.'

'I like your thinking.'

'I could even be persuaded to lose.' The emphasis she placed on those last two words was pure seduction.

Something soared through Sean's chest, before zigzagging lower. He could touch her, take possession of those perfect thighs with his palms. Pull her close so she could feel the chaos she caused.

But that wouldn't be half as much fun as strip poker. Holding on a bit longer, really earning that right.

'How about we change the rules slightly?' Cherry ran her tongue along the inside of her lower lip.

'Explain.'

'It's like this. We each draw a card from the pack. Whoever's is the lowest takes off an item of clothing of the other person's choosing. Makes it a little fairer.'

'I see. It's almost like you want to take your clothes off.'

'My husband is learning.' Cherry lifted the deck and riffled the cards before sliding off the barrel, brushing down Sean's front as she went.

'You still on form, Butler?' It was clear she was referring to what she'd just made contact with rather than his poker game.

'Aye. Never been better.' *Total lies.* He was a tortured mess but would hold it together.

Cherry moved to the opposite side of the barrel, placing the deck face down between them. Across from her, Sean was aware of the weight of his breath. In all the years working at the cooperage, he'd never stood in this warehouse and been remotely aroused. Until now. Until facing his molten-hot wife in the dim light of the cask warehouse, the draw of the cards the only thing between their being clothed or unclothed.

'Do you want to go first?' Cherry blinked soft and low.

'No, you go?'

She laid down the first card from the top of the deck.

King of Clubs.

He was fucked.

Sean picked a card.

Seven of diamonds.

Cherry hummed. 'Mm-hmm, Butler. Sorry about that.'

'Aye, right. What you after then?'

'I am after...this.' She looped her finger around Sean's chest. 'Get it off.'

Without missing a beat, he pulled off his polo shirt and threw it onto the warehouse floor, glad to be rid of it amidst a Cherry-induced heatwave. And the way she looked at him, like she craved what she saw, fired him up hotter than the cooperage kiln on full heat.

'Loser goes next.' Sean flipped over the next card without being invited. The six of diamonds. 'Is this deck rigged or what?'

Cherry revealed a five of clubs. 'I guess not.' A lascivious smile curved her mouth upwards. 'Name your price, baby.'

Holy fuck! She didn't need to take anything off. Calling him baby like that drove Sean to distraction.

'The t-shirt.' His command came out hoarse but assured.

And when she cast off the tee and threw it onto the floor next to his, a low growl tore through Sean's throat. Fuck. The way her breasts, soft and generous, rose like pillows inside the black-lace cups of her bra. And the mellow tan of her beautiful skin – how did she get colour like that playing poker?

'Have you been sunbathing nude while I'm at work?' It came out with a hint of accusation.

She shook her head slowly. 'Oh, no. No one gets to see these.'

'No one?'

'Except my husband.'

Sean took a deep breath to ensure he could stand upright. 'Is that bra the right size for you?'

'Yep, why?'

'It's like there's a lot of breasts and not much bra.'

'It's a plunge bra, sweetheart. But maybe the plunge is what you're most focused on.'

'Could be. They're beautiful, you know.'

'Thank you.'

'Welcome. Pick a card.'

Cherry's French manicure slid over the top card. It didn't matter what the card was; all their clothes were coming off tonight. There was no way anything but would be happening. The anticipation, though...

'Ace of Hearts.' Cherry traced the shape of a heart over the card. 'You're getting that belt off right now.'

'I haven't picked a card yet.' Sean reached for the deck, selecting the Ace of Clubs, rendering them equal. He laughed, and the light in Cherry's eyes was like a fireball. She was loving this.

He fumbled for his belt, focus diminished because all he could think about was what was underneath that phenom- enal plunge bra.

'Do you want a hand with the belt, honey?' Before there was time to answer, she was in front of him, unbuckling his belt without looking away from his face, yanking it tightly from his jeans. It clunked to the floor. 'That's better. Now, I believe I owe you.'

'Aye.' Sean motioned to her bra. 'I need this gone, like, fucking last week. Show your husband, the only man who gets to see you.'

Reaching round, Cherry unclipped her bra and let it cascade to the warehouse floor. Sean watched it dropping onto the dust and dirt. But immediately, his eyes were ascending Cherry's body to the most incredible pair of breasts he'd ever seen. Journeying over the smooth curves and inhaling the olive skin, the perfect deep-honey coloured nipples, pert in the cool oaky air.

He reached out.

Reflexively, she caught his wrist. 'No touching. It's the rules.'

'I must have missed the bit where we discussed the rules.'

'Nonetheless, that's one of them.'

Sean read her easily this time – her mask was nothing like the one she'd worn at the poker table. She was teasing, holding back deliberately.

'Fine,' he said. 'That's fine. Pick another card then. Back to the game.'

Cherry turned towards the barrel, away from him, showcasing hourglass curves he could lose track of time in and an intricate floral tattoo on her lower back.

'Nice tat. Get to your side of the barrel, Paradise. Facing me.'

She did as he ordered. Sean was rock-hard looking at her. Stunning didn't even cut it. Cherry was picture perfect. Those tits were going in his mouth later, no doubt about it. In his hands, in his mouth, his cock sliding between them.

'You thinking filthy thoughts, Butler?'

'Of course I'm thinking filthy thoughts. All yours pure, are they?'

'Not exactly, no.' Cherry chose the next card, Sean's eyes flitting up and down between her face and her beautiful breasts.

Who gave a fuck what the card was? Not him. Not now.

'King of Hearts,' she said. 'It's like a sign.'

'A sign of what exactly?' Sean placed a card on top of Cherry's. The Queen of Hearts.

'Isn't that funny?' she said. 'The queen on top of her king.'

'Aye, isn't it just?'

'Jeans, Butler. Unbutton. No need to take them off fully.'

Holy crap. Sean reached for the buttons at his straining crotch. It would be nothing but a relief to get these loosened.

Cherry caught the softness of her mouth between her teeth, lids heavy like a drunken butterfly, as she watched him, his arousal more than obvious through his underwear.

She moaned.

'Jesus. You turned on, Paradise? Turned on watching your husband turned on for you?'

A biting down and a shudder-sigh. Yes, then.

'As it should be.' Moving to her side of the barrel, he rested his hands on her hips from behind, dipping his mouth to the soft skin of her neck. He breathed her in – the potent floral scent like opium. Coasting upwards, he kissed softly under her ear.

Another moan stirred the air.

Hands braced on her hips, he brought her round to him, hoisted her onto the barrel, reaching for her breast.

This time there was no protest, only a whimper.

Sean slid the pad of his thumb over the tip of Cherry's nipple, palming the other. So soft, so generous, so firm.

So his.

Plunging down, he sucked hard. Cherry's tits were heaven. He could feast on them all day. He palmed her other breast. A firm, bountiful handful, made for him.

'Oh, Seany.' She grasped at strands of his hair, tugged as he swiped his tongue across the peak of her nipple, more blood rushing to his cock. He tightened the other between his thumb and forefinger, testing how far he could take it.

Quite far, it seemed.

'Mmm, harder, Seany. That's so good.'

She was going to have to stop calling him Seany, or he would shoot his load.

As if he was going to tell her to stop.

Breast still in his grasp, Sean dropped his mouth to Cherry's. Kissing his wife at last. Devouring his wife. Possessing his wife. Their tongues hot and desperate together.

'I need you so much, Cher. I really fucking need you.'

'Take me.'

Jesus! Was this an offer to fuck her on this barrel? Seeing himself plunging in and out of his wife on the result of hours of his own labour would be nothing short of spectacular.

Sean flicked open the button of her jeans and unzipped them, a triangle of black lace visible now, hard to define in the dim light what was beneath it.

He reached for the waist of the jeans.

Like she knew what was coming, she toed off her Converse.

'Lift,' he said hoarsely, and Cherry hoisted herself up on her arms, affording Sean the chance to pull her jeans over that decadent backside and down those beautiful, tanned legs.

The panties were all lace and the only thing that stopped Cherry being completely naked.

'Stand.' It came out as more of a command that he'd meant, but she stood without argument. He pulled her flush to him. This decadent creature, so fierce yet so fragile, skin next to his skin. The size of his body eclipsing hers so fully.

He slid his hand inside the lace – palm hot against her mound, fingers diving into her soft, wet heat.

Soaking heat.

Their poker foreplay did this to her? He did this to her. Their need was mutual. Sean wasn't sure he'd fully grasped that until now.

With one digit, he glided Cherry's wetness over her clit. His fingers felt like giant invaders inside the soft, delicate mounds and dips of her pussy, but she appeared to welcome the invasion.

'Oh fuck, Sean. Oh God! I've dreamt about this.'

Those words. The power of those words. All he could do was watch that divine face as it melted at his touch. His wife crumbling under his fingertips.

Fuck, she was so beautiful.

Sean pushed two fingers inside her, thrust them deep, plundering her softness, finding the place to make her fold, his hand dripping with her slick arousal.

She ground down into him, searching for a solid surface.

With the heel of his hand, he gave it to her, simultaneously finger-fucking her. 'Rub your clit right there, Cher. Soak my hand with that beautiful dripping pussy of yours.'

'Mmm.' She writhed into his palm. 'How do you know it's beautiful?'

'Because it feels fucking out of this world, and if it's

anything like your face, it'll be the most beautiful thing I've ever seen.'

'Oh, Sean. I want to see you too. Need to... Show me... Show me.'

With his free hand, Sean pulled back the waistband of his underwear and lowered it. His cock stood long and thick, a bridge between them both.

'Oh God! Imagine that stretching me, fucking me.'

'I have done, Cher. A lot.' Sean drove his fingers inside her. 'Have you thought about it? Thought about being fucked by me, like this but harder? You must have, right?'

'Maybe.'

'Yes, then. You touch yourself and think of me?'

She nodded.

'Show me. Play with yourself like you would on the other side of that bedroom wall.'

Cherry reached for her clit and slicked her wetness over it. 'This is what I do. This is how I touch myself when you're right there through the wall. Do you have that beautiful cock in your hand at night, thinking of me?'

'Jesus! You know I do. I don't think of anything else.'

'Show me. Show me what you do when you think of me.'

Sean groaned, grasping his cock in his palm, working his hand up and down his straining shaft, this time with the creature of his imagination right here. But it wasn't enough.

'Oh, Cherry, fuck. I need more of you.' He dropped to his haunches and, taking the band of the panties between his teeth, dragged the flimsy, saturated lace over her pubic mound, nose trailing through the soft line of hair, over the beginnings of her divine slit.

Torturing himself, he refrained from dwelling on it.

Down the panties came over her hips, knees, ankles. Then he balled them, brought them to his face and inhaled.

Fucking Jesus! He had peaked.

Almost.

Except the real thing was here.

He opened his eyes and let himself finally see what was undoubtedly – as he had known it would be – the most beautiful pussy he had ever seen.

His wife's.

Wasting not a second further, Sean buried his face between Cherry's legs.

It was everything he had imagined and more. Soft, slick and monumentally swollen. For him.

She cried out. He swiped his tongue over her clit, then round it and back again, repeating and repeating until she segued from moaning hard to noises that could not be described in words but which sent shockwaves through his balls, and his hand to his cock again, the need dire.

Palming himself while he sucked and licked at her soaking-wet core, Sean knew that when Cherry came, it would catapult him over the edge. And he needed her to go there so badly because, although he never wanted this to end, the pleasure was next to torment, and he desperately needed to release everything building since the moment he'd met her.

He worked his tongue inside Cherry, over her, flicking, licking, sucking. She bucked and writhed into him, straddling her legs wider so he could get in deeper, give her more, see every pink and swollen crevice.

It was the stuff of his fantasies. But better. So much better.

'Get back on the barrel, Cher, and spread these legs wider for me.'

She jumped up, legs parting for him.

'Wider. Show me it all.'

And she did, every slick, glistening, swollen moment of her.

'That's it. God, you're perfect. Let me fuck you.'

'Keep sucking my pussy,' she said. 'It's so good.'

Sean wasn't about to argue. This could be the starter. He fell to her again.

The sounds they made together filled and heated the warehouse – her needy moans, his uninhibited grunts as he buried his face deep in her, lost and unleashed – until her legs shook, her whole body capitulated, and her climax ravaged her.

'Oh, oh, oh, fuck, oh, Sean. Yes! Oh God!'

At that moment, Cherry's arousal lush on his lips, Sean fisted himself hard and fast, the sound of her orgasm driving out his own – wild, savage, unstoppable – bringing a hot primal rush of cum shooting out, over his hand and onto the stone warehouse floor.

The best day at work, ever.

'Sean, that was incredible.' Cherry zipped up her jeans and adjusted her breasts back into the cups of her bra.

'Aye, it was.' Why did this feel like there was a 'but' hovering in the air?

She pulled her t-shirt on but didn't say anything more. And perhaps it was the stillness after an evening of constant motion in a place where normally all he heard were male voices, but suddenly Sean was acutely attuned to her frequency. As he replayed what had just happened between them, something struck him. Something she'd said.

'Cherry, can I ask you something?'

'Of course.'

He stepped towards her. 'Answer me honestly, please. Did you not want to go all the way because of the stupid marriage annulment?'

She didn't even need to reply. The widening of her eyes to deer-like proportions at his question told him everything. Still, he slung his polo shirt over the crook of his elbow and waited.

'It complicates things, doesn't it?' she said. 'Not just legally. Emotionally.'

'And what we did here keeps things simple?'

'No, of course it doesn't.' Cherry's tone was so matter-of-fact, as if she could easily detach from the complications. He wondered what her trick was.

'You know what would be simple, Cher? If it makes you feel things, just feel them. You feel everything else. You felt enough for some other guy to try and have kids with him. You married me. Is that not enough, feelings wise?'

She stared at him, silence hanging between them, as she weighed up where to take this. What to give him in terms of an explanation. She pushed her hands into her jeans pockets and shuffled awkwardly.

'I do feel things, Sean. That's the problem.' Her voice cracked a little. This wasn't as easy for her as he'd thought. 'But my feelings don't match what the world has dealt me. How it has shaped me. I got carried away tonight because I want you, but in the aftermath, I'm ashamed of myself.'

Fucking hell. 'Why would you be ashamed? We want each other; that's normal.'

'Because every desire I have now comes with conse-quences. If I let myself have you, then I'm putting down the bricks of a house I might not be able to fully build. The woman you see – the one you met in New York, the one who just unabashedly enjoyed her husband – is me, but she's a part of the old me. There's a whole other Cherry under the surface.'

'Isn't that true for everyone?'

'Yes, of course. But this is bigger than the outer face and the inner world.' Cherry sighed as if she'd reached the edge of a cliff and didn't want to go on, but she did so, for which he was grateful.

'Look... From the moment you know you're carrying a life inside you, your idea of future-you shifts. When that's ripped away, you can't swim back to where you came from. There's a raging river of trauma in between Cherry before and Cherry now. Like it or not, I'm changed forever.' She moved into a darker corner of the warehouse and trailed her hand across some casks. Sean understood that the candid nature of what she was saying must be taking all her courage. He wasn't expecting more, but something had opened in her.

'You know, sometimes people tell me I'm lucky to have my freedom, so I try to appreciate it.' Cherry looked at the barrel as she spoke. 'But it's not freedom when you wake up every morning weighed down by grief and terrified for the future.'

Sean nodded as if he understood, but how could he?

'My friends' worlds are revolving at a million miles an hour; they're frantically making packed lunches, at soft play on a loop, their kids giving them grey hair. I stand still in my hot pants, clutching my poker cards, not belonging at soft play and feeling out of place at the poker table. Don't get me wrong; I'm no victim, but I am in a whole other dark, murky universe with weeds and cold, deep currents where I'm trying desperately to tread water, never mind swim. Cherry traced her finger across the word 'Butler's' on the face of one of the casks, like she was considering all that it meant –

his family name, her name – her family – if she wanted. Something hot tugged at Sean's chest and the room seemed to tilt.

She turned back to him, raw and vulnerable, her sweet floral scent floating across the space. 'Every month that passes, it gets harder, and I need to prepare myself for finding a way not to sink – not to feel less – for the rest of my life. And it's exhausting. Utterly exhausting. So, you see, I'm still me, but I'm broken in ways I can't fix, and everything about who I am feels unsettled, like my world is shifting and cracking every single day.'

Holy fuck. The fragile strength of this woman never failed to steal breath from Sean's lungs. It ripped at his heart that she was going through this. He locked onto her gaze, today more steel than sparkling cobalt. She met him right back, possibly waiting for him to run a mile. Which he would not be doing.

'You're fucking incredible, Cherry.'

She nodded tightly, blinked at him, that steel blue glistening a little now. 'Am I? Yeah, maybe I am.'

'Of course you are. To stand here and open your heart like that, making yourself so vulnerable but showing nothing but strength. Not everyone can do that. And for what it's worth – and I don't say this to negate a single second of what you feel – you could never, ever be less. *You* are "more" than anyone I have ever met. You fucking shine, woman.'

Thank you, she mouthed.

He went to her, the pull to hold her more than magnetic, but she stepped away.

'I can leave Kinshore. If it's getting too much.' To her credit, she met him dead on as she offered this. 'Organise the tourney remotely. It's not fair to bring my mess into someone else's life.'

'No, I don't want you to leave.' Sean moved back himself and leaned on a barrel, mimicking casual, hands grasping the solid oak – the thing *he* controlled, had mastery over, could create something out of that would last for hundreds of years. 'You need some stability, and the money for charity is my main objective, so...let's stick to the original plan. Rings on, hands off, poker, the end. No flirting, nothing. Okay?' If this kept her here and kept things safe for them both, then that was how it would be.

Cherry searched his face. Something in his words had surprised her. But she nodded.

'Okay, I want to do the tourney, too. For you. Let's count tonight as getting things out of our system and move on.'

'Aye, sounds like the best way forward.'

Does it, Sean, aye? Sean wasn't sure that the words 'out of his system' and 'Cherry' belonged in the same sentence, but he would give it a go.

And he would try his best not to lose his mind in the process.

Chapter 17

Sean

The house was empty when Sean got home two weeks later. He kicked off his trainers at the door and padded through to the kitchen, where he poured a glass of water down his throat at record speed. Prepping to cycle one hundred miles was thirsty work.

Beyond the patio doors, he saw the summerhouse door was open. Cherry would be in there, in her new poker HQ. Something about her presence comforted him, took the edge of his loneliness, even though he would have preferred her in the house with him.

It was amazing how quickly you could get used to someone being there, even when they weren't always with you. The glass with the succulent red lipstick mark on it by the sink, her tiny denim shorts and glittery vests hanging on the clothes airer, the smell of floral shower gel wafting out of the bathroom.

Her energy was everywhere, even when she wasn't.

But this wasn't how it should be between newlyweds. He shouldn't be here alone, wishing he was that glass. Maybe after ten years together, but not now.

They weren't like normal newlyweds, though. It was better to think that they weren't married at all.

He didn't want to think that. He wanted his wife. Was that so wrong?

Sean went upstairs, took a shower, came back down, and with a bowl of potato salad in one hand, opened his laptop and navigated to the email he hadn't done anything about yet.

The one where had he to go online and book an appointment for his American visa interview in London. He ought to get cracking on that, although it didn't seem so appealing anymore.

A sea of dates swam in front of him; most of them were a few months away, but there was a free one in two-weeks' time.

You're going to have to go for it, Seany, because if you don't, you could end up with nothing.

He booked the slot. If she gave him a sign, he could cancel it.

He really hoped he would have to cancel it.

Sean placed his empty bowl on the table and picked up a book and tried to read. But his mind wasn't focused enough, so he began to scroll through the photos on his phone. He came to one of him and his dad standing together in their kilts at one of the annual distillery Burns' suppers. Eighteen-year-old Sean had been so proud to attend as Jimmy Butler's son and over the moon that he'd been allowed to do the *Address to a Haggis* that year. His dad had even coached him.

Fair fa' your honest, sonsie face,
Great Chieftain o' the Puddin-race!
A sucker punch of grief hit him right in the solar plexus.

Shit. Grief could hit you at the most inopportune times.

He didn't want to cry when Cherry could walk in at any minute. That would be embarrassing.

On the internet tabs on his phone, he flicked to some stuff he'd been browsing over the past couple of weeks, dipping in and out and wondering what to do with the information. Articles and blog posts about the effects of miscarriage on relationships. He wanted a deeper understanding of what it meant because, with that, he had a better chance of holding onto his wife.

There was no denying it was depressing stuff. It seemed that the strain could tear even the strongest couples apart.

But he thought he'd found something that might give some hope.

The patio door clicked, and Sean turned to see Cherry. God, she never failed to take his breath away. Tonight, she was softer, more vulnerable-looking than the public-facing version. Her face was clear of make-up. A flowing black skirt fell to her ankles; her feet were bare, with pink-polished nails. And heaven help him, was she wearing one of his work polo shirts?

Yep. Due to the size of the shirt on her, the Butler's Cooperage name was on her right breast.

A powerful wave of something unfamiliar crashed through Sean. What was that? It was as if the cord of energy between them had thickened. Was it primal? Like she was sending him an invisible message that she belonged to him.

But she didn't. This was one giant tease.

But what could he say? It was just a t-shirt.

'Hey,' he said, lowly. 'How's it going?'

'Hey.' Cherry ran her hand through her mermaid waves. 'It's going good. I came in for some water. Did you get something to eat?' She held her glass under the running faucet.

'Aye, old potato salad. Nice top.'

She glanced down at the shirt, more precisely at the logo on her breast. 'Oh, yeah, sorry. I found it hanging on the clothes airer. You don't mind, do you?'

'Nope. It suits you. Keep it if you like. I've plenty more.'

He wondered if it smelled of him. It was clean, but maybe wearing it reminded her of him. God knows, if he had an item of her clothing pressed to any part of his body, he'd have her on his mind.

'How was training tonight?' Cherry perched on the arm of the couch, then leaned back a little as if noticing something wasn't right. 'Are you okay?'

'Aye, I'm fine. Just been thinking about my dad and getting sentimental over old photos.' He motioned to his phone. 'Training was good – cycled forty miles with Nate. Hard work, mind you. Don't know why but I'm struggling a wee bit.'

'Oh.' Her brow furrowed. 'How so?'

'Och, I'll be fine. It's normal to have peaks and troughs and feel a bit like a teenage girl at a boyband concert.'

'Eh?'

'Bit dizzy at times.'

'Jeez! You need to see a doctor.' She touched his arm, softly, like she did care.

'I'll be fine. It was probably low blood sugar or something. Nothing a can of Bru won't sort out.'

'Sean! Come on. See a doctor, please. People need you.'

People. People needed him. Was she referring to everyone else but herself? 'Are you one of them?'

Her hand moved back faster than he could have anticipated, and she gave him words in place of physical affection. It would have to do. He was right. She did at least care.

'I know how much this bike ride means to you, and I

want to see you succeed. Your family needs you. Your dad, I'm sure, is watching you and cheering you on, too.'

'Aye, maybe. Or he's up there telling me to "Calm doon, son".'

Cherry smiled, and Sean realised how much he needed to see that. It was like oxygen being injected into his bloodstream. 'Did he say that a lot?'

'All the time. I got a tattoo of it.' He rolled up the arm of his t-shirt and showed her the inking of his father's words. 'Got it done about six months ago. I wanted him to see it.'

'Oh my God, I adore it.' She ran her finger under the tattoo. A tiny gesture that burned fire right through him. 'It's so sweet of you. And it's hilarious, too. Did he like it?'

'Aye. Rolled his eyes and told me I was as daft as a brush, but he laughed, too. Safe to say he loved it. Anyway, I didn't listen to him any of those other times he told me to calm doon, so I'm not about to start now.' Sean pulled his sleeve down. 'I'll rest when this thing's over.'

Her concerned gaze roamed over his face, an emotional engineer examining him for signs of malfunction.

'Really, I'm fine... Enough about me. Cher, listen...' Fuck it, he'd grasp the nettle while he had her here. 'I've been doing some reading—'

Cherry glanced at the airport thriller on the table. 'Any good?'

'Not that. On the internet.' No point beating about the bush. 'About...miscarriage.'

'Oh.' Her mouth froze on this word. And did that one syllable hold tinges of betrayal? Was he overstepping the mark by doing this? As she rose from the arm of the couch, he feared he had his answer. 'Sean, I have a tourney in twenty minutes. I can't start on tilt.'

'Oh, right. Another time then.' The last thing he wanted was to fuck up her game.

But then she sat back down again. 'Sorry, that sounded dismissive. What... What did you read?'

'Are you sure...?' He waited for her nod of agreement before sitting forward and tapping at his phone. 'I found something kind of promising. It was in this article about this woman who'd had five miscarriages before she had a baby. It mentioned new treatments that are coming to analyse the womb lining and—'

'Sean...' Cherry inhaled deeply and let the breath out on a slow exhale. 'You've no idea how amazing you are for reading that. But I'm thirty-seven. It's too late for me and new treatments. Those things will help women in their twenties who don't even know yet that they're going to have problems. People my age, who exist in this dead zone when it comes to understanding, are fucked. On our own.' She raised her palms up in the universal shrug gesture. 'This is the medicine logo for me. It doesn't know the answer and isn't in enough of a hurry to help.' Rising from the arm of the couch, she covered his hand with her own and gave him a bittersweet smile before trailing her fingers away. 'Thank you for caring. You're gorgeous, inside and out. Sorry, I have to go to work.'

Sean so badly wanted to grab her hand and tell her to stay. Pull her down to the couch, onto his knee, breathe her in deep and slow, kiss her in the same way, crack his heart wide open and tell her how he would try with everything he had to make it okay.

But that would be naïve.

So, he let her go.

The patio doors closed, and he watched her drifting

back to the summerhouse, her honeysuckle scent still floating tantalisingly in the surrounding air.

Fuck. He leaned back on the couch and let out a deep sigh of his own. That was heavy, heavy stuff.

He needed a beer.

As he rose to get one, something by the printer caught his eye. A pile of paper. He moved closer and, Jesus, if his heart didn't stop beating in his chest.

He'd known it was there, but what was on the top sheet made him aware of every muscle in his body, yet aware of nothing but the two words glaring at him.

Nullity Application.

The step that Cherry, his wife of nearly one month, had taken in ending their marriage.

Nothing could have prepared Sean for how heavy this made him feel. He picked up the paper and flicked through the sheets.

She'd filled the whole fucking form in. There had been no mention of that. Twenty pages of boring, formal detail done and dusted. A box ticked for the reason it was all ending before it had begun.

The marriage was not consummated owing to the wilful refusal of the respondent to consummate it.

That was true.

But how depressing. All their passion and fireworks boiled down to this cold, black and white document, so some judge somewhere could make a decision on whether their marriage was a mistake or not.

It wasn't a mistake. Not as far as he was concerned.

Sean hated this.

Loathed it.

Nonetheless, there was one question niggling at him.

Cherry had dotted every I, crossed every T and left the

form sitting by the printer for him. But there was nothing left to fill in. So why hadn't she posted this or pressed him to do so?

A suspicion crept through him that Cherry was struggling to decide. Somewhere deep inside her, she didn't want this either. Perhaps she was hoping he would post the form for her and take the decision out of her hands.

Or chuck it in the bin.

Who did she think she'd married? Mr Give Up After The First Hurdle?

Sean was not that guy.

Then he had an idea. A wee thing to test her out.

It was a gamble, but how Cherry responded would speak volumes.

Chapter 18

Sean

I t was six p.m. by the time Sean reached the distillery, sweat prickling on the back of his neck from the run from the cooperage. Jamie was in his office, shirt sleeves rolled up, winding up a video call of some kind.

Sean would forever be grateful to his older brother for taking on the role of Chief Operating Officer then the distillery CEO as their father became too ill to do it himself. Besides getting the rest of them off the hook from working in an office in a suit and tie, it meant that there was family at the helm of the business.

And that mattered. A lot. The distillery wasn't merely business. It was blood. From the barrels Sean sweated over, to the flavours his mother as Master Distiller selected, to the bottles of the stuff Cal sold in his bars in Edinburgh.

Jamie motioned for Sean to sit down, but he jogged on the spot and pointed at his watch. Jamie, ever the professional, nodded at the screen and continued to speak in what Sean called 'business drivel' but which he knew was a necessary part of keeping the company running. Jamie did, however, manage a subtly raised middle finger under the desk.

Sean grinned. He loved how he could reduce his sensible big brother to behaving like a teenager again.

'Right, let's go!' Sean clapped his hands when the call ended. 'You were meant to be ready at six.'

'Alright, calm doon, son.' Jamie echoed their dad's words and softened Sean's nervous energy. 'Give me five minutes to get into my short shorts, and we're good to go.'

'Jesus, not the short shorts. Suppose you'll be wanting to run past the nursing home.'

'I have had a few requests this week, but okay, I'll wear normal shorts, and we'll avoid the village.'

Thankfully, Jamie kept his word, and soon they were pounding along the shoreline road, the evening breeze working as nature's air conditioning on their warming, clammy skin.

'So,' Jamie said, 'how's married life? Are things okay? I've been a bit worried about you. We all have.'

If there was one person Sean could tell the truth to, it was Jamie. Niall was often his closest confidante, but he and Carli were visiting her sister in Australia, and Jamie had a head that was way older and wiser than his years.

This was hard, though – admitting that his marriage was a sham to the brother who had it all. Loved up with a Hollywood star he'd met while snowed in at a Highland hotel, who'd given it all up to come to live in Kinshore. It was like Jamie was born with the script and stage directions and just needed to arrive for curtain up.

'No need to worry; it's all good.' Sean upped the pace, almost too obviously, noticing as he did a solitary hare sitting in a nearby field, ears up, on high alert for predators. 'Shall we go harder here?'

'Thought we were still warming up?'

'Ach, warm up, schmorm up. C'mon.' He jogged backwards, beckoning to his brother to hurry, before turning around and running on ahead. Anything to outpace the subject hot on his heels.

Who was he kidding? All he was doing was buying time. Jamie was no idiot, and he'd known Sean his whole life – watched him slide carrots off his plate and into his school shorts pocket, seen him try to hide his heartbreak by acting like James Bond when his first girlfriend dumped him. If Sean thought he could kid him now, he was delusional.

For three miles along the coastline road, they ran in near silence, the evening sun providing encouragement, and the wide ribbon of sand and sea a familiar friend training alongside them. Sean tried to lose himself in the rhythm of their breaths, in the sound of their trainers thwacking on the tarmac, in the pointing out of kestrels, pheasants, grouse and carelessly discarded bits of litter. Anything.

'See that Snickers wrapper?' He pointed to the verge. 'Every week I pick it up, and the next time I'm out, there's another one in its place. Why can't folk take their litter home?'

'It's annoying, alright,' Jamie agreed, an edge to his voice that hinted he knew this was the symptom not the illness.

As their journey brought them back to the outskirts of Kinshore, Jamie suggested they take the pace down a bit.

'How about we go onto the beach, get some breeze in our ears and sand in our face?'

'Aye alright.'

'And you can tell me what's really going on?'

'No idea what you mean, but sure.' Sean wanted to talk to Jamie, but the Captain Coping persona Cherry had recognised was strutting about the scene, and taking off the cape was far harder than it seemed. How long had he been doing this? Helping others with their problems and shoving his own in the to-do pile? It was a strategy that showed cracks when your dad had died and your wife was leaving you.

Jamie's voice sharpened and softened at the same time. 'Don't fob me off, Seany.' He stopped shy of the path through the sand dunes, pinning Sean with his serious older-brother stare. 'Something's not right. Let it out.'

The nearby waves roared in Sean's ears, like the truth he was avoiding. He was cornered, back at school, caught by the teacher with no way out. But unlike any teacher of Sean's, Jamie didn't push it further. It was his style. He opened his door and let you come to him.

This was hard, though. Massive. Nobody needed his self-created drama when they were all grieving their dad.

But Jamie read his face. 'And if you're holding back because we're grieving dad then forget it. That is precisely why you need to share.'

Sean rested his vision on a spot far out at sea where a wave was cresting, about to break perfectly. He felt a lot like that wave, besides the perfectly bit. *Thank God for Jamie.*

'My marriage is fucked.' The wave peaked, curled and rolled towards shore. He could be riding that right now. Whatever happened, surfing was never one of his problems. 'We're getting it annulled.'

'Eh?' Jamie frowned. 'But you guys are smitten. There's no way that's fake. No way.'

'Aye, we are. It's not that. She's incredible, J. I'm nuts about her. Never felt like this about a woman, ever. And I know she feels the same.'

'Alright. So what's going on?'

'Hee haw, that's what. I'm living in a sham marriage.'

'What? So, you haven't...?'

'Aye, besides a wee thing the other day, we haven't. Not for want of sexual chemistry. It's complicated. It was all going great until we went to see Cherry's mum, who set off a bunch of fucked-up thoughts Cherry has about not being a good enough wife. She's convinced that she can't be what I need.'

'Which is what exactly?' Jamie removed his baseball cap and streaked his hand through his dark, sweat-damp hair.

'A "normal" wife, a mum. Her own mum kind of reinforces the ideal, doesn't believe in her own daughter.'

Jamie stared at Sean for longer than Sean was entirely comfortable with. His brother was reading him, scanning all the data and about to deliver a sensible, measured solution. Nevertheless, it was intimidating.

'Okay, ignoring the bit about you having a "normal" anything... The mum thing... What is that?' Cap back on, Jamie embarked on some quad stretches, perhaps to make this easier for Sean.

Sean absent-mindedly stretched too. 'It's complicated. I don't want to say too much. But it's kind of linked to her poker player lifestyle, other things that happened in her past.'

'Ah, okay, say no more. You don't need to share her private stuff with me.'

Jamie's near sixth sense was helpful, meaning Sean could avoid explaining the finer detail. 'I've tried telling her that families are built in different ways, that my half-brother is my cousin, three of us are adopted, etcetera. But it's like meeting you all has made things worse. She sees the family as too perfect and is convinced I deserve better. Basically,

I've persuaded her to stay for two months and do the poker pro-am thing. I'm hoping it might make things a bit clearer for me, too. But after that, she's gone. I'll never see her again. I'm taking her to meet Mum on Friday and dreading it.'

'Okay, okay.' Jamie raised his palms. 'Let's back-pedal a wee bit and unpack a few things.'

'Uh-oh, the business speak is out.' Sean's jest betrayed his worry that he was about to be hit with wisdom he'd been hiding from.

But Jamie ignored the playful jibe. 'That wee hidden nugget in what you said tells me a lot. *You* need things to be clearer. On one hand, you're telling her it's all fine and you can adopt or something, but you need time to think. Why is the "you" in this equation buried so deep it's practically hidden?'

Sean had to concede. 'That's a point I don't have an answer to.'

'Right. First things first, do *you* want to adopt kids? How much have you thought about that?'

This was such a simple question, yet it went right to the crux of the matter. 'I dunno. I suppose we grew up with it, so I thought why not?'

'Because it's a massive deal – you don't need me to tell you that – and if you need to think on things, then perhaps that's not the best solution to chuck out there right now.'

'Aye, fair enough. I've thought about it from time to time but haven't had to go too deep.'

'And maybe it's not what Cherry wants,' Jamie added another salient point. 'So, putting that to the side, what is important is how you and Cherry feel about one another.'

Jamie's positive tone gave Sean cause for optimism. 'Care to expand?'

'As a matter of fact, I do.' He smiled that warm, wry smile of his, and Sean loosened further.

'Listen,' Jamie said, 'when I met Alicia, I didn't get given a folder with her history to peruse, and I certainly didn't have a time machine. I had no idea what our future would be like. All I knew was how I felt about her. She's the love of my life, plain and simple. Maybe we'll have a family, maybe we won't, but no way am I letting her go. Not now, not ever. And you've, unfortunately, come into this a completely different way around. Armed with some sort of knowledge that confuses things. What I say is, put that aside and focus on how you and Cherry make one another feel. She's the one, right?'

'Aye. Hundred percent.'

'Great. She needs to know that. If she believes it, she might feel more confident in staying. She's only known you five minutes, remember? She's still feeling her way to see if she can trust you. Be there for her if she wants to open up. When I met Alicia, she was holding onto stuff about her past. I could sense it, but I couldn't force it out of her. Luckily, we got there in the end, albeit with a bit of drama along the way. Being snowed in with nowhere else to go might have helped.'

'Aye, no chance of any snow in this weather.' Sean dug his foot into the warm evening sand. 'Thing is, we're living in the same house, and the tension is insane. She's right on the other side of the bedroom wall, J. It's too fucking much.'

Jamie scrubbed his jaw. 'Trust takes time. Stop trying to fix things and go with the flow and show her you're there for her. To talk if she needs to talk. And, you know, Kinshore has this way of getting under people's skin.'

'Aye, that's true.'

'Whatever you do, take it easy.' Jamie rested a reassuring, solid hand on Sean's shoulder. 'It's been a full-on few years, not to mention the last six months. You've been dealing with tons of stress.'

'Och, I'm fine.' And there he was, Captain Coping again. Why did he do this, in front of his big brother no less? It was so hard-wired into his brain that it was hard to let go of.

Jamie quirked a brow. 'Mibbes aye, mibbes naw. Look after yourself, wee bro. Mum doesn't need to lose a son as well as a husband. You can cancel the poker tournament, if need be, and focus on the cycling.'

'Aye, I could do.' Not for one second would Sean consider this; it would be like dishonouring his dad. 'But I plan to raise a shitload of money for the charity. Cherry's got great connections.'

'So do you. Connor, for one. And his pal. The Duff guy.'

The Duff guy. This made Sean laugh. Jamie might have married into a celebrity family, but his knowledge of anyone famous could barely be considered as such. He didn't own a TV and made sure his priorities were what he considered real-life matters – the distillery, family, love. Not that different from Sean, in many ways. It was refreshing. His advice was like the cool coastal wind in the warm evening air.

'Aye, I've half the A-list on speed dial. What it boils down to is I need this poker tournament to happen, and I need Cherry to sort it. I'll have to accept the pain of living with, but not being able to, touch my smoking-hot wife. Which is a whole new kind of frustration.'

'I can imagine.' Jamie's concerned older-brother face

was back. 'Who knows, she might be lying in her bed, wishing you'd knock in Morse code and ask her to come through.'

'Ha. Is there an app for learning Morse code? I'll download it tonight.'

Chapter 19

Cherry

'This is where you grew up?' Cherry stared up at the handsome house with its historic stonework, spotless Georgian windows and rainbow of neat window boxes on the outer sills. There must be at least ten bedrooms inside. It was a far cry from the small colonies house that she'd grown up in. The place her mum had always said there wasn't room to swing a cat. 'It's stunning, Sean.'

'Aye. I can't complain about growing up here. And down that way are the old barrel store and the distillery.' He gestured to a path that led down to a smaller, lower stone building, the Buddhist-temple-style pagoda roof of the distillery rising up dramatically in the distance.

'I'd love to have grown up somewhere like this.' Cherry was still marvelling at the house and grounds. 'It's like something out of a soap opera about a Scottish distilling family. Kintyre's answer to one of those glossy American shows.'

Sean chuckled. 'Sign me up to play the evil heartbreaker.'

Evil wasn't in Sean's playbook, but heartbreaker could

easily be. He scrubbed up exceptionally well in jeans and a light blue button-down shirt, stubble trimmed neatly for a respectable, casual look.

Cherry's express order of 'impress your mother-in-law' clothes had arrived that morning. She sported a deep-red sundress offset with a cream cardigan, soft nude nail polish, red wedge sandals and the same nude polish on her toes. It was strange being dressed up in Kinshore, but surely it was better to overdo than under-do things on an occasion such as this.

'You look absolutely beautiful.' Sean allayed her fears, not for the first time that evening. 'Come on.' He reached for her hand – all part of the marriage sham, of course, but reassuringly strong and steady around her own. With his other hand, he pushed open the solid front door of the Butler family home.

Inside the house, the temperature was several degrees cooler than out, but warmth enveloped them. This was a home. Dependable and safe. Was it the smell of statement wooden furniture? The cushions upholstered in durable luxurious fabrics? Or could it be the shift in her husband's demeanour, the confidence in his gait, as he walked through the hall of a place he undoubtedly felt most comfortable?

A place he was raised with love to be the incredible man he was today.

Cherry cast a sideways glance at Sean. To think she'd married him. And into this amazing family with its history and achievements. She could be part of this forever if she knew how to stop feeling every day like she didn't belong here, believing that she was too different. A factory second, standing on the outskirts as the other wives and girlfriends lived up to ideals.

As if reading her thoughts, Sean smiled. 'Don't worry, it's just my mum, and she's going to love you.'

'It's so calm in here.' *Like the calm before the storm?*

'Aye, weirdly so.' Sean upped the pace a little. 'Normally, there's a radio on or something.' He dipped his head into a room that Cherry could see was the kitchen, called out to his mum, but no response came. 'Place looks like a bomb's hit it, but no one is here.'

'Could she be in the garden? It's a lovely evening.'

'Maybe... Come on.' Sean led Cherry further down the corridor and into a large drawing room with Georgian French doors. Closed blinds masked the view, and he reached for the cord. 'Why has she got the blinds down?'

'To stop the furniture from getting faded?'

'Hmm.' He yanked up the blind, simultaneously pulling at one door.

As it swung open, it brought into view the most vibrant and riotously coloured garden Cherry had ever seen. Trellises of exotic white jasmine, beds of yellow and purple pansies, as well as trails of pink honeysuckle, to name but a few, bordered a perfectly manicured lawn.

It also spilled with nearly every single member of Sean's immediate family and their respective partners, each one of them beaming radiantly and holding aloft a filled champagne flute, the chime of their 'congratulations' bouncing off the garden walls.

And Amanda Butler was in the middle, looking the happiest of them all.

Oh my God!

'Oh fuck!' Sean's utterance would only be audible to Cherry. 'Sorry, Cher. She said it was just the three of us.'

A quick glance at his stunned face, and Cherry knew Sean was telling the truth. He wouldn't put her or himself in this position on purpose, meeting all the family who wouldn't be her family in a few months. He appeared more devastated than she felt. And she was monumentally terrified.

'It's okay.' She massaged his knuckles with her fingers, wishing she had someone to massage her own. 'I'm a big girl. Come on, take me to meet the clan.'

'You sure?' He glanced down at their hands together as if the answer lay there.

'Yes, of course. Let's go.' Somehow, placating Sean diverted her attention from her own worries. Who knew this would have bothered him?

'Thank you. They're all harmless, really.'

Cherry knew that Sean's family would be charming. Jamie and Alicia were lovely when acting as wedding witnesses, as were the others whom she'd met briefly in the blur of her first encounter with Sean.

But the first and most important person to meet was his mum. Elegant, graceful and as friendly as her garden was colourful.

Guilt wracked Cherry as Amanda Butler embraced her then chatted away with genuine delight and curiosity. She had recently lost her own beloved husband but had the mettle to hold a surprise party like this. To put effort and energy into meeting her new, soon to be ex, daughter in law.

It felt cruel. Wrong. Ungrateful.

'Welcome to the family, Cherry. I believe it's been quite a baptism by fire. I hope being married to my son is a good experience so far.'

'Of course it's a good experience, Mum.' Arm cinched around her waist, Sean pulled Cherry in tight. 'Right, Cher?'

'Nothing quite like it, Seany.' Nothing quite like the

heat of this man's body conducting to her own. Nothing quite like being parachuted into the heart of his family, where warmth and love spilled as freely as the evening's champagne. Nothing quite like the alluringly addictive rollercoaster that was their marriage. 'Wouldn't swap it for the world.'

Sean's hold on her waist shifted, and she caught mild bemusement on his face.

'I admire your optimism, but has he cooked you a steak or run you a bath yet?' Sean's sister, Cara, drifted into the conversation. 'You'll get underdone on both counts.'

'When did I ever run you a bath?' Sean asked. 'And what's an underdone bath? Don't listen to her, Cherry. This is coming from the woman who once tried to boil a steak.'

Cara laughed. 'Okay, hands up. I did that.'

'Anyway,' Jamie cut in. 'We don't want to put you off Sean when you've only just joined us. Welcome to the Butler family, Cherry. It's fantastic to have you as a sister-in-law.' He raised his glass and proposed a toast to the married couple.

Everyone lifted their drinks and echoed his words, and Cherry flushed crimson at the focus being on her. Sean's family were lovely, and they were so curious, asking all sorts of questions as the evening went on – about her life, her work, her background.

'And what about your family?' Amanda asked. 'Sean says your mum lives in Fife. What does she do to keep herself busy?'

Oh, the 'What does your mum do?' question. Not that Cherry minded, but it was never as straightforward as 'She's a teacher' or 'She likes to bake scones and knit sock puppets for the grandkids'.

'She was a nurse, but now she's a self-employed psychic, etcetera.'

A hush descended across the garden, enough to amplify the tweeting of the birds in the trees, as if she'd admitted her mother was an assassin or a gangland leader.

'That's fascinating.' Amanda's voice rung with genuine curiosity. 'And what, may I ask, is the etcetera?'

'Things like aura reading, astrology charts, colour matching stuff. You know, where you find out which colours suit you best and what season you are. She loves it, and it keeps her out of trouble.' Cherry laughed nervously.

Amanda laughed too, but with conviction. 'I'd love to meet her one day. Have her over to stay, even. I know a lot of people who would pay for some of her advice. And some who might need it.'

'Aye, I'm sure she'd love that.' Cherry focused on the sweet scent from the plants, trying to separate the notes of honeysuckle from the sweet pea and the jasmine. 'Amanda, this garden is wonderful. The sweet pea is gorgeous, and the broom is like plantable sunshine.'

Mirroring the gold of the broom, a brightness lit Amanda's face. 'You sound like you might know a little about plants, Cherry.'

'I do. I love gardening. My dad taught me when I was younger, and it's stuck with me, but I'm on the road so much, and I miss it. Virtual garden apps don't cut it.'

Amanda glanced at Sean, who was now chatting to Jamie and Nate. 'I know of a garden that might need a bit of an overhaul. He's done so much to that house, but he wanted to spend as much time with Jimmy in his last months. And now he's working and training all hours. He bends time as much as he can, but the garden's one thing too many.'

'Ah, well.' Cherry smiled warmly at her mother-in-law, wanting to make her – and her son – happy. 'I could take some of that load off. Leave it with me.'

A short time later, with drinks and conversation still flowing, Sean's sister, Cara, was swinging on the two-person garden swing.

'Hey, you honeymooners should sit on this love swing,' she called to Sean.

'It's okay, Car. I think you're having too much fun to interrupt.'

'Nope.' Cara jumped off the swing, almost falling onto the grass as she did so. 'Please be my guest. It's a family tradition.'

Sean laughed. 'Mum bought that swing last summer.'

'Aye, so it was ready for the first lot of newlyweds. You're technically the second, but I'm sure Cal and Bea are having fun on a swing of their own on Mustique. Anyway, please...' Cara held her hand out as if presenting the swing to Sean and Cherry as a wedding gift. 'Be my guest.'

'I'm game. Come on, Sean.' Cherry hauled him up. 'We can't break family tradition.'

'Exactly,' chimed Cara. 'Thank you for not being stubborn like my brother. Sean, you sit first, and Cherry, you sit on his knee.'

'Jesus, Car, you're not planning on working as an intimacy coordinator, are you?' Sean asked. 'Your manner might need some refining.'

'No, but what a great idea. I'll let you get comfy, and then we'll get started on the photos.'

Sean stopped short of gracing his sister with a response, but he got on the swing.

'You don't have to sit on my knee.' He steadied Cherry with confident hands on her hips as she climbed on, too, the swing lurching in response to the shifting body weight.

But Cherry lowered herself onto his lap, onto her husband's thick, solid thighs – possibly a little too pleasant a place to sit when in the presence of his family. She had not thought this through at all.

Still, she was in it now. She curled her hand around his neck and spoke lowly enough so that only Sean could hear.

'Madly in love, Seany. A madly in love wife would sit on her husband's knee.'

'If you say so, sweetheart.' He looked up at her with a roguish glint that made her fantasise about being both a good wife and a naughty wife.

God, he smelled so delicious up close. His scent knocked her sideways as much as it had at the wedding in New York. The warm skin, redolent of Scottish summer evenings – of spicy whisky kisses, stealing into wooded glades and slinking behind oak trees for delicious, illicit moments.

'Careful what you're doing with those fingers, Paradise.'

Unaware she was trailing her fingers up and down the back of Sean's neck, Cherry stalled.

'Sorry.'

'No need to apologise.' His voice rumbled low enough to be audible only to her. 'You know I like it.'

'I thought we weren't flirting anymore.'

Sean placed his hand on her knee, moved it up her leg a fraction. 'I'm a man, you're hotter than the sun and you're practically sitting on my cock.' He stared robotically at his family as he said these words, checking that none of them were listening. They all seemed occupied with their own chatter, and Cara had gone to get a charging cable for her phone.

'Okay, darling. I'm sorry.' Cherry's words bubbled with sweetness. 'I'll keep my hands safe in my lap from now on. And when I say lap, I mean down by my knees, not on my pussy.' She affected a sweet, feminine laugh.

'Cherry, fucking hell.' Sean's mouth barely moved as he growled these words. 'This is a family fucking gathering. Mind your language.'

'Sean, you started it. And stop saying "fucking" so much. It's a family fucking gathering.'

The full-beam smile that spread across Sean's face at this interchange was like a shot to Cherry's heart. God, he was gorgeous, and hard-wired to her mind. Unable to resist, her mouth fell to his.

Just for a moment.

And there it was again, that feeling of being right where she was meant to be. How could a man's lips feel so much like home? The soft warmth of his breath on her skin making her so conscious of the beating heart of this man. And his craftsman's hands skimming her waist – hands that would protect but that also wanted to explore, to claim her.

All of this spoken silently in the seconds of a small kiss.

A family gathering kiss. Giving them what they wanted. Clean and presentable.

Enough for a million sparks, though. Enough for a small groan, audible only to the person closest, to escape from Sean's throat.

The tapping of the family's phone cameras began.

'Come on... Look this way... Another wee peck.'

'Keep it family friendly,' Sean mumbled as they moved in for another kiss. 'For my sake, not theirs.'

· · ·

'I take it Tennessee's off the table now?' Nate asked Sean as they tucked into a mouthwatering buffet of rainbow salads, succulent chicken and verdant greens.

Tennessee? Sean was going to Tennessee? Cherry tried not to appear confused, but what the hell were they talking about? Sean had mentioned nothing about Tennessee. Was this something she, as a wife, should know about, at least for the sake of keeping up appearances?

'Aye, um, I'm not sure to be honest. I might still go.' Sean shuffled in his seat, and Cherry suspected it was something that he would have mentioned had their marriage been going to last. 'The job swap is still on the table. Cherry and I are discussing it. Her work is portable, so it makes things easier.'

'Yes,' Cherry dissembled as much as possible. 'Although, poker is illegal in Tennessee and the bordering states, so we would have some hoops to jump through there. I could travel to the six states where it is legal, but I'd miss Sean too much.'

A flash of surprise crossed Sean's face at this information, which threw a spanner into his story.

'But I don't want to hold him back from doing something he had his sights on before he met me. I know how much he likes to keep life varied.'

'Never one to stay still for too long,' Nate agreed. 'Always on the hunt for the next adventure.'

'I married the next adventure.' Sean didn't miss a beat. His hand slid onto her knee, like he was saying thanks for her smooth response to the topic of Tennessee.

And guilt swooped down like a vulture at the buffet dinner because what Sean said was kind of true. Except the marriage, which should have been the adventure of lifetime, had turned into a crocodile-infested cruise in a leaky boat.

He deserved so much more. A union that included the joyous anticipation of growing a family. Not a marriage where you sat in a post-adrenaline slump at the end. And this was why she couldn't let him settle for her as enough. Because, one day, she wouldn't be. One day, lovely Amanda would be surrounded by grandchildren, and she couldn't bear to be responsible for Sean not being part of that because he'd chosen a liquidation risk as his wife.

Cherry drained her champagne glass. 'Speaking of adventure, I hope you're all going to attend the charity pro-am poker tournament I'm organising.'

'Too right we are.' Cara immediately reached to top up the empty vessel. 'I'm brushing up on my poker skills already.'

'I love your enthusiasm.' Cherry turned to Sean's older brother. 'Jamie, I was wondering...might the distillery consider donating a prize, as a draw card for high-rolling guests?'

'Absolutely.' Jamie put down his drink. 'What were you thinking? A bottle or two?'

'I was thinking more of a cask. We can raffle it since it's probably too expensive to legally offer as a prize.'

Sean appeared to either choke or laugh into his beer, possibly at how brass-necked she was being. 'Excellent idea, Cher,' he said. 'What do you say, J? It's for charity, after all?'

'Aye, it shouldn't be a problem if it's going to bring in the money.'

'You know, I can offer you something,' Alicia said. 'My brother, Connor. He's a well-known actor, films a lot in Scotland and loves poker. His attendance could raise the profile of the event.'

'Connor...um?'

'Connor Donoghue.'

Cherry nearly spat out her drink. Connor Donoghue was a massive star, an A-lister of Hollywood A-listers from the legendary Donoghue acting dynasty. His attendance would be a huge boon for the event.

'Wow! Thank you so much, Alicia. That would be incredible.'

'Oh, and he's good mates with Campbell Duff,' Alicia added. 'I'll see if Con can get him on board, too.'

Sean cracked open another beer. 'Ah, Campbell Duff – the boy from Newton Mearns who pretends he's fae Drumchapel but talks like he moved to LA when he was nine.' Clearly, he was not a fan. Not that Cherry had time to dwell on this.

'C-Campbell Duff? Oh, fab.' She could have kicked herself for stuttering, but the last thing she was expecting was for that name to crop up. Fuck. She would have to contact him now. It was either that, or reject Alicia's offer and explain that he was her ex and his presence roused ghosts she didn't want awoken, which would seem selfish when charity money was on the table.

'Having Campbell there would also be amazing,' she said. 'Thanks again.'

Alicia beamed. 'Connor loved Jimmy, so I know he'll be keen to raise money to stop other families from going through what this one has.'

Cherry agreed with a nod. 'Of course.' Sean's family had been through so much. She hoped that, even though their marriage was a mess, she could bring some value before she left. It was the least she could do for this beautiful bunch of people who had welcomed her so freely.

Chapter 20

Sean

Back at Sean's house, he pulled a beer from the fridge and held the bottle out to Cherry.

She took it, grateful for the cool touch and the promise of more edges softening. 'Thanks.'

'Have a drink with me, yeah?'

'Okay.'

Sean sat on the couch, and she plonked down next to him.

'So,' she said, 'Tennessee, huh?'

'Aye.'

'What's all that about, Butler?'

'What that's all about is, I needed to get out of Kinshore. Wanted a change.'

'I thought you loved it here.'

'I do love it here. It's very much home. But I'm also kind of bored cooped up – no pun intended. I needed a new challenge, and the opportunity to do a year's exchange at a cooperage in Tennessee came up. So I went for it.'

'And it's still on the table?'

'Aye. As long as I pass the visa interview, I go next year, and an American lad comes here.'

'Well, you should definitely go.'

He searched for something in her eyes – that her encouragement was fake, perhaps?

'Nothing holding you here, is there?' she added.

God, Cherry, what is wrong with you?

'Nope, I suppose not.' Sean slugged back a large mouthful of beer. 'Certainly not a woman.'

You deserved that.

Between them, his words hung like a wrecking ball.

'That was one reason I decided to leave,' he said. 'I was pretty fucking lonely here. I can keep myself going like the Duracell bunny, but I want someone to come home to at night, to sleep next to. To love. You know?'

Oh God. His honesty cracked her open, pulled her heart out from her chest and screamed at it: *What the hell are you doing?*

'I get it.' She did. That was what she needed, too. And where would she get it from, if not Sean? If she walked away from the love of her life to protect him, the odds were high that she'd end up alone. No one else compared to him, and the reasons for leaving him would still stand with any other man.

'Because I've a lot of fucking love to give to the right woman,' he added. 'To give to my wife, actually.'

Cherry's lips quivered. She knew he had that love. Of course she did. Sean's ability to love oozed out of him; it was one of the things that had drawn her to him. If only she could find some way of them moving forward together, but she couldn't see what that was.

'I know you do.' She swigged her own beer, scratched at

the wet label, tearing a strip through it with the rounded edge of her nail.

'And if you can't come with me then Tennessee is a tentative.' Sean layered on more acute, endearing honesty. 'In case that isn't obvious. Because you make living here entirely different. We might not hang out all the time, but I really, really like having you around, and even if I went, I'm sure we could find a way to make it work. Anything is possible.'

Cherry tried to blink back a stinging, salty tear. Fruitless, because where there was one, there were hundreds more. 'Oh, Sean...'

'Hey...' He reached out and wiped the salty drop with his thumb – the best and worst thing he could do.

The temptation to seize that hand as it withdrew, pull it back to her cheek, let him dissolve his mouth into hers and give her one of those ruin-you-for-anyone-else kisses was tugging at her like an anchor in a sea storm. She turned away, brushed her hands down the crimson broderie of her dress.

Sean seemed to sense her discomfort. He relaxed back into the couch as if he knew it would put her at ease. Drank his beer quietly before speaking again. 'You know, I think you have a hidden talent you're not telling me about.'

This got Cherry's attention. She swung round to him. 'What talent?'

'This "colour my thingy" thing that your mum does, and my mum is all intrigued by. You must be able to do it too, because everything I see you in, you look incredible. The fit, the style, the colour.'

'Oh, thank you. I might have picked up a few tricks from my mum. I used to sit in on her parties.'

'Amazing. You could host an evening of it here. Cheer my mum up.'

'Och, I'm not sure I'd be much good.'

'Don't be humble. I bet you would.'

'I dunno. I might send everyone home with the wrong colour palette and all the villagers would hate me.'

'You might inadvertently improve some of the dress sense. And I'm sure they'd all have fun. Tell you what, give me a mini consultation right now and I'll be the judge of your skills.'

Some of Cherry's vibrancy returned at this idea. 'Seriously? *You* are going to judge *me* on this?'

'Deadly serious.'

How did he do it? He had this way of bringing her round and making her heart happy again. 'You're on, Butler. Go grab some of your favourite t-shirts, and I'll sort you out.'

'Far be it from me to argue with a woman who wants to sort me out.' Sean jumped up from the couch and took the stairs two at a time, returning less than sixty seconds later carrying a bundle of t-shirts in various muted shades.

'These are your favourites?' Cherry arched a brow at the garments he'd handed her. Everything was blue, white or khaki.

'Something wrong with them?'

'Nope, they're just very same-y.'

'Even more of a reason to have a consultation.'

'True. Okay, we need to decide which of each colour is right for you. Let's start with blue.' She draped the t-shirts over the arm of the couch. 'You've got three blue t-shirts here, all in slightly different shades. I'm going to need you to try them on for me, and we'll see.'

'We'll see what?'

'Which one suits you best...obviously.'

'Oh, obviously. Forgive me for thinking you wanted me out of my clothes so you could ogle me. Right, come on then. Tell me what to do.'

'Take this off.' Cherry gestured to his current button-down shirt. 'You can go to the other room if you need to protect your modesty.'

Showing no sign of moving to the other room, Sean began to unbutton his shirt. 'Do people normally take their clothes off in these things?'

'No.'

'Just me then.' His fingers moved rapidly through the buttons. 'Why do I feel I'm being taken advantage of here?'

'Because that's what you want.'

'Wow!' He beamed. 'Victim blaming.'

'Sean?'

'Aye?'

'Shut it and take your shirt off.'

Without another word, the shirt was off.

'And...um, now choose a t-shirt to put on.' Cherry did her best to haul her eyes away from the beautiful specimen taunting her. From the body she dreamed every night of touching.

'You alright, Paradise? Your voice went all wobbly there.'

Lucky you don't have access to my heart rate. 'I'm fine. I'll look away now and give you some privacy.'

'Why? You just saw everything. Again.'

'Okay, fine.' She fanned her face. 'Is it hot in here or...?'

'No, it's called chemistry. Anyway...' Sean swung the shirt he'd removed round his hand. 'How do I find out which shade of blue suits me best?'

He was such a flirt whilst pretending not to be. She took the shirt from him and cast it onto the couch.

'You put on your first blue t-shirt.' Cherry selected one off the chair and handed in to him, electricity zipping through her as their hands brushed. 'This one is a basic navy.'

In a few stolen moments while he pulled the t-shirt over his face, she allowed her feral side to run rampant at the sight of his many tattoos, his underarm hair, of the way the upward stretch of his arms pulled his abs taut, the sculpted V that led down to his waistband where...

Eyes. Eyes. Eyes on his face, Cherry.

'Okay! Let's see.' She stepped towards him, even though a step back would afford her a better view.

Sean said nothing. Simply met her gaze. Stood still for once, letting her do her job. But his gaze never left hers, watching her watching him.

Energy thundered between them.

Up close, she drank him in. His skin was flawless. There were a few freckles around his nose and expected lines from a life spent outdoors and laughing a lot, but nothing could diminish the brightness of those eyes. And the generosity of the mouth. A mouth that kissed like it meant it.

Cherry flicked her tongue onto her cupid's bow.

Sean dipped to this movement, then back up as if to challenge her. 'What do you think?'

She slunk her tongue behind her top teeth. Nodded slowly. 'It suits you. Brightens your skin and makes your eyes more green. But I need to see the others.'

The air between them was heavier now, weighing down their desire to speak. Words cost energy. In silence, Sean pulled the t-shirt off. Cherry looked down to the floor, but the size of his feet reminded her of the size of other parts of him.

As Sean leaned down for the next t-shirt, her eyes

darted to his neck, the hair shaved close, skin tanned. She remembered how strong and warm it had felt to the touch when she'd kissed him, when they'd danced in the ballroom at the wedding, when she'd gripped onto him in the elevator and in the cooperage. It could be hers again if she said the word. He could be hers.

To have and to hold.

The next shirt was a deep petrol blue.

She went to him and brushed the fabric of the garment over his hips as if to flatten it. Sean stiffened.

'Relax, Seany.'

The sound he made could only be described as a dismissive grunt. A dismissal at being told to relax in circumstances that promoted anything but relaxation.

Back to his face. To the strong jaw, the complexion. Looking at him now, it was like going back to New York, staring into each other's eyes for three minutes. Waiting to fall in love.

Some people waited a lifetime.

Not her and Sean.

Cherry lifted her left arm around the back of her head, twisting her hair up into a makeshift bird's nest. She stood examining him, lips slightly parted in contemplation.

A small smile crept over his face.

'What?' Her question came out as a whisper.

'That's a sexy look. You're sending pheromones my way. Why are you shaking your head?'

'Because the colour isn't quite right. This one is more of a "summer" blue, and I'm not getting summer vibes from you.'

'What vibes are you getting?'

'Not sure yet, but I'm thinking "spring". Shall we try one more?'

A heavy inhale from Sean, like this was getting to be painful. 'If you want. I'm quite certain I'm a spring, though.' He exhaled heavily and adjusted his jeans.

Catching a flicker of amusement on his face, she knew this was nothing to do with the colours.

'Something in your jeans giving you a spring vibe?'

'Aye. I might need an expert to sort it out.' The need in him beckoned to her without a single word spoken.

Cherry dropped her hair, let it cascade down, closed the inches between them with a silent, barefoot step.

'I'm an expert; how can I help?'

Softly, he considered her and the question. 'You can start by taking this off for me. It's the wrong shade of blue, and I can't be seen in petrol when I'm a periwinkle guy.'

'Mm-hmm.' Cherry skirted her hand along the hem of the t-shirt, glancing across the thick cotton that clung to her husband's body in all the right places. The blue might be wrong, but the fit was incredible the way it hugged his barrel-making arms, hung over those surfer's abs. Cherry slid her hand under the hem, round to the small of Sean's back, the curve and dip of the muscle there strong and fevered. She ventured her touch further up the geography of the body she hadn't yet explored properly, like a foreign land in an atlas.

A land of hot plains and valleys of muscle.

Palm splayed on his back, she pulled him in, needing the closeness, their combined temperature far beyond toler-able already.

The whole time, he watched her.

Dropping her hand to the hem again, she tugged his t-shirt up as far as she could reach until he brought it over his head, letting it drop to the ground.

'It really didn't suit you.' She trailed her finger around

the Celtic band tattoo on his wide, muscular arm. 'This, though, is perfect; tell me about this.'

'Mmm.' Sean's voice was low and deep like a loch. 'It represents my family. You know, the love that wraps all the way around you.'

'That's lovely.' Cherry was mesmerised by the beautiful artwork on his arms. 'Which did you get done first?'

'Hmm, there's an ugly thistle right there.' He cocked his head towards his bicep. 'We don't make the best decisions when we're seventeen.'

'Those decisions are you. I love them all.'

'Thanks. There's always room for you on here, when you're ready.'

She shot her gaze to his. It was bold; it was tender; it was trademark Sean. It shouldn't be a surprise, given that he'd married her after two days, but that he would get a tattoo for her, if only she said the word, rendered Cherry speechless.

The awkwardness flared between them for a moment or two before dissolving.

'What about you?' He ran his hands down her arms. 'Tell me about your tat. The one on your back that I saw on poker night.'

Now this was taking things down a different route. Did she want to do this? 'You might think it's naff.' Her chin dipped, coyly. 'But it's special to me. I'll tell you if you promise not to laugh.'

'I'm not going to laugh, Cher. I can assure you of that. Come on.' Sean craned his neck to meet her eye, and she lifted her head to him.

'It's a string of forget-me-nots. In memory of my dad. We used to see them when we walked on Corstorphine Hill together. And I wanted to let him know I'd never forget him.'

He smiled.

'See? Told you it was naff.'

'It's not naff at all. Would you show me it again?'

Cherry's stomach roiled a little at the intimacy of this request. Talking to anyone about her dad was intimate; showing someone the tattoo she had done in his memory was another thing. Sure, it was on display when she wore low-cut jeans, but this, with Sean, it was different.

'Um, sure. I'll need to lift my dress up.' She turned away from him, lifting the hem, the white lace of her underwear very much visible.

Apart from the low, steady breath of her husband as he contemplated her lower back, the room was deathly still. She should feel exposed, but somehow there was no rawness, no vulnerability. Only tenderness.

'It's beautiful, Cher. A really lovely tribute.' Sean's voice thrummed behind her, through her, mellowing her.

She could tell him the rest now. This was as good a time as any.

'There are four extra flowers,' she said, hardly believing herself. 'Can you see them?'

She couldn't see his face to give a hint of what he was seeing or thinking, but he must have found the flowers.

'The white ones?' he said.

'Yes, they're...' The words hitched in her throat. 'They represent...my...my babies.' Pressure surged behind her breastplate. Saying that out loud would never be easy, which was why she rarely did.

Babies. Fine, downy hair, unaffected giggles, chubby arms – those things she longed for, slipping from her grasp every time.

Sean was silent. Cherry drew in a slow breath and wondered if this was a mistake. It was hard enough to deal with her own emotions without having to navigate other people's difficulties.

But then something happened. It was soft, it was simple, but it meant the entire world.

'Can I touch them?'

Oh, Jesus! No one had ever asked that before. No one. Not even Dale. But Sean wasn't Dale; that was very clear. Cherry managed a nod. Then she felt the pad of his thumb on the small of her back, assured but tender, tracing across each of the flowers, one by one, warm, stabilising comfort over her unimaginable, life-altering loss.

Her urge was to spin round and fall into his wide chest. Have him hold and tell her he would take care of her, shield her from any more pain. But she knew those words would only ever be words, and this wasn't Sean's hurt to shoulder or heal. That felt acutely true.

'I'm so sorry you went through that, Cherry. I can't even imagine the pain.' His voice vibrated at the perfect timbre to soothe.

'Thank you.'

Silence filled the air as he gave her time, as she let the feelings bubble up to the surface, allowed them to form words that might explain what it was like. Explain what most people never heard about because it was too sad, too uncomfortable.

'I never thought I'd get through it,' she admitted, quietly rubbing the fabric of her sundress again. 'Every time, it felt like the world was kicking me black and blue and laughing at me, saying, *"What did you think, that it would actually work out? Don't be so fucking stupid, Cherry."'*

'Oh, Cher.'

'I can't explain how attached you get to this idea of being a mum. So quickly. And every time, I believed. I had to. But I almost wished I hadn't been allowed to believe, so the fall didn't hurt so much. But then I'd have blamed my own lack of belief for the outcome. Do you see?'

'Aye, I see.' Sean's voice was calm and reassuring over her shoulder. 'Sorry for upsetting you.'

'It's okay. I'm okay now... Sorry.' She worked her jaw. 'But that's how it was; it's the worst thing – things – I've ever gone through. That and my dad dying.'

Sean glanced his fingers over her skin again. 'You've been through devastation, Cher. White forget-me-nots are perfect.'

She swallowed hard, wanting to stay composed. Tears were not always the answer. 'Thank you. I put them with my dad so they could all be together.' The cracking in her voice told her it was time to stop talking. Sean's strong hands dusting and smoothing down on her shoulders steadied her. So bittersweet.

'Thank you for letting me share with you,' she whispered.

'Thank you for telling me.' Softly, he kissed the curve of her neck. Just once. Then he reached for the sides of her dress, which were bunched inside her fists, and gently eased them from her, lowered the skirt so it dropped and covered her exposed skin. When she came back round to him, his expression was soft and serious.

'Do you want to talk any more?' he said. 'Or go to bed?'

She stalled. He must mean going to separate beds, but they could walk upstairs as husband and wife. There was so much unspoken yet spoken in the silence between them. The way he looked at her, like she blew his mind but completely broke him. It was almost impossible to bear. She could make it better. They could heal each other.

But she didn't want grief sex. Or pity sex. And if they did it tonight, that's what it would be. Sean feeling like he had to treat her with kid gloves, as if she would break were he anything but gentle. Everything was overshadowed by the past, her shame over her body failing her, her fears for the future, and the chance of waking up an emotional shambles, not knowing which way was north anymore.

Keeping her gaze fixed on Sean's, she said, 'We should both get some sleep.'

'Aye, okay.' He took their beer bottles to the bin. 'Come on, I'm knackered too.'

Together, they ascended the stairs. Stopping at the top, they faced one another, the landing dim but the atmosphere burning.

'Night, Cher.' Through the smoky light, Sean's voice was deep and protective, and she wondered if he could give her an orgasm just by talking.

Probably, yes, but get a grip, Cherry.

'Sleep tight, Sean.'

'Aye, you too.' His breath was warm, his rough stubble comforting, as he leaned in and kissed her softly on the cheek.

And he might sleep well, but she bloody wouldn't. How on earth could she do anything but lie in bed, her to-die-for husband in the next room, and think of him?

Chapter 21

Cherry

Ten days later, the squawking of Kinshore seagulls drew Cherry into Monday wakefulness. Last night, the bedroom was too warm, so she'd left the window open, and now a refreshing breeze feathered her skin, her legs tangled in the bedsheets as if her dormant self hadn't known if she was too hot or too cold and opted for half and half.

The hot half being the part that dreamed of her husband.

Every night, there he was, moving around her subconscious in some form or another, and it took mere moments before he appeared in her waking thoughts, too, making barely noticeable the transition between sleep and consciousness.

Cherry slipped out of bed, tugging down the long white t-shirt that hung barely below her backside. Not that it mattered since Sean was on his way to London. She missed him already. It had been over a week since their 'almost' moment after dinner at his mum's, and she'd done nothing but think of him.

She padded down the hall to the bathroom, splashed her face with cold water and worked her toothbrush around, before making the detour that was becoming something of a very bad habit.

Although Sean's bedroom remained a constant – the solid oak floorboards, the trusty surfboards leaning on the wall, the sweet, woody scent of his pillow – one thing kept changing.

Cherry's feelings.

With every day that passed, she hugged his pillow tighter, inhaled deeper, ached harder.

She was pining so hard for the man she lived with. The man she was married to.

As she did every day he wasn't here, Cherry sat on the edge of the bed, smoothing her hands down the duvet, grasping it in her fist, imagining doing this with Sean buried between her legs. Remembering the time he was.

So good. It was so good. He was as dextrous with his tongue as he was with those cask-crafting hands.

Closing her eyes, Cherry tipped her chin to the ceiling, inhaling hard, her mouth tightening briefly before she let out the breath.

Firmer, she pulled the pillow against her breasts, imagining him yanking her t-shirt off, pushing her back onto the bed, his impressive cock springing free from his underwear.

It was an arresting sight, the image of it soldered into her mind from the cooperage.

'Fuck, Sean,' she intoned.

'Aye. What can I help you with, Paradise?'

Cherry's eyes flew open and shot to the location of the voice, where – what did you know? – there was her husband, leaning on the doorframe all scrubbed up in jeans and charcoal t-shirt. Oh, holy shit! He was meant to be on his way to London.

Sean ran his hand through his clean, shower-damp hair. Amusement teased her while he waited for an answer. But what could she say? Cherry had styled out a lot of embarrassing situations, and this was going to be difficult to troubleshoot.

Nothing would wash.

Nothing.

So, honestly, why bother?

'Morning, Butler.' She threw him a smile, still holding onto the pillow as if all she'd been doing was changing the pillowcase. 'How goes it?'

'Aye.' Sean nodded, swimming into her flow and moving into the room. 'It goes pretty great, thanks. Forgot my phone, but don't let me disturb whatever it is you're doing.' Retrieving the handset from the top of the chest of drawers, where she should have seen it, Sean slid it into his pocket and stood facing her. 'You missing your teddy bear?'

Cherry stifled amusement. 'By teddy bear, do you mean an actual teddy bear or is the teddy bear in this instance you?'

He laughed that joyous laugh that she loved. 'I'm not sure. I'd say it's you who needs to clarify that to me, seeing as you're the one in *my* bedroom cuddling my pillow.'

'I'm not "cuddling" your pillow.'

'No? My bad. What are you doing? Taking its pulse? Checking the thread count?'

'Don't be daft. I mean, "cuddling" is a bit much. I'd say I'm hugging it.' Cherry held steadfast to the pillow as if shame was never an option.

'Aah, okay, hugging. Fine. Listen, Jamie's giving me a lift so I've got to go, but I have to ask before I head off... Are you okay?' Sean tapped at his temple, sparkle in his eyes. He was humouring her.

'Yes, of course. I'm absolutely fine.' Cherry blew her fringe up and hopefully her cares away with it. 'I'm going to get going in a minute.' Extracting the pillow, she placed it back where it came from, raising her arms above her head before remembering her lack of underwear and stretching the t-shirt down her thighs. 'So stiff today.' She deflected a bit more with some twists.

Sean watched with the same subtle amusement as before, biting his bottom lip. Damn, he was a sight and a half for morning eyes.

'Anyway, I'd best get on and get a shower,' she announced as if he were the one delaying her.

He reached down. 'Need a hand up, seeing as you're a bit stiff?'

'Thank you.' She slipped her palms into his – large and calloused with strong, thick fingers that had explored the most intimate parts of her body – gaze darting to the corded muscle of forearms flexing under his tattoos as he hauled her towards him. She could smell him from here – so clean and fresh.

So fuckable.

As she rose, something flickered in Sean's eyes before he raised that summer-rock-pool-gaze to meet hers. It dawned on Cherry immediately. No bra + white t-shirt + morning breeze + sexy-as-fuck-husband = tight little nipples poking through the fabric for sexy-as-fuck-husband to see. She'd been so worried about her pussy being on show she'd forgotten about the other stuff.

'Oops.' She didn't move a muscle, in an ever-ludicrous attempt to style this as *nothing out of the ordinary.*

Sean smiled. 'I've had worse oopses.'

'Glad to get things off to a perky start for you.'

She could have sworn that, as he was about to leave the room, Sean stopped for a moment, deliberating over coming right back to her and slamming that gorgeous mouth into hers.

And if she was honest with herself, she was half hoping that he would.

But all he said was: 'Aye, anyway, I'd better get going. Have a good few days without me. And behave yourself.'

Cherry sipped her coffee and regarded the jungle that was Sean's garden. The grass was so long it was doubling back under its own weight; wild foxgloves danced unchallenged with stinging nettles and gangs of rebellious weeds. It was wild and rich and teeming with life.

And a complete state.

But it was a project that Cherry relished. Visions of how she could change it were already bubbling in her brain. About what could go where. And if she worked really hard, she could have it done by the time he got back from London.

His face would be priceless.

Showering away the morning's embarrassment and dressing in khaki shorts and a black vest with her usual high tops, Cherry drove five miles to the garden shop on the outskirts of Campbeltown. She bounced through the door, optimistically clutching a list of plants she hoped she could find at least half of.

Inside the shop, her mind was blown.

Lush greenery spilled from every shelf, bracket and inch of space. The fragrant aroma of lilies, verbena and orchids filled the air. Cherry closed her eyes, cast back to her small childhood garden with her dad, playing her favourite game of identifying the flowers from their smell, picking out the subtlest tones from so many overlapping and intermingling layers.

'Morning!'

She opened her eyes.

'Oh, hi.' It was no wonder she hadn't noticed the assistant sooner. In her floral blouse and green overalls, blonde hair spilling out from the confines of a brightly coloured scarf, earrings resembling hanging baskets, she was like a plant in motion. Peering at her badge, Cherry could see that her name was – fittingly – Summer.

For a hot, fleeting moment, Cherry wanted Summer's life. The seemingly easy existence of pruning and misting plants in a garden shop on a peninsula on the west coast of Scotland. Of not having to worry about winning or losing at work, about tells, bad hands, poor decisions.

Of course, appearances meant nothing; she was well aware of that.

'Is there anything you'd like help with today?' Summer asked.

'Yes, I'm overhauling my husband's garden, and I need all the things on this list.' Cherry held out the piece of paper to Summer, who scanned it quickly.

'We can do most of these. Come with me.' She began pushing a trolley through the centre with fluid efficiency, placing things in or asking Cherry if this thing or that thing worked for her. In went potting compost, garden tools, geraniums, impatiens, lavender, pansies, sweet pea, honeysuckle, jasmine. Plants and flowers that were bright or smelled intoxicating and divine. Cherry threw in additional items as she saw fit – a bird bath, feeders and seed, and wind chimes.

As they moved around the shop, Summer chatted away. 'Do you live in Campbeltown?' she asked with a vibrant inquisitiveness, which Cherry liked. She craved an easy-going female friend to talk to.

'I've just moved to Kinshore, actually. Married a local.'

Summer swung round, her eyes even brighter than before. 'No way! You're not Sean's wife, are you?'

'Yes.' Cherry raised her palms. 'Caught red-handed.'

Summer laughed. 'Sorry, sorry, that came out a bit stalkerish. I didn't mean to alarm you. I'm friends with the Butlers, and since Nate told me about the wedding, I've been dying to meet this amazing woman Sean married. I'm Summer.' She tapped at her badge. 'As you can see. Right, I think we have everything now.' She swung the trolley back towards the checkout.

'How do you know the Butlers?' Cherry asked as they settled into a rhythm at the till – Summer scanning and Cherry packing things into boxes.

'Ah, it's a long story, but I've known them all since I was a teenager. My adoptive mum fostered Nate, Cara and Eilidh as babies. When I moved to Kinshore as a teenager, we got to know each other and into this habit of meeting for tea once a week. All the foster babies together. Sean too, actually.'

'Really? But he's not...'

'No, he's not, but he came all the same. That's Sean for you! Love him.'

'That's fascinating. I'm still learning about him. Do you all still have tea together?'

'I wish. It's rare that it's ever the five of us now that Eilidh's in Edinburgh and Cara's busy filming. Nate visits when he can... Works a lot of lates. Sometimes it's me, him and mum, which is...' She trailed off, holding the scanner in one hand and a geranium plant in the other. It didn't take close scrutiny to see that her mind was distracted.

'Is...?' Cherry prompted.

'Sorry.' Summer's eyes readjusted from somewhere far away. 'It's lovely...really lovely. Anyhoo, Mrs Butler, pop back if there's anything else you need. Or give us a call and someone can deliver.'

Ten minutes after returning home from the garden centre, motivated and restless, Cherry started on the lawn. She hacked back the grass with a scythe, then hauled out the lawnmower from the shed and ploughed it up and down until the grass was a respectable length and the flowerbeds reachable at last.

Unfortunately, reaching them also meant weeding them.

With the sun at its highest point in the sky, she was a sweaty, grass-stained mess, but invigorated. Alive.

Around 4.30 p.m. as she was laying out all the plants and equipment for the next part of the job, she realised she'd forgotten to bring home the bird bath and feeders. She would need to collect them tomorrow.

After clocking off around 7 p.m., Cherry took a cooling bath, watched a little TV whilst eating a sandwich and thinking about how empty the house was without Sean.

As she was about to head to bed, her phone pinged with a message.

Campbell Duff. *Jesus Christ.*

Or so he likes to think.

> CAMPBELL: Cherry, hey. Long time, no see. How are you? I've been invited to your pro-am poker tourney in Kinshore via Connor Donoghue (his sister is shacked up with your husband's brother or something). I hear you live there now. I've been filming up near Dornoch, but have a gap in my schedule if you fancy a wee dram? C x

What? Did she fancy a 'wee dram' with her ex from ten years ago? The short answer was no. The more considered response was: say yes, clear the air before the tourney and ask the question that had been bugging her of late.

> CHERRY: Hey, Campbell. It has been a long time. I'm good, thanks. It'll be great to see you at the tourney. My schedule is a bit busy before then, but a coffee would be fab when you're here.

That stalled the problem for a while. Bought some preparation time. She would tell Sean when he got back.

The following morning, Cherry headed back to the garden centre to pick up the forgotten items.

'How's the garden shaping up?' Summer asked.

'Cherry tucked a bird feeder under her arm. 'I'm happy with progress so far. I just have to work super hard today to make sure it gets done by the time Sean comes home from London tomorrow.'

'Listen, I'll tell you what…' Summer spoke in her bright, sing-song lilt. 'I could come over this afternoon and help you, if you like. There's folk here who can mind the shop. I could even bring homemade ginger wine for when we're done. Or for while we're doing.' She wiggled her eyebrows.

'Seriously? Help would be amazing, and I'm not going to say no to ginger wine. Thank you so much, Summer.'

Summer grinned and clapped. 'Amazing! I love a good garden project. Can't wait!'

As Cherry was toiling in the midday sun, the doorbell signalled the arrival of Summer. She was effortlessly vibrant in her green overalls, carrying the promised bottle of ginger wine. Two grab bags of crisps spilled out of her overflowing tote bag.

'I've brought snacks.' Summer put the crisps down on the counter, followed by dips and biscuits. 'These can go in the fridge.'

'You didn't have to do that, but thank you.' Cherry was blown away by this generosity. Life really was different in small-town Scotland. For every busybody in the local store, there were five people who excelled in loveliness.

And Summer was so easy to talk to. No sooner had they pulled on their gloves and begun tugging out the last of the weeds than they were chatting away like they'd known each other forever.

'I've never met anyone who got married after two days,' Summer said as they raked back the soil in the flowerbeds. 'What's that like?'

Cherry leaned on her rake. 'Honestly, it was one of the easiest decisions I've ever made. *The* easiest. From the moment I saw him, I was gone. We have this mad connection, you know?' This was all true; it was what came after that crazy connection that was difficult.

'If you know, you know, I guess,' said Summer. 'Sean is a kind of a fly-by-the-seat-of-his-pants type of guy, so it doesn't surprise me he got married quickly.'

She must have seen some hesitation on Cherry's face.

'I mean, he makes decisions fast, but he's not rash,' she added, hurriedly. 'It's like his operating system is built of faster RAM or something. He knows what he wants, and he doesn't waste time deliberating over things – or regretting them afterwards. Not that everyone believes that about him.'

'I guess you've known him a long time.'

'Since he was a teenager, but it doesn't feel like that much has changed. He's still handsome, still the life and soul, with a reputation as "boyfriend material". Although he doesn't always get the girl. I think what's changed is his decisions don't land him in hot water like they once did. Take this house – when he bought it, it was a shell and people thought he'd made a huge mistake, but they're eating their words now.'

'The house is incredible,' Cherry agreed. What Sean had done here was impressive. 'He does work super hard and put his whole heart into things.'

'And it's a huge heart,' Summer added. 'Sean is a smart guy, just not in a conventional package. He's unique.'

Cherry wouldn't argue with that. How funny that the love of her life lived here, on this little village in this remote peninsula in Scotland, and she'd met him in New York. If fate was something she believed in, she might say it was lending a hand.

'Are you and Nate an item then?' Cherry asked a little later, pushing the familiarity but acting on a hunch.

Summer began to dig holes in soil rather more busily than before. 'Er...no, we're close but just friends.'

'Okay. Sorry, that was rude of me.'

Surprisingly, Summer didn't change the subject, but flushing from something more than the early afternoon sun, she talked whilst bedding impatiens.

'Nate is incredible. The way he is with animals would melt anyone's heart, but I've known him since I was thirteen years old and he's almost like a brother to me.'

'Mm-hmm.' There was something there, floating so close to the surface; it was like Summer wanted to talk to someone about it. 'Almost?'

She laughed and shrugged coyly. 'Well, he's not my brother. He was adopted; I was in the foster system for a long time. He gets what that does to your psyche; not everyone does.'

'No, I'm sure they don't, and I can see why that would give you a strong bond.' Cherry saw the irony of her trying to read someone else's love life when her own was barely legible. But reading people was fun; she liked Summer, and it was a nice diversion.

As the sun rose higher in the sky, the two women dug and planted and talked, until their skin was burning. Cherry was settling plants in the flowerbeds while Summer, guiding honeysuckle up a bamboo trellis, asked if she wanted some ginger wine. This was another thing Cherry wasn't putting up a fight about.

'The Butlers are an amazing family, aren't they?' Cherry said, leaning back on her elbows on the grass, emboldened by half a glass of the alcoholic drink.

'They are,' Summer agreed. 'I love them so much.'

'Yeah.' Cherry noticed how truly potent the buzz from this wine was. 'I know they've had their problems – big ones. Jimmy dying, for one, but sometimes I feel I'm short-changing Sean.' She glanced at Summer, who was listening with interest, giving her encouragement to continue. 'He's bringing warmth and love and this amazing clan to the table. I've come from a rollercoaster life playing poker that my mum, the tarot reader, likes to remind me is no good for anyone.'

Summer turned on her side to face Cherry, strategically bringing her wine with her and not spilling a drop. Her expression was warm but serious.

'I don't have a vast amount of successful experience to draw from, but don't we bring different things to a relationship? You don't need to give Sean exactly the same thing he gives you. He has a big, strong family, and that's there for you. And you, gorgeous Cherry, are bringing him all this vibrancy and grab-life energy and this beautiful soul of yours. I don't know if he's ever had that.'

Vibrancy and grab-life energy and a beautiful soul? These words were so kind that Cherry wanted to weep and hug Summer. This was exactly what she needed to hear – that she was more than what she was not. It was so simple, thinking of what she did bring to Sean's life, yet she had become fixated on what she might not give him.

'Thank you, Summer. That's so incredibly kind of you to say.'

'It's true. I can easily see why he married you.' Summer sipped her wine, pacing herself better than Cherry was. 'And listen, Sean might come from small-town Scotland, but he's got a worldly head on his shoulders. This amazing mix of stability and insight. He has so much love to give, and he'll be your rock. I hope I'm not overstepping the mark in saying that.'

Cherry wiped at her eyes with semi-muddy fingers,

then pulled up the hem of her vest to wipe away the dirt. It stung, hearing what Sean had tried to tell her about himself. 'You're not overstepping the mark at all,' she said. 'Thank you so much, Summer.'

'Oh, and one very important thing about him that you ought to know...'

This sounded ominous, but the excitement in Summer's voice suggested otherwise.

'He can do the lift from *Dirty Dancing*. Well, his part. If you've got good core muscles then he'll have you up there. In the water... But not many Scottish men can say that.'

Cherry laughed and inwardly thanked Summer for breaking the tension. 'Ah, didn't he just keep that one a secret? I'll need to speak to him about that.'

'You definitely should. Now, would you like a top-up?'

'Absolutely, I would.'

And as they were going for the bottle, a streak of different ginger weaved through the flowerbeds. Long-haired, sleek and curious, sniffing at the new array of plants.

'Oh! A kitty!' Summer shimmied on her stomach towards the cat, hand outstretched. Immediately, it came to her. 'I wonder where it's from. It's skinny and so matted. Have you seen it here before?'

'No, never.' Cherry remembered her dad chasing away several strays from his allotment, despite her protestations to adopt them. 'Could it have been dumped?'

'Possibly.' Summer scratched at the cat's chin, and it took the affection with ease. 'People tend not to drive down here to dump their cats, although I wouldn't put it past some arseholes.'

'I'll text Sean and ask if he's seen it before.' Cherry

picked up her phone, attaching a picture of the cat to the message.

> CHERRY: There's a stray cat here. Big ginger floofster. You know it?

A few minutes later, Sean replied.

> SEAN: Aye, Meowchel J Fluff. He stops by sometimes.

She relayed the message back to Summer, who laughed.

'Ask him if he's ever put a paper collar on "Meowchel J Fluff".'

> SEAN: No, I thought it belonged to Drumlinnie Farm. They have a lot of cats.

'Should we feed it?' Summer would hopefully know what to do.

'It looks young but hungry.' Summer examined the cat as she showered it with neck scratches. 'We should try it with a paper collar first to establish if it has an owner. But let's give it a little something, just in case.'

Cherry texted Sean.

. . .

CHERRY: I'm going to feed it that tin of salmon in the cupboard. I'll get more later.

She went inside, fixed a bowl of salmon, taking care to remove the bones, and came back to the patio, where the cat shot straight to the fish.

Sean replied with a GIF of a man shaking his head.

SEAN: Salmon doesn't grow on trees, you know.

Cherry shot back a laughing emoji.

CHERRY: What? I can't ignore a hungry pussy, can I?

The answer came instantly.

SEAN: Absolutely no fucking comment.

By this time, the cat had devoured the food.

'He's clearly starving, right?' Cherry hoped Summer knew more about this than she did.

'Maybe,' said Summer. 'He's young, so it's unlikely to be thyroid. I'll make him a collar. Do you have some paper, a pen and a wee bit of tape?'

'Hang on, I'll get some from inside.' Throwing back the last of her wine, Cherry ran into the house and over to the printer. Where she came thundering to a halt.

Oh my God!

Sitting right there on the printer was the marriage annulment form she had filled in a few weeks ago. But now there was an added envelope. And, on the front, written in a handwriting that could only be Sean's, the address of a local solicitor to send the form to. Plus, a stamp.

Fuck me. Smart move, Butler.

And now it was hers.

Cherry reached to the printer to steady herself. This was not what she was expecting. Not at all. The annulment was turning into a game of will, with Sean almost certainly testing her.

It should have been simple. Stick the form into the envelope and post it.

But this wasn't simple at all.

Dread curled behind Cherry's ribs. If she made her move, that would be it. Marriage over. Goodbye Sean.

Lovely, lovely Sean. The man she'd seen forever with across that shimmering ballroom. The god in a kilt who made her feel safe and protected and the centre of his world. The huge-hearted man who was loved and cherished by so many. He had chosen her right back, and now he'd essentially given consent to sign it all away.

Was it the ginger wine, or did her husband's gesture make her feel like throwing up?

'You alright in there?' Summer's voice floated in like hot honey from the garden.

'Yeah, coming.' Cherry folded the form and slipped it into the envelope. Lifted it to seal it, an action she'd carried out hundreds of times in her life.

But not this time.

Leaf flapping open, she dropped and abandoned the envelope, grabbed a sheet of paper from the printer tray and headed to the kitchen drawer for some tape.

And when she thought she'd had the biggest surprise of the day, what was in there threw her even further.

Oh, bloody hell! He didn't? Cherry wanted to sob and laugh at the same time. *Oh, Sean, you wonderful human.*

She blinked hard. The tears would flood her face if she didn't force them back and concentrate on the cat. Grabbing the tape and a pen, she slammed the drawer closed and, pulse still ricocheting from what oddly felt like a run-in with a bear, took them out to Summer.

The cat was rubbing up against Summer's legs when Cherry stepped out onto the patio.

'If no one claims him,' Summer said, 'you could get him checked over by Nate and then adopt him as your family pet.'

Cherry considered the sweet, affectionate creature. It broke her heart that someone would abandon a cat like this, although the idea of adopting him warmed her to the core. Sean and her sitting in this garden, a little cat sniffing at the flowers and chasing butterflies.

'That would be lovely.' Her mind drifted momentarily to everything she had seen inside the house. 'Really, really lovely.'

Chapter 22

Sean

Behind Sean, the front door clicked shut, the serenity of Kinshore almost ringing in his ears after the noise of the past few days' travel. It was the perfect welcome home, although there was one thing he'd like more. One thing he'd thought of constantly whilst away.

No sign of her, though. Not standing making toast in those denim hot pants he loved, or dancing to country music whilst dunking a tea bag in a cup. And certainly not waiting to kiss him and let him tear her clothes off like he'd imagined for most of the journey home.

Dropping his bag, Sean moved to the kitchen and poured himself a glass of water, downing it in a few gulps. Only then did it come to his attention that the patio door was slightly open.

He slid the door open and, for a second, forgot to breathe as the sight of a transformed landscape hit him, including slender soil-stained legs bathing in early-afternoon sunlight and equally filthy feet resting on an old garden chair.

Standing unnoticed, he took her in. From behind, covered in dirt, his wife was still the most captivating woman he'd ever seen. He let out a long, low whistle.

'Woah! What happened here?'

As Cherry glanced back, joy and delight shimmered in her eyes. 'Oh, hi!'

'Did you do this?' Sean moved to the edge of the patio, drinking in his newly made-over garden. The answer could only be yes, unless she'd hired a gardener, but she looked like she had been in amongst it.

'Maybe,' she teased. 'With a little help from my new friend, Summer.'

He spun back. 'Summer? Summer Munro?'

'Yes, she works in the garden shop. Speaks very highly of you.'

'I speak highly of her, even higher now that you've both turned the place into the Garden of Eden. I'm speechless. I mean, as speechless as I get, but you know...'

'You like it?' Cherry brightened.

'Aye. It's incredible.' He stepped onto the lawn, then stopped. 'Can I go here with my shoes on?'

She laughed. 'Of course you can. It's grass, not diamonds.'

Sean did a little dance on the lawn. 'Check out this normal-sized grass... And all these plants that aren't weeds... You've got honeysuckle!' He walked over and called to her from the fence as if she weren't the one who had put it there. 'Honeysuckle!'

'Yes, like at your mum's house.'

This caught him off guard for its thoughtfulness, and all he could do was stare at her. He thought of her constantly, but to know it might be mutual moved him more than he could say.

'There are bird feeders and a birdbath.' Cherry pointed to the rowan tree in the right-hand corner where the bird paraphernalia was set out. 'This place is going to be a wee winged creature's paradise.'

'Did the wee winged creatures vandalise this one already?' Sean stared down at the unassembled birdhouse sitting on the patio.

'No, I ran out of steam and into the ginger wine. I thought you might like to put that one together.'

'Ah, okay, I'd love to... Ginger wine?' He pulled a chair up next to Cherry's. 'The psycho juice Patsy makes? I've nearly had my stomach pumped on more than one occasion from drinking that.'

'The very same. Would you like a glass?' She lifted the bottle. 'There's still some left.'

'I'll stick to beer, thanks. Maybe you should too since I don't have time to take you to A&E.'

Cherry reluctantly relinquished the ginger wine, and Sean went inside and got two beers from the fridge. Sitting in the old garden chairs, they slugged from the chilled bottles, the lush, verdant world humming around them.

'Tell me how the interview went,' she said, her tone forced casual. She would know that the chances of him being rejected for a visa were so small that he was almost certainly going to the States.

'Aye, good. Visa granted. That'll be me away to Tennessee next spring.' He snuck a sideways glance at her, keen to see her reaction.

'Ah, amazing. You're going to have a blast out there. All the Tennessee girls won't know what's hit them.'

This response wasn't what Sean hoped, but he knew she didn't want him going with other women. And how could Tennessee girls compare to this – dirt-streaked legs, chaotic hair, hypnotic femininity? They couldn't. He swigged from his beer and changed the topic of conversation. 'Thank you for all the gardening you did here. Although, I believe there's another name for all of this.'

Cherry lowered the bottle she'd been about to drink from. 'Oh, right. What's that then?'

'It's nesting, isn't it?'

A smile danced playfully at the corner of her lips, like she'd been sprung naked but quite liked it. 'Nesting? Never heard of it.'

Aye, right. 'It's when a woman buys lots of scatter cushions and candles to make the house all cosy 'cause she wants a nice place to settle down. Jamie tells me Alicia does it at his place.'

But Cherry continued to play innocent. 'I can't see any scatter cushions out here.'

'Not yet, but I'm telling you, this is nesting, Paradise style. You want to stay here and feel at home, but you're holding back, so instead of making the inside of my house all cosy and girly, you come at it from the side, going for the garden like I won't notice. And you won't notice yourself. But I've noticed.'

Cherry tugged at her shorts. 'Oh, you're smart, Butler. So smart.'

'Aye, I am. We might not have been married very long, but I can see into your soul, woman.'

'You wish.' Now she adjusted her neck a little awkwardly. For a professional poker player, she had a fuck-load of tells.

Sean reclined, took a sip of his beer. It was so nice to be back with Cherry and fall into their teasing banter.

'Anyway, darling husband, do you fancy a game of

Swingball?' She motioned with her foot to the game she had pitched in the centre of the lawn.

Darling husband? Was this some sort of progress? 'Swingball?' he said. 'Are we expecting some children around?'

'It's not just for kids.' She pulled on her baseball cap, bounced up, and began lightly batting the ball back and forth to herself. 'I got it as part of your training regime. Don't you like Swingball, Mr Poopy Pants?'

'Regime?' Sean laughed. 'Aye, Mr Poopy Pants likes Swingball. I killed at it when I was nine. Come on, then.' He lifted the other bat from the patio. 'Let's see who's the winner round here!'

'I think we know it's me.' Cherry bounced on her tiptoes and served the ball to him. Sean hit it right back.

'We'll see about that,' he said. 'So, are there any more surprises for the garden?'

'Yes, there's an unboxed garden swing in the summer-house. Like the one at your mum's.'

'Like the one we were sitting on the other week?'

'Yes, the same. I thought you might like one for your own garden; it was comfy.'

'Sure, a love swing for me and myself. Thanks, Cher.' He segued from this into the topic that was at the front of his mind. 'By the way, did you see I put out a stamped envelope for the annulment form?'

'Oh, did you?' The cutest rosy blotches, which he could have kissed, bloomed on Cherry's cheeks as she stared at him almost too intently.

Sean grabbed the tennis ball on the end of the line – he needed all of his faculties for this. 'Aye, about two weeks ago. I'm amazed you haven't noticed, given that you put the form there in the first place.'

'Sorry.' She deflected her sights to the patio doors as if someone was about to walk through them. 'I did see it.'

'Good. Are you fine to post it then?'

'Sure, I'll do it tomorrow.'

He stepped closer to the pole. 'Only if you want to.'

Cherry's baseball cap shielded any subtle eye movement that would betray hesitation. There was nothing on the rest of her face. This is what you got for marrying a poker player. But something told him to stop this line of inquiry. After all, her not posting it was what he wanted.

'So' – he prepared to serve – 'we've managed to qualify for an annulment based on not consummating the marriage. Tell me, how the hell do they prove if you've slept together or not?'

'I'm not sure they can.' Cherry rolled her shoulders. 'Guess it's like lying in court – you're breaking the law if you do it.'

'Right, well, we'd better continue to keep our hands to ourselves. But be warned, Paradise, if you can't, then you're paying for the divorce or you're stuck with me.' He swung the ball round the pole in her direction.

She grinned. 'I promise to keep my hands and all other body parts off you. Wouldn't want to commit perjury, after all.'

Sean would happily risk perjury when his wife looked the way she did, her breasts bouncing lightly as she braced like a tennis player batting the ball to him. Those tanned, smooth legs, the low-cut vest and the hair swinging in a ponytail under the baseball cap. Who cared about a little lawbreaking when your wife resembled a poster girl for very adult Swingball?

'I've got a top line-up for the tourney so far.' She jolted him back to reality.

'Oh, aye?' Sean tried to think about poker. It wasn't easy.

'Yes, Connor is confirmed, which is freaking awesome, as is Campbell Duff.'

'Well, as much as I think he's a knob, he is a huge star, so even better.'

'Sean, you should probably know something...' Cherry's tone dipped a little alarmingly. 'Campbell Duff and I used to date.'

Fucking what? He whacked the ball hard. 'Seriously? When?'

'About ten years ago, before he was a massive star, but we were in the gossip mags and stuff.' She kept the game going, like she didn't want the whole focus to be on this conversation.

'I don't read the gossip mags. Was it serious? Where did you guys meet?'

'He liked to go to edgy poker games in the back of pubs. I met him in Shoreditch, and we dated for about a year and a half. The nature of his work and my work is the reason it ended, and the reason it lasted.'

'Okay. I guess it's good publicity.' Sean had to think of the bigger picture. Money for charity. To help people like his dad. He began to hit the ball on autopilot, trying hard to focus on everything that was going on. His wife's body, how much he didn't want that annulment form posted, his wife's body.

'Hot, isn't it?' Cherry swiped her hand across her forehead.

'Pretty hot. Guess I'd better get used to it since it's going to be way more sweltering in Tennessee.' He hit the perfect serve, but she missed it. 'You okay?'

'What?' Cherry's cheeks flushed rose again, and he thought she was the most beautiful thing he'd ever seen.

'You're not overheating, are you?' He batted to her gently. 'Need a drink? A wee lie-down?'

'No, I don't need a wee lie-down.' Cherry swung hard.

'You can always lie in my room if you're more comfortable there. Hold my pillow.'

'Shut the front door, Butler!' She laughed, hitting the ball so badly that it flew upward and the rope tangled. Sean watched as she tried to undo her work.

'Need a hand there?' He reached for the rope, their hands overlapping – his large and rough, hers small and soft, clear pink gloss on the nails.

'It's fine. I can manage.' Their fingertips touched in a rare, electric moment.

'I know you can. Doesn't mean I can't help you.'

'Yes, yes. Let's play.' Cherry unwound the cord and stepped back.

'You know, it's okay if you're bothered about stuff,' Sean said. 'About annulling the marriage, me going to Tennessee. It's okay to admit you don't want either of those things.'

'Don't make this more difficult, Sean, please.' She lifted her cap and adjusted her ponytail. He took the moment to reassert his feelings.

'For the record, I don't want either of those things half as much as I want to stay here and be married to you.'

Cherry held her hands at the back of her head, allowing his words to hit her, until the ponytail slowly dropped back down, swinging in the wake of his honesty. 'That's an incredible sentiment, but what am I meant to do? Ask you to give it all up for a car crash of a wife?'

'Yes, that would be the perfect thing to ask.'

Up went one indignant eyebrow.

'*You* said you were a car crash. I was agreeing to the "giving it up" bit.'

She pouted. 'Just serve, Butler!'

He stepped back. 'Fine.'

They volleyed in silence for a while, the repetitive thwack of the tennis ball against the hard plastic bats giving a steady rhythm. The sun beat down, turning the garden game onerous. After a time, bored with the quiet and hoping to break the tension, Sean asked, 'Have you seen the hungry pussy today?'

Cherry laughed and missed the ball. Her smile lit up her entire face; he could watch it all day.

'Sorry, did that put you off your game?'

'You know it did.'

'So sorry.'

'You know you aren't.'

'Aye, true. But have you seen the cat?'

Cherry looked around the garden and then back to Sean. 'No,' she said, licking sweat off her top lip.

'Must be sheltering in the shade somewhere. It's bloody hot.' He took off his t-shirt and cast it to the side, caught Cherry's eyes widening as he did so, and a thrill cut through him.

'You're okay if I take my top off in my own garden, right?'

'Yep, all good. Stop trying to put me off my game with your salacious shenanigans. I've seen half-naked men before, you know – including you.'

'Fine. C'mon then.' Sean pelted the ball. Cherry smashed it back to him with equal force. Again, they lapsed into quiet, the only sounds the thud of the ball against their bats and the sharp, syncopated rhythm of their breathing. Eventually, Sean hit a volley that Cherry missed.

'Game, set, match, Butler!' He threw his bat in the air; it spun back down, and he caught it one-handed.

'Such a gracious winner.' With a small bow, Cherry tipped her baseball cap at him before sticking her tongue out, throwing her bat on the ground and strutting away in an affected huff, her perfectly round arse wiggling inside her 'gardening' shorts, so tight they should be outlawed.

He went after her, stopping her with the simple motion of sweeping his arms around her waist. 'Where do you think you're going, Paradise? Stay and worship the champion.'

'No way.' Cherry wriggled with admirable effort, her laughter holding her back. Sean lifted her off the ground, spun her around to face the way they'd come.

'Get back there and kiss my bat, woman.'

'Never! I will never kiss your bat.' Her laughter pealed around the garden. It was music to Sean's ears to hear her happy. 'Let me down, Butler. I command it.'

'Command all you like. I'm going to need a promise about my bat?'

'Okay, okay, I'll kiss your bat.'

'Alright then.' He lowered her to the ground. In one motion, she spun round, giving him the finger before taking off down the garden, lifting his bat and throwing it to the side.

'You wee minx.' He ran after her, catching her again, but she was already on her way down, having not recovered from lifting the bat. This time they fell to the ground together, Sean landing on top of her, his heart thundering next to hers.

'Sorry,' he said.

'You sound so sincere.'

'I am sincere. I wouldn't want to put either of us in a position where we might be at risk of committing perjury.'

'Right, yes, perjury.' Her voice trailed off, but she wasn't thinking about the finer points of the law; he could see that.

'Because committing perjury is the last thing either of us wants, right?' Sean, leaning on one hand, raked the other through his hair. He could use a shower. One with the woman who was underneath him would suit him down to the ground. Although, flirting with her was also fun.

'Do you want me to get up?' he asked.

'Maybe.' With a small wriggle, Cherry made a vain attempt at movement, like having him on top of her was far more pleasurable. He was with her on that one.

'You know, Cherry, it's okay to want this. I am your husband.' He eased her cap off, laid it to the side and trailed a thumb across her cheek. Her skin was warm and glowing from the heat. 'You're allowed to enjoy being touched by me.'

She stared up at him, that delectable cleavage heaving, small beads of perspiration between her breasts, his chest mirroring the action back to her.

'You want this?' he asked. *Say yes, woman. For the love of God, say yes.*

A shake of the head. 'No.'

But her eyes were roaming all over him – his hair, mouth, chest, down to the place where their bodies were flush. She shifted her hips.

'Do you want up?' Sean sat back, lifted his own hips to let her go. But Cherry didn't move, only stared at him, so he lowered himself down again, leaning over her again, hot breaths mingling.

'You know what I think, Cher?'

'What?' She blinked up at him.

'I think fuck perjury. No one will ever know. And if they do, I'll gladly pay for a divorce just to have this with you for one afternoon, because the idea of never knowing what it's like to touch you, to be inside you, to fuck my beautiful wife, is unbearable.'

Her nod was reflexive. She got it. Understood. Struggled with the oppressive weight of trying to resist as much as he did.

'But you know what's more unbearable?' Sean continued. 'The thought that you aren't letting yourself have what you want now because of some fear of the future. Live for now. You deserve to be loved and fucked by the man you married...to scream down the walls while he's deep inside you, living for every moan and whimper you make. Because that's what I want, and I know it's what you want.' Sean dipped his head and kissed the soft curve of her collarbone, where the scent of honeysuckle lit a fire inside him. 'Of course, you can correct me if I'm wrong...'

A tiny moan escaped Cherry's throat – her body wanted this, even if her mind fought against it. How he longed for her to let go. For both their sakes.

'I'm still scared, Sean.'

'Of what?'

'Of hurting you. Leaving you with nothing. It's so hard to shake.'

Pain was etched on her face. He reached for her hand, and she let him. He wished he could do more than this, promise it would all be okay. Give her exactly what she wanted. But all he had was his words.

Four of them.

'I only want you.'

Tears spilled into Cherry's eyes. 'But what if you stop wanting me...?'

Sean shook his head. 'This only happens once in a lifetime, Cher. And it's forever.' He found her hand with his.

'No matter what happens, I hope you never go through that pain again. But if you do, then let it be with me, because I don't trust anyone else to look after you like I can. Okay?'

Those brilliant blue irises searched his face for reassurance that he meant this, that she could believe. She truly could. He had never meant anything more in his life.

And finally, she said the words – a vulnerability so tangible he knew he would do nothing but honour it, forever.

'Okay,' she whispered. 'Okay.'

'You sure?'

'Yes.'

Sean lowered his mouth to Cherry's. For a fragment of time, he stopped and waited there, giving them both a moment to understand this. The implications.

She took the moment. Breathed and waited. For him to kiss her.

So he did.

In a response Sean was only half expecting, Cherry kissed him back, tentative for a split second then with a hunger she seemed barely able to contain, her hands sliding up over his neck, into his hair, grasping the strands, moaning into him like she'd been waiting for him her whole life.

And he got it, because if they were about to do what he hoped they were, then this was everything. At last, this was everything. Everything their marriage should be.

He boxed her in with his elbows. Showing what he could give her.

Strength. Safety. Belonging.

And a tightness straining inside his jeans that desperately needed release.

Cherry's small body was fierce and hot under his, but also so soft, underscoring her vulnerability. This was a woman of such stark contrasts, so impossible yet so lovable. Nothing made Sean feel the way she did. Every yes, every no, every come, every go, every night spent on the opposite side of the wall from her, his hand moving in frantic rhythm, thinking only of his wife, made being with her now, at last, all the more mind-blowing.

It had been a rollercoaster, but Sean wouldn't have had it any other way.

'God, Cherry.' Lifting away from the kiss, he touched his forehead to hers, words hot like the perspiration that glittered on both their brows. 'Let me fuck you. Let me show you how I fuck my wife.'

'Seany, Seany, as long as you fuck like you kiss,' she murmured as if half intoxicated, draping her arms around his neck, legs curving across his back, drawing him down to her again.

She was no match for him in strength, but Sean wasn't fighting this, not for one second.

Chapter 23

Cherry

The sun burned overhead, but her husband burned hotter. His heavy, half-naked weight pressed down on Cherry, grass pricking her skin. She arched up to meet him, the air thick with the scent of oak and sweat and raw man, waiting to claim her.

He already had. The moment they met.

But this now was sealing the marriage contract.

Letting him ink his signature all over her.

It was impossible to deny it any longer. To deny herself. To deny him. She needed the man she had chosen to be her forever. The man wearing the solid gold ring that was glinting in the sun with his commitment to her. She needed him to put his mark on her, sear that promise onto her skin. Needed the rough, possessive hand that was sliding up under the hem of her top and inside her bra, taking her nipple between his fingers and squeezing.

Holding it there. Pressing a little firmer. Owning her a little more.

'Oh God, Sean.'

'This is fucking incredible, Cher. If I die now, I'll die a happy man.'

'Don't you dare die.' The words came out a trembling command. She couldn't lose him now, not on this monumental precipice.

'No chance.' Sean yanked up her top, pulled her bra down from both breasts and took one in his palm, the nipple of the other in his mouth. Sucked hard.

And my God, it was so good.

So fucking good. Everything he did with that part of his body drove her wild. From his kisses, to his jokes, to his sincere sentiments, to this. Thank God the house was isolated from neighbours because the sounds of nature, the chirruping of the birds and the cool rush of the sea couldn't compete with the noises she was about to make.

Taking her nipple between his teeth, ever so gently, Sean bit. Cherry stifled the moans battling to escape her throat. A force of habit, perhaps, but her husband was here to remind her to let go.

'Don't fight it, Paradise. No one is here. Only the birds.' He switched to the other breast, propping himself up on one of those gorgeous, swollen biceps inked with stories of his soul, his depths, his feelings.

Cherry's fingers roved over the sculpted planes of his back, sliding across the hot, damp skin. Raising her hips, she spread her legs to let Sean settle, hot and hard, against the thin barrier of her shorts.

'Fuck, Cherry. Fucking you might end me.'

Intoxicated by his arousal, she tilted her hips again and saw the masculine drive teetering on the edge of a crash. The pulsing in his throat as he fought for control. The flex and tense of his jaw. All the strength he was battling to hold onto. It only tightened the hold he had on her. By simply being himself and falling apart in front of her, he made her lose herself to him.

'God, Cherry. I need you. I need you. I need to see you. Show me,' Sean babbled but ended on a rough growl as he sat back and tugged at her shorts and white knickers, slid them over her hips and ankles.

Tipping her knees apart, he drew in air. 'Fuck me... Look at you... You're a goddess.' In a beat, he dropped between her legs, licking and lapping feverishly at her soaking core, sucking her clit, winding his tongue through her swollen, aching folds, drinking her in like he might never get the chance again.

'Cherry. Oh, Cherry,' he groaned. 'Say this pussy is mine.'

'It's yours, Sean. I'm yours.' Oh, the rush at being able to tell him that, at last. Catching him checking she was serious, she nodded assent, because this was about so much more than one part of her body. This was about being his wife.

He spread her apart, buried his face in her. 'I could die here.'

'Stop talking about dying and suck my clit.' Cherry's nerve endings were burning up, flames licking through her as her husband stoked the fire with his tongue. They were right when they said Sean did nothing by halves. God, she'd lucked out when she'd met him. Whatever else went wrong in her life, he was the universe's gift for all the trouble it had caused.

And he was wholly ruining her.

Entirely destroying her.

Wrecking her for the rest of her days.

And if being wrecked felt as good as this, Cherry would gladly be eviscerated by Sean. She was soaking. Molten arousal, dripping heat. He drank in every last moment, stubble rasping over her skin as he planted kisses on the inside of her thighs, across her stomach, travelling back to her mouth.

'Taste your pussy, Cherry. Taste it with me.' The glaze of his eyes revealed how far gone he was. And fuck, if she wasn't falling off a cliff for him. This man sent her spiralling. Everything about him – the way he gave, the way he took, his laughter, his candour, his passion, his drive, his tongue, his hands, hot and deserving, but worshipping only her.

Fuck, she loved him. She really did. It was impossible not to.

And wherever he was now, whatever place he was travelling in, finding and losing himself between her thighs, she only loved him more for it.

'Fuck, Sean, if I'd known... Oh!' Cherry grasped for sheets but found only grass.

A hot tongue circled her clit, and she bucked up. 'Known what?'

'If I'd known how good this would be, I would have let you fuck me weeks ago.'

'I've not even fucked you yet. This is nothing.' Sean returned to his place of worship, giving all the saints and sinners a run for their money.

Cherry palmed her breasts, sunshine torrid on her skin, nipples hard even in the afternoon sun, tension looping and swirling like sand martins above. Suddenly, she needed nothing more urgently than Sean. Until now, she'd held him at arm's length, but at this second, the need for her husband inside her was ravaging her.

'Sean, I...' She tried to inch away from him so as not to come.

'What? What is it?' Worry flashed over his face.

'I want you inside me. I need to feel it so, so much.'

Palms confident on her hips, Sean pulled her back down. 'We'll get to that – soon. Don't be so desperate, Paradise.'

'You what?' She lifted her head and saw the familiar Sean, bold and winking. Fuck. Trust him to turn this back around with his trademark cheek.

'Ugh.' She squeezed his shoulder, firm but playful. 'So rude.'

'Aye, rude but good.' He swiped his tongue again, reaching up and grasping her nipple at the same time. Branding every bit of her he touched.

'Oh!' Cherry's head tipped back. 'So good. So... Oh, Sean. Fuck! Please!' How had she ever held back from this? And more to the point, why? This man was everything. Every instinct in her body had told her that when she met him.

'That's it, Cher. Grind into me. Show me how much you love your husband sucking you.'

And he was right. That was it. Holding back was over. Done. He had her now. Cherry was barely aware of Sean's palms gripping her hips as her whole body came swooping and soaring, and she ground and rocked and fractured into a million pieces with him right there drinking it all in with a savage groan.

Moments later, there was nothing but warmth coursing through Cherry. From the sun, from the orgasm she'd just had and from her gorgeous husband smiling up at her.

'How's life in paradise?' he asked.

'Come find out.' She ran a finger from between her legs up to his mouth.

'You sure?' How the hell was he still managing manners?

'Of course.' She reached for him, but her arms weren't long enough, so Sean did the work, flicking down his zipper.

'You wouldn't rather do this in bed?' he asked. 'Might be more comfortable.'

'I didn't spend hours mowing this lawn not to be fucked by my husband on it.'

'I'm so glad you had an ulterior motive.' Sean rolled his jeans over his ankles, underwear following in hot pursuit.

And then he was there, in all his glory. Long, thick and perfect.

My beautiful Scotsman.

'Cher, condoms. Believe it or not, I didn't think I'd need them for Swingball, but there's about five hundred packets in the house.' A pained smile twisted his lips. Like he didn't want to part from her now. She knew the feeling.

'I've got a coil. And I'm clean. I want to be skin on skin with you. You?' How she hoped he would say the same thing. That he needed that closeness, too.

'Aye. I'm clean. I can't promise I'm going to last long, though, especially bare.'

'Honestly, I'm nearly gone for you.'

'Again?'

'Again.'

He lowered to her, firm chest pressing insistently against her breasts. Forehead to forehead they met, breath hot in the warm summer air between them.

'Cherry.' Sean spoke hoarsely. 'You ready to consummate this marriage?'

Sliding her hands to the base of his spine, she felt the firm muscle there about to power everything he would give her. She had never been more ready for anything in her life.

'God yes.'

Slowly, Sean edged the head of his cock into her.

Cherry clenched around him, her body instinctively knowing this was something – someone – to hold onto.

He stopped. Teasing or taking it in? One glimpse of the strain on his face confirmed the latter.

'I sound like a broken record, but this is going to fucking end me,' he groaned. Not that it stopped him pushing in further.

Cherry had spent plenty of time imagining what this would be like, but nothing matched the real thing. The thickness of him stretching her, filling every inch of her, reaching parts no man ever had.

Nothing compared to being with Sean like this. Nothing. Not a million royal flushes. Because this, right here, in this hot little garden on a remote peninsula in Scotland, being joined with this huge-hearted man – the closest they could be – was like winning all the glittering poker bracelets in the world at once.

Sean rolled his hips, the motion bringing him deeper.

Cherry gasped, hands finding his shoulders, craving a solid hold. The way he filled her, it completed her. She could never be anyone else's, not now.

'Sean, I've never felt anything like this. You're huge.'

He let out a strained laugh. 'Jesus, don't flatter me, Cher. I'm on the edge here.'

'Let go. Fuck me like you've wanted to for weeks.' Seeing him rampant and unbridled was the stuff of Cherry's fantasies, and she couldn't wait for it.

Sean moved out an inch, then slid back in – slow, measured, excruciating. She tightened around him, and he dropped to her, possessing her with raw kisses, throbbing insistently inside her.

'Oh... Oh, Sean.'

'You like that? You like my cock in you?'

'I fucking love it. It's the best I've ever had. You make me so...' She dragged her nails down his back.

'Fuck, that is so fucking good.' Sean picked up the pace, each thrust he gave to her a chasing of lost time and a taking of everything, in case she changed her mind again.

How could she change her mind about this?

'You belong in me, Seany.'

'I'm going to come here and now if you keep that talk up.'

'Do it. I'll come right round you. Fuck me like you mean it, Butler. Show me why I married you.'

Something cracked in Sean. He grabbed her thigh, hitched it higher to his waist and began powerful, rhythmic strokes. Fucking her like it was his only mission in life.

'That better? Is that how you like to be fucked?' He ground into her like he was going to penetrate right through her.

'Yes, more, more.' Her fingers splayed across his back, over the powerful muscles working under the sweat-slicked skin. 'Yes, Sean, yes. More. Harder.'

He slammed into her. 'I knew you could take my cock like this, Paradise. Knew it from the moment I met you. My fucking beautiful wife.'

'Yes, yes, Sean, oh my God, oh my God, yes.' Cherry was abandoned somewhere beyond reality now, her husband fucking her untamed, feral, hips grinding, jaw flexing, biceps swelling, deeper, harder, driving into her pussy, grinding against her clit. She threw her legs up, bringing him deeper still, desperate for all of him, everything he could give her. Needing him to know that he had her, that he'd won her with everything that he was.

'Come for me, Cher. Let me feel this tight pussy coming around me.'

Those words were it. Cherry shuddered and, with a ricochet of moans and gasps, she clamped down around Sean, her back arching, head tipping, mouth parting on a shrill cry, everything shattering seismically under her husband.

'Oh God, Sean! Fuck yes!'

It went on forever. Like nothing she'd ever known, from a man like no other.

A primal groan, fierce and feral, rocked and shook Sean's whole body as he came hard and deep, hot seed spilling into her, strong hands bracing her so firmly she thought he might leave an imprint on her skin forever.

Another one. To go with the one he had on her heart.

Because Sean Butler had her.

Unequivocally. *Till death do us part.*

Birds went about their daily lives. The ocean continued to roll into shore. Sean stilled, breathing hard against her neck, the nearly full weight of his body pinning and steadying her. Sweat and heat mingled in the air between them, entwining with so much love and adoration.

He mumbled something she could barely discern into her neck.

'Hmm?'

'I said, I've lost the ability to talk.'

'Allow me... You're a great fuck, Sean Butler. The best I've ever had.'

Sean raised himself up on those god-like arms and regarded her, still seemingly struggling to form words. But the bright tenderness on his face spoke volumes. He leaned down and pressed a loving kiss to her forehead, the tip of her nose and then her mouth.

'No one comes close to you, Cherry. No one at all.'

And Cherry thought she might combust into flames and die in her husband's arms.

Chapter 24

Sean

'You know what you've not said yet?' Sean planted little kisses on Cherry's earlobe, listening for that little whimper that caught in her throat when he did that. The love swing swayed gently beneath them.

'Thanks for assembling the swing?' she offered.

'No, you thanked me for that.'

'I haven't suggested we do it on the swing?' Cherry deliberately rocked the seat so it swayed a little more.

'You haven't, and if that's a suggestion, then we can do it in, say, half an hour.' Sean tipped his chin to the incipient moon slowly emerging into the evening sky. 'But what you've not said is that any of this was a mistake.'

'Oh, I see.' Cherry pulled up the throw as the air cooled around them. 'I don't think it's a mistake. How could something so good be wrong?'

'See, this is what I've been trying to tell you...' Were they at last on the same page? Could this be the breakthrough he'd longed for?

'Are you absolutely sure, though?' She leaned away from him a little. 'You certain you can handle life with me?'

He knew what she meant when she said 'life with me', but so many things combined now to tell him that life with her was exactly what he wanted, no matter the shape or size. Her strength and courage. Her wicked sense of fun. The way he couldn't be away from her for a day without aching for her. And the sex. If Cherry walked out of his life now, Sean might become a monk, because being with anyone else would be a crushingly empty experience.

As for the tough stuff...

'Cherry, I was born to handle life with you. But the things you talk about "handling" are a hypothetical for us.'

'I know, but you don't know—'

'Okay. Let me stop you there.'

She stalled. 'What?'

'You are going to have to stop assuming I can't cope with things, especially things that haven't even happened. I've just watched my dad die from one of the most unforgiving illnesses there is, and I'm still standing.'

'That's true.' She leaned over and kissed his cheek. 'Sorry.'

'Lie down.' Sean motioned to his lap.

'What?'

'Lie down. I want to tell you a wee story and see your beautiful face.'

Cherry manoeuvred her head into his lap, like she had in Central Park, blanket tucked under her arms. 'Is that better?' She gazed up at him.

'Aye.' Sean softly swept at her hairline with his thumb. 'You know, when I was in my twenties, I went out with this woman who was a few years older than I am now. Went off to London to be with her. You could say it was my awakening in many ways. She showed me quite a few ropes.'

'Ah, well, that might explain a few things.' She touched his jaw. 'Sexy man.'

'Thanks. We're always learning. Anyway, she ended things after six months, told me that I wasn't the sort of guy she could see herself settling down with. Not that I wanted to settle down with her, but it grated, because she said I was fun, the sex was great, but that she had higher ambition than a village boy. Like I was some sort of idiot with straw coming out of my ears.' This was too long ago now for it to bother Sean, but it was the right tone to illustrate his point to Cherry.

'The wee cow. You know I don't think that about you, Sean.'

'Do I?' Sean spoke without accusation, but seriously. 'I think you think I'm made of straw – that I'll give under the slightest bit of pressure, that I don't have the capacity to cope. You've decided that and, quite honestly, being under-estimated pisses me off because I'm not that guy. I'm not your ex.'

'I know, but you've told me you want a family and——'

'Cherry.' Sean had listened to Cherry a lot, but now it was his turn, so he forgave himself for interrupting her. 'All we need right now is me and you. Our feelings for one another. Nobody knows what's in the future. Not Jamie, Alicia, Cal, Bea, Carli. Niall, anyone. And quite honestly, if there was ever a point since meeting you that I could have let you go, it was probably around the vol-au-vents, and even then, I doubt it. If it was a question of some woman I had diluted feelings for and ten kids, or you and none, I'd choose you. Every fucking time.'

'Oh.' Her eyes darkened a little with surprise. How could she not know this? Had he not shown her the depth of his feelings?

'Aye, oh. Tell me, what would you have done if the shoe had been on the other foot? If I'd told you, say, in that elevator, that I was shooting blanks?'

Now she brightened. 'I'd have done anything with you in that elevator. It was you with all the self-control.'

Sean mentally banked to go back there one day and finish what they'd started. 'There you are.' He teased out some leaves and garden detritus from her hair.

'I know, Seany. I know.' She found his hand and gently stroked it in a way that almost had him stirring into the back of her neck. 'Can we take it slow? The annulment is up in smoke, but I don't want to mess this up. I don't know how we work that exactly – maybe we keep separate rooms or something – until I get my head round things.'

'Sure.' Sean placed a leaf from her hair onto the blanket. He wouldn't remind her of the irony, given that they'd had sex three times in one day. It was a move in the right direction. He'd give her time. Although, not forever; she would know that. 'I'm going to take separate rooms as a reason to do it in lots of other places besides the bedroom.'

She laughed and rolled her neck very deliberately over his lap. 'Sure, let's start with love-swing-sex in, say, half an hour?'

One thing that was important to Sean, regardless of how fast they moved and where they ended up, was Cherry's inner peace. It hadn't escaped his thoughts that sorting one other aspect of her life, might help her peace of mind and their marriage.

'So, listen, have you spoken to your mum since we saw her at the caravan site?' he said a short time later as, still on the swing, they drank beer. The temperature was dipping considerably, and love swing sex hadn't quite happened yet. There was always the couch.

'Nope. She sent me a text about something to do with the tides, but we haven't engaged in any meaningful conversation.'

'Right, well, I was thinking...'

'That's really not necessary.' Cherry blew across the opening of the beer bottle.

Sean smiled and kissed the crown of her head, catching notes of her blossomy shampoo. 'Believe it or not, I think on a daily basis, so it wasn't a stretch.'

She gazed up at him lazily, beer-softened. 'Go on, then.'

'Okay, you know the "colour my thingy" thing you're hosting next week? Why don't you invite your mum? She can stay here, get to know everyone and you guys can spend some quality time together.'

'Mmm.' Cherry nuzzled into his neck. 'I'd like to colour your thingy.'

'Cherry, I'm actually being serious here.'

'Sorry.' She pulled her face into a more sombre expression.

'You might have a nice time with her. I know you think half of what she believes is bollocks, but it's not like you're buying into some sort of extremist ideology by inviting her round with her colour swatches, is it?' God only knew what it would be like having Cherry and her mum together in the house, but if it helped mend their relationship, he would do it. He'd do anything for her.

'No, I suppose not. But, Sean...'

'Is this a new argument?'

'No, but I can't have her coming here and reminding me why she thinks I'm such a failure in life.'

Cherry's insecurities ran deep – her mum was her only

parent, and things had clearly been strained for many years – but all Sean had was straightforward solutions. Sometimes those were what worked best. 'So, you tell her not to. You write her a letter—'

'Nobody writes letters anymore.'

'Your mum's generation do. And it's way more personal than an email. Write a letter inviting her here for a weekend. In the letter, say that you don't want any card readings, but to focus on the positive – which is your marriage to me – and the future.'

Cherry raised an eyebrow. 'Our marriage is the positive?'

'Of course.' He took her wedding finger between his thumb and forefinger and lightly twisted her ring. 'Be honest with her because that is the only way this is going to work. Tell her you need to know she doesn't think you're a failure and you'd like to go some way to healing your relationship. Do it the Sean's Simple Psychology way and see if it works.'

Cherry sat in silence for so long that Sean could swear he heard both their heartbeats. He could only hope she was thinking about it, giving it a chance to work. Eventually, she leaned closer into him. 'It terrifies me. It could all backfire and set me back again. I'm only now recovering from the last time I saw her.'

Sean took her hand and interlocked their fingers, hers both warm from their contact and cold from confrontation. 'I know. You've come a long way, Cher, but she's your mum and she's going to have a big sway on how you feel. There's a chance you'll have to work through things alone, but maybe she'll come to the table. And I'll be here if it gets tough. I think you have to try.'

. . .

That evening, as Sean cooked dinner, Cherry sat at the kitchen table and wrote a letter to her mum. By the time the meal was in the oven, she was surrounded by at least thirty bits of crumpled paper spilling onto the floor.

'Ugh. Why is this so hard? Everything I write sounds pathetic. *I'm sorry we haven't*-this. *I truly hope we can*-that.'

Sean sat down opposite her at the table, dishtowel slung over his shoulder. 'Listen, there is no way that every single one of these drafts is pathetic. Whatever you write, you will think it sounds that way. I want you to write one more, and before you even think about crumpling it up, you are going to fold it and stick it in an envelope and put the address on the front. You can tell yourself it's not perfect, but then again, neither are you or your mum. Okay?'

It was as if he'd revealed the secrets of the universe to her, the way she gaped at him, eyes all shiny and bright.

'You make it all sound so simple.'

'Sometimes that helps you get by. As I said, Sean's Simple Psychology. Brought to you by a very complex man.'

'You are, aren't you?'

'Not really, no, but I do care, Cher. A fuck-load.'

He could have sworn he saw tears in her eyes, but she focused on putting pen to paper like a small child practising her handwriting. He got up and left her to it, but as he prepped the meal, he could see her signing the letter, sliding it into an envelope and writing the address on the front.

'Go post it now. I'll have a glass of wine waiting when you get back.'

'Really? Now?'

'Aye, there are stamps somewhere in that drawer over there. If you don't do it now, you might never do it.'

'But the postbox... It's in the village. And it's sort of raining.'

'So, put your trainers on and run. That way, you qualify for two glasses of wine. Oh, and Cherry...' Sean remembered something else.

'Aye.'

'There's another letter over by the printer. Can you do something with it?' He focused sharply to see how she would respond to this. Sure, the annulment was fucked, but that she might still want to commit perjury or get a divorce lingered treacherously in the back of his mind.

'Oh, yeah.' Slowly, Cherry moved to the printer and picked up the envelope Sean had put the annulment forms in. It was still open, and he watched her lick the seal and fix it down, watching him right back, over the edge, like someone blatantly committing a sin they wanted to be punished for.

Sean's heart was beating like a racehorse at the steeplechase as, envelope in hand, his wife walked back to him, seemingly in the slowest motion that had ever existed. Reaching the kitchen island, she pressed her foot to the pedal bin. Up popped the lid. Pulse thumping, he watched as she hovered the envelope over the abyss – their future a piece of paper dangling over a black plastic bag. Until, finally, she parted her fingers, and the envelope tumbled down into the murky depths.

Sean tried not to let out too audible a sigh of relief as it became clear the annulment forms were where they both wanted them to be, mingling with the rubbish at the bottom of the bin. But when Cherry blew him a kiss, he knew the stupidest smile had lit up his face.

Her mission seemingly not yet complete, she walked towards the bottom kitchen drawer, the one where Sean kept tape and other odds and ends. The place where he'd stashed something he wasn't sure what to do with. Something he'd assembled shortly after she arrived here but had never found an opportune moment to give to her. He'd considered leaving it next to the annulment form but had chickened out, wondering if the whole thing wasn't a bit insensitive.

But it seemed she had found it before now and was not upset in the least.

Carefully, Cherry pulled out the weighted-down piece of paper, laying it on the counter while she rummaged in the drawer for Blu Tak. Then she took both items over to the fridge, where she stuck the paper to the door.

'I bloody love this.' Standing back, she examined his handiwork like it was *The Mona Lisa*. 'It's just like me. The balance of wholewheat and plain spaghetti for the hair is perfect. You've captured my arms and legs so flatteringly with the penne. And the textured curl of my eyelashes with the fusilli and this farfalle croupier bow tie? Genius!'

At last, Sean let himself laugh – such sweet relief. 'How do you know it's you?'

'As I said, it looks like me. And because it says "my wife" in spaghetti at the foot of the page. Do you have another wife?'

'Nope, just you.'

'There you go then. And now I have my macaroni art on the fridge. Life is pretty damn good.' She beamed at him.

And he beamed right back, a thousand times as bright.

Fuck! He loved this woman.

Chapter 25

Cherry

A week later, Cherry drifted downstairs to make a coffee. As she did most days, she would sit on the patio in the morning sunshine, letting the birds' early twittering soothe her, meditate on squirrels scuttling across the grass and scaling trees as the caffeine filtered in.

But something was already different.

Sean was still at home.

'Oh, hey. Morning.' Cherry rubbed her eyes, her nipples peaking at the sight of her husband drinking coffee all casual and perky like they hadn't been up until the wee hours together. The whole separate rooms thing was a joke, seeing as how much time he spent in hers and how much she thought of him when he left. Whether or not staying married was the right thing to do, she was losing sight of anything else but Sean.

'The clocks didn't go back, did they?' she asked.

He eyed her over his coffee cup. 'Nah, I took the day off work. Wanted to fit in a run – and it's quieter than the weekend. Bonus is seeing you, of course. I missed you the past four hours.'

And the bonus for her was seeing him. 'Me, too. You want some company?' If Sean could have a day off work, she could too. That was the benefit of being her own boss.

He put down his cup. 'Seriously? You want to come for a run?'

'That wouldn't be too awful, would it? I'd like to get into an exercise habit again since I've left hotel gyms behind. And spend some time with my husband? Plus, you need a PT, right?'

Sean came to her, and she saw in the softness of his expression how much this meant to him. 'It wouldn't be awful at all, Cher. And I'd love to spend more time with you. I'm planning on running up to Inchfallon Falls today. It's a beautiful waterfall with a swimmable pool. Much like these.' He motioned around his eyes.

'Ha! I stand by what I said in New York.' She pulled in close to him, rose up on her tiptoes and kissed him. 'Skinny dipping it is.'

Sean gave a throaty chuckle. 'Don't make promises you can't keep, Paradise.'

'Guide's honour, I won't. Now, show me where your bike is.' She playfully pinched his bum, and he extricated himself from her.

'Bike? You didn't say you were a lazy PT!'

'It's motivational for you. I'll ride, and you run alongside me.'

'Do you want a megaphone to bark orders at me?'

'If you've got one, then sure.'

'I don't. If I thought you'd believe me, I'd tell you I don't have a bike either.'

. . .

'This beats a hotel treadmill any day,' Cherry cycled at a moderate starting pace along the shoreline road. The morning sunshine sparkled across the still blue waters of the sound.

'Aye. We're lucky.' Sean jogged alongside the bike. 'My dad brought me running here as a kid. We'd do wee jogs on the beach and mini-sprints, and he'd tell us we had to build our stamina for the three-legged race at school sports day. It's bizarre that a man who ran a distillery was fighting fit, until he wasn't, and that some of the old soaks he knew are still cutting about the place. Doesn't make sense.'

'No, it doesn't.' Cherry could relate. 'My dad seemed in fine health, and then the heart attack hit. I'll never forget getting home from school, excited to show him my project on the history of poker, only to see the ambulance outside the house. He'd been climbing mountains on the weekend, so I assumed it was the old bloke next door. Then I saw my mum on her knees in the hallway...'

Whenever Cherry recalled this memory, she so often focused on her own grief, but today, for some reason, her mum came into sharp focus. Pam always said she didn't have much in the world but what she had, she loved ferociously. And that day, one of those things was snatched from her forever. She had never dated again, her existence completely shaped by grief of losing the love of her life.

'Shit, Cherry. I'm sorry.' Sean placed a hand on her shoulder, briefly, until the motion of the bike parted them.

'It's okay. It was a long time ago now. Shall we talk later and concentrate on the running for now? Focus on your breathing and...um...keeping up the good work.'

It was strained, but Sean laughed. 'Amazing pep talk, Coach.'

'Sorry. Think how tight your buns are going to be after this.'

'Tight buns?' More laughter punctuated his sharp breaths. 'You've been living in the States for too long.'

'What I meant was a toned arse."

'You do know I'm not cycling 100 miles for a toned arse.'

'Of course, but it's a good incidental benefit. You know, what you're doing is amazing, Sean.'

He eyed her askance, amusement on his face. Cherry did her best to look at him whilst cycling at a similar pace and not falling off the bike.

'I know you think I'm being daft,' she said, 'but your motivation *is* inspiring. The way you're pushing yourself on so other people don't suffer like your dad, how you get up every single day and keeping going, your mind on that goal… It's incredible. If there were more men like you in the world, it would be a better place.'

She wasn't sure if the pained expression on Sean's face was at her words, concern about her falling off the bike or something else.

'Thanks, that means a lot.'

Cherry prepared to pedal harder, perhaps to get to their destination and the turning point she was about to instigate. 'I'm going to cycle up ahead.' She pointed to the road in front of them. 'I want you to sprint to me. Then when you reach me, you can moderate the pace, and I'll cycle on again and we repeat the process.'

Keeping his eyes on the road, Sean hit back. 'Sounds like a metaphor for our marriage.'

It was hard not to laugh. 'Don't talk, sweetheart. Save your breath for the sprint.' She blew another air kiss his way and focused on the road. His observation was both amusing and incisive. And a little heartbreaking. It was time to try and mend that heart today.

The main road meandered along the coastline for as far as the eye could see. But about half a mile after they had passed the distillery, Sean told Cherry to turn right. The incline was steeper; there were fewer dips, and mostly they were travelling uphill. She put all her focus into the cycling and found her thighs burning as they headed towards the thicket of trees in the distance.

Finally, the incline plateaued, the road became more of a dirt track and the warming sunshine disappeared as the trees merged into a canopy overhead.

The quiet stillness of August fields segued into gushing water and the low rush of wind through summer foliage. Moments later, they reached a clearing where a waterfall, about twelve feet high, tumbled into a wide blue pool below.

'Welcome to Inchfallon Falls.' Sean's voice vibrated low like the hum of nature around them. 'My dad named a whisky after it, but it's stayed a bit of a local secret. All it would take is for someone to film a Netflix series here and it'll never be the same.'

'It's stunning.' Cherry straddled the bike, mesmerised by the babbling of the water below and the rustling of the leaves. The air was cooler under the shade of the trees, but there was a gap where the sun shone through at the right angle to hit the pool and brighten the waters.

'I love it here.' As if drawn by memories, Sean drifted to the rocks overlooking the pool, and Cherry followed. 'We spent hours splashing around here as kids. It must have been a health and safety nightmare, but Mum and Dad never complained.'

'We should've brought a picnic,' said Cherry. 'Made a day of it.'

'I've got some Irn-Bru in my backpack. Thirsty?'

She narrowed her eyes. 'You're training for an endurance race. You should be drinking water and eating bananas.'

'Aye, I do that, too. C'mon, let's sit.'

They found a couple of flattish rocks above the water, laid the bike down, and Cherry took Sean's lead in letting her feet dangle over the edge. The water was refreshing without being bitingly cold.

'How deep is it?' she asked.

'Depends. Maybe neck height for you today. The warm weather means there's less water than usual.'

'Did you learn to swim here?'

'Nope. In the sea.'

'Have you ever had sex here?'

'Ha! Just as I thought your questions were getting boring. In the pool or under the waterfall?'

'Either.'

'Neither. And I'm saying no more than that.'

'A few cheeky wee snogs?'

'Aye, maybe a few of those. This is the Kintyre equivalent of a drive-in movie for me. You park up and watch the waterfall.'

'I don't understand how it's not rammed full of people. Where is everyone?'

'No idea. Folk do come here, but it's a bit off the beaten track. The Butler family were, and still are, frequent visitors. Maybe other families aren't as hardy as us.'

'One day, we could come here,' she said. 'With...our kids?'

Sean eyes found hers, and she saw such a vulnerable mix of confusion and hope there that it stalled her heart. 'Our kids? Cherry?'

Cherry blinked back the fiery bite of tears, and focused on the sunlight twinkling on the water. She had planned to say things today – things about making a go of it with Sean – but not those specific words. They must be her subconscious talking. Like an iceberg cracking apart, things were shifting under the surface, Sean's kindness and patience affording her the confidence to believe.

'I know I need to be more positive, Sean. You have no idea how hard this is for me, but you believe in us, and I want to believe, too. You deserve that. We deserve that.'

'Fuck. That means so much, Cher.' He took her hand, and she was so glad she'd got to this point. 'I've mostly hidden it,' he said, 'but this has been a journey for me too. I have thought about things. I'm not being some naïve idiot who hasn't considered the way it might go. But, as I said before, no one knows what's in the future, good or bad. My dad didn't. My mum didn't when she married him. It's all unknown. I might... Fuck, I hate even saying this, because deep down I'm scared it might make you run, but it's important – what if I get it, too?'

'What? MND?' She hadn't even considered he might be worried about this. It was a real oversight on her part that someone as insightful as Sean wouldn't be acutely aware of his own mortality after painfully watching his father's demise.

'Aye.'

'Is it hereditary?'

'Sometimes. In our family, there isn't any history of it, but that doesn't stop me wondering. I don't talk about it, though, 'cause no point worrying yourself stupid over something you can't control.'

'I never even thought, Sean. I'm sorry. I'm so wrapped up in myself sometimes. Are there things you can do to minimise the risk?'

'Aye, I eat healthy-ish, exercise a lot.'

'You could be healthier. Cut out the Irn-Bru, for one.' It was a hypothetical, but now she knew she wanted their marriage to work, the thought of losing Sean as her mother had lost her husband became a more frightening possibility.

'Och, a man's allowed one vice, right? Which reminds me...' Sean reached into his bag, retrieved and cracked open a can of the soft drink.

'Depends how many cans a week that vice is.'

'Cherry Paradise, are you worried about me?' He held out the drink to her.

She took it, swigged and handed it back. 'I am, actually, Sean.' With her other hand, she brushed over his. Her feelings for him grew so fast, like the emerald moss on the rocks, but she could slip and fall at any time, and that still terrified her.

'Anyway, this pool... Cold, is it?'

She stood up and glanced down at a silent Sean. He was staring up at her, blinking hard, suggesting surprise at her honesty and worry about her breaking away so soon.

'It can be,' he said. Was he talking about something other than the pool? 'But the strong survive.'

'Let's go then.' Cherry toed off her trainers and slipped out of her t-shirt and shorts. She lowered herself onto the edge of the pool in only her white cotton pants and bra – a choice that would render them very transparent if anyone else appeared.

'It's safe to go in, right?'

She saw those green eyes shimmering softly, melding with the cool forest light. And fair play to him – his eyes were on her face, not anywhere else.

'It's safe,' he said. 'But I've no towels, so once you're wet, you're wet.'

'Ah, that's fine. I'm not afraid of being wet.' Then, as the double meaning of what she'd said hit her, Cherry was sliding off the rock and down into the bracing cool of the waters below.

Taking the plunge into the unknown and acclimatising to the feeling. Of freezing cold water.

She rose out of the pool, her laughter and breath coming in rapid bursts.

'Oh my God.' Finding her feet, she looked up to where a once-again-joyful Sean was standing on the rocks above.

'Bit fresh, eh?' He beamed that heart-stopping smile of his.

'Fresh, but also amazing.' She spun around and took in the dense greenery of ferns, rock foils and sorrel that surrounded the pool. Woodland birds chattered in the trees. How was this Scotland? Flipping onto her back, she let herself be mesmerised by the bright cerulean sky through the trees. This summer was one in a million.

'You coming in?' Her voice echoed off the rocks.

'I'll finish my juice, then I'll be right with you.'

'Strip and get in, Butler! You can finish your diabetes water afterwards.'

'Strip, eh?' This invitation was clearly like encouraging a fish to swim.

'Well, you know, within the bounds of what's decent. Or indecent. I don't mind.

Sean was close enough for Cherry to see his smirk before his face was obscured by his t-shirt. And there was that body. The ladder of abdominal muscles that you could climb to the sun on. Holy moly! She could never get enough of those.

He swigged the Irn-Bru, well aware he was being ogled. But it was delight, not arrogance, that suffused his movements. Then, in an unexpected move, he lifted the drink above his head, closed his eyes and tipped the can back, letting the bright orange liquid cascade down his face. He licked some of it away, the remaining rivulets rolling down onto his chest.

Cherry's laughter bounced off the rocks, and she was about to clap and whoop him on when a sharp voice split the air.

'Sean Butler, what on earth are you doing?'

Sean spun around as two women – one with bobbed grey hair, the other with bouncing curls of the same colour – came into view, a small black Cocker Spaniel pulling at the leash wrapped around the former's hand.

'Oh, hullo, Val...Gloria.' He fumbled for his t-shirt. 'Sorry, I didn't know you walked your dog around here.'

Cherry tried to stifle her laughter, watching Sean hug the t-shirt to his chest and prepare to be reprimanded.

Gloria remained quiet while Val spoke, but Cherry could swear there was a smile drawing her lips upwards. 'Sean, you're pouring Irn-Bru over rocks that have stood here for hundreds of years, that people like to come and sit on expecting they will not leave with a sticky bottom. Not to mention you're nearly naked in a public place. I appreciate you're grieving, but what do you think your father would say to this?'

To give him his dues, a shell-shocked Sean looked the woman dead in the eye as he spoke. 'I dunno. Probably tell me to calm down, as usual.' He shrugged and then, in trademark Sean-style, added, 'And spank my sticky bottom?'

Val was struggling not to laugh, but she shook her head disapprovingly. 'I can't imagine he ever stood up here and poured Irn-Bru over his head.'

'Um...' Sean's mouth tightened, possibly at the image of his dad doing this. 'No, he never mentioned it.'

'Having known your father most of my life, I think he'd say two things here. One: what are you doing wasting a good can of Irn-Bru? And two: make sure you take your litter home with you.' Val raised her eyebrows as if waiting for agreement.

Sean's brow creased in puzzlement, evidently not sure whether he was being ribbed or not. 'Aye, right, okay, Val. Both fair points.'

'Glad we agree... Oh, hello!' Suddenly bored with Sean, Val waved at Cherry. 'I didn't see you down there. You must be the new wife?'

'Yes, that's me.' Cherry waved back. 'Don't worry, I'll make sure he takes his litter home.'

Sean narrowed his eyes, as if she were a co-conspirator with the women, but he was half smiling, too.

'Lovely. We'll leave you to it. I expect you'll need to get in the water and wash all that juice off.' Val examined Sean up and down before turning to Cherry again and winking. 'We won't be back this way today. Enjoy married life, won't you? I'm sure Jimmy would approve.'

'Aye, thanks, Val. See you, Gloria.' Turning away from the women, Sean bent over, bracing his hands on his knees, and Cherry couldn't tell whether he was laughing or catching his breath. There was a mixture of amusement, relief and disbelief on his face.

When the dog walkers were out of sight, she swam backwards to make space for him in the water. 'Come on in,' she said. 'Wash that beamer off your face and calm doon.'

Chapter 26

Cherry

If the Sean on the rocks was an advert for Irn-Bru, the one drenched in fresh water was a living, breathing promotion for the great Scottish outdoors.

'Has your family ever used you as the face of Butlers?' Cherry forgot the cold now she had a sexy, wet Scotsman to gape at. He had all the right angles to promote the family drink. In fact, who better than the man who crafted the barrels the whisky was matured in?

Sean scraped his wet hair back from his forehead. 'No. I don't mean anything to anyone. We're using Alicia's brother, Connor, though. He's Hollywood hunky, a walking orgasm, y' know?'

'I guess.' She rubbed her foot on the silt at the bottom of the pool. The sun was warm on her skin, but she would need to keep moving to stay warm in here. 'At least they got someone young. If I'm going to be persuaded to drink whisky, then it needs to be by a guy whose abs I could drink the stuff off.'

'Fair point. Whisky advertising has started moving with

the times, but it's still geared towards men. Getting women to drink the stuff is a slow burn.'

'Hmm, you know who'd drink whisky off your abs?'

'You, I hope?'

'Those ladies up there. What were their names? Val and Gloria. They were ogling you.'

'I don't think so. They're lesbians.'

'I'm sure they can still appreciate you objectively. There's a lot to appreciate.'

Sean dragged his hand through his hair again, affording Cherry a first-class view of his underarm hair and curved biceps which sent her into cavewoman mode.

'You know,' he reminded her, 'this is the place where you could tick two things off your bucket list – sex with a younger man *and* under a waterfall.'

'Hmm. It's a bit cold. I kind of imagined a waterfall in the Caribbean or something.'

'I'll take you there one day... Listen, Cherry.' She heard the semitone drop in his voice, and she knew joking-Sean was gone. 'What you said up there? Does this mean you want to be my wife?'

'I am your wife, Seany.' True, but not what he was asking. It was only fair that he press for an answer on this one. In fact, she wanted him to.

'Aye, I know that but, like, forever?' He eyed her sharply. How did he manage to look seductive *and* interrogative at the same time? 'Do you want *this* forever?'

Cherry's feet were sinking into the silt. Goosebumps rose up on her skin; her nipples were like frozen peas skimming the water's surface. And her gorgeous husband was waiting for an answer on whether she wanted to be his wife forever. He didn't seem to be remotely cold, like he could wait all day.

She crossed her arms over her breasts. Sean glanced at them and then back up to her eyes. He waited. Patient. Determined to elicit the answer that she was pretty sure he already knew – the answer she wanted to give him. Like the leap into the cold water of this pool, she would need to take the plunge because fear might always breathe somewhere inside her.

'Yes,' she said, the words shivering warmly off her lips into the air between them. 'Yes, I do want to be your wife forever, Sean. I really do. And I want us to...to make a go of things.'

Sean's face softened with relief and Cherry's heart soared. But he stayed where he was. Waiting for more from her. What more could she say? What did he want? *I love you?* It felt wrong to blurt that out now, in case she was spooked again. She bit down.

Don't cry, don't cry.

Sensing her inability to move, Sean came to her. Stood over her. She considered that she'd never seen him so serious, not even when he'd told her to stop being a massive prick tease. Gently, he reached down and prised apart her arms, opening her to him in a way she seemed to struggle with. Cherry let her arms fall, and Sean pushed the stray streak of damp hair from her forehead, examining her with so much tenderness it nearly broke her. Then his arms were curving round her, and he was pulling her close. Right into that solid chest of his, bringing her cheek to rest on his beautiful muscular shoulder, allowing her to freely lose herself in the sweet, woody scent of his skin.

She curved her arms around him, too. Oh, thank God for the boundless heart of this man – for never giving up, letting her reach him in her own way and time, and meeting her at the last stretch. Being held by Sean was exactly what

Cherry needed, what her body craved. He was everything. Safe, solid, warm. All she had longed for, but had been too scared to believe she deserved.

'Cherry, Cherry, Cherry.' Sean's chest vibrated as he spoke her name, low and assured. Gently, he manoeuvred her to face him, kissed the top of her head, slowly ran his nose down her forehead, over the bridge of her nose, their breath synching, the cool water on his face mingling with the warmth of his skin.

She whimpered in appreciation. It might not be much, but Sean read it correctly and swept her mouth into a kiss, hot tongue insistent against hers, rough stubble grazing her cupid's bow, those hands that hammered and sculpted all day cupping her face like she was the most precious thing he'd ever held.

To love and to cherish.

She knew he would. If she could get through life's tribulations with anyone, it was with Sean. He was strong, safe and supportive and, most importantly, aware of what might lie ahead.

Cherry pressed into him. Sean gave a low groan in response, going deeper, harder with the kiss, before he raised her onto his hips in one swift motion. She clamped onto him with her thighs, the water giving her buoyancy, hands on those muscular shoulders surprisingly tanned for a Scotsman.

'Fuck, Cherry. You're so fucking beautiful. My perfect wife.' Sean lowered her slightly, cradling her backside and urging against her. The Butler jewels pressed insistently at her centre. He reached round, unclipped her bra, peeled it off, and cast it onto the rocks behind him, never taking his eyes from her breasts.

Pressing into him, she found a rhythm as he leaned back and watched her, his face etched with arousal.

'Fuck, that feels so fucking good, Cher. Keep going. I need you so much.'

'I need you too, Seany.' She ground against his shorts, moans vibrating into his neck, soft kisses morphing into gentle bites on the tender skin, the tougher sinew of his muscle.

Arousal swirled in her belly and flowed down to her core. No man had ever done to her what Sean did. He was the lost other half she'd longed for all her life. She moulded her hands into his back, craving that oneness again – he was already under her skin, but it wasn't enough.

'Mmm, more,' she moaned.

'You want me?' Sean's voice was hoarse as he grasped at her hair, an untamed need shimmering on his face, the embers of control leaving his body.

'Of course I want you.' Her legs coiled around his waist, grinding against him with a methodical rhythm. 'I want you so much, Sean. I want everything with you. Forever.'

At her words, she watched him tighten to the point of near release, jaw tensing, flexing, tensing, flexing. He was trying to fight it.

'Come for me, Seany. Come hard and make me come watching you.'

On a tight, suppressed groan Sean unravelled, an intoxicating fusion of pleasure and pain in his face. Cherry was there with him as he ground against her, eyes fighting and losing the battle to stay open, his climax ripping through him, racking his body as he shuddered into her violently. It was so unbearably intimate. The friction rubbing onto her clit, took Cherry right to the edge, her aching need culminating in the tension draining from her limbs, talons carving into his skin and her core tightening and pulsing, over and over.

As their climaxes abated like ripples on the water, Sean laughed softly, tiny water droplets vibrating on his skin, his hold still solid on her thighs. 'Wow! That was unexpected, but incredible.'

She leaned into his neck and kissed it. 'I loved coming with you, hubby.' This was what they did best – enjoyed each other.

He groaned. 'Fuck, you'll set me off again.' Stroking his hand down her hair and over her back, he said, 'You have the smoothest skin.'

Cherry uncoiled her legs from his waist and slid to her feet. Pressed her breasts to his chest. 'You have the smoothest moves.'

'Ha. You're implying I had some control over what happened there. I can assure you I had none. You're a devil-woman, and I'm absolutely fucked when you're around.'

'Next time, let's ensure we both are absolutely fucked.' It didn't escape her notice that she was talking about the future, together. *Progress, Cherry.*

'Aye. That would be awesome.' Sean reached for her chin, tilted it up to meet his face. The sunlight caught his wedding ring, and it glinted. She realised she'd never seen him without it since they'd married. It was just a ring, but this mattered. She suspected it wasn't a coincidence.

'You never take your wedding ring off,' she said. 'Not even at work?'

'Of course not. I made a commitment to you. *For better or worse.* If it gets battered, then that's a metaphor for life. Right?'

Was he for real? Was Sean Butler for real? Those words

were like a wedding vow in themselves, falling out of his mouth like poetry.

'I mean it, Cherry.' He spoke as if she might doubt him. 'This isn't a joke to me. It's not a wee bit of fun, although that was a lot of fun. I want to be your husband, and I want that for the rest of my life, whatever that might look like.'

'Oh, Sean. I believe you.' That was never the problem. He was never the problem. He was anything but.

'I've noticed you never take yours off either.' Finding her left hand with his right, he slid his fingers through hers.

'Mmm, busted.' She didn't want to remove the wedding ring. It was beautiful, but it was more than that. It was her link to Sean when he wasn't there, whether that was at work, in London or in the next room. Removing it was like giving up and accepting they were over.

'Aye, busted, Mrs Butler. I know, I know... Ms Paradise, but humour me here because there is something so fucking hot about calling you Mrs Butler.'

'I agree.' The whole time she'd doubted her ability to stay with him, Cherry had never been able to stop thinking of Sean as her husband, of herself as Mrs Butler. The hold was too strong.

'Oh, you do?' A cheeky sideways smirk brought the carefree Sean swimming to the surface.

'Mmm, maybe. I kind of like it. But I also like being Cherry Paradise. It's unique. Like me.'

'So you be Cherry Paradise. Far be it that being married to me should rob you of your unique identity. But allow me to think of you as Mrs Butler in here from time to time.' Sean tapped his temple. 'Because I'm not going to lie, it's hot as fuck.'

'Speaking of being hot.' Cherry shivered.

'Aye, it's baltic. Come on, let's get out.' Sean retrieved

her bra, Cherry put it back on, and as he braced her from behind, she climbed up the rocks to dry land.

When they arrived home, a package had arrived addressed to Cherry. She sat at the table, a letter in perfect cursive script open in her hands, surrounded by swathes of colour swatches and a framed photograph her mum had sent – oddly an enlarged version of the one she carried in her locket.

'This looks pos—'

'She's not coming.'

'No? How not?' Still damp from the waterfall, Sean placed a beach towel on the chair opposite her and sat down. He was wearing only shorts, and she recalled the amber beads of soft drink trailing down his chest. There was no competition of what she would rather look at in a contest between him and the letter. Nonetheless, she read the letter out loud.

Dear Cherry,

Thank you for your letter, sweetheart. I am glad to hear you are settling into Kinshore with Sean. I would love to come, but I am afraid I won't be able to travel that far to the Colour my World event. My arthritis is giving me awful gyp, it's a long way to travel, and to be honest, I'm not as good with new people as I used to be. But I will be there in spirit, and

*I am sending my swatches for you to use, as
well as full instructions on how to run an event.
Also enclosed is a photograph. It's the larger
version of your locket one, although you might
wish to change the frame to suit the decor in
your new house.*
*Never give up hope. Things may be okay in
the end.*
Have fun next week.
All my love, Mum. xxx

'I'm sorry, Cher. I know you wanted her to come. But those aren't bad reasons.'

'I know, I know. But...I...' Cherry's voice tightened, raw emotion constricting her. 'I kind of got my hopes up a bit on this one, not going to lie.' To be able to present her small but imperfect family to Sean's was important. And now it wouldn't be happening. Her mum had put her own needs first and left her daughter looking like a motherless child.

'But she sent you the swatches?' Sean fingered the rainbow of samples labelled "Autumn". 'So pretty. I'm sure I'm a November.'

'Yeah, all the swatches for all the seasons and sub-seasons, and about twelve pages of instructions. She says to call her if I need any more guidance, or some woman called Gina Gilhooly, a qualified colourist who lives in Oban.'

Sean sat back in his chair and surveyed it all: the letter, the swatches and the photo. 'I suspect this is her way of saying she cares.'

'I think you're right.'

'And listen, we don't need Gina Gilhooly, but it's good to know she's there as a backup. You can do this. You still want to?'

As resigned as she appeared at her mum not taking up the invitation, Cherry rallied, helped by Sean's positivity.

'Of course.' She watched his thumb on the swatches before forcing out a smile. How could she not when there was that face, shining with his own beautiful brand of optimism? 'It could be fun, and she's gone to the trouble of sending me these, so I should use them.'

'Brilliant. I'll tell you what else you can use.'

'What's that?'

'Me. No pressure, but if you need a sommelier or even a model, then I'm on it, okay?' Sean raised his hand to his forehead like a ship's captain staring out to sea.

'A model?' Cherry laughed.

'What? You don't think I could be a model?'

'Oh, you are model material, Butler. Get you, sitting here topless in these shorts, pretending you don't know what it does to me. But at an event where your mum and sisters and probably some rabid old grannies from the village are going to be present, it would be wrong.'

'Shame. I'd be a good model.'

'Aye, I know. Probably a bit too good. Best you stick to bringing the nibbles.'

Sean rose, leaned over the table, palms flat on the surface, and spoke with a rough twinkle in his voice that could almost certainly induce ovulation.

'That doesn't sound half as clean as you think it does, Paradise.'

Chapter 27

Cherry

'I was not expecting this many people. Or for them to enjoy themselves quite this much,' Cherry confided in Summer during a quiet moment in the kitchen the following Sunday. As quiet as it could get in an open-plan house with at least twenty women and two men in the lounge, clinking wine glasses and chattering animatedly about colour palettes, seasons and silhouettes.

'This could be a new career line for you,' Summer said. 'You could open a boutique in the village and run workshops.' She raised her hand and drew a horizontal line in the way people did when indicating signage. 'Colours by Cherry.'

'With a free glass of ginger wine for every customer,' Cherry joked. It was completely not her but sounded idyllic. It was possible for both to be true at the same time. Most things in Kinshore ticked the idyllic box so far.

'Amanda looks happy,' Summer noted. 'It's lovely for her to have this sort of distraction. Nate said she's been just about hanging on since Jimmy passed.'

'Yes.' Cherry thought Amanda was lucky to have a

supportive network around her. Pam Paradise had found her fulfilment in tarot and Colour my World when her husband died. It gave people contact, but it wasn't the same as friends. If only she had a better relationship with her daughter.

'Right, you're going to have to help me here.' Eilidh bounced over to the kitchen with an empty champagne flute. 'Is it possible to be a different season from your identical triplet sister? Because Cara won't let the winter thing go, and I say we are both summer.'

Cherry refilled Eilidh's glass. 'You guys are definitely both summers; the deep rose did it for me.' It was amazing how much of this stuff she had taken in from her mum, how naturally it came to her. People loved learning which colours suited them best and which style of clothing flattered their body shape.

'Brilliant.' Eilidh tripped off again, but not before declaring, 'It's amazing having a sister-in-law who knows all this stuff.'

A surge of warmth spread through Cherry at the ready acceptance that she was now someone's sister-in-law, the closest she had been to having a sibling at all. To having a family full of love and acceptance. Kinshore was a lovely place to be this evening.

'This has been such a great night,' one of Amanda's friends, Pauline, said as they were getting their coats. Sean had arrived home from a night out with some friends and had already asked everyone what season they were. 'I hope you'll host more, Cherry.'

'Can do if there's an appetite for it,' she said.

Pauline beamed. 'Brilliant! You could do hen do's, baby showers, even an event at the nursing home...'

'Funerals,' Sean added, and Cherry tried not to laugh

too hard.

'I could do,' she said to Pauline. 'Happy to see where the wind blows me.'

'Wonderful. Your children will be colour-coordinated in the best clothes.' Pauline studied the house as if imagining children running about the place wearing matching sailor outfits in the perfect shade of blue.

Cherry swallowed hard. *Deep breath, deep breath. It's a small town, and this comes with the territory. In the grand scheme of things, it's low-level stuff.*

Pauline wouldn't have known the inherent presumption in what she was saying. To her, it was a throwaway comment – Cherry and Sean were a married couple, so the next stop on the journey must be children. Fortunately, as Cherry was pinning a rictus smile to her face, Sean caught the comment like a baseball out of left field.

'Absolutely,' he said to Pauline. '*If* we have them, they will look great.'

It was only a small rejoinder – an emphasis on the *if*, but Pauline noticed, and Cherry wanted to hug Sean into next week for what he'd done. She tucked her hand into his waist to let him know how much his words meant.

Doubtless, it wouldn't be the last time this would happen. This was a reminder of how small this place was, how traditional the ideas of roles were, and it gave a little hint of what village life might be like when her colours didn't match the season of her life. But with Sean by her side, she could try her best to manage.

The day before the poker tournament – the following Friday – Cherry awoke around eight a.m.. She opened the curtains and sat on the side of the bed, checking her phone. There was a message from Campbell.

CAMPBELL: Psyched for the tourney, Chez. I'm staying at Jamie's house with Connor. Let's do that coffee today. I've got a proposition for you.

There was no getting out of this. Campbell's presence was a boon for the tournament, and what harm could a coffee do? She would admit to being both trepidatious and curious about the proposition.

She hit back a reply, arranging to meet him at a local café. Best to keep these things out in the open. She would tell Sean later.

Exhaling and putting the phone aside, Cherry settled her eyes on the photo on the bedside table. The larger version of the one in her locket.

'Hey, Dad,' she whispered, picking up the photo. 'Good to see you. Hope you're keeping busy in the big garden in the sky.'

Cherry's focus shifted to her mother's image: the curve of her smile, the glow of her cheeks, the light in her eyes. All the things she hadn't seen in her locket picture because it was too small. My God, she didn't think she had ever seen her mum as radiant as she was in this photo.

The frame was awful, though – clear plastic moulded and coloured to look like gemstones. She would have to get a new one. Turning it over, she unclasped the latches. But when the frame came off, Cherry saw there was blurred but legible writing on the back of the photo. The familiarity of the words struck her.

A mother is not made by a footprint in the sand.
Love does not begin with a clasping of the hand.
I carried you inside me, your heart beating with mine.
And though I never held you, I'm your mummy for all time.

This was the poem her mum had given to her the last time she'd seen her. She read it again, and there was no stopping the tears that fell from her eyes, thick and fast. Shit. This sort of thing always got her.

But then her blood chilled at a realisation.

Sniffing and rubbing her face urgently, Cherry flipped the photo over.

The first thing that hit her again was how much her mum was glowing – like in no other photos, except maybe the ones when Cherry was born. She had always thought Pam's sadness in later pictures was because of the loss of her husband. But the maths didn't compute. Her mum had been sad long before then.

I always wanted a big family. Some siblings for Cherry. That was what she'd said.

And slowly but surely, realisation dawned on Cherry.

This photo with the poem on the back wasn't an accident. Her mum had put it there very much on purpose. To communicate the facts she couldn't bring herself to say face to face.

The facts that hit Cherry like a juggernaut slamming into her whole body.

'I know what you went through because I went through it myself.'

Chapter 28

Cherry

There was a tangible festival-like energy in the village because of the impending poker tournament – a lightness about the villagers. Even the girl serving in the coffee shop seemed overly excited about taking their order. Then again, that could be related to Cherry's coffee buddy.

Scottish movie star and her ex-boyfriend, Campbell Duff, sat across the table in the pointless disguise of a baseball cap and sunglasses. Given that nobody in a small Scottish village dressed in such a way, especially indoors, all it did was draw attention.

'You'd have been less conspicuous if you'd worn a tartan bunnet and a pair of plus fours.' Cherry noted at least five people staring. 'Given the impression of being an ancient golfer instead of a movie star.'

'The stookie would spoil the ruse.' Campbell indicated the fibreglass cast on his leg – a result of breaking his ankle on set. 'I won't be on the golf course for a while now. Luckily, we'd wrapped most of the filming.'

'That does suck; I'm sorry, Cam. But you'll make it tomorrow, right?'

'I wouldn't miss Scotland's first-ever celebrity pro-am poker tourney. Good on you for organising it.'

'Ah, it was my husband's idea. He wants to raise money for MND charity. His father recently passed away from the disease.'

'That's noble, Cherry.' Campbell fiddled with a sachet of sweetener. 'I was surprised to hear you'd got married so quickly. You were always one to calculate odds and take your time over things.'

'In poker, yes, but not in everything. I believe I told you to give acting in LA a chance. And I calculated the odds very fast when I met Sean.'

'So, he's the one then? It's not a shotgun wedding?'

'Um, yes, he is. And no, it isn't.' Why was Campbell questioning her marriage? The rebuttal was easy to give, but it was none of his business.

'Ah, good.' Campbell thanked the waitress as the coffees were placed on the table. 'Since you guys are apparently solid, I have a proposal for you.' He sipped his flat white and leaned forward conspiratorially. 'How would you like to come to dinner with me at the Balmoral in exchange for £150k to the MND charity?'

Fuck! Who needed coffee when you had a shot like that to the heart?

'Are you serious?' Cherry wished he'd take his stupid sunglasses off so she could see his eyes. '£150k?'

'Aye, serious as a broken ankle. Jamie and Alicia were talking about Jamie's dad and the impact of the illness. It sounds horrendous, and I want to do something to help.'

This was incredibly kind of Campbell, but something about it didn't sit right. It was a bit seedy.

'So why not just make a donation?'

'That's a good point.' He ran his finger round the rim of his cup. 'I like to eat out, I know you're fond of a spot of luxury, and it's a chance to catch up with an old friend. Is that so wrong?'

'I like to eat out?' Fuck's sake.

'Campbell, I'm married now. I can't go fleeing off around the country for dinner with my exes, even if it is for charity.'

'So bring your husband, too. I'm happy to meet him.'

Cherry took a steadying breath. Something reeked of bullshit. 'Let me speak to Sean,' she said. 'The money would be great, but I need him to be okay with this. Things are—'

'Oh, aye – things are what?'

'Nothing. It's important that we're open with one another, that's all.' There was no need to tell Campbell that they had only started finding their feet in the marriage.

'Sure. Let me know tomorrow then.'

Cherry surveyed the coffee shop. She'd be happy to swap this conversation for any of the normal ones these people were having. 'I'm surprised there isn't another woman in the wings for you to go to dinner with,' she said. 'You're still a committed bachelor then?'

'Aye, that's me. I mean, if I met my dream woman then great, but I'm starting to think she isnae out there...' Campbell stared over Cherry's shoulder as if disappointed his dream woman wasn't on Kinshore High Street. She suppressed a smile and opted to soften him a little more.

'You and Shanola Smith seemed like you had a good thing going on for a while.'

'Och, Shanola is great, but she wanted a family, which she has now.' Campbell shrugged, and Cherry heard a faltering in his voice, which gave her a subtle in-road. She pushed her chair closer to the table and lowered her voice. 'Cam, this is probably not the place to ask you this, but you know when we were dating and how we used to have "Russian Roulette" sex?'

Campbell's face lit up, and he finally took off his sunglasses and pushed his own chair in, too.

'Hardly going to forget it, sweetheart.'

'And how I was late with my period a few weeks but then it came?'

'Um, aye, in Sun City, wasn't it?' He leaned back a little as if remembering the sex.

'Yes... I'm sorry to pry, but did you ever have anything like that happen with anyone else?'

'Not sure this is the place to be having this conversation.' Campbell recced the coffee shop. People were almost taking it in shifts to peer at them, but no one appeared to have a phone out. You never could tell, though. He turned back to Cherry and, despite talking in code, put his hand on his chin to hide his mouth.

'I never played Russian Roulette with anyone else. Never wanted to get into that level of debt again.'

'I see.' Cherry had been half hoping that Campbell had found himself in that position again, only in as much as it might indicate that her body was not the issue. Grant her some peace of mind. But it didn't look like she would be getting that here.

'Are you sure everything is hunky-dory?' Campbell seemed to get what she was talking about, as well as assuming a little beyond this. 'If you ever need any money for medical stuff or whatever, let me know.'

'We're fine, Cam. Just fine.' Cherry hated having to ask Campbell about this at all, and she certainly wouldn't be taking any money from him for 'medical things'. 'So, tell me about this golf rom com you've been filming. I'm curious as to how you make golf sexy.'

'This is it, sweetheart.' Campbell grinned and made some *Vogue* dance moves around his face. '*This* is how you make golf sexy.'

Thank goodness the man was easily distracted. Cherry had asked her awkward question, and now they could move on.

Chapter 29

Sean

Sean stood at the lounge window and contemplated the dark clouds lurking ominously over the water. You couldn't have as much sunshine as they'd been having of late without a storm as payoff. The surf forecast was pretty gnarly – waves up to six feet. Once he'd shown his face at today's poker tournament, the beach was his first stop. He'd take his chances on lightning and thunder for the reckless thrill of those waves.

Speaking of taking chances and reckless thrills, the poker tournament was the deadline that had been circled in red ink in his mind for the past two months. The day his wife could walk away, having done what he'd asked her to do.

But now... Now things were different. Cherry was settling, agreeing to give things a shot, accepting at last that they belonged together. They slept all night in her bed and spent time together curled up on the sofa watching movies, ate meals together, drank beer and wine and laughed a lot. And her bags weren't packed to leave after the tournament.

They hadn't discussed Tennessee and her future in the poker world, but they had agreed they would after today.

Sean turned at the creaking of the stairs.

And there she was, stealing the breath from his lungs as always. The solidity from his legs. Giving him so much to be thankful for. The future was luminescent, like his wife. Although, there was something more understated about Cherry today. A short black skirt still showed her tanned legs, but she wore a long-sleeved white blouse, and her face was make-up free. She radiated a natural glow, and it would take a strong man to look away.

Sean's thumb traced the inside of his wedding ring, as if to assure himself it was real. He smiled at her.

'Morning. I made you a coffee. It's on the side.'

Coffee in hand, she came over and leaned into him. He swung his arm around her. God, it felt good to do this.

Soft cobalt eyes framed by vulnerable lashes met his. 'Thank you. I need this today.'

'You okay? You seem a bit on edge.'

'Just a bit nervous. I want to do you and your dad proud. I know this sounds daft, given that I never met him, but I sense his presence.'

'You do?' Jesus! What was she doing, telling him this at 8 a.m.? It was enough to give him a breakdown before the day had begun. His dad had been right there with him since he'd woken up, and now it was like the three of them were standing in the room together. Jimmy clapping Sean on the back and telling him he was proud of the man he'd become.

'I hope that's not a ridiculous thing to say, or cheeky, seeing as I never knew him, but I've heard so much about him. And there is so much love for him in this house. In here.' She placed her palm over Sean's heart, causing him to bite down hard on his inner lip. If he got emotional today, he might never stop, like the rain hammering down outside. It was going to be one of those on-the-edge type of days.

'That means a lot, Cher. It's not cheeky. You feel what you feel. Dad was a powerful presence.' He could see his father chuckling proudly at him, at how far gone he was for Cherry. Because, far from it being a weakness, his father saw being in love with a strong woman as an achievement in life.

'A powerful presence, like his son,' Cherry said, palm warm through his shirt.

And there she was, lassoing his heart with her words. He pulled her into an embrace, arms across her chest, so they were both gazing out to the beach. In silence he held her, always wanting it to feel like this. Like she was his to love and protect. Cherry might be an independent fire-cracker of a woman, but she needed him. He knew that.

'Sean, listen.' Foreboding laced Cherry's imperative, like when his mum was about to tell him that an old person she knew had died.

'Mmm,' he mumbled into her hair. 'I'm listening.'

'Connor is confirmed for the tourney today. There's no clause in his advertising contract that says he can't be seen gambling at the distillery.'

'Great. He's a massive name. Thanks for getting him on board, Cher. It's going to mean a big deal for the charity.'

'Och, it was mainly Alicia. There is one other thing I have to tell you.'

He wished he could see her face to check for a sign of what was going on. 'Aye? You alright?'

'I'm fine. It's Campbell Duff.'

'What about him? He's not dead, is he?'

Cherry laughed. 'No, he's not dead. I didn't tell you this yesterday because I wasn't sure how to broach it, but when I met him, he said he wants to take us out to dinner after the tourney, in exchange for money to the MND charity.'

Sean broke from her, and she turned to face him. He was aware he wasn't exactly radiating happiness, but he needed to hear more about this.

'It's in Edinburgh, at the Balmoral,' she said, clearly knowing this add-on was not going to soften the blow.

'The Balmoral?' *Of course.* 'Is he flying you there in his helicopter?'

'Yeah, that's the idea. But he's invited you, too.'

Sean laughed, but it was hollow and mirthless. 'The fuck he wants me there. And the fuck I am going.'

Cherry moved so that her back was to the window and she faced him, a little tense, as if she was about to reveal the kicker. 'The thing is, the amount he's willing to pay is £150k.'

'Aye, right. You believe that?'

'Yes, I do. He's honourable when he needs to be.'

'When he needs to be. Like when he wants something.' Sean moved to walk away then spun back almost immediately. 'Cherry, this is all manner of fucked-up. I've spent the last two months being pulled through the wringer and back again by my wife, who maybe did but probably didn't, but actually did, want to be my wife. Yes, it was my choice, and yes, I want to raise money, but I have to draw the line somewhere. Not even for a million quid to the charity am I flying to Edinburgh in that guy's helicopter so he can wish I wasn't there while he takes my wife out to dinner.'

Cherry nodded her understanding. 'I get it. But do you want *me* to go? It's a lot of money.'

'You know the answer to that question.' She knew. She had to know.

'Alright, good.' Cherry visibly loosened. 'I'm actually

quite relieved. If you'd said you were happy for me to do it, I would have gone, but it wouldn't feel right.'

Sean went to her, still recovering from the half heart attack he'd had for nothing. 'Cherry, if you don't want to do a thing like that, then you don't do it, end of story.' He tipped her chin up to meet him. 'The tournament is enough. Duff Campbell can find another dinner date or cry into his expensive soup alone.'

'Campbell Duff.'

'Aye, I know.' He examined her. 'Let him spend as much money as he likes on the tourney and the raffle and whatever, but don't do something you're not comfortable with. It's not what my dad would have wanted, and it's definitely not what I want.'

The main function room in the distillery, where Sean had often thought his wedding reception would be held, was doubling as the casino. If his dad's presence was powerful in the house, it was cask strength here – in the business he fortified and gave the oak-solid reputation it boasted today.

Round tables draped in green baize were arranged across the polished wooden floor as if for a function with an edge. Stacks of coloured poker chips sat in neat towers next to illuminated brass lamps, and decks of cards still in cellophane lay ready to be unwrapped. Locals Sean had known all his life were dressed in the customary white shirts, waistcoats and bow ties of croupiers. Cherry had outdone herself here.

And there was no casino in the world with a backdrop like this one. Ceiling-to-floor windows proudly framed the craggy Kintyre coastline. The churning waters of the sound stretched out to where smokey clouds hung perilously low, bruising the horizon.

A storm was on the way.

By mid-morning, people were filtering in and filling the space. Locals arrived bubbling with excitement. The most action this wee village got was when someone got married. There had never been a poker tournament where members of the public would mingle with celebrities.

Two Hollywood stars, no less.

Less recognisable were the poker players, whom Sean identified by the way they greeted Cherry. Hugs were shared, handshakes given, laughs filling the air. Gone was the vulnerable Cherry he'd embraced this morning. She was back to the glittering, vibrant scene-stealer. The worst was over. She was settling and letting herself be happy in Kinshore.

Some familiar faces arrived: snooker players, reality TV personalities, DJs, Scottish TV presenters and soap stars. The latter were courtesy of his actress sister, Cara, who was now getting smaller roles in movies. She lived between Edinburgh and her latest filming location, but came home to Kinshore as often as possible.

'Did I do well?' Cara swept her hand out as if to present the band of players to her brother.

'Of course, Car'. You did incredible. You're playing, right?'

'Absolutely. Wouldn't miss it for the world. Can you remind me what's better, a straight flush or four of a kind?'

Sean grinned. 'Straight flush. Want me to sit with you and keep you right? It's a free service.'

'No, thank you. I'd rather lose than be that lame. Who else is coming?' Cara scanned the room like security detail, not anything out of the ordinary for someone who liked to keep her finger on the gossip pulse. But Sean had his suspicions about what was on her mind.

'He's been staying with Jamie and Alicia, so he'll be here.' He eyed his sister with amusement. She and Alicia's brother, Connor, had met at family occasions a handful of times. The energy between them was tangible.

Cara was sharp, and she caught her brother's undertone straight away.

'I'm sure *Mambo Number Five* can get here fine. Don't go making drama where there is none, little brother.'

'*Mambo Number Five*? And I think you'll find I'm your big brother.'

'What fiancé number is he on now? Four? And you're older by a mere scraping of days, therefore the eldest is whoever acts more mature, and that's definitely not you.'

Sean laughed. 'If you say so. I never actually mentioned Connor's name, but I believe he's single and bringing his pal, Campbell Duff, with him.'

'So there's going to be two massive egos cutting about the place.'

'I'm sure you can put them in their place – wherever you decide that might be. Take it easy on Connor, though.' Sean gave his sister a playful nudge. 'I think he likes you.'

Cara's mouth dropped open. 'What? He does not?' She looked away and then back on a beat. 'Does he?'

He laughed. 'Dunno, but made you look. Actually, I think he does.'

'Oh.' Shock muted Cara as she processed this idea, drinking it in, letting it settle. 'Oh.'

Sean smiled. It was nice to focus on someone else's love life instead of his own.

· · ·

It wasn't long until the Hollywood cavalry arrived in the form of Connor and Campbell – last and, of course, the biggest draw. The men had presence; Sean would give them that. Even dressed casually in jeans and button-down shackets, they were unmistakably movie stars. Although, the jury was out on whether sunglasses indoors on a stormy day before the poker had started didn't just scream 'wanker'.

And Campbell had gone one better with a broken leg accessorised with black carbon-fibre-effect crutches to add an accidental stylishness to his look.

Sean steeled himself for watching his wife interacting with her movie star ex. Not any old movie star either. Hollywood's hottest eternal bachelor. Sean didn't do jealousy, but given the dinner proposal, he would be watching closely.

'Hey, hey, Seany!' Connor Donoghue, the brother of Jamie's fiancée, Alicia, bounded into Sean's vision – although the man commanded attention from across the room by merely breathing. Some mistook it for arrogance, but Sean knew better. He'd met Connor enough times to see that his presence came from a natural, grounded confidence borne of growing up in Hollywood acting royalty. The glitzy Donoghue family made the Butlers look like the Waltons.

'Alright, Connor. Thanks for coming. I appreciate your support. It's raised the profile hugely.'

'Wouldn't miss it, bro. Any excuse to come to Kinshore and see my sister and my favourite second family. Also, I hear there's a chance to win a cask of whisky; that's mighty generous of Jamie.'

As Sean was about to confirm this, Cherry sidled up, with hobble-along Campbell Duff leaning into his designer crutches for all he was worth.

'Sean, this is Campbell,' Cherry announced, meeting Sean's eye long enough for him to see she was valiantly trying to mask nerves. 'Campbell, this is Sean, my husband.'

Sean held out his hand and, after making an exaggerated fuss about what to do with his crutches, Campbell shook it, his handshake surprisingly firm.

'What happened to your leg?' Sean thought he ought to ask, although he didn't especially want to know.

'Och, I lost control of my golf cart. Filming a rom com, of all things.'

Sean's urge to laugh kicked in hard, but he noticed Campbell was deadly serious.

'Really?'

'Aye, I drove it into a bunker during a wee chase scene,' Campbell drawled, his accent adrift on the Atlantic somewhere between Glasgow and Chicago.

'Oh, right. Sorry to hear that.'

'Aye, I do all my own stunts, you see.'

'I see. Maybe best you don't. Was everyone else okay?'

'Och, aye, the extra playing my caddy got knocked over, but he got away with a few wee cuts and grazes.'

Sean found it amusing that Campbell kept over-seasoning his speech with Scottish words like 'och', 'aye' and 'wee' as if he needed to prove his Scottish nationality after spending so long in the States. He probably had a trenchant opinion on Scottish independence, too, despite not living here.

'I hope you heal well and are better soon. I'm sure the Scottish air will help.'

'Aye, that and I'll drop in for some of my maw's food. Thanks, big man.'

This parting shot made Sean grind his molars. 'Big man'

might be a Scottish term of endearment, but he and Camp-bell were not on that footing, and Campbell was not the salt-of- the-earth Glaswegian he was playing here. Plus, his ex was Sean's wife. The overfamiliarity curdled in Sean's gut.

'Sooo… You married Cherry?' Campbell posed a point-less rhetorical question. Which would be fine if he hadn't followed it with: 'Congratulations. Never thought I'd see the day when "Gangsta" Paradise settles down.'

Cherry visibly tensed at being talked about as if she weren't here.

'Settling comes to us all eventually,' Sean said, 'like wrinkles and saggy balls.'

'Ach, not to me, pal. Wrinkle-free, perky-balled bach-elor 'til I die.' Campbell winked firmly and pointed to the side of his eye as if to show that there were no crow's feet on him. 'Some of us aren't made for the mundane life. Variety and action for me, like in my movies.'

'I see. Well, some of us get that variety and action in our married lives.'

It was hard to miss Cherry's disapproving glare, which Sean fully understood – veiled comments about their sex life weren't called for here – but surely he'd earned the right to prod this man a little.

'I can well believe it,' Campbell said in another inappro-priate turn. 'I expect you won't mind a night off that action. Enjoy the care home ceilidh, or whatever counts for enter-tainment around here, while I take your wife to dinner in the big bad city. All platonic and for charity, of course.'

What the actual…? Surely Cherry had told him this was not happening. But for Sean to demur this second very public invitation would be churlish – even if he evidently wasn't being asked to join them this time, because he'd be busy at the "care home ceilidh".

Turning to Cherry, he saw the faltering in her eyes. Campbell had caught her off guard, too. Sean softened his expression, letting her know she didn't have to do this – the extra money wasn't important.

'It's very generous of you, Campbell,' Sean said, 'but we couldn't ask you to donate all that money. It's too much. Your presence here is enough.' That would hopefully keep him quiet.

But Campbell was one step ahead.

'Och, that's a shame. The charity will be disappointed. I called them, you see, and had a good chat about what that money could do. An awful lot, as it turns out. They're very excited.'

You gallus wee fucker. Sean was furious at being backed into a corner like this, but he would not put Cherry in a compromising position, no matter whether Campbell had talked to the charity or not.

'I'm sorry, Campbell,' he began.

But Cherry cut in.

'Maybe we need to rethink, Seany? It's super generous of Campbell. And the charity would really benefit from that money. Think of all the lives it could help – people like your dad.' She smiled a little too sweetly.

'Aye, such a good cause, such a good cause.' Campbell nodded reverently. 'Motor Neurone Disease ravages so many lives. So sorry about your father. I enjoy a wee dram of his whisky.'

Sean was at sixes and sevens. First there was Cherry pretending she was up for this, and then his dad thrown into the mix by Campbell.

Dad, if you're up there, make this shit be over, for the love of God.

He took Cherry to the side and spoke to her in hushed tones. 'Cher, you said you didn't want to go to dinner. What's going on?'

'I know.' She stood on her tiptoes and adjusted the collar of his shirt in a way that was far too sexy for optimum concentration levels. 'But I won't let that amount of money go by, not when I know how much it means to you. You get that, right?'

'Aye.' What else could he say? Well, probably a lot if she hadn't been working her fingers over his collar like she was about to undress him.

'By all means, press for more, though.' Cherry winked a heavily mascaraed, glittering eye at him.

Fuck. How can one eye be so seductive? But she has a point.

Sean turned to Campbell, the words spilling out of his mouth before he could stop them. 'How much was it again?' he asked. '£500K?'

Campbell laughed, but Sean held fast to gravitas. He had one chance, and he would not back down. If this man wanted to fly his wife to Edinburgh in a helicopter, and she was willing, he could cough up to charity. Big style.

'Aye, okay, you could be right.' Campbell leaned on his crutch and appeared to think. 'Maybe I did say £500k. And you and Cherry can take a bit off that for yourselves. You know, for "painting the nursery" or whatever.' He nodded sagely at Sean as if they were sharing some sort of secret.

What the actual fuck?

"Painting the nursery"? What the hell had Cherry said to him? It sounded very much like she'd told him about their marriage hanging in the balance. Quite how much she'd revealed was uncertain, but Sean already knew it was too much. Even when he'd spoken to Jamie, he at least tried to keep things as coded as possible. And Jamie was his brother; he could be trusted, implicitly.

'We're fine, thanks, Campbell. But I'm sure the charity will appreciate the money. I don't see why you shouldn't go out for dinner with Cherry, as long as Cherry's fine with it.' He could barely look at her, so seeing her flying off in a helicopter might be a good thing. 'I would come, but old Agnes Anderson has me booked for the Gay Gordons at the care home every Friday night.' Sean hoped Cherry noticed he hadn't called her 'my wife'. He was not in the mood. The money for charity would be good – he'd be a fool not to take it – but it felt weirdly like she'd been spilling about their private life to Campbell, who seemed completely indiscreet.

He caught her eye and, funnily enough, she tried to smile, but she would not be getting one back from him after that.

'Now we've got that sorted, I think I need a drink.' Oblivious to the tension he'd caused, Campbell scanned the room. For him, being half a million quid lighter was like a normal person emptying their pocket of a spare tissue. 'Where can I get a whisky sour around here? Can Jamie get one for me? Jamie!' Campbell raised his arm like he was calling a waiter, and Jamie, who was standing near the bar, saw but simply waved in return.

Sean leashed back the amusement that threatened to burst out. Campbell and Connor were staying at Jamie's house, so Jamie would have the measure of him.

'Jamie's not here to wait on us, bud,' Connor interjected. 'Plus, you're already off your chops on pain meds, so

I don't think a drink is a good idea if you want to get past the first table. And lunchtime.'

'That is a fair point,' Campbell conceded.

At least Connor seemed to have him under control, and perhaps Campbell's terrible judgement could in part be explained by pain medication.

As for Cherry, he wondered what her excuse was.

Chapter 30

Cherry

Sean was furious with Cherry, and she knew exactly why. It wasn't the dinner with Campbell. She's persuaded him on that front. No, he was furious with her because Campbell had intimated that she'd been chatting about their personal life to him.

And she could see exactly why it looked that way. She would need to talk to him later and tell him exactly what had gone down, that Campbell had read between the lines of barely any information on her part.

Campbell could stick his dinner. Although, she'd need to find another way to get the money to the charity.

One thing to be pleased about was the tournament turnout. Over one hundred players were in the distillery. From the sidelines, scores of Kinshore locals watched, alongside photographers from poker publications and local newspapers. Freelance paparazzi and social media influencers were clamouring outside to get snaps of Connor, Campbell and Cara. It was priceless publicity for the charity.

But as she sat at her table with a mixture of locals and

professionals, Cherry was struggling to think of much except Sean. He was chatting animatedly with his table buddies. She willed him to look at her.

It took some time, but as the table hushed for play to begin, for the briefest of moments, their eyes met and emerald flint bored into her. Then he bent his head down. No smile. No nod. Nothing.

Cherry let out a ragged breath. Okay, she'd played on tilt plenty of times. Gone to the table upset and compartmentalised. Why did this feel so different? Why was this like the entire world, not only the room, was tilting under her?

The dealer – a local man called Gordon – dealt the first hand, but Cherry could barely look at her cards, never mind consider how to play them. For the first twenty minutes, she was on autopilot, folding numerous hands, even those she might normally call or raise on, and then she started over-compensating and calling without thought. All she could think about was Sean.

He appeared to be completely focused on his game as if, by giving it his full attention, he was punishing her. But, like someone doling out a physical lashing, she could see the tension in the way he held himself. He hated this, too. Had to.

It broke her heart. He'd given her so much, and now he thought she'd betrayed him.

As she was folding another unremarkable hand, Jamie's voice cut through the speaker system. 'Sean Butler and Campbell Duff to Table Three.'

Table Three. That was her table. Sean and Campbell were being reallocated to her table.

Cherry watched them approach, Campbell hobbling across the room on his crutches, supposedly oblivious to being watched, Sean more interested in greeting some locals on the way and updating them on how he was getting on.

As they converged, Campbell nudged Sean. 'Alright, pal. Looking forward to this.'

Cherry cringed, but an unflustered Sean took a seat with no more than a nod and an 'aye' in response.

Folding her fingers together, Cherry rested her chin on her hands, watching her husband settle into the table, smoothly stacking his chips with those beautiful strong hands. For a moment, his eyes glanced over hers but not long enough for anything to be said. They were strangers here. This was the side of him she'd seen during the poker game at the cooperage, and it was strong.

Tenacious. Focused. Determined.

Cherry kept her composure. She could do this. She'd been here a thousand times before with tenacious players.

But not when the tenacious player was her pissed-off husband.

Campbell sipped his whisky as if he were sitting on top of a mountain being filmed for an ad. Cherry tried not to let it distract her.

Come on. Focus. Win.

But she couldn't care less about winning the tournament, or even this table. All she wanted was Sean.

Out of the tournament, Cara came over to the table. 'Why so serious, Seany?'

'Just concentrating, Car'. Try it.' He at least gave his sister a smile.

'How's it going, Cara?' Cherry asked her sister-in-law.

'I'm loving this event,' Cara said. 'You excited about winning?'

Cherry smiled and shrugged. 'It's anyone's game.'

'I think we know it's your game,' Campbell said. 'But don't take it for granted, Chez.'

This got a flick of the eyes from Sean to Campbell. Cherry shifted in her seat. Campbell calling her by a random nickname from a decade ago was not great when Sean was at the table.

Not that Campbell noticed. For a man who made a living by pretending to be other people, he was disarmingly oblivious to the human psyche today.

As they played, Cherry found her rhythm again. She won a few small pots, boosting her own confidence. Her focus wasn't where it normally was, but for a celeb pro-am tourney, it was possibly enough. She took in her latest hand. Jack and ten of spades. Not great but not awful.

Everyone called, and the flop came down as the king of diamonds, queen of clubs and queen of spades. A board abundant with the promise of a straight or even a flush for Cherry.

She checked to keep the action moving. She had a heavy suspicion that, with Campbell in the game, a raise here was not necessary. He would do all the work on that front.

And she was right. He shoved a heavy stack of chips forward without hesitation. Possibly, he had a king or a queen, or even pocket queens or kings, giving four of a kind or a full house. Or he was he bluffing hard, like he used to do.

Smoothly, Sean called, his eyes never leaving Campbell. He could also have big pairs.

And seeing him win with those was infinitely preferable to seeing Campbell rake in the chips.

Everyone else folded and Cherry called the bet.

The turn brought the six of hearts.

'All in,' Campbell said after a brief pause, pushing his stack forward with the smirk of a man who was certain he was the winner here. What the hell had the six brought him? Did he have pocket sixes and now a full house?

Cherry thought for a while. She could keep playing in the hope that a nine or an ace came up to give her that straight. Or she could fold and let the two men rough this out. They both seemed so confident. One of them could very well have a big hand.

She folded. Watching this play out could be enjoyable.

Sean barely blinked before calling. She dearly hoped he wasn't bluffing because Campbell as a gloating winner was not something she wanted to witness.

The river brought another six. Clubs this time.

Campbell, with a solemn expression, turned over the King of clubs and King of spades. 'Full house, baby.' He leaned back in his seat like he was the king of the world.

But then Sean flipped up his cards, and everything changed. Oh, thank God.

He had pocket sixes.

Which meant he had four sixes. The two on the board and the two in his hand. Four of a kind. Beating a full house and, more importantly, beating Campbell.

Yes, yes, yes. You beautiful man!

Campbell's grin faltered as he realised his monster hand was nothing more than a butterfly.

Cherry could have jumped up and kissed Sean. But, unlike the day he'd won at Swingball, her husband was all composure and restraint. Calmly, he slid the mountain of chips to his side of the table, like he knew he deserved this win but would not be making a song and dance about it.

In contrast, trying to mask his bruised ego, Campbell shifted in his seat. 'Nice hand, big man.'

'Thanks, Pal.' Sean's retort was quick, and Cherry could swear he was suppressing amusement. She almost laughed out loud. He'd handed Campbell his arse on a plate, and for that she was so proud.

'Ach, well, now that I can get lashed, I'm going to get a drink.' Campbell stood up, scanning the room. 'We're still on for that dinner, aye?' He placed his hand on Cherry's shoulder.

She spoke stiffly. 'I'll talk to you after.'

Briefly, Sean glanced at her, before turning back to his chips. He obviously didn't know that she meant giving Campbell a piece of her mind. After the game, she would need to find him and explain.

It was Sean and Cherry left on the table now, but Jamie didn't make the call for them to sit at other tables. Heads-up it was.

Cherry's hand was queen-jack suited. Spades again. She slid some chips into the centre of the table and tried not to be too distracted by her smouldering husband opposite her, chewing his lip and examining his cards.

She'd seen him chew his lip like that before, been stopped dead by it at home. He did it when he was looking in the fridge, staring out the window deciding whether the surf was decent, examining the sky for clouds to see if his bike ride would be rained on. She'd even watched him do it this morning as she'd come down the stairs. He was contemplating. Uncertain.

Which probably meant his cards weren't a dead cert.

But he pushed in a pile of chips, raising her. Like some

kind of metaphor for their marriage. Raise big, even if you don't know what the cards hold.

Playing poker, not metaphors, Cherry called. The flop of the jack of diamonds, eight of hearts and three of clubs gave her a pair of jacks – decent, but nothing spectacular. Although playing against amateurs, it could be enough.

But Sean raised again, inviting her to do the same. Why had he been so worried before the flop? Was it a bluff to confuse her?

She called.

The turn of the five of spades put nothing definitive on the board. Again, Sean raised, so she called once more. He could have a pocket pair, giving him three of a kind. He was raising with such confidence.

The river was the two of clubs, and Sean went all in. There was a strong possibility that he had a straight now, aces low.

Either that, or there was something else going on here. She hadn't known Sean long, but she knew some things about him. About his heart. About how much he was prepared to give to her, but also that he had a limit. This behaviour was a strange mix of both.

She called and flipped over her queen and jack pair.

Sean did the same to reveal a nine of diamonds and a six of clubs. No straight. Just a hardcore bluff from the start. Like he was quite prepared to hand the game to her if it made a point.

Gordon slid the winning stack of chips across the table to Cherry.

Sean stood up, gave Gordon a friendly clap on the back. 'Cheers, Gordy.' He pushed his chair in, walked round to Cherry's seat. Standing behind her, he leaned in and spoke into her ear, his breath warm and soft. 'Well played,

Paradise.' Tenderly, he kissed her on the cheek, stubble bristling assuredly over her skin, sending a shiver through her soul.

And then he walked away. His words holding no weight whatsoever. She hadn't played well at all. He'd given the game to her like he was all out of fucks. Let her take it but shown her what she'd lost in the process.

The one thing that mattered more than anything else.

Him.

Two hours later, and out of the tournament herself, Cherry looked around the room for Sean but found only Campbell.

'Commiserations, Chez. That was a bad beat you had there.'

Cherry couldn't care less about the bad beat.

'Gives you more time to get your bags packed for Edinburgh,' Campbell added. 'I can have the helicopter ready to leave, whenever you are.'

'I'm not coming to Edinburgh, Campbell.'

'Ah. Problem?'

'Yes. I'm not doing this to Sean.'

'Doing what? He said he was fine with it.'

'Of course he bloody said that. You left him no choice. I would have thought that a sensitive actor such as yourself would be able to read the body language to see that neither of us were comfortable with the situation. Also, that comment about painting the nursery. Seriously! Our conversation the other day was in confidence.'

Campbell straighted on his crutches. 'Och, sorry. It won't mean anything to anyone. And I meant it about the money – and when I said his dad's whisky is awesome.'

'Well, it meant something to Sean, and he's fuming. I

honestly think the least you can do is pay the amount you said you would to the charity. That's five hundred, by the way.'

'So, you are coming to dinner?'

'No. I'm not. I'm going home with my husband. Don't worry, you can make the donation public. Think how good it will be for your image. Who knows, it might even put you on the map to be the next face of Butler's. But I'm not coming with you tonight. This isn't some movie. It's my life – my marriage – and it matters to me.'

Campbell puffed and nodded. 'Alright then. You always did know how to wind me round your finger. I'll make the donation and see if there's anyone nice here who wants to come to dinner instead.'

Cherry resisted the temptation to suggest he seek out Shona and Elaine. Instead, she gave her attention to finding Sean. But there was no sign. There hadn't been for some time now. One of the reasons she'd busted out was because her focus was divided between the game and where her husband was. Every time she lifted her head, he was nowhere to be seen.

A bolt of lightning – white and razor sharp – cut across the sky outside, followed by the loaded rumble of thunder.

Where was he?

Amidst a media frenzy for her attention, Cherry posed for some photographs, forcing happiness onto her face.

Give them soundbites, say things about the charity, present the right image. It's all about image.

But her mind was on Sean. Where was he? Where was her husband?

'What made you decide to organise a charity poker tournament for MND fundraising?'

'Do you plan to do anything else to raise funds for MND?'

'I believe you used to date Campbell Duff? Is there tension with your ex and new husband being in the same room?'

Where is Sean? Where is Sean? Where is Sean?

Cherry answered the questions as politely as she could. And when she got away, the rain now thundering down outside, she found Jamie.

'Jamie, where's Sean?'

'I'm not sure.' Jamie checked the room once, then back again, the second time his eyes settling on the window. He paused, and Cherry watched as something changed on his face. A darkening in his eyes.

'What?'

'Fuck!' Jamie swept his hand through his hair. 'He wouldn't.'

Cherry didn't know what Jamie was getting at, but her first thought was that Sean – never one to walk away from a challenge – probably would. She followed Jamie's eye line to the window. To the rain teeming down, to the dark smoky skies, to the enormous waves churning into the shoreline far in the distance.

Huge, gnarly waves.

Surf that was going off.

Storm of the year.

He wouldn't.

But Cherry knew he would.

She turned to Jamie.

'He's gone surfing, hasn't he? He's actually gone surfing in this fucking weather.'

Jamie nodded. 'Aye.' He thought for a moment, pressed

his tongue into his cheek and took a deep breath. 'Shit. Right, come on. I'll drive.'

Chapter 31

Sean

It wasn't the first time Sean had surfed in conditions like this. But it was the first time he'd done it with a storm going on inside him to match the weather.

The first time with a helicopter rising up in the distance possibly carrying his wife and her movie star ex.

She hadn't cheated on him and wouldn't. He knew she wasn't interested in Campbell. But Cherry had betrayed him in a different way. She had told Campbell about their private life. The man knew way more than he should.

All these weeks of mining his soul for strength to deal with Cherry's trauma on top of the grief over his dad, of grafting to show her that she was all that mattered, that he would be her concrete foundation when she felt like she was standing on sand.

Apparently, it meant nothing. Sean was just a slot machine that kept on spitting out the jackpot.

He was done. Done with suppressing his own needs for her to have her act like he was an emotional blow-up doll who would bounce back up again with a stupid grin on his face.

He'd respected her every inch of the way. And not been granted anything of the sort in return.

Sean paddled hard. The rain was battering the sea, battering his skin. Doing this without a wetsuit was the stupidest idea, but straight thinking wasn't on the table anymore.

What was on the table? Forgetting Cherry, that was what.

Paddling harder. Away from her, away from Kinshore, away from the grief and the pain of everything he'd lost and was about to lose.

The waves were wild. Huge, seven-foot bastards. You didn't mess with waves like these.

But Sean wasn't here to mess about. He was here to surf. To do the only thing that reliably gave him unabated satisfaction.

In only board shorts and a rash vest, his skin was already raw from the cold water and the pounding rain. There was a strange pleasure in the pain. He realised that this was what he did. Put himself in stupid positions like this, laid himself open to the danger in the hope of an adrenaline payoff.

It was exactly what he'd done with Cherry.

Except, with her, the adrenaline had come first. And he'd been stupid enough not to realise how hard the pain was going to hit when it did. Marrying someone on a whim wasn't like moving to London or buying a house. It was so much more. Why was he arrogant enough to think that it would work out? She was a professional emotional athlete. He was a giant blazing heart on a humongous fucking sleeve. All his life, he'd been warned about getting ahead of himself. Like his teachers had told him at school, and like his dad had said every second day during Sean's teenage years, he only had himself to blame.

'*Calm doon, son.*'

After this surf, Dad. I need this one to calm me down.

One more wave, and he was out the back, ready to pivot that board, to paddle until his arms burned and use every muscle he had to keep himself standing while he rode that wave to wherever it went.

It wasn't a death wish, but Sean was happy to be taken on a ride where he didn't have to think about anything anymore.

Didn't have to think about Cherry.

About how much he loved her.

Wild, untameable Paradise.

He saw it when it was two hundred metres away. The swell. It was his. No one else was out here. His wave. His ride home. Or to nowhere. Who cared?

Sean paddled like the devil was on his back, emptied his mind of anything but getting onto the enormous dark belter rising behind him. Growling at him to get going.

And then Mother Nature was cresting beneath his board and hammering down from above. You didn't take anything for granted out here. She was a punishing matriarch, and you worked for every second you were on that board, earned every ounce of exhilaration storming through your bloodstream. If you wanted the headlong rush of surfing waves like this, you'd better take it seriously, because if you went down, you would know who was in charge and it wouldn't be you.

Sean respected the fickle nature of Mother Nature, especially the Scottish version. You didn't pick a fight with a Scottish maw.

The cold of the water was bracing, the recent hot

temperatures a far-off memory. That version of Kinshore was a different world. Gone were garden sprinklers, sun-scorched roses and clear blue skies. Today was an iron sea, steel grey clouds and a mood like a torn-up Ace of Spades.

Knee deep in the shallows, the first ride over, Sean turned his back to the village and waded out to sea, primed to go again – the gargantuan breakers beckoning him back with their curled fists, saying, 'Come and have another go, Seany. We promise it'll be worth it.'

He didn't doubt them for a second. It was always worth it. Since he'd first stood up on a surfboard, his dad and older brothers cheering him on, Sean had lived for the rush of it. Surfing wasn't easy, but nothing good ever was.

Like his wife.

Out the back again, rain hammering like nails onto the petrol blue surface of the sea, so dark and deep, he identified the next wave from its incipient swell and, turning his board, paddled again.

'*Come on, Sean. Paddle, paddle, paddle.*' His dad's voice was right by his side, straight out of his eight-year-old's memory bank.

'I got it, Dad. I'm good, I'm good... I'm the fucking wave master.' Except he hadn't sworn in front of his dad because that would have landed him in serious trouble.

Like they understood one another perfectly, in completely synchronicity as if it were all choreographed beforehand, Sean's board caught the peak of the wave, he jumped up and wave and man were as one, tearing away from the deep, dark waters of the sound and into shore.

Into Kinshore.

And, as it happened, to Cherry waiting on the sand with a face so distressed that he wondered if someone had died. Was it him? Had he drowned out there and was watching all this from the afterlife? Watching her grieving his loss?

He slapped his face.

Cherry, shivering in the rain in a Butler's Whisky cagoule she must have got from the distillery shop, shot him an expression that said, 'Have you lost the plot?'

Okay, he was alive. He didn't bother to explain, didn't owe her anything.

'Sean, what're you doing out there? There's a mad-arse storm.'

Ah, she *was* worried about him.

'Aye, I know. I've been surfing it. Fucking incredible. Why aren't you in the helicopter?' He motioned to the sky with his chin.

She ignored the question. 'I didn't know where you'd gone. We were worried about you.'

'We?' Surely not her and Campbell fucking Duff.

'Yes, me and Jamie. And the others.' She glanced back up the beach to where Jamie was standing, giving them space but no doubt wondering if everything was okay. Sean gave his brother a salute that told him he was good to leave, before Cherry drew him back.

'Jamie said you're fucking mental to go out there in weather like this.'

Sean shrugged. 'Jamie's right.' He considered for a moment. How honest did he want to be with Cherry? How much more of his energy should he give her? Hadn't she already stolen enough?

'So Jamie's right, but you do it anyway?'

'Aye, of course. I thought you, of all people, would get that. The high. Dopamine hit. Whatever. All the good chemicals shooting around in your veins. Today's been a wee bit of a fucker, and *out there* is the only place where I don't think about you all the time, where my brain stops the storm and focuses on the waves.'

These words seemed to reach her, to strike somewhere within. 'And here?' she asked, eyes glassy, voice raised to compete with the rush of the rain and roar of the sea. 'On shore? What happens?'

'Here, on shore, you're all I think about. It's relentless. It's incessant. It's killing me, Cher.' Now that he was face to face with her, all he could do was hit her with honesty. It seemed to be the way they worked. She brought out the least dilute version of him.

'I'm sorry, Sean.' She took a step closer, lips bearing a mild stain of peachy lipstick now, eyes smudged with remnants of smoky make-up only accentuating her beauty. She was fucking radiant like this, rainwater dampening her face. 'You know, I have no escape at all. Poker isn't even cutting it. I can't think straight; my body is a cocktail of hormones and insanity for you all the time.'

'Really? Even when you're having dinner with Duff?'

'I'm not having dinner with Duff. How could I after today?'

'You're missing out. The Balmoral is the finest dining in Edinburgh.'

Cherry shrugged. 'My husband is the finest dining in Scotland.'

'That doesn't even make sense.'

'The taste of you is always on my tongue.'

Fuck.

'Anyway, I'm sorry, Sean. I know you think I've been spilling my guts to him about babies and stuff, but I haven't. The truth is, when I dated him, I had what may have been a very early miscarriage, and I was trying to get out of him about whether that had happened with him and anyone else. To see if the problem was him. He read between the lines. I'm sorry; I shouldn't have put you in that position.'

Sean dug the tail of his board into the sand. 'Jesus, okay. It might have helped to know all this before we went in today.'

'I know. Sorry. He is still donating to charity, though.'

'He is? The £150k?'

'No, the number you quoted him.'

'Fuck!'

'And that was after a serious ticking off from me. I told him never to put us in that position again. Said this was a really important event for you and that it surprised me such a sensitive actor was so unable to read the room. And that the donation would enhance his profile. I think he fancies himself as the next face of Butlers' whisky when Connor moves on.'

'Like hell that is happening. But thanks for getting the money out of him. I'm glad you're still in touch with his weak spots.' Sean looked down the beach where sea sprayed onto sharp, jutting rocks. 'Maybe you guys are a good match. A confirmed bachelor and all that. Funsies in the city. Travelling across the world.' He looked at Cherry to see her gut response.

She shook her head, moved in closer towards him, tinges of sweet summer honeysuckle mingling with the tang of seaweed and saltwater, and placed her palm to his cheek. So warm and dry, a contrast to his cold wet skin. He held his nerve and tried not to shiver.

'I'm a good match for my husband. I'm so in love with you, Sean.'

Sean nearly staggered back into the sea. That he was not expecting. Blinking, he stared at her in wonder. 'Jesus, Cherry.' How was it he was so in love with her, too? The ride he'd been on with her was more tumultuous than the waves he'd almost drowned in.

'But I need to head away for a bit to sort some things,' she said.

'What things?' She'd told him she loved him, and now she was talking about leaving. Why was this not a shock?

'I need to see my mum, talk to her about some stuff, think about things somewhere that isn't here, play some live poker, see some friends. Get some perspective on who I am. Where I fit in. I was grasping at straws with Campbell, and I can't keep doing things like that. Because, invariably, I end up hurting you, and that's the last thing I want.'

Sean wedged his board further into the sand. 'I thought we'd moved forward with this stuff, were making a go of things.'

'I know, but the thing is, Sean, grief isn't linear. You should know that. And I don't even know what I'm grieving half the time. The babies I've already lost? The ones I might never have? The mother I may never be, the poker queen I once was, my identity as a woman, the wife I wanted to be to a man I thought was made for me? You. Every precious moment of you. All those tangled strands of grief at once. What happens if I have none of those things at all? Who am I? I'm confused and I'm aching, and I need a break to see it all from a different perspective. And I so truly hope that you'll be here for me, as my husband, when I come back.'

Sean dug at the wax on his board. 'If you're leaving, I'm going to go to Tennessee.'

She searched his face, maybe hoping he was joking. 'I have to go, but I will be back. I just need some time.'

Sean sighed heavily. 'Cher, I get that things are difficult for you, but the past few years haven't been a stroll by the seaside for me either. My dad died, and I'm trying to get myself through that whilst supporting my family and battling to show you how much you mean to me. But that seems to get forgotten half the time. I'm fucking terrified of losing another person I care about, but you're wrecking my heart. The thing that makes me so alive is also the thing that's killing me.'

She wiped her eyes. 'What are you saying? I'm not welcome back?'

'I'm saying I've given you space and time and patience and love. But for once in my life, I need to put myself first, otherwise I'm going to break and be no use to anyone. And you have no idea what it takes for me to realise, never mind admit, that.'

Sean fixed on her, letting the words sink in. He wasn't exaggerating when he said that admitting this was huge. Coping had always been the name of his game.

'Believe it or not, I need you as much as you need me.' He took a step closer. 'If you're sure you'll be back then why go? You belong here. With me. You know you do.'

She half nodded, half shook her head, seemingly torn, her mascara more smudged than before from the rain and her tears. She swiped at her cheek with the heel of her hand. 'I can't lose you, Sean, but I have to do this. For me, for us, to make us stronger.'

'Trust me, Cherry, you don't have to do anything for us except stay.' Sean searched her face, hoping desperately to find even a fragment of hope. 'I can give you so much, but after everything, I can't hang on here wondering if you'll come home.'

'I... I can't. Not yet. But I am always here for you, Sean.'

'Nope, you aren't.' Sean slung his board under his arm and started walking up the beach. 'When exactly are you leaving?'

She followed alongside, matching him pace for pace. 'I'll get the bus in the morning.'

Sean didn't say anything else. What more could he say? This was it. Game over. They'd ridden their wave, come tanking down the side of it, caught another belter for a while, but that had crashed down into itself, and now they were sinking to the ocean floor.

And, like the Titanic, it was time to let it rest.

Chapter 32

Cherry

Cherry's mind was like a snow globe, except with the snow replaced by driving Scottish rain. Everything was clouded, visibility fogged, and all she wanted was to find her way through the storm to warmth and safety.

To break down the glass barrier that prevented her from getting there.

To Sean.

Because the one thing Cherry knew, clearer than anything else, was how much she loved him.

But he was unreachable. Closed off. Shutters down – Cherry prohibited.

She'd never seen him like this before. It was always a thinly veiled attempt at resistance from both of them.

This was cold, hard glass.

He was giving up.

Like she'd been terrified he might all along.

Still not talking, they crossed the road from the beach to the house. Sean put his board in the garage while Cherry went inside. She stood in the lounge, considering the place that had become home.

Home she would never see again after tomorrow.

A minute later, Sean appeared, closing the door behind him.

He was soaked through in boardies and rash vest, feet bare, dripping seawater onto the kitchen floor. His face was as striking as ever, and though she preferred the happy Sean, the pensive, brooding man was beyond breathtaking, too.

He pulled his rash vest off and threw it next to the washing machine, where it landed with a wet slap. But this was no body tease. This was Sean living his life in his own house, making no accommodations for her presence in a place where she was no longer welcome.

Cherry was glued to the spot watching him. She should go upstairs and give him space, pack the last of her things, numb herself on her phone, but her husband's energy consumed her.

Despite knowing she was there watching him, Sean didn't seem concerned with Cherry at all, and she was certain that was what drove him to do the thing he did next. The thing she was not expecting.

He reached for the gold band on his left hand.

In a stride, she was on him, coming from behind and grabbing him. 'No, Sean, please don't!' Cherry tugged his right hand away from the left. 'Please don't do that. Not yet.'

He spun to her, his face set with challenge. She let her hand fall.

'Please,' she said, breathless.

'Please, what? What is it that you want so badly, Cherry?'

'Please don't take your wedding ring off.'

The electricity between them crackled with such intensity she could almost smell the burning. They held each other there. She was powerless to move, even if she wanted to.

'You've never taken it off...and... We've never.' Her words tangled on her tongue. 'Please, Sean, please, don't.'

'Why not? We're done.'

'Because we're not done. Because I promise you I'm coming back. Because I love you, Sean. So, so, so much, and the idea of life without you now is unthinkable.'

All she saw reflected back was disbelief – shock, turbulence, the muscle in his jaw ticking, his throat bobbing violently, fingers still hovering over the wedding ring.

He shook his head.

Why did he not believe her? She mouthed back, *Yes*, the words like a silent prayer. Of course it was true. Of course she bloody loved him.

Then, as if Sean understood everything in the small movement of Cherry's lips, he took a step towards her, grabbed her face in his hands and crashed his mouth into hers, the ferocity of the kiss nearly knocking her off her feet, before driving them up against the kitchen wall.

Oh my God!

Interlocking her right hand with his left, ring still on, Sean pinned them together against the wall, the symbolism not lost on her. His tongue was hot and desperate against her own, a counterpoint to rough stubble on cold skin grazing against her.

She slid her free hand to the cold, damp small of his back, dragging him closer, every hot inch of him pressed against her.

Her husband, hard and primed.

She was soaked inside and out.

Sean's hand dropped to her thigh and then slipped beneath her skirt. In one swift motion, he hoisted the fabric up around her waist and yanked down his board shorts. Gripping the underside of her thighs, he lifted her off the ground with a low grunt, and she wrapped her legs instinctively around him.

Pressing her higher against the wall, he anchored her with his hips. One hand moved between her legs, sliding her panties aside before he slid two fingers inside her, testing to see if she was ready.

Cherry gasped, head tipping back. Oh, she was ready.

Lifting those fingers, she drew them into her mouth, meeting Sean's challenging gaze. She knew what he was saying; he didn't need to say it.

'You want to leave the man who makes you this wet in seconds? Who soaks you through by standing looking at you? Go on then, I dare you.'

Cherry sucked his fingers, and Sean absorbed every moment, his expression fascinated, satisfied, pained.

Then, barrelling his hips to hers, eyes never deviating from her own, he thrust upward.

Giving her everything.

Every inch of him.

So fierce. So dominant. So fucking incredible.

Cherry slung her arms around his shoulders, steadying herself on the man whom she needed more than anything in the world.

The rhythm Sean found was almost possessed, every drive into her pushing out his need, his effort, his aching for her. A confused tangle of lust and something that felt to Cherry so potently like love it couldn't be anything but.

'Fuck, Cherry.' He snapped against the soft skin of her

backside as he took her, eyes near feral. 'Can you live without this? Can you?'

He must know the answer. She shook her head and tried to speak, but words failed to come. Sean hardened to steel inside her as arousal carved itself on his face.

He ground in deeper, primal need possessing him with a tortured sound that coiled up need in Cherry. She loved hearing him so turned on for her. Clenching him tighter inside, she sank her nails into his skin. Sean's intense expression of pleasure and pain pinned to hers, she dug firmer and watched the remainder of his composure fracture.

His eyes fell to the place where they met.

She looked, too. Whimpered.

'Cher.' Sean ground into her, growled in low broken breaths. 'Look at us together; we're made for each other.'

She grabbed the back of his head – the hair there damp from the sea and sticky from the salt water – and pulled his face back to her. 'I love you, Seany. Come in me. I want to feel it so much.'

And with those words, she'd hit the mark.

A guttural sound, raw and rough, broke from Sean. His breathing altered – sharper, tighter – and with one last chance to show her how he could fuck her better than any other man, he slammed up inside her. Then once more. And again, before his body quaked and his release came shattering out of him, ragged, hot and primitive.

The animalistic roar of Sean coming sparked a primal flame in Cherry. With barely any warning, her climax hit her hard, relentless, desperate, nails clawing at his salty skin, her heated cries ravaging the space between them. My God, she was never letting go of the man who could fuck her like this. Never, never, never.

Her man.

Her love.

Her everything.

As Cherry's breathing settled, she found Sean watching her, eyes glazed but attentive, absorbing every movement on her face. Nothing but bare, unshielded love in them.

Maybe he would tell her how he felt. That would make this perfect.

But he didn't say anything.

Instead, silently, he lowered her to the ground, his release slipping down her leg. He leaned forward, boxing her in on either side, palms against the wall. Kissed her softly on the cheek, holding there a moment, tender and safe. She hoped he might whisper something in her ear, but he pulled back, walked to the kitchen island and returned with a warm wet towel.

Before he could do anything more, Cherry took the towel and dropped it to the floor.

Ravaged from the storm and the sex, Sean – a tousled, dishevelled prize of a man with the purest of hearts – watched her, confused, definitely not expecting what she did next.

Cherry slid her hand down the inside of her thigh, through the viscous liquid dripping there, and slicked a generous amount onto her finger. Then, meeting her husband dead on, she raised that finger and sucked.

'Tastes like paradise...' she murmured. 'Just so you know how I feel about you, Sean.'

Sean's chest was still heaving a little, his eyes darting in line with every move she made. He raked a hand through his hair, jaw ticking, like he was torn about what to do.

He hesitated for a moment, and she wondered if he might be about to concede something.

But then he spoke.

'That was something else, Cher. All of it.' Tenderly, he trailed his fingers through the lower strands of her hair, before they fell away, his touch drifting down her arm and leaving only the memory of his warmth in its wake. He blinked slowly, hesitating before clearing his throat and speaking again. 'I know you have to go, and I won't stand in your way. But I'm not a hundred percent convinced you'll be back, so I think that it's best that we aren't in touch. I need to maintain some sanity, you know?'

Cherry could hear the seams of her heart tearing, slowly. The prospect of being without Sean, even at the end of the phone, was devastating. But what could she do except respect his wishes? He was right; she couldn't ask him for anything more when he'd given her so much of himself.

'Sure, Seany.' Her hand wobbled by her side, hoping to find his again. 'I guess we just had the best goodbye-for-now sex ever.'

'Aye, Paradise, I hope that's what it was. I really do.'

Chapter 33

Sean

Sean considered skipping the usual Sunday drop-in at his mum's house to avoid questions about Cherry. But that meant lying to her and sitting at home alone, so he opted for the lesser discomfort.

Of course, one of the first questions Amanda asked before he'd sat down at the kitchen table was: 'How's Cherry after the tournament yesterday?'

'Aye, fine, I think.' For all he knew, she was. 'She raised a lot of money, Mum. A lot.'

'That's fantastic. But you *think* she's fine?'

If they were breaking up, then he may as well pull the plaster off. It was hard to mask everything right now. And it could be time he stopped.

'She's gone to see her mum,' he said. 'She left this morning.'

Amanda watched Sean intently. His heartache was probably written all over his face. He shrugged. 'I'm not sure she'll be back.'

'Oh, Sean.' Far from an *I told you so*. Amanda was nothing but compassionate. 'What happened?'

Burdening his mum with the news that Cherry had left was unfair, especially as his dad's birthday was on the horizon, so he wouldn't go into any more detail.

'I'd rather not talk about it. Let's focus on the ashes.' Normally, at this time of year, Amanda would be busy organising a huge party for her husband. But the plan on Jimmy Butler's birthday this September was for the siblings to get on their surfboards and to scatter his ashes at sea. It would be a moving tribute, but there was nothing to plan, except to get everyone in the same place and on a surfboard, including – at her own insistence – his mum.

'Listen to me,' Amanda soothed in the matter-of-fact tone that had given Sean an immense amount of comfort his whole life. 'Everyone is heartbroken, so we need to support one another. Your *Sean the superhero* act won't save anyone, so please, if you won't talk to me, talk to one of your brothers. They all need it as much as you. Do you understand?'

Suitably humbled, Sean mumbled, 'Aye, I do.'

'Good.' Amanda leaned against the oven and watched him.

He picked at crumbs on the table, hoping she would stop soon. When things became unnervingly quiet, he looked up to see her flexing her biceps Charles Atlas style. It was sweet and playful and made him smile. She always knew how to do that.

'Do you think I've got what it takes to paddle out the back?' she said.

'Mum, you won't need to do anything. I'll do all the work, or whoever's board you want to ride on. But, as I've said before, we can get you a boat.'

'Oh no. Your dad wasn't interested in boats. We agreed on surfing.'

'Alright then. You can come with me, and I'll make sure you're safe. But wear your armbands in case.'

Amanda playfully slapped Sean with a dishtowel. 'I'll armband you! I've been swimming since before you were even an idea.'

'I know, I know. Just teasing.'

After they had finished their meal, Sean stacked the dishwasher and was getting ready to leave when his mum stopped him.

'I have something to give you. From your dad.' She disappeared for a minute or two before returning with an envelope and a small jewellery box.

The last run-in Sean had with a jewellery box didn't end so well, and if what was in this one was what he thought it was, he had to do this alone.

'You don't have to open anything here.' Amanda sensed his hesitation. 'But I wanted you to have it now. It seems like the right time.'

'Is everyone getting a letter?'

She nodded. 'Yes. Everyone is. And everyone is getting something. This' – she pushed the box into his clammy hand – 'is yours. It's nothing big, and we'll do the will reading soon, but now feels like I should give it to you.'

Holding whatever this mini heirloom was, Sean thanked his mum. 'I'll open it at home. I think I might need a reinforcement dram.'

'Yes. You could see if your lovely wife could be there, too.' Amanda skimmed her eyes over his left hand but said nothing about the missing ring.

Thank goodness.

'Aye.' He styled it out and tried his best to meet his

mum's eye. His 'lovely wife' was one reason he knew he couldn't deal with this anywhere besides alone.

Back in his own house, Sean steeled himself for opening the letter and box. Despite what he'd said to his mum, it wasn't his style to sit down with a cup of tea or even a dram. He wanted to see the contents now.

At the kitchen island, he tipped back the lid of the jewellery box. Inside was, as expected, jewellery, but the appositeness of the item threw him, and he stepped back to take it in.

A sapphire bracelet with deep blue stones that sparkled like the inky Kintyre sky. It was exquisite. It would look beautiful on...

Someone whose job was to win bracelets.

How could his dad have known? He couldn't. It was a poetic coincidence. Sean slid his finger under the seal of the letter and pulled out the thick, creamy notepaper folded inside. One solitary sheet. Long missives weren't his dad's thing. He leaned his back against the island and read.

Dear Sean,

This was your grandmother's bracelet. I would like you to have it, to give to a someone as precious and iridescent as the bracelet itself. I know, one day, you'll find that person. Perhaps you already have. Whenever it happens, hold on to her and love her with every ounce of passion

*and energy you have in that enormous heart of
yours.
Dad.*

Oh fuck! He could see his dad sitting at his desk writing this letter, before he lost the ability to write, having no idea how much his son would almost succeed on those wishes. The sharp sense of having failed his father clawed at Sean. Shards of salt water stabbed at his eyes, his legs opted out of normal functioning and gravity slid him down the wall, the letter crushing in his fist.

Fuck!

How was it possible to feel this empty and still have air in your lungs? To be so hollowed out and still have a pulse beating in your chest? Everything was gone – his dad, Cherry, his hopes of honouring the wishes in that letter. The regret was phenomenal.

Sean staggered one fist to his abdomen and forced himself to breathe and count.

In, two, three, four... Out, two, three, four. *Come on, Seany, you've got this. You do. You do.*

He didn't. Meditation was never his strong point, and now was not the time to master it.

'I tried, Dad. I did.' Through blurred vision, Sean flattened the letter out onto his knee, like he'd done with Cherry's bucket list the night they met. 'To hold on to her and love her with everything I have. I can't even explain how much I love her.' His head fell back against the island. 'I have no idea if she's coming back.'

Tugging at his hair, the only tangible thing he could find, Sean let the volcano inside erupt, tears spurting. Hot.

Burning. Inevitable. Months – years – of holding everything in, being a hero for everyone else, hurtling out, emotion no longer permitting suppression.

'Fuck! Dad, I miss you... I miss you.'

A great, heaving breath shuddered through his whole body. An earthquake upending everything he'd fought so hard to keep solid and stable.

'I love her so fucking much. What have I done?'

Another quaking sob racked him. Sean let it come. And the next one and the next one. Until there were none left. Just a man, ordinarily larger than life, now a defeated, crumpled mess slumped against the kitchen island.

Lost, heartbroken and alone.

Chapter 34

Cherry

Cherry stepped inside the caravan, the cloying scent of incense and amber catching in her throat. The memory of being here with Sean was potent. She remembered his hand wrapped around hers, her free fingers fiddling with the tassels on the garish cushions, while her mum gave him the third degree. His body was warm and comforting next to hers as she'd thought about everyone missing from the photographs – those passed on and those who had never got to be here at all.

She rubbed at the wedding band – on the same chain as her locket. Not her own ring but the one she'd found in the front pocket of her bag during the bus ride from Kinshore to Edinburgh.

Sean's wedding ring.

Cherry stepped into the warm, whisky-coloured glow the September sun cast across the caravan's interior. It, too, reminded her of Sean. Whisky would forever remind her of Sean. Sunsets over the Forth would remind her of him. Everything reminded her of him.

Pam, back to her normal dress code of lounge pants and

a long wrap cardigan, filled the kettle and flicked the switch to boil. 'Where's that lovely husband of yours?' she asked.

'He's back in Kinshore, Mum.'

Pam paused, halfway in her pursuit of Jaffa Cakes from the cupboard above the kettle. 'Is everything okay? How is he?'

'He's still lovely, inside and out.' Waves of pain and regret surged behind Cherry's ribs. 'But I dunno what's happening with us.'

'Oh, Cherry, for goodness' sake.' Pam nibbled on a Jaffa cake as if a marriage stalling was another cab off the rank in a long line of Cherry's trivial mistakes, like the time she'd dyed her hair yellow.

'Please don't *for goodness' sake* me, Mum.'

Pam studied her daughter and then sighed. 'I can see you're upset; I'll get the cards.'

'No, Mum. No cards. They don't help. Not your kind, not my kind. Both of them are just blocking things out right now. Things that need facing head-on. Talking about.' Cherry's voice cracked like the hairline fractures in her mum's Doulton figurines.

'Fair enough. But sit down.' Pam gestured to the banquette. 'Are you staying the night?'

'No, I don't think so. I don't know, maybe. Listen, there's something I need to ask you.' Cherry sat and reached into her bag, pulling out the photograph her mum had sent. It felt heavier than usual. She softened her voice, apropos of what she was about to broach. 'You sent me this photo with this poem on the back for a reason?'

Pam glanced at the photograph then back at Cherry. 'It's the same one that's in your locket,' she said, a little too airily, the gaps between her sentences betraying her discomfort. 'I thought it was about time you had the proper version.' She sipped her tea but didn't mention the poem. She didn't need to.

Cherry nodded, her throat tight. God, this was difficult. Her heart was beating so loudly it almost drowned out the sound of someone singing badly in the next caravan, as they always did when she visited. This conversation did not need a soundtrack, and definitely not Kenny Rogers.

She bit the bullet. 'Mum, in this photo, were you pregnant?'

Pam stiffened. It was a microscopic shift, but enough to suggest that she'd known the question was coming and that the answer was more than a simple no.

The room was silent for a short time until she relented and nodded. 'I was, darling, yes.'

Cherry's mind was a time lapse of possibilities. Images of what might have been flickered by. A sibling? Someone she had carried in her locket unwittingly all these years who could have stood here with her now, because unless her mother led a double life, then there was only one ending to this story. It was the last thing she wanted to do, but she had to pull the Band-Aid off.

'What happened to that baby, Mum? Did it... Did it not make it?' The words caught in her throat, so inextricably linked to her own experience.

Pam picked at another biscuit and then put it down again. 'It wasn't meant to be.' She forced a smile that she may as well not have bothered with. 'We don't always get what we want.'

Cherry swallowed. Stared at the rejected Jaffa Cake. Over thirty years ago, her mum had gone through the same thing Cherry had endured. A miscarriage, a bone-shattering loss, becoming a carved-out void. This explained so much.

Her mum's sadness and difficulty dealing with Cherry's own situation.

Yet made no sense at all. Where was the compassion? The understanding?

'I'm sorry, Mum. Truly sorry. I wish I'd known. I have so many questions.'

Pam swallowed and spoke as if she wanted the questions dealt with as quickly as possible. 'Three months. A boy; we named him Owen. I never fell pregnant again.'

Tears burst through Cherry's defences. 'Owen.' A baby brother called Owen. 'Did they tell you why it happened?' She rubbed her eyes with her cuff.

Pam shook her head. 'They mentioned stress. They also said I got very lucky having you at all.'

'I'm so sorry. That's not helpful advice at all.'

'No, no, it isn't, but I accepted it because I had you. I took the word lucky and focused on that.'

'That makes sense. But all this time, you've known exactly what I went through. Why did you never tell me? It might have helped us both feel less alone. Helped me feel less like it was my fault.'

Pam held her cup in both hands. Her face held an expression of sadness that provoked the hope of honesty. 'Some things are too difficult to talk about, even years later. I've never thought it was your fault, only that there were certain things you could have prioritised to help yourself fulfil your dreams.'

A sharp tang of laughter burst from Cherry. 'That *is* blaming me.'

'It isn't meant to. There are things I could have done, too.' Pam smoothed the handle of the cup. 'Like asking your dad to stop working all the hours, stop smoking in the house, stop drinking so much as it caused me stress. But I didn't.

So, all I ever wanted was for you not to make the same mistakes I did.'

Cherry studied the glowing woman in the photograph. How had that happy lady, excited for the future, become this troubled, complicated person sitting before her now?

'By never telling me why you were so critical of my lifestyle?'

'Was I?' Pam seemed genuinely puzzled.

'Yes. Cherry lifted her fingers into air quotes. '"Travelling around the world playing poker is no way to carry a baby to term." Criticising my choice in men.'

'Well, how many pregnant women play poker for a living? And Dale was wrong for you. Take it from someone who married a man who liked a drink. I loved your dad dearly, but his bad habits ruined us. Sean, though, I like him.'

Cherry took a long blink, recovering from the words that scalded. 'That's nice, Mum. I like him too. I love him, and I need him. You know, I thought it was all going to be fine, then you did that reading with the death card and you said that I had to leave some things behind me. Some dreams.'

'That can mean so many things, Cherry. I want you to go into the future with your eyes open.'

'Eyes open to the empty road ahead? The empty nest? I have dreams, Mum. Sean has dreams. And when I don't think you believe in me, it makes it so hard to let someone else put their faith in me.'

'Oh, Cherry.' Pam adopted a soothing tone, but Cherry heard the patronising undercurrent. 'You know that my saying you're worth something won't solve things if you don't believe it yourself.'

'I get that, but it would be the start I need. You're my

mum. If anyone is meant to believe in me, it's you. Do you know how crushing it is to think that your own mother thinks you're wasted potential? No potential?'

The light in Pam's eyes darkened. 'I don't think that at all. But we don't all get our own cheerleading squad. It's not something I heard a lot from my mother, you know? Nobody said "I love you" to their children when I was growing up.'

'Okay, fine, but did she tell you to let your dreams die? Did she watch you lose four babies and tell you to accept? Mum, I had four miscarriages. Four! Did you ever think that might be an ever-so-slightly insensitive way of helping me cope?'

Pam rose from the banquette, started tidying away the biscuits and mugs. 'I've only ever dealt with life in the best way I could. I know everyone is more open these days, talking about their feelings and sharing everything, but that isn't me, Cherry.'

Cherry rubbed the scratchy fabric of the seat. It was hard to be emotionally open when you hadn't had a role model since you were thirteen. 'Allow me, Mum. I love you. And I'm sorry you went through that and that it's taken until I'm thirty-seven to find out about it.'

Silence. Even the neighbour had stopped singing. Pam looked at the table and at Cherry, her eyes glassy. Those three words might have flicked a switch in her. Cherry waited. Her mum fumbled with the mugs before letting her hands rest on the counter surface.

'I'm sorry, too, darling. But I'm just... Oh, it was your dad who was good at all this stuff.'

'But he's not here, Mum. He's been gone for over twenty years. It's only us now.' Cherry stood to meet her mother.

'What is it you need from me, Cherry?'

'I don't know. To know that you have my back. The doctors said it wasn't my fault, but I feel like you think it was. These things happen, right? To good people who didn't do anything wrong. And some people have lots of miscarriages and go on to have babies.'

Pam nodded. 'Yes, that's true. Please, don't listen to me; listen to the doctors. I come from a different time where everyone blamed women and nobody talked to counsellors like they do now.'

Cherry was sad for her mum, for the pain she had gone and still was going through. The small shaft of openness helped her, though. She needed to hear that it wasn't her fault.

But it wasn't a magic cure for her lingering feelings about not being enough for Sean, feelings that were going to crop up when people made thoughtless comments, or she saw a mother cooing lovingly at her child, or a plotline on TV triggered her. That was something she would have to decide about on her own. About whether she could let him love her and forget about the outside noise.

Chapter 35

Sean

The colours of the seasons were slowly shifting, with summer giving way to autumn. There would be no more unseasonably balmy days, no more scorched grass. The petals of the flowers Cherry had planted in his garden had tumbled to the earth, soaking to near mulch after a deluge of September rainfall.

Sean stood on the patio drinking his morning coffee, the Swingball set still pitched on the lawn. A few days ago, he'd prepared to pack it into the shed but ended up batting by himself and losing track of time as he remembered Cherry on the opposite side of the pole, laughing and whacking the ball into next week, breasts swaying softly in her bra cups. And, of course, the feel of moving inside her, her moans as she came around him.

God, he missed her.

No time for reminiscing today. Sean threw back his coffee and headed into the house. After six months of gruelling training, the day had finally come. He was embarking on 100 miles of thigh-burning pedalling through Kintyre. All day, he and his six siblings would cycle over undulating hills, through deep forests, coast by rugged castles and secret coves. But it was no leisurely tourist ride with stops to photograph squirrels or turrets. They would pedal until their legs were jelly. It was the least they could do for a man who had endured far, far worse.

The man who had raised them and whom they'd said goodbye to far too soon.

Sean was so ready for it.

But he was also ready for it to be over.

Since Cherry had left, two weeks ago, sleep had also deserted him. There were too many late nights, drinking beer, staring into space – a pursuit Jamie had told him was great for clearing the mind, but that Sean had never quite mastered – and playing online poker, the latter a stupid thing to do when he was trying to stop thinking of her.

Pinning down and boxing to death the temptation to text her one night when he got a royal flush was a challenge in itself.

But he'd won it.

Didn't stop her being on his mind constantly.

Didn't stop him going into her bedroom, laying on her bed and imagining her beside him. Now he understood the pillow thing, although he drew the line at cuddling hers. The scent of her was enough, slipping into his senses, invading his bloodstream, making him feral for her all over again.

Where was she now? There were no calls or texts. She knew the ride was today.

In his pocket, his phone vibrated.

Morning gorgeous. Feeling pumped!

.   .   .

It was from Jamie.

Fuck's sake. Right vibe, wrong person.

Sean dumped his coffee cup in the sink. Outside, he strapped his bike to the back of the car and swung out of the drive onto the rain-slicked road towards Jamie's place. From there, he'd drive them both to Tarbert, where they'd convene with the rest of the family and ride.

Tarbert harbour was calm and placid, like a sensible aunt who would never cycle one hundred miles in a day. Boats bobbed gently, their reflections wavering in the clear water, and people milled around drinking takeaway coffee and chatting.

The race started with little fanfare – a peaceful beginning to match his dad's end. Sean caught a tear in his mum's eye as he and his siblings coasted off, the fresh autumn wind providing a baptism into the day. He hoped they could finally make something positive from the pain of the past few years.

From Tarbert to Claonaig, they cycled close to one another, occasionally chatting or joking, but often pedalling through a comfortable silence that you could only have with your closest loved ones. The panoramic views across the Kilbrannan Sound to the jagged green mountains of Arran were enough to keep anyone quiet.

From Claonaig they coasted along open moorland past Loch Ciaran where, on any other day, it would be great to stop and listen to the lapping of the water and the call of birds. He bet Cherry would know the names by their calls.

The route from Clachan took them over to the east

coast, where the Atlantic buffered the shorelines with an endless, rhythmic rush. They were thirty miles down now. Ready for refreshments, they pulled into the small village of Tayinloan and sat on rain-soaked fold-up chairs outside a coffee shop, drinking weak coffee and eating sandwiches from floral crockery that had seen better days.

Sean checked his phone to see if there was anything from Cherry. He'd settle for a simple *I miss you.*

Nothing.

But he was the one who'd told her to go. If he'd given her leeway to take the time that she needed, she might be here now. It was just that he'd felt like a lobster being boiled alive by that point, and more upheaval was unbearable. He needed his wife there with him.

And now she was gone. Who knew where? Thriving again in the poker world? Or lonely, like him, longing to wake up together again.

Sean shoved his phone back in his pocket. He was breaking his own race rules thinking like this.

'You're awful quiet, Seany,' said Eilidh. 'Not tired already?'

'What, because I've not spoken in three minutes, I must be tired?'

'Yes.'

The rest of his siblings laughed.

'Don't worry about me. I'm conserving my energy for the next seventy miles.' Sean wrapped a slice of millionaire's shortbread in a napkin and stuck it in his pocket. 'You should all do the same.'

'Nice energy boost strategy,' said Niall. 'Don't talk. Stockpile shortbread.'

'Aye, I'm sure I heard Sir Chris Hoy say that once.'

For all its faults, the coffee had touched the edges and

given Sean a small lift. Combined with the morning sun edging the rain off its patch, his mood improved as they set off again, up into the hills, rising to Carradale, where you could see the rugged volcanic dome of Ailsa Craig rising proud in the sea.

For some reason – not that he needed a prompt – Ailsa Craig brought Cherry to mind. A solitary, strong, fearless presence.

Fuck it! After the race, he'd get in touch with her. He needed her. Missed her. He loved her. That was the truth. If he'd told her that, she might have stayed instead of needing to venture out to find her certainty. He'd claimed to have given her everything, yet he'd held those words back, needing to know she wasn't leaving him.

Before fucking her against the wall.

What an arse.

But the future could be bright. Right?

A packed lunch and more coffee, forty-six miles in – nearly halfway there. Energy levels were where they should be, and they boosted each other's spirits. It would power them along the twenty-two miles of craggy shores to Camp-beltown, past more castles, woods and lochs and onto the curved, golden shores of Dunaverty.

'Hard to believe a massacre happened here, eh?' Jamie swept his hand across the beach over to the grey crags of Blood Rock, like an enthusiastic history teacher at the end of a very long school day.

'My legs feel like they've been massacred,' Cara groaned.

Sean was with Cara on this one. Normally full of boundless energy, he was so ready for this to be over, to see the bright lights of Kinshore on the horizon. To get home, fall into a bath and text Cherry.

But it was as they were leaving Southend and barrelling down to the southernmost point of Kintyre, the landscape wild and unsheltered, golden eagles wheeling ominously above, that Sean wondered if the bright lights were happening already.

A glare caught the edges of his vision.

What was that? He shook his head but continued pedalling.

Then there was a sensation of the ground being further away than before. Sean blinked hard, puffed out a sharp breath or two and adjusted his hold on the handlebars.

Focus, Seany.

'You alright, bro?' Nate sounded more serious than usual.

'Aye, aye, fine. Just a fly.'

But the strangeness swept in again, and this time there was no mistaking it for dizziness. Sean gripped the handlebars, noticing distinctly the fading tan mark where his wedding ring had been. Sweat beaded on his forehead. Strange, as he'd been taking it easy. Was he dehydrated? Coffee wasn't great for hydration, and he'd had a fair few cups today. He reached for his water bottle.

But there was no time to drink. It all happened in a split second as the gleam of afternoon sunlight cut across his eyes, and his vision spun again.

This time, his balance faltered and the front wheel of his bike caught the edge of gravel where it sliced into slippy, wet mud.

Underneath Sean, the bike twisted, front wheel first, and he was falling – off the road and down into the ditch – the sound of Eilidh calling his name the last thing he heard before he hit the ground.

And everything went white and still.

Chapter 36

Cherry

Cherry turned the key in the mortice lock of her Bruntsfield garden flat and listened for the reassuring clunk that always made her feel safe in the historical solidity of Edinburgh.

Today, it sounded like the empty sound of a key turning in a lock mechanism.

As she strolled onto the Meadows and across to the coffee shops of Quartermile, the cool autumn air was a refreshing balm. The view of Arthur's Seat – the emerald-green extinct volcano which rose majestically across the skyline – invigorated her. Edinburgh was a city that sat cheek by jowl with nature.

But the truth was, even in one of the most beautiful cities in the world, after Kinshore it felt bleak and lonely. Without Sean, she was like one of the trees on the Meadows with their leaves falling off. In a month or so, they'd be completely bare.

It was a short walk in the other direction to the casino where Cherry had joined the poker tables in the evenings. Her presence turned a few knowing heads, but she'd focused on the game and walked away in the green every night. Ultimately, though, it was depressing to be surrounded by strangers – men, mostly – some hiding from their wives, some posturing and losing, some tech students avoiding sweating away in a bar or a restaurant for minimum wage. And, every night, she journeyed home in the low September light with an emptiness inside that couldn't even be filled by a large serving of chips from the fish bar – even if they were piping hot, salty, vinegary deliciousness.

The answer to whether she was still a party poker queen was that she could be if she wanted to, but it simply wasn't her priority anymore.

At the door of the coffee shop, time slowed down as Cherry spotted Kirsty inside. Buggy next to her, wriggling toddler on the neighbouring seat.

And the bump.

It was barely noticeable, but she knew it was there so sought it out as if to prepare herself. She could walk away now. Not have to put herself through the pain of hearing about the ups and downs of being a mum. Because it wasn't only hearing about the ups that was hard. It was all hard. The thing about wanting it so much was that you wanted the bad stuff too. You wanted the whole package, no matter what people told you.

But this was one of her oldest friends, waiting to meet her. She couldn't ghost her.

Cherry took a deep breath and opened the door.

It was like slipping into an old pair of shoes. Conversation came so easily, and Kirsty was more interested in hearing about Cherry's life than talking about herself. But Cherry found that she wanted to know about her friend.

'So how is Marty?' she asked of Kirsty's husband.

'Oh... I forgot you don't know.' Kirsty handed a plushie duck to her daughter. 'Marty and I broke up.'

'What? When? Why?'

'He left me about a year and a half ago for one of the teachers at Kallie's nursery. She's twenty-six. It's tragic. For her.' Kirsty laughed.

'Oh, Kirsty, I'm so sorry. What a loser.'

'It's fine. I'm over it. He's a dick, and I'm well shot of him. I've a new man now. Well, an old man, actually. Joe McNeill, the one from uni who got away, and father of this little one.' She curved her palm over her bump.

'Oh my goodness! I remember Joe. You guys reunited. That's incredible.'

'Yes, if I'm honest, I thought about him a fair bit over the years, always regretted letting him go. And turns out he thought about me too. Although we have a spanner in the works, in that he's just been given a diagnosis of MS. This time next year, life is going to be a lot harder. We're currently trying to put some reinforcements in place to prepare.'

Cherry was truly saddened by Joe's illness, but two things struck her about Kirsty's situation. The regret she talked of about letting the love of her life slip away. And her attitude to the future. She was planning, not running. She and Joe were in things together.

Cherry rubbed at her wedding ring. *'No one knows what's in the future, good or bad.'* Those were Sean's words.

'Tell me about your husband,' Kirsty said. 'I want to know everything.'

'Well...' Cherry sipped her hot chocolate. 'His name's Sean, he makes whisky barrels, his family owns Butler's Whisky, he's tall, handsome and hilarious, and I love the pants off him, which might be why I married him after two days.'

'Oh my God, Cherry. Listen to you; look at you. You're glowing.'

'Sorry, sorry. I'm like one of those lovesick idiots.'

'No, no, it's wonderful. I don't mean "listen to you" in a bad way. I mean, how amazing that you've found this. Who finds that? Not everyone. You're so lucky and so deserving.'

Cherry's hot chocolate nearly became a salted one as a tear dropped from her eye.

'I am lucky, aren't I? I've spent so long hoping for someone like Sean, and I get him, and to be honest, I've spent a lot of time worrying that I'm not good enough for him.'

The surprise on Kirsty's face threw things into a different perspective. For a moment, Cherry was standing outside her life staring in, seeing a woman who deserved the love of the man she'd fallen in love with at first sight. Of course, it was a little more complicated than that and she didn't want to talk about that with Kirsty, not when she hadn't seen her in years and Kirsty was expecting. But if you looked at it in a pure way, without all the baggage, you had two people who were besotted with one another. Plain and simple.

As Kirsty had just reiterated, some people waited a lifetime.

'I could tell, by your wedding photo, you guys were smitten. You looked so happy.'

'We were.' Cherry watched Kirsty's small daughter playing with a toy. She smiled at the little girl, who smiled back at her. 'We are. Very happy.'

'He sounds like a total keeper, Cherry. I hope you plan on never letting him go.'

Cherry imagined herself replying to this with: *Well, I've been thinking about it.* It sounded so ridiculous. And if she did let him go, she knew that, like Kirsty with Joe, she would never be able to erase the memory of him. Sean Butler was seared into her heart forever. If she left him, she would feel the tug of the scars every day for the rest of her life.

She was so very nearly there. But there was still a streak of fear sitting in her gut. How did she reconcile with that?

'Are you staying the night?' Pam asked again when Cherry returned to her mum's caravan later that afternoon. 'I'll make your favourite for tea.'

'Sure, but what is that?' Cherry didn't even know what her favourite meal was anymore.

'Macaroni cheese.'

Gosh, she had forgotten about her mum's macaroni cheese, or mac and cheese as everyone else seemed to call it. 'Thanks, that would be really nice, Mum. Can you grill the cheese on the top so it's kind of burnt, but only a wee bit?'

Pam smiled. 'I'll see what I can do.'

Cherry rubbed at her wedding ring, getting to be a force of habit now. She had left Kinshore to find her identity, and around the poker table wasn't enough. She'd made peace with her mum and recognised that, to some extent, she had to find her own way forward. The babies thing might always trigger her. The only question remaining was where did Sean fit into the future? It would be rough at times. Could she bring him onto a ship that would potentially weather storms, knowing that there would be beautiful, placid waters too?

Pam came over to her, glanced at Cherry's hand and

lifted it to the light. 'You know, I never said before, but this is a beautiful wedding ring. He's spared no expense on you.'

The observation struck Cherry like the sharp glare of the evening sun on the white diamonds. Sean really had gone all in on her, taken a huge gamble, bigger than most men would have. Because he wasn't most men. And she'd done the same for him because she'd been twenty-four-carat certain he was the one.

Still was.

A man she'd do anything for, and who would do anything for her.

'That ring tells you a lot about the man,' Pam added. 'But I told you before he's the King of Cups. A solid man. Not that you need me to tell you that. You're the one who's good at reading people. Tells and all that, if you're explaining it in poker speak.'

Cherry huffed out a laugh that was nearly a sob. 'Aye, Mum, tells.' Jesus, was there ever more truth spoken by her mother? The tells were there, plain as day, every time she looked at Sean. Sure, marrying him was a reckless gut decision, and logic had been whispering to her ever since. But if she thought Sean played their marriage based on gut, she'd underestimated him. Repeatedly, he'd shown that his choices carried thought, weight and love. She needed to accept that he could make decisions about his own future; he knew there would be rough and smooth. It was vital she learned to trust him.

Otherwise, she might live with the regret of losing him, forever.

The decision was made, and the weight off her shoulders at that was immense. She would call him and speak to him this evening.

'Shall I help you with tea, Mum? Peel the potatoes or something?'

'Thanks. That would be great, love.'

Cherry was reaching for the peeler when, on the table, her phone vibrated. For a moment, she stared at the screen in puzzlement. Summer's name lit up the screen.

Why would Summer be calling?

It could only be something to do with Sean.

Oh fuck.

'Are you okay, love?' Her mum's voice filtered through from what sounded like miles away.

'Yeah... It's a friend from Kinshore, and it's weird that she would call me.' Cherry stared blankly at the handset.

'Answer it.' Pam lifted the phone and held it out to her daughter.

Cherry took it and fumbled her finger to the green button whilst attempting to smile at her mum.

'Thanks.'

But when Summer's voice came through the line with the news from Kinshore, Cherry's smile plummeted through the caravan floor.

Chapter 37

Cherry

Cherry arrived back in Kinshore late. The call from Summer about Sean's accident came at 4 p.m., and now it was gone midnight. She slowed the hire car as she passed his house. There was a dim light on in the lounge. He might still be up, but he could have forgotten to switch off the lamp, and she wouldn't disturb him if he was already in bed, recovering. She hadn't told him she was coming because seeing him in person was the only way to do this.

She took a big-girl breath and drove on to Summer's house.

Summer was padding around in bright green pyjamas with lambs on them. A cat was following her around, rubbing against her ankles and purring.

'Love the PJs,' Cherry said.

'Thank you. I've made up the spare room for you. There's a towel on the bed. Bathroom is at the end of the hall. You might have a sleeping companion; I hope you don't mind.' She motioned to the cat at her ankles. 'Butterscotch likes to sleep in there sometimes.'

'Not a problem at all.' Cherry had to ask the question that was niggling at her mind. 'How is Sean? Do you know?'

'I think he's okay. Bruised and stuff, but still talking about finishing the race. That's Sean. His foot could be hanging off, and he'd still be climbing Kilimanjaro.'

And that was her man. It was a comfort knowing he was near again, but she ached to see him. To spend the night with him, in that bed that she'd never been in.

Never slept in the same bed as her husband,' she considered, as she snuggled under the duvet a short time later. 'How was that? So symbolic of their relationship. Fucking everywhere but his bedroom. She'd give anything to be in Sean's bed right now. Next to him.

God, she was torturing herself, although it made a difference from pleasuring herself on the small bank of memories and a backup generator of fantasies.

Ugh. She groaned quietly and rolled over in bed, leaning to turn off the lamp. At that moment, her phone lit up. She grabbed it so fast it nearly fell to the floor.

SEAN: You come to Kinshore but you don't come to see your injured husband? Rude.

Tears stung Cherry's eyes as a small laugh choked out. Oh my God! She fumbled across the keys, tapping out a response.

CHERRY: You still think of yourself as my husband?

> SEAN: Have done since the moment I met you. Don't make me come over there and get you, wife.

A huge, goofy grin spread across her face. He wanted to see her. He'd pushed her away, but now he was asking her back. And calling her his wife.

> CHERRY: Are you okay to have after-dark visitors?

> SEAN: It's not a booty call, you wee minx. I just want to see you. But I am going to bed if you're not here in ten minutes.

She shot out from under the duvet. Joggers and a tee would do. Summer was still in the kitchen, making a herbal tea, when Cherry practically fell down the stairs.

'Sorry,' Summer said. 'I might have told Nate, who might have told Sean, that you're back.'

'No need to apologise.' Cherry panted, grabbing her bag and pulling on her trainers. 'I'm popping over there for a bit. I'll be back soon.'

Summer beamed. 'Take as long as you guys need. I'll leave the door unlocked for you.'

It was strange to knock at the door of Sean's house, where she'd come and gone so freely for two months.

When he answered, he was wearing navy jogging bottoms, a black t-shirt clinging in all the places that rendered her defenceless, and the colour under one of his eyes sat somewhere between the two shades.

She gasped.

'Alright, Paradise. I know I'm handsome, but I'm not that handsome.'

'Sean, your eye.' She drew in closer, her instinct being to touch it. Touch him. Her hand got as far as his chin before she pulled it back, afraid it was the wrong thing to do.

'I'm fine.' She noticed his eyes move from the chain around her neck, where his wedding ring hung, to her wedding finger and the white diamond ring he'd given her. There was a fragmentary hesitation as if he were about to say something about this, but instead he said, 'Come on in.'

Nothing much had changed in the house, which still had that warm, woody Sean smell. He motioned for her to sit on the couch and sat down at the other end, turning slowly to face her.

Now it was her turn to catch sight of his hand. Wedding ring free, of course.

'Are you okay?' she asked. 'Summer said you took a nasty tumble off your bike.'

A softness in Sean's expression suggested appreciation of her concern. 'I'm fine. Had a bit of an old-lady fainting spell because of low blood pressure. Fell off my bike into a ditch. Came round with a black eye and bruised ribs, went to hospital and here we are. The doctor advised me to rest for far too long, but I've a ride to finish, so I'll be going against doctor's orders.'

And wasn't this the man she loved all over? 'Oh, Sean. Are you sure?'

'Aye.'

She twisted her lip. He shouldn't be thinking about the cycle, but it was too much to expect him not to.

'I'm fine,' he said. 'Don't worry. I presume that is worry I'm seeing.'

Cherry wiped away a tear before it tumbled down her cheek. 'Of course it's worry, you daft muppet. You could have died.'

Sean dismissed the possibility with a light laugh. 'Not from a wee tumble into a ditch, although the doctor did tell me to sort myself out or I could be marching into pre-diabetes land.'

'Fucking what?! Sean! They told you you've got pre-diabetes?'

Sean shook his head from side to side in an indefinable way. 'No, they didn't, but I need to be a bit healthier. Lower stress, less Irn-Bru and a better diet. It's no biggie.'

'It is a biggie. What caused all this? Overdoing it?'

He caught her concern. 'Stuff we talked about, I think. Me looking out for everyone else but myself. But don't worry, Cher, please. I've learned my lesson.'

'Have you, though? There are a lot of people who care a hell of a lot that you're around, you know. Me included.'

'Aye, I have. And I'd trade all the Irn-Bru in Scotland to have you here every day. Zero contest.'

God, she wanted to wrap herself around him. Have him squeeze her right back. Being on the other end of the couch was too far away.

Sean read her expression. 'I'd come closer,' he said. 'But, you know…'

'The black eye?'

He laughed. 'No, not the black eye. You. I want you, Cherry. But I'm a bit debilitated, and if I go near you, I might disappoint both of us.'

'I highly doubt you would disappoint.' Cherry smoothed down a cushion, holding it as a very poor second to her husband.

'Jesus, the way you're stroking that cushion is turning me on, so you might want to stop it.'

'Oh. Sorry. I didn't realise a cushion could be such a trigger.'

'Of course you didn't. But now you do.'

'But listen... There are some things I have realised.' Cherry pulled the cushion in closer.

'Go on.'

'The first thing is that I'm sorry for all the ups and downs of being married to me. I'm so sorry. You mean so much to me and...' Her voice wobbled.

'Cherry, come on. Don't cry. Unless you want comforted by a very horny man.'

She laughed. 'Is he you?'

'Aye, he's me.'

'I would actually love that.'

Sean raised his eyebrows, but his expression morphed into serious. 'Tell me what you realised.'

She found herself reaching for the cushion again, but stopped. 'The short version is I've realised that I have to stop letting my fears hold me to ransom, otherwise it's going to ruin my life. I have to choose loving you. Because being without you, Sean, is so much worse than my worries for the future, and I couldn't bear the regret of letting you go without trying. I honestly believe that you and I were made for each other. I love you so, so much, and I missed you every second of every day I was away from you.'

For one heartstopping moment, she wasn't sure of Sean's response to this. He was staring at her so intensely that it was hard to tell if he hated her words or loved them.

Hated or loved her. Then he reached across the couch, and it became obvious which it was.

'Cherry, sweetheart, it was torture without you. I'm sorry I laid down the law about you coming back. I was an emotional mess and petrified of losing you.'

'It's okay. I understand.' She took his hand, her wedding ring glinting with a reminder of what she was holding – not just the metaphorical.

Sean touched the ring.

'I have yours,' she said.

Glancing at her neck, he said, 'I noticed.'

'Would you like it back?'

'Ha. Aye. Letting it go was the stupidest thing I ever did. I'd kill for it back.'

Cherry faced away from him and lifted her hair so Sean could unclasp the chain. His warm fingers glancing over her neck gave the sweetest relief. Turning back to him, she slid the ring off the chain.

'Can I...?' She motioned to his hand.

His eyes shone. Despite it seeming like it was too much, he never took them from her, chest rising and falling, face softening, right hand steadying his ribs. 'Of course you bloody can.'

Cherry rested his left palm in her own and, as he watched, pushed the ring up his wedding finger. This almost felt more significant than the first time.

'For better or for worse, I love you, Sean Butler.'

Sean flexed his fingers, examining the gold band. 'God, I've missed this thing.' He raised his gaze back to Cherry. 'I've missed you, Cherry, my beautiful, wild wife. And it might not surprise you to learn that I am out of my mind in love with you, too. Thank you for coming back, for caring and for being so honest. Have I ever told you that marrying you was the best thing I ever did?'

His words almost knocked the breath out of Cherry. He loved her. He wanted her back in his life. He regretted nothing. 'Y-You truly think that?' she stammered.

'Of course I do. You're perfect for me. And if you're sticking around then so am I. Tennessee can get tae. Most respectfully, of course.'

'Oh, Sean.' She clasped his hand. 'I'd love to stick around.'

'Oh, fuck it, would you come here?' He motioned to his lap, where Cherry didn't hesitate in curling up.

'No hanky panky, okay?' He teased a finger down her jawline. 'Just a wee kiss.'

She fixed on the steadfast angles of his face. Could she do just a kiss with this man? She could try.

'Fuck,' Sean groaned before their mouths had even met. 'This was a mistake.'

'Oh, well, we don't have to...'

'I mean that I'm not sure I can just kiss you.' He pressed his forehead to hers. 'I'm going to need either self-control to stop this or working ribs to keep going, and I have neither. My God, woman, you turn every part of me on.'

He pressed his lips to hers and held them there. Soft and firm. Reassuring. No tongues, no wandering hands. Just Sean. It was perfect.

'Let's go upstairs,' he murmured.

'Mmm... I want to, but no.' Cherry summoned every ounce of willpower she had and slid from Sean's knee, his hand still in hers.

'I am going to be a good wife and walk out of that front door to let you get some sleep tonight.'

'Are you kidding me?'

Her face split into a grin. 'Of course I'm kidding. Now, what would you like?' She shimmied back from him. 'Cherry pie or Cherry blossom?'

He beamed. 'What's the difference?' His eyes were fixed on her from the couch as he cradled his ribs.

'I actually have no idea. But they both involve this...' Cherry whipped her t-shirt over her head.

Sean sat up straight, wincing but suddenly very alert at the sight of her in plunge bra and joggers. 'And the rest, Paradise. And the rest. Or I'll come over there and eat them off you.'

As tempting as that sounded, Cherry knew that Sean deserved her on a plate. He'd waited long enough; they both had. She unclipped her bra and let her breasts spill free.

He sucked in a long breath. Nodded to the jogging bottoms.

Cherry brought them down over her hips, but only a notch, letting them linger above her pubic bone. A tease, just for him, because she knew he loved it.

She definitely had his attention. 'Are you not wearing any panties, Cherry? Did you come to a man with bruised ribs in joggers with just that beautiful pussy underneath?'

Cherry flicked her eyebrows up. 'I thought it might help with your recovery. I needed to be sending you the right energy.'

Sean laughed hard, the same way he had the very first night they'd met in New York City, but also winced and reinforced his hold on his ribs. 'That is – as the Americans would say –total baloney, but who am I to argue?'

She shrugged. 'Indeed.'

'Show me.'

Sliding her hand inside the waistband, Cherry gently shimmied the joggers over her hips so that, slowly, Sean got to see everything he was so patiently waiting for. Her husband's worshipful gaze and the mild September air fuelled her as she stepped into full nudity.

'Come here!' he beckoned hoarsely.

Softly, she went to him, watching him watching her, and knelt between his knees.

'Cherry.' He skimmed his hand over her breast, down the middle of her stomach, trailing into the most sensitive area right between her legs, but only giving a dusting of a touch. It was clear as the night sky, by the tent pitching in his own joggers, what this was doing to him. 'This might not be the time to say this – I'm torturing myself here – but when I married you, I was so in love with you. Crazy to some, but you get it, right?'

Cherry nodded, swelling with heat and adoration where his finger stilled. 'Of course I do. I fell for you the moment I laid eyes on you.'

'I would have married you that night if I could.'

'Me too, Seany. I'm sorry it's taken us so long to get here. I'm sorry for being a broken mess.'

'Don't you dare apologise.' Sean lowered his hand, along with his voice, and brought it to rest on her hip. 'You're not broken; you're fractured, like all of us. To me, you're the most captivating woman ever. You're a fucking goddess in motion, and I got to marry you. Things haven't exactly taken the traditional route, but I wouldn't change it for the world. You are so beautiful, Cherry, inside, outside, up, down, back to front...'

'There's been a lot of that.'

'Aye, our journey to get here has been nuts, but I've loved every second. I'm addicted to this. Addicted to you. I'd explode if I felt any more for someone than I do for you. This is enough. It's everything.'

'Oh, Sean. A thousand times all of that. I've never met anyone I've felt for even a fraction of what I feel for you. Nothing on my bucket list can compare to you. Nothing.'

'Not even swimming with dolphins?'

God, he was beautiful. No one could make her melt or laugh, or come until she was hoarse calling his name, like Sean could. 'That's not on there, and you know it.'

'I know. Is having an orgasm while a Scotsman tells you how much he loves you?'

'It should be.'

'Well, let's go upstairs, Mrs Butler, and check that item off right now.'

Chapter 38

Sean

'Is this real?' Cherry whispered against Sean's neck in his bedroom. 'Am I naked in your room, with you?'

'Aye, you are.'

'Aren't you tired after your fall?'

'Listen, woman, I've got lightly bruised ribs, but this ain't no care home. Do I seem tired to you?' He raised his eyebrows and then dipped his chin downwards. Cherry followed its path to where he looked very awake.

'Just checking, but I think you should have a rest.'

'I don't need a rest.'

'Not that kind of rest.' Her voice dropped a semitone. 'The kind where you let me do the work.' Without waiting for him to take his orders, Cherry hooked her fingers into the waistband of Sean's jogging bottoms and eased them down. He sprang free, hard and ready. It was sweet relief, even in loose clothing.

'Oh, this will always take breath away.' Cherry wasted no time curving her hands around his girth and working him as he stepped out of the trousers. 'You're perfect.'

'Jesus, Cherry.' He almost fell over. Those hands of

hers. How did she know exactly how to touch him? Exactly how he liked it?

'Sit on the bed.' Soft palm insistent on his pecs, Cherry encouraged Sean back towards the pillows, where she crawled up towards him from the foot of the mattress, before straddling his lap. Draping her arms around him, she found her north.

It was him. And he was hers.

As Cherry lowered herself onto his erection, Sean took the soft olive skin of her cheeks in his hands, hardly believing they were here, traced his thumb back and forth, affirming this wasn't a dream. For a man rarely short of things to say, he was speechless.

With his palms on her backside, bolstering her rhythm, Cherry found a cadence, moans soft like whipped cotton. The bruised ribs had done him a favour because this inti-macy – being wrapped together with her, inside her in this way – was mind-blowing.

It occurred to Sean he should be on top, showing his wife how he could love her, but his ribs were protesting, and something told him she wanted it this way. Truthfully, he did too. He'd never made love to a woman before. Until Cherry.

With one confident hand steadying the dip of her back, the other drifted to her clit, thumb circling softly. The smallest gesture, a fragment of the power he used in the muscular graft of coopering, but it was enough.

'Oh God, Sean. Never stop doing that. My pussy fucking loves you.'

Sean groaned hard. Talk like that fired him up, and she knew it. He grasped her breast, tweaked the nipple tight, the way she liked, and listened as she moaned in synch with his touch.

Grasping his shoulders, she slid, tight and snug, up and down his cock, the soft breasts of his dreams within sucking distance, her adoring smile leaving his self-control in shreds. For years, the one thing Sean wanted more than anything was a woman to share every liveable moment with. And now here she was, riding him like a spirited goddess who was in love with every bone in his body. He would never get enough of this.

Letting Cherry take the rhythm alone, Sean tangled up a fistful of her dark golden hair and brought their mouths together. His kiss was a little rough but fuelled with so powerful a love that he could barely breathe.

'Cherry, sweetheart... My wife.'

'Seany.' She brought her hand to his. 'Love of my life.'

The words were everything. She was stunning, the apricot glow of the lamp accentuating her curves as she met his somewhat tempered thrusts. Wild, loving, fantastical. The golden strands of her hair shimmered like the moon that glowed over them. He coasted his hands over the sublime curve of her hips. Held them there as she lifted and dropped onto his cock, moaning freely.

'That's it. Ride me, Cherry. Let that beautiful, wet pussy take everything it needs. You're close; I know it.'

'I am, I am. Oh God, Sean.'

The sight of her, lithe and frantic, giving her all for both of them, nearly ended Sean. Being inside this woman wasn't close enough. He wanted to be everywhere with her. Every whimper, every moan, every syllable of his name falling from her lips was like a prize. He was so close to losing it, but he had to see her go there first.

And damn, when it happened, if it wasn't the most stunning sight ever.

'Oh fuck, Sean. Oh God!' Cherry's climax seized her,

clench after desperate clench, her manicure daggering into his forearms, forging marks he'd treasure like temporary tattoos. Hell, he'd get tattoos over those marks.

There was nothing he wanted more than to watch every moment of his perfect wife stripped bare and coming around him. But it was impossible. She was quivering and moaning and clamping onto him, breasts rising and falling, and he was powerless to do anything except come hard, deep inside her, all the tension shooting – thick, urgent and determined – from his body at last.

'Oh, Cherry. Fuck. I love you.'

And as her own peak abated, with him stilling inside her, Cherry threaded her fingers through his hair. 'I love you, Sean.'

Finally, they stopped, her eyes drifting open bright and dazed, latching onto his, almost causing his heart to shudder to a standstill.

'Oh, hey, Butler.' Her smile was so intoxicating it should be illegal outside the bedroom.

'Aye, hey, Paradise. Come here.' He cradled her face. 'I love you so much.'

'Mmm, coming with you inside me is out of this world.'

Together, they lay down and, tentatively because of his ribs, Sean pulled her close, cherishing her small frame in his arms again. At last. He tucked her head under his collarbone and kissed her temple.

For a minute, they lay there in the silence, absorbing it all, until Cherry circled her palm as far as it went round the Celtic band on his bicep. 'You have the best arms. I'd love for you to tattoo me there when you're ready,' she purred lazily.

Sean had to check. 'Seriously?' This was better than the roar of surf going off. She was comfortable being inked onto his skin, to accepting that he wanted her forever.

'Yes. You can decide what it is, but I want to be there when you get it done. I'll bring you rationed Irn-Bru and hold your hand. Dry your tears when it gets too sore.'

Sean smiled, but he was choked with emotion. 'That means so much, Cher.' He breathed in the sweet floral scent of her hair. 'You letting me love you means the fucking world. You won't regret it. And there's no tattoo that hurts as much as not having you around.'

Cherry dusted her hands down his chest, softly over the hollow between his ribs, south and back – drifting, exploring, adoring – as they talked and touched and laughed, at last able to focus on being together. Until the hot brushing over his skin became too much for Sean. He barely needed any recovery time with this woman.

'You ready again? Let me show you how much I love you.'

'I thought you'd never ask. I'll go on top.'

'Ha. Nice, but no. I'm taking this, Cher. No arguments. It'll be slow but good. I promise.'

A softened, flushed Cherry hummed in ascension, rolling onto her back, and as Sean tentatively pressed his weight onto her, he considered he'd never seen her so demure. It wasn't a taming, simply that this was different and they both knew it. This was their first night in his bed.

Their bed.

As he pushed deep into her, their eyes locked together in the golden glow of the room, he could tell by the quivering of her cupid's bow that she was ready for him again.

'I love seeing your face when I'm inside you.'

'Mmm, it feels sooo good. You make me so happy, Sean.'

'You make me very fucking happy, Cher, looking like

you belong right here.' He shifted his hips in one deliberate movement, sending a searing pain shooting through his ribs. This position might be untenable, but it was worth it to see her reaction.

'I do. I... Oh God! Oh fuck, Sean. What are you doing to me? That's incredible.'

'Just ruining you for anyone else.'

'There's really no need to try. The battle's lost and won.'

Chapter 39

Cherry

Two weeks later

A soft wind whipped up the sands of Kinshore beach like shortbread dust. From the shoreline, the Butler siblings were tiny figures bobbing on the waves, but the poignancy was more overwhelming than if Cherry had been out there with them. Goosebumps prickled her arms. She pulled her beanie down over her ears and rubbed the sleeves of her thick knit sweater, wondering if any of the other WAGs were feeling the same surge of emotion.

Of course they were. They were real wives and girlfriends, woven into the family tartan. She was a recent addition to the clan.

And for that reason, she didn't refer to them as WAGs out loud, only to Sean in private. It would undermine the privilege she felt standing here on the sand with Bea, Alicia and Carli, watching Amanda and her children scatter the ashes of their beloved husband and dad. Someday, when she knew them better, maybe they'd laugh about being WAGs together.

Hopefully.

'The conditions are great,' Bea, a keen surfer, noted. 'I'm so pleased they've got weather like this on Jimmy's birthday.'

'Me too.' Bea's words reinforced to Cherry how important it was that this went right for the whole family, not only Sean. 'I'm sorry I never got to meet Jimmy. Although, Sean has really brought him to life for me.'

'He was incredible,' said Alicia, who was busy taking photographs of the scene, to capture in a painting. 'I see so much of him in Jamie: the hard worker and down-to-earth generosity.'

'Yeah, Cal has his drive and no-nonsense attitude,' Bea added.

'For a long time, Niall thought he was nothing like his dad,' Carli said, 'but he has the same driven heart.'

'And Sean is Jimmy all over.' Alicia lowered her camera. 'The energy, the spark, the "never stop moving" vibe. A bit more talkative but the same essence.'

They stared out to sea, Alicia clicking at her camera, as the siblings and Amanda cast their hands out to disperse ashes, silver murmurations floating over the waves. Cherry's eyes were on Sean. How was he? Last night, he'd slept fitfully. At 3 a.m. she'd tucked in close and wrapped her arm around him.

'Thinking about tomorrow?' She kissed the soft skin on the nape of his neck.

'Aye.' The deep gravel of his voice suggested he'd been drifting in and out of sleep for hours. 'I just want it to go right, for his birthday – his memory.'

'It will, Seany. And I'll be there watching from the beach, thinking of you the whole time.'

He found her hand. 'You've no idea what a difference that makes, Cher. When Dad died, I had no one to hold like this. I felt alone, but I always thought, *Don't complain. Mum has it so much worse.*'

'I'm here now.' She placed a tender kiss at the top of his spine, softly nuzzled her nose there. 'Hold me anytime.'

'Thanks.' He turned to face her in the dark, pulled her in close and kissed her. And that was it; they made love there and then, Sean's physical and emotional urgency for her barely reined in. She understood. If she were grieving, she'd have grasped for every moment of him in the same way.

In the morning, you'd never have known anything had been wrong. Cherry made coffee while Sean stared out the lounge window, fingers lazily rubbing the nape of his neck. It was a fine substitute for the lip chewing.

'Surf looks perfect. You look perfect.' He took the cup from her. 'This coffee looks...okay.'

'You cheeky wee...' She elbowed him softly.

'I'm kidding. The coffee is perfect, too. What more could a guy ask for?'

There wasn't much more either of them could ask for. The privilege they had was understood.

On the sand behind came the soft crunch of footsteps and the puffing of someone in a rush. Cherry spun round to see Summer jogging towards them with her dog.

'Sorry I'm late. Barley got a thorn in his paw. How's the surf?' She scanned the waves, probably for Nate, in the same way that each of them did for their own man. It was sweet and telling that she'd come to support him.

'It's going well. They've got individual tins of ashes to scatter.'

'Oh, wow.' Summer fixed hard on the figures out in the water. 'What an awesome thing to do.'

'Are you coming to dinner at Amanda's tonight?' Alicia asked.

Summer shrugged. 'Och, I'm not sure. Nate mentioned it, but it's a family thing. I'll give you guys some space.'

They watched as, one by one, the surfers pivoted shoreward and rode into dry land, Sean first with Amanda on the back of his longboard. Cherry walked down to the waterline to meet them, noting how different it was from the last time she'd met him after a surf.

'How did it go?' she asked, her sweater getting soaked in seawater as she hugged him extra tight, but the salty kiss he planted on her more than making up for it.

'Jimmy would laugh his head off at me on the back of that board.' Amanda swept her hair out of her eyes. 'But it went well.' She touched Sean's shoulder. 'Thank you, sweetheart.'

'Aye, no bother, Mum. Dad would have loved it, especially the bit where I got a face full of ashes.'

One by one, the others followed, welcomed back with kisses and hugs. Bea and Cal, Alicia and Jamie, Carli and Niall. Cherry noticed Nate's face brighten at the sight of Summer, and their hug lasted a beat too long for only friends.

'You're next, by the way.' Sean slipped his hand into hers.

'What do you mean?'

'You're getting on a board. In fact, lessons start tomorrow.'

'Tomorrow? Sean, it's nearly winter!'

'It's early autumn, woman. And we've got to get those bucket list items checked off, one of which was "toughen the fuck up".' Playfully, he squeezed her cheek.

'Oh, and what happens if I say no to surfing lessons?'

'Then I'm afraid your punishment is sleeping in the other room again.'

'Aye, right. As if you'd ever let me go back there.'

He grinned. 'Fair enough. I might be that transparent. I'm actually terrified that if I'm naughty, you might go back there to punish me.'

'And what about if I'm naughty?'

'If you're naughty, Paradise, then your punishment will be doled out in every room of the house and will involve all those things you once promised to my pillow.'

Cherry laughed and leaned into him, so glad to have the real thing to hold. 'You don't even know half of what I promised to that pillow.'

As the late afternoon sun gilded the waves behind them, Sean slung his arm around her. 'That's exactly what I want to hear. Now, let's go home and you can tell me all about the other half – and then some.'

Epilogue

THE FOLLOWING JULY

'You ready?' Sean's deep voice thrummed as if vibrating from the depths of the loch.

Cherry nodded. Was this nuts? Yes, this was nuts. She was chest deep in loch water in a matching white vest and leggings. Her husband was facing her in nothing but swimming shorts and a white Jacobean Ghillie shirt, now drenched, affording her a front-row view of every rippling muscle in his upper body and shadows of his tattoos through the soaked fabric. The dream had been him in a kilt to go with the shirt, but the weight made it a drowning hazard, and they were too deep in the water for it to show in any photos.

The photos that all of Sean's family would be taking from the shore of the loch.

Also holding a camera was Cherry's mum. Who would have thought Pamela Paradise would be standing there, side by side with Amanda Butler as if they'd been friends forever rather than having met last night? It warmed Cherry's heart, even if it also made her a little nervous. If all they talked about was colour swatches, fine. She couldn't contemplate anything else, not today.

Cherry turned to her loch-soaked husband, the man taking her breath from her one married day at a time. And none more so than today, for his willingness to say yes to her whimsy.

She cradled her arms around his neck. 'Thank you, Seany.'

He pulled her in. 'What for?'

'Everything. For marrying me one year ago, for sticking with me, for loving me, for renewing your vows today and, mostly, for humouring me on this.'

'Listen, nothing makes me happier than doing this, Cherry. I could never for the life of me work out what was the point in me learning how to do it. Cara and Eilidh always told me that it would help me sweep some woman off her feet one day, and now I realise that, for once, they were right.'

'Come on!' Voices called from the shoreline. 'Do the lift! Do the lift!'

Sean leaned back a little and smoothed Cherry's hair from her hairline. 'Before we do this, I have something to say, too.' He lowered his hands to cup her cheeks. 'This past year has been the best of my life. Right after the worst thing happened, the very best thing came along. Sometimes I look at you, and I don't actually know what to say. Hard to believe, right? You fit so perfectly into Kinshore, into my family, my life. I love you, Cherry, so, so much.'

Cherry smiled, salt tears mingling with fresh loch water down her cheeks. 'Oh Sean. You make loving you so easy. I love you, too.'

Tenderly but briefly, he kissed her. 'Let's get going

before we freeze to death. I'd like to know more than one wedding anniversary.'

Cherry was keen to get moving, too. It might be July, but the loch water was cool and pooling even cooler around her feet. Cramp was the last thing either of them needed.

Once again, powerful, muscular hands rested on her hips, this time with intent. Intent to raise her right above his head – with a little assistance from those barrel-making arms.

'Is this how you hold one of your casks?' she asked.

'You're obsessed with how I hold my casks. Are you jealous?'

'Damn right, I am.' For a year, Cherry had playfully been asking Sean to do foreplay and make love to her in the manner of building a whisky barrel. The only response she got was laughter and him telling her he was more than willing to cater to any of her bedroom fantasies, but he had no idea how exactly that one would play out.

'With craft and precision,' she'd said.

'Don't I always bring craft and precision to the bedroom? You want me to bring a hula hoop and pretend it's a barrel hoop?'

The answer to the first question was undeniably yes. The second one... She told him she was willing to try anything. The hula hoop was on her shopping list.

Sean waved to his expectant, exuberant family on the shoreline. 'They're causing noise pollution, so let's go. Bend your knees. That's what Johnny says, right?'

'Yes. And they're bent.'

'Okay, one, two, three...' And in one swift, confident motion, Sean lifted Cherry out of the water, the temperate July air skimming warmly over her skin as he raised her with complete confidence over his head, holding her there, balanced like a soaring ballerina, arms out, gazing across the glittering blue of the summer loch towards the distant heather-dusted mountains.

A moment she would treasure forever.

A few metres away, on the pebbled shoreline, the Butler family were cheering, whooping and shouting things about the time of their lives. But Cherry concentrated on how complete, safe and fortunate she felt with Sean holding her. And the beauty of the dramatic Kintyre landscape. Gazing to the wonder ahead, not down. Never looking down.

'Let me know when you've had enough.'

'What if I never have enough?'

'Then I guess we stay here forever. It's not a problem for me, although we might get hungry. And Meowchel will wonder where we are.'

Wee Meowchel J Fluff, very much part of the furniture and fabric of their home now. And who made sure, by the timbre of his meow, that he never went without a meal or snack.

'Just a moment or two more. I never want to forget this.'

And Sean held her there, until she asked him to bring her back to him, down and into his arms again. Because that was where she belonged. No one held her like Sean did.

And as it happened, no one dunked her under the water like Sean did and lifted her back up, laughing and carrying her to shore like he'd carried her over the threshold one year ago.

No one did anything quite like Sean Butler.

And no one could love him right to his very heart quite as much as Cherry Paradise.

Amber Cooper

The End

Thank you

Thank you so much for reading *Wild About my Scotsman*. I truly hope you enjoyed Sean and Cherry's story. If you did, please consider writing a review as it would (hopefully) make me smile and help other people find the book. The world deserves to know about Sean Butler, right?

Thank you again.

Amber xx

About Amber Cooper

Amber Cooper is Scottish lady who lives in a wee flat in Edinburgh, Scotland, with a Scotsman and a Scotscat. She took to writing when chronic illness put paid to her becoming a theatrical star – and she loves it (writing, not chronic illness – chronic illness sucks). Romance writing is even better. When not writing, Amber can be found stressing about not doing enough writing or obsessively watching every series of The Traitors ever made.

Sign up to Amber's newsletter for all the latest updates on books, cats, Scotland and more.

www.ambercooperbooks.com

Books by Amber Cooper

The Spirit of a Scotsman. Prequel to the Butlers' Romance Series.
Free to download.

Surfing with a Scotsman: The Butlers' Romance Series 1

Snowed in with a Scotsman: The Butlers' Romance Series 2

Reunited with my Scotsman: The Butlers' Romance Series 3

Wild About my Scotsman: The Butlers' Romance Series 4

The Butlers' Romance Series 5: Nate and Summer

The Butlers' Romance Series 6: Connor and Cara

The Butlers' Romance Series 7: Eilidh and mystery man

Free Prequel

If you enjoyed this book, you can download the free prequel to the series at my website, www.ambercooperbooks.com or here. Read on for sample chapters.

The Spirit of a Scotsman

Chapter 1
Amanda

April

'Got your wee notebook?' Bill Kincaid asked his daughter, Amanda, as she stood waiting for the 6.30 a.m. bus. The crack of dawn service from Glasgow was the only way of arriving for the opening of the Kintyre Whisky Festival at midday and Bill had escorted his daughter to the bus station to ensure she made it.

'Aye, Dad,' Amanda replied. 'And the wee pen, too.'

'Good. Mind and note down aw they're up tae, fae the notes in the whisky tae the colour of the tablecloths on the tasting tables.'

'Um, okay then.' Amanda couldn't always tell what was her dad's dry sense of humour and what was his dogged desire to tear down the competition. She erred on the side of the latter.

'I'm joking aboot the tablecloths.' Bill clapped Amanda

on the shoulder. 'But not the rest of it. Just see what they're daein and what this festival is all about. I willnae have Butler's whisky outshining Kincaid's.'

'Do we need to spy?' Amanda asked, albeit with a lump in her throat. You didn't question Bill Kincaid. 'And if we do, would Micky or Billy not be better at this?'

'Aye, we dae. And they're daein something else for me today.' Bill's tone shut the conversation down. Amanda knew her dad and brothers were heading to the bookies and the pub, while she did the donkey work for the business. 'Oh, and mind and only use the camera if you have tae,' her dad added. 'Film's nae cheap.'

'Okay, bye, Dad. See you tomorrow.' Amanda was grateful the bus driver had arrived with his coffee. She was also glad her dad had coughed up for a night in a B&B, so she didn't have to get the bus home tonight. 'A chance to write up your notes and competition analysis,' he'd said. Just the word *competition* filled Amanda with dread. What was the obsession with beating everyone else? And why couldn't she have chosen her own career? Not that being a brand ambassador for Kincaid Distillers, a Glasgow-based whisky company, was a bad thing. Amanda got to travel a bit, enthusiastically promoting Scotland's national spirit. But brand ambassador was a misnomer. It would have been more honest to give her the title *promotional dogsbody*.

'Oh, and Mandy...'

'Aye?' Amanda swung back to her dad. Maybe he would tell her she was doing a great job, or to have a nice time while she was away. Give her a hug.

'Bring us back a dram or two. Wangle a free bottle out of them somehow.'

'Sure.' Amanda turned away so the expression of disappointment and frustration on her face was hidden. Her sole worth to her dad was as a spy for the business. It was as if having a daughter was only useful because you could plant her in rival whisky camps and nobody would bat an eyelid.

By the time Amanda had taken her seat on the bus, her dad was sauntering away from the stance, confident that his only daughter was on her way to do his bidding. Now, he had a few hours until the pubs opened. Amanda pulled a book out of her bag. It was the best way to block out the hurt.

Two and a half hours later, she closed the covers of the well-worn novel, having finished it for the fifth time in two years. Every time, she was right there with the sculpted and commanding Texan ranch hand, tipping his Stetson, cupping her cheek and telling her he was going to take care of her in more ways than one. Along with the other romance novels that lined the shelves of Amanda's bedroom, it was the perfect escape.

Amanda dropped the closed book to her lap and gazed out the window as they passed rolling green fields, dotted with sheep and cattle on one side, and rugged, wildflower-strewn coastline on the other. She'd lived in Scotland her whole life, most of it spent in Glasgow, but the view from her bus seat was like a window into a new land. It was also a stark contrast to the wide, dusty expanse of Texas she'd been reading about, although just as breathtaking

The idea of the whisky festival filled Amanda with dread, but she was also excited about it. Away from her dad, she could try to enjoy the freedom this wild peninsula offered. She'd fill out the notebook he'd given her, with the bookies pen, but she'd pretend she was doing it for a reason other than competition notes. Maybe it was research for a novel or a diary entry of a whisky enthusiast. Maybe she'd be scribbling away in a corner with a dram on the table beside her when a striking man with broad shoulders and a chiselled jaw would approach and ask what she was writing. She'd look up into his piercing blue eyes and say 'whisky'. He'd appear surprised, hold out his strong hand and ask her if she wanted to come and see his barrel store. Then they'd get into the dark depths and whisky would be on neither of their minds anymore.

Amanda sighed. The whisky, at least, was a guarantee.

Another ninety minutes of winding country roads, and the bus arrived in the coastal village of Kinshore. It was an adorable place where old stone cottages sat side by side, their brightly coloured doors and flower-lined paths saying come and live here. Amanda lugged her overnight bag through centuries-old streets to her B&B, gazing into curious shops and cafes on the way. After checking into her room – and ingesting a pick-me-up coffee and piece of plastic-wrapped shortbread – she headed out to catch the shuttle bus to Butler's Distillery.

As far back as Amanda could remember, her dad had scoffed at the name Butler's whisky. According to him, the Kintyre operation was nothing to worry about in terms of competition, but recently, he had mentioned it more. The ownership of Butler's had recently changed from the late James Butler, Senior, to his sons, Jimmy and Archie, who were only in their twenties. While James Butler was content to let the company coast along with moderate sales, in the wake of his untimely passing, with his brother having emigrated to Canada years past, his sons were intent on moving things into the present. There was to be an upgrade to the distillery, a new visitor centre and now the Kintyre Whisky Festival, a promotional vehicle for the brand. It was impressive stuff, although Amanda would never say that to her dad.

As she stepped off the shuttle bus at the distillery grounds, the delectable scent of malted barley hit Amanda. She stopped and embraced the midday sun on her face. It was strange: although Butler's was a rival distillery to Kincaid's, it immediately felt more like home. Could that feeling bode well for the day? Maybe her visit could be more like a holiday than work — if only she could forget why she'd been sent here.

The Spirit of a Scotsman

Chapter 2
Jimmy

Jimmy Butler strode through the distillery scanning every corner of the building for anything out of place. The Kintyre Whisky Festival started in – Jimmy glanced at his watch – ten minutes. Where the hell was Archie?

That was the eternal, and infernal, question these days. Where was Archie? Jimmy's younger brother's name was on the Butler's paperwork, but the man himself was rarely around. Jimmy had organised this festival single-handedly. Archie, instead, had his father's interest in the business, that is, none. He had as much drive as a scrap car and expected Butler's to run passively, or that someone else would do all the work. And that was exactly what was happening. Since their father had died, Jimmy was the one making all the decisions because no way would he let Butler's go to ground. His grandfather would turn in his grave if he thought the company was at risk.

Jimmy slipped into his office and dialled Archie's home

phone. No answer. He wouldn't ring more than once. The last time he'd done that, he was accused of being a 'nagging auld wife'. Archie had probably been out late the night before and was still in bed, possibly with a woman. There were a few tourists in town for the festival and his brother had talked about 'getting laid', no doubt parading out the 'I own a distillery' line to help his cause. Jimmy liked getting laid as much as the next man, but you didn't let family down like this. And what was all this for, if not family? Even his father had an ambivalent attitude toward the business. In happier times, Jimmy and Archie had darkly joked that he'd died to get it off his hands. Jimmy missed his dad; however, he could imagine him sitting on his shoulder telling his eldest son to sell the distillery and go fishing instead.

But fishing wasn't in Jimmy's blood. Whisky was. Business was. He sucked in a breath. There was a work to do, and he couldn't let his emotions or his brother's irresponsibility get in the way. One day, there would be a family of his own to pass all this onto.

Jimmy made his way to the tasting room, where he would showcase some of the distillery's best whiskies. The room was set up perfectly, with rows of glasses and bottles neatly arranged on the stands. Everything was in order: well, apart from the fact that Archie should be here to run the Butler's tasting. No doubt he'd find his way to the ceilidh tonight, not wanting to miss the chance to eat stovies, drink barrels of whisky and bother women. Already, tickets were sold out and Archie would hate to miss out on a key social event.

Jimmy had invited some other local distillers to set up stalls at the festival. They might be his rivals, but it made business sense to support them. Putting Kintyre on the whisky map was important and working as a team could only make it more of a destination. People might not come for one distillery, but they would come for several. Jimmy was confident enough in Butler's to acknowledge that others made good whisky, too. He checked they were all okay and raring to go.

'Cannae wait.' Gordon Dukes of Dukes Distillers raised an empty Glencairn glass to Jimmy. 'This is a rare idea, Jimmy. Thanks for the opportunity to set up here.'

'Aye, let's show them the Kintyre spirit.' Jimmy tried to sound rousing, despite inner uncertainties. He glanced at his watch again. Two minutes. 'Right, I better let in the punters.' He strode to the main entrance of the distillery, where the piper was striking up. The sound always sent goosebumps through him. But Jimmy was metres from the door when a loud banging assaulted the air and almost drowned out the piper.

'What the hell is that?' Jimmy suspected he knew the answer.

'Do you want me to let folk in, Mr Butler?' asked Peter, a young employee poised to check tickets. 'They sound keen.'

Jimmy raised an eyebrow and listened to the intensifying banging. 'Maybe a bit too keen, would you no' say?'

'I don't know, Mr Butler.' Peter shuffled and eyed his boss with uncertainty. 'Keen is good, no?'

'Aye, keen is good if it's a customer.' The faint suspicion of who it was grew. How many folk would be outside, witnessing this? Glancing out the side window, Jimmy could see people milling around. The shuttle bus was leaving to bring more from the village.

Bang, bang, bang. Jimmy had to put a stop to this before it drove people away. He unlocked and hauled open the heavy oak doors to confront, as he suspected, his brother standing on the other side.

'Thank God, where've you been? I've got a tasting to run.' Archie brushed past Jimmy into the building.

Despite growing up around whisky and being at this present moment in a distillery, Jimmy could smell alcohol on his brother as he wafted by. Stale alcohol. Archie appeared to have put on clean clothes this morning, but his hair was like a bird's nest and there was a six o'clock shadow on his jaw. And there was the faint hint of arrogance that always emanated from him, more pronounced when he'd had a drink or was still drunk from the previous night.

A few other people took Archie's entrance as a sign that the festival was open and moved into the building too. At one minute to twelve, Jimmy wouldn't refuse them.

'Good afternoon! Welcome to Butler's Distillery. I'm Jimmy Butler.' While Peter checked tickets, Jimmy said hello to each guest who crossed the threshold of his distillery. It had always been his intention to greet as many as he could. After a few minutes, the car park was quiet again and there were only a few people milling around the outdoor stalls on the lawn and one woman staring at the view. Jimmy headed off to find Archie, hoping his younger brother hadn't had time to undo the hard work put in to make the festival a success.

The Spirit of a Scotsman

Chapter 3
Amanda

Amanda could never tire of this landscape. The glistening blue waters that stretched out from the foot of the verdant distillery lawn were mesmerising. She had to tear herself away and get to the whisky, but away from her dad's direct expectations and scrutiny, she could slow down and enjoy the experience.

Inside Butler's Distillery smelled of stone and old oak, similar to the Kincaid distillery, but something here was softer. Amanda couldn't say what exactly. Maybe it was the lighting or the lower ceilings or the staff's infectious enthusiasm.

In the reception and shop area, rows and rows of gleaming bottles of Butler's whisky lined the shelves, like spotlessly uniformed soldiers. There were a few other items for sale, the customary glasses and tasting notepads. Amanda spotted some older expressions in glass cases, such as Butler's Eas Inchafallon, the most prestigious of all the

Butler whiskies. She had never tried any of Butler's expressions, but their reputation went before them.

Amanda signed up for a distillery tour with a cheerful guide. The distilling process was ingrained in her mind, but she wanted to take in as much of this place as possible, to discover if they did anything different on their tours. Her dad would grill her and if she said she hadn't taken the tour, the repercussions wouldn't be worth thinking about.

Down in the depths of the distillery, the tour group learned from a young man named Peter that Butler's whisky was founded in 1798 by Jack Butler, who set up the distillery on the current site. 'Jack was a pioneer in all things whisky,' said Peter, 'and Butler's was the first distillery on the Kintyre Peninsula. He grew the business by word of mouth and even held events which could be described as festivals similar to the one we are having here today, where he invited his friends and friends of friends round and they drank a lot of whisky, told stories and gambled. The distillery was passed onto Jack's sons, and their sons, and so on, until most recently to Joseph and James Butler, who built on the legendary reputation. Joseph emigrated to Canada, and it was left to James to keep things going, but Butler's reputation has only grown. Sadly, James recently passed and the distillery ownership has moved to his sons, Archie and Jimmy, who you may meet here today. They are excited about the future of whisky and see many opportunities for development. Butler's is a business with a bright future.'

This was all business rhetoric, but Amanda could also sense the opportunity and excitement in the air. However, as Peter guided them through the rest of the tour, her attention wandered from his words about the distilling process. Once you'd met one mash tun you'd met them all. Instead, she cast herself into an imaginary world running tours here, engaging the customers with tales of distillers of old. There would be a roguish distillery owner who poached her away from her own family distillery. He'd hide in the crowd to witness her show-stopping delivery and as the customers filtered out of the old dark barrel store, there would be a rough grip on her soft palm pulling her back into the dark. Then firm lips on her own, the graze of rough stubble and the scent of whisky mingling with the scent of a brawny Scotsman.

Amanda sighed heavily.

'Is everything okay?' Peter frowned.

'What? Oh, absolutely fine.' Amanda's face flushed, as if people might read her mind. 'Sorry, don't stop, it's fascinating.'

Peter recommenced his talk about the fermentation process. Amanda tried to maintain an interested composure, whilst her mind ran wild with the feverish idea of the distillery owner taking her over a barrel of his most expensive malt.

Once the tour was complete, Peter led the group back into the reception and gestured to a set of double doors at the back of the reception room and shop. 'Through there is a banquet of delights. Please sample away, then come out here to purchase your favourite Butler's whisky.'

As Amanda stepped through the double doors to the tasting room, her eyes widened. There were stalls adorned with the familiar names of whisky companies, and glistening bottles waiting to be emptied into tasting glasses. The air was thick with the malted scent of whisky, and the sound of enthused chatter filled the space. People were sniffing and gesticulating and swallowing and nodding. She moved further into the room, her heart racing at being part of this.

There was so much to take in that Amanda couldn't settle on a stall at which to begin, instead digesting everything but nothing. But enthusiasm was only part of the reason she didn't stop at any of the tasting stands. She was worried she'd give the game away and introduce herself as a brand ambassador for Kincaid's. People might be interested – they usually were – but what if they worked out she was there to spy or steal ideas? So, she wandered anonymously, observing and absorbing. What surprised her most was that there were several distilleries running tastings. What would her dad make of the fact that Butler's embraced the competition?

Eventually, Amanda drifted towards the largest stand in the room – The Butler's whisky stand – which, oddly, was unmanned. Perhaps they had nipped away for a minute. She examined the bottles sitting on the counter. The traditional Butler's logo that remained loyal to the origins of the company gave a classical elegance to the bottles, yet they still fit with the contemporary direction of the company. Next to the bottles, there was an array of tasting glasses waiting to be filled with whisky for thirsty customers. Amanda glanced around hoping someone would appear to offer her a sample.

'Why don't you help yourself?'

She spun on her heel to see a gentleman with a kindly face and large moustache smiling at her from the neighbouring stall.

'Archie Butler was here a minute ago, but he had to nip off,' the man explained. 'Help yourself to a wee dram.'

Amanda hesitated for a moment, then agreed. 'If you're sure.'

'Aye, that's what the day is for.'

'It is, indeed.' Amanda lifted a luxuriously heavy bottle of Butler's ten-year-old single malt, loving its solidity. Popping open the cap felt a little sinful as, despite being invited to do so, it was like trespassing on private property. Still, she followed the familiar routine of pouring a small measure into the curvaceous Glencairn glass and holding it up to the light, witnessing its amber glory, before swinging the glass to her nose and inhaling scents of vanilla, apples and burnt toffee. As the dram hit Amanda's taste buds, she was bounding through golden fields of wheat, biting down on crunchy apples and lying on a blanket eating toffees. This whisky was delectable. For a moment, she savoured the aftertaste. The ten-year-old expression was Butler's flagship malt – simpler than the others – but anyone who took one taste could tell that Butler's didn't do simple in the understood definition of the word. Amanda understood now why she'd been sent here.

When the ten-year-old had relinquished its hold on her palate, Amanda reached for a Butler's twelve-year-old. She was enjoying the promising rush of another dram pouring into her glass when a voice made her jump.

'Excuse me.'

'Oh, I wasn't stealing the...' Amanda stopped. There was a young Japanese woman staring at her, expectantly.

'May I taste some samples?' the woman asked.

Does she think I'm in charge here? Well, I suppose there's no reason I can't help her out.

'Sure, try this one.' Amanda pointed to the first whisky she'd sampled. 'It's delicious. Has a creamy apricot finish.' She poured a glass and kept talking to her rapt audience. 'For a ten-year malt, it's quite a complex expression. On the nose there's vanilla, apples, maybe even a hint of pear.'

The woman nodded and stuck her nose so far in the glass, Amanda thought she might get stuck.

'Oh, yes,' she said.

'Then, take a drink and see if you can notice those things. You might even get a hint of cloves.' Amanda scrutinised the woman's face as she swallowed the whisky, nodded and smiled.

'Delicious,' she said.

There was nothing quite like the expressions of pleasure when people enjoyed a good malt. How Amanda wished her dad would let her do more tastings rather than spying trips.

'So, let's move on to this.' Amanda pulled forward the twelve-year-old single malt and poured two glasses. 'Mmm.' She inhaled what smelled like a punchy nectar. 'This is a bold one. Sea spray, brine and peat. I love a big peaty lass.'

Again, the woman laughed and poured back the whisky.

'This area used to be a hotbed for whisky,' Amanda explained, deciding to complement the tasting with some detail she'd learned about Kintyre and the type of whisky it produced. 'But things declined. Butlers is one of the few distilleries operating out of Kintyre, and from drinking this, it's easy to see why.'

Soon, Amanda's rhapsodising drew a small crowd, people assuming she was in charge. Emboldened by their assumption, she continued sharing her thoughts on the different tastes and flavours of the whiskies. As she spoke, her confidence grew, and her speech flowed effortlessly. The visitors leaned in, hanging onto her every word. Amanda was surprised at her own eloquence and how at ease she felt, considering this was not her home ground.

'Okay, folks, well, the only expression left to try is this

one here.' Amanda reached for a bottle of Butler's Eas Inchfallon. 'This is the crème de la crème of the Butler's flight. A big peaty seafarer that packs a punch.' What was she talking about? She hadn't even tasted the drink yet.

At least ten people were waiting expectantly for their glasses to be filled. Amanda decided it would be easier to get behind the stall and pour from there. But the crowd was building and she'd need extra tasting glasses.

'Just a moment. I'm sure there are some fresh glasses down here. Amanda disappeared under the stall to search. But as her eyes settled on the glasses, a commanding male voice resonated from up above her.

'Can ah help you find something?'

Amanda, remembering where she was and why she was here, and realising she was probably in trouble, travelled her gaze slowly upwards, her heart beating hard. The first thing she clocked were sturdy tree-trunk legs in thick woollen socks. *Oh my God, those are exceptional legs.* Then she hit a hem of tartan. A kilt. *Well, he's got the legs, so let him.* And a sporran slung under a tightly leather belted waist. Strange things were happening to Amanda looking the waist of a man whose face she hadn't yet seen. She cast her sights up some more, her eyes scanning over a crisp white shirt and pressed waistcoat covering a chest broader than the peninsula. Then there were shoulders as wide as the channel. *Oh my God! He's built like a distillery truck.* And when she moved beyond his shoulders and neck, Amanda's breath hitched in her throat as she locked onto intense green eyes of possibly the most handsome face she had ever seen. A man with a jawline rugged like the Kintyre coastline, lightly tanned skin, and an expression that said business is my priority. Amanda dropped her gaze back to his chest and the badge pinned to his waistcoat that said *Jimmy*.

Oh God!

This was Jimmy Butler. The owner of Butler's Distillery. *Shit! Shit! Shit!* Would he turf her out of the festival? What if he found out she was an interloper on a mission from Kincaid's? Would he take her to his study and question her intentions? Maybe then he'd kiss her and ask her to join his team instead. Amanda would do it. If things happened like that and he was a good kisser, she would definitely do it. Then she remembered she'd hijacked Jimmy Butler's whisky tasting. On jelly legs, she stood to meet his piercing, emerald gaze.

Keep cool, Amanda. Be the heroine in your own story, for goodness' sake.

'I was getting some Glencairn glasses,' she said. 'We've got quite the crowd.'

'Aye, *we* have.' Jimmy's tone was steely and hard to decipher. 'Far be it from me to interrupt your tasting session. Please...' he stood back and gestured with a wide arm, 'continue.'

Amanda examined his expression for signs of sarcasm. She was used to insincerity from her dad, and wasn't sure how to react. One minute he encouraged her and the next he tore her down.

'Och, no. I couldn't. I shouldn't. I'm sorry for taking over. The man over there said I could try a dram, someone thought I was in charge, and it all snowballed from there.'

Jimmy Butler scanned the crowd and spoke slowly. 'Aye, it would appear it has snowballed. Luckily for you.' His gaze bore into her. Never had such alluring eyes intimidated her so much. 'So, why don't you carry on with the tasting and show me what you know about Butler's whisky.'

Amanda took a moment to consider if she should run. This Jimmy was a formidable character. But she had muscled in on his tasting stand. Her dad would have come down far harder on anyone who'd done that at Kincaid's. So, forcing herself to unfix her gaze from those gorgeous but intimidating eyes that were staring at her so intensely, she turned to the whisky, twisted open a bottle of Butler's Eas Inchfallon and poured.

***

If you enjoyed the opening chapters of The Spirit of a Scotsman, you can download the full prequel for free at ambercooperbooks.com or here.

www.ingramcontent.com/pod-product-compliance
Lightning Source LLC
Chambersburg PA
CBHW020900060726

47591CB00004B/1023